THE ANATOMY OF FOREVER

THE ANATOMY OF FOREVER

T.B. MARKINSON
MIRANDA MACLEOD

The Anatomy of Forever

Copyright © 2025 T. B. Markinson & Miranda MacLeod

Cover Design by Victoria Cooper

Edited by Kelly Hashway

This book is copyrighted and licensed for your personal enjoyment only. All rights reserved. No part of this publication may be reproduced, stored in a retrieval system, or transmitted in any forms or by any means without the prior permission of the copyright owner. The moral rights of the authors have been asserted.

This book is a work of fiction. Names, characters, businesses, places, events, and incidents are the product of the authors' imagination or are used fictitiously. Any resemblance to actual persons, living or dead, events, or locales is entirely coincidental.

CHAPTER ONE

"Do you need some help in there?" Simone hesitated at the bathroom door. It remained open a crack, having failed to latch shut after Erica made a mad dash inside. "I could hold your hair back if you want."

Erica's only response to the offer was a pitiful groan, followed by a cacophony of retching sounds that made Simone take an involuntary step back. She paced in front of the door, torn between respecting her friend's privacy and her natural inclination as a doctor to comfort patients in distress.

Her high heel caught on the edge of the rug, nearly causing her to wipe out. She responded by sending one shoe after the other sailing down the hallway toward the guestroom, where she would be staying for the next few nights. She wished she could ditch the skintight dress, too. Scrubs were more her style, but Erica had insisted on her donning a slinky black number and a pair of stilettos for their girls' night out.

Some night this had turned out to be.

Simone leaned against the wall, closing her eyes and taking a deep breath to dispel her current sense of helplessness. As the seconds ticked by, the worst of the sounds from the bathroom subsided, eventually replaced by the gentle hiss of running water. Simone was about to call out again when Erica appeared, her face deathly pale.

"Give it to me straight, Doc," Erica croaked. "Am I dying?"

"You ordered raw oysters from a random cart on the side of the road." Just in case it wasn't obvious, Simone felt compelled to add, "Stupid, stupid idea. I haven't seen anyone throw up this much since that Halloween party when I was the RA in your dorm."

"Oh, God. Freshman year. I should've listened to you then, just like I should've listened now." Erica slumped against the doorframe. "Your last days of freedom are being ruined because of me."

"Freedom? I'm going on a humanitarian medical mission with Global Health Frontiers, not heading to prison or being conscripted into the army." Simone slipped a supporting arm around Erica's waist as she helped guide her friend's unsteady steps toward the living room. "Why don't we get you settled on the couch? I'll grab some water. Do you know if your dad keeps a bucket somewhere?"

"No clue." Collapsing on the couch, Erica gave a dramatic toss of her hand over her head. Simone was taking it as a good sign. If Erica had the energy to be theatrical, she was probably on the mend. "I haven't spent much time on the Cape since he moved to this crappy condo after refusing to kick my ex-stepmother out of our house on the beach. That was where we were supposed to be spending the weekend."

"I'm just grateful your dad offered to let us stay here, since he was going to be out of town. It's so much nicer than that motor inn near Logan airport I'd been eyeing."

"Anything is better than that. But the point is, it's been six months since the divorce. He needs to grow a pair and kick that woman to the—oh, God." Erica pressed a hand to her mouth, turning as green as a character in a cartoon as another wave of nausea overtook her. "This sucks."

"Hold that thought. I'll be right back with something for you in case you need to throw up." Simone dashed to the kitchen to find a suitable container. Not that she wanted her friend to be sick, but she couldn't help her relief at avoiding yet another diatribe about Erica's father's recent divorce. It had been the topic of conversation the entire drive down from Boston, even though Simone had never met either of Erica's parents. But from what she could tell, her friend had taken their breakup personally and was doing her best to direct her anger away from her father, demonizing her stepmother in the process.

Not that it was any of Simone's business.

There were no buckets to be found, but after rummaging through half the cabinets, Simone spotted a large mixing bowl that would do in a pinch. With a glass of water in hand, she returned to find Erica curled into a tight ball on the couch, her arms wrapped protectively around her midsection.

Simone set the bowl on the coffee table and knelt down on one knee, placing her hand on Erica's forehead. "You're clammy, but you don't have a fever. That's a good sign."

Erica managed a weak smile. "Always the doctor, aren't you?"

"Can't help it," Simone replied, gently brushing a strand of hair from Erica's face before offering her the glass. "Small sips, okay?"

Erica shook her head, pushing the glass away. "I don't think I can keep anything down right now."

"You need to stay hydrated," Simone insisted, her voice taking on the firm but compassionate tone she used with stubborn patients. "What if I ran to the store and got some ginger ale?"

"You don't have time to go to the store. The Velvet Sirens' first set starts in less than an hour. You can't miss that."

"No way am I going out tonight. After I get back from the store, I'm gonna change into some pajamas and watch movies while you rest."

Erica lurched into a sitting position on the couch. "Don't you dare take off that dress. One word: smoking. No, that's not enough. Fuckable. That dress says let's fuck. Go. Find. Woman."

Simone laughed. "I don't live in a cave, nor do I plan on hitting someone over the head and dragging them to my bed."

"No clubs necessary. If she doesn't beg to get into bed with you when you're looking like that, she's not the woman for you."

"It's a moot point, because I'm not leaving you here to puke your guts out by yourself."

"But it's gay night at The Driftwood Lounge, and they've got one of the best queer bands in New England playing tonight. They also happen to be your favorite. You should be cutting loose, getting laid, and living it up. I'll be fine." As a matter of fact, Erica's color was no longer as green as it had been.

"I appreciate you looking out for me, but I'm not interested in random hookups. Besides, I'd much rather be here taking care of my best friend."

"I appreciate you looking out for me, but I'm fine," Erica protested weakly, her eyes already drooping. "You're leaving for Haiti in three days. I'm ruining your big send-off."

"Will you stop beating yourself up? Life happens. I wasn't even supposed to be here this weekend. You saved me from getting a hotel room in Boston after my program postponed my departure because of the tropical storm that's hitting the Caribbean. I don't need you to treat me to a night out on the Cape, too."

"But you have to go out and have fun." Erica's eyelids fluttered closed, succumbing to exhaustion.

"You need some sleep."

"Fine. But you go to the bar. I won't listen to any arguments. Please or I'll hate myself forever."

"You're not going to let this go, are you?" Simone sighed, knowing her friend's stubborn streak all too well. "Alright, I'll make you a deal. I'll go to the bar for one drink—just one—and then I'm coming straight back here to check on you. Deal?"

"Deal," Erica mumbled, burrowing deeper into the couch cushions.

Simone shook her head as she grabbed a light throw blanket from the back of the sofa and gently draped it over Erica's torso, giving her friend's shoulder a fond pat. "Fine. I have my phone. If you need anything, give me a call."

Erica cracked open one eye. "And if you meet a hottie who wants to take you back to her place, I expect you to forget all about me and go."

Chuckling softly to herself, Simone retrieved her shoes from the hallway. She stopped in front of the mirror to smooth her long blond hair, torn between her promise to go out and her instinct to stay and be a caregiver. But Erica was right—Simone needed to unwind a bit before her upcoming mission.

Once she arrived in Haiti, she expected to work around the clock, with little time for relaxation or socializing. Becoming a doctor and providing emergency medical relief to victims of natural disasters was the only thing Simone had wanted, ever since the hurricane that had devastated her family, taking her father from her and washing away her old life in New Orleans when she was young. But she wasn't naïve enough to believe it would be easy. The work would be grueling, both physically and emotionally.

Maybe one drink wouldn't hurt. She could pop into the bar, listen to a song or two, and be back before Erica finished her nap. With a final glance at Erica's sleeping form, Simone slipped out the front door and into the warm summer night, heading on foot in the direction of The Driftwood Lounge.

The salty sea air filled her lungs as she walked, her heels clicking against the sidewalk. Thankfully, her destination was only a few blocks away, because her usually sneaker-clad feet couldn't handle a longer walk. Tourists and locals alike packed the streets, all out to enjoy the balmy evening. While her outfit was anything but comfortable, the not-so-subtle looks of admiration she received as she walked boosted her confidence. It's possible Erica was right about the dress.

The pulsing beat of music spilled out of the bar onto the street as Simone approached. The Driftwood Lounge overlooked the water, and the view of waves crashing on the seagrass-dotted sand took Simone's breath away. After relocating from the Gulf Coast to northern New Hampshire at age twelve, she'd had little opportunity to spend time near the water. The sight of it now stirred something deep within her, a mix of nostalgia and longing that she quickly pushed aside.

This was not the time to dwell on all she'd lost. There was too much in life to look forward to, and her father wouldn't want her to be sad.

A line had formed outside the entrance, but it was moving quickly. Simone joined the queue, her stomach fluttering with nerves. It had been ages since she'd gone out to a bar, let alone one catering to queer people.

Since the Velvet Sirens were a popular lesbian band, it wasn't surprising that more than half the crowd was female. Given that it was a busy weekend toward the end of the summer high season, there were also more than a few tourists of both sexes, looking vaguely befuddled by the abundance of rainbow decor as they waited their turn to enter. From what Simone could tell, however, she was one of the few people flying solo.

Just as well since she had no intention of hooking up. No matter what Erica thought she should do. Even if Simone hadn't had a sick friend at home, she wasn't the type for one-night stands. She preferred meaningful connections, which would be scarce in a crowded bar and inconvenient given she was days away from embarking on a nomadic lifestyle.

After reaching the front of the line, Simone made her way inside. The restaurant area and the deck in the back were both packed, and people moved in sync to the driving rhythm of the live music coming from the stage at the far end of the bar. The band was already in full swing, the lead singer's powerful voice soaring over the crowd as she belted out lyrics about love and heartbreak.

The band was her jam, for sure, but all Simone really cared about was getting that one drink she'd promised her friend and then heading back home. This wasn't her scene.

Simone squeezed her way through the throng, heading outside toward a smaller bar inside a tent. It was every bit as crowded as the one inside, perhaps made worse by the limited space and complete lack of airflow. She angled herself into the only open spot beside a tall woman with deep crimson curls who was so far out of Simone's league it was almost laughable.

Not that Simone was looking, of course. Strike that. Simone was staring so hard her eyes might pop out of her head. Which meant she was admiring, not intending to get laid. It was impossible not to notice someone so striking, even if only from an aesthetic point of view. The woman appeared to be in her late-thirties, maybe five years older than Simone, though it was hard to tell for certain. It was less about actual age and more an attitude of maturity that drew Simone in, a quality she admired but didn't herself possess.

Even the woman's posture exuded confidence, and her clothing was both timeless and sophisticated. She wore a fitted black blazer over a low-cut emerald green top that accentuated her curves. Dark skinny jeans hugged her long legs, and she stood with a serene confidence that drew the eye. While most women her height would have opted for flats, this woman wore heeled boots that added another three inches to her already impressive stature. Now that took guts.

Was she here for the band? Almost certainly not. The woman gave off an air of sophistication that was at odds with the raucous atmosphere of the bar. She looked like she'd be more at home sipping martinis at an upscale jazz lounge than downing beer while vibing to queer pop.

Probably a tourist, and a straight one, at that. Despite that, Simone found herself inexplicably drawn to this stunning stranger.

The frazzled bartender jerked her chin in Simone's direction. "What can I get you?"

The woman beside her gave a frustrated sigh. Simone couldn't blame her. Given the packed space, it was difficult to get anyone's attention, and the bartender had skipped right over the other woman, even though she'd been waiting longer. Simone glanced at the specialty drinks written on the chalkboard behind the bartender's head. "A Cape Codder's Dream for me, and whatever she's having." Simone motioned to the woman beside her, whose green eyes widened in surprise.

"That's very kind but not necessary," the woman said.

Damn, a husky voice like hers was like an aphrodisiac. Bold and in control. It made Simone wonder if she was always so composed, or if there were moments that voice could become breathy and desperate. Even without closing her eyes, she could imagine urgent whispers in her ear, sending shivers down her spine.

Simone shook her head, trying to clear away the inappropriate thoughts as she forced herself to meet the woman's gaze. "Please, I insist. I'm sure it was your turn."

The woman edged a step closer to Simone. "In that case, I'll have the same. Thank you."

"Make that two Cape Codder's Dreams," Simone shouted

to the bartender, who had turned her back to begin making the first drink.

Even though she had sworn not to do it, Simone scanned her brain for a pickup line. Unfortunately, the best she could come up with on short notice was the truly terrible, "Are your feet tired? Because you've been running through my mind all night." Wisely, Simone opted to stare straight ahead and keep her mouth shut.

The band began to play a new song, and Simone broke into a grin. "'Echoes of Her Smile,'" she said to the woman beside her. "My favorite song."

"I don't really know it," the woman said with a shrug.

That settled it. The stranger was definitely straight.

The bartender set the drinks down, but before Simone could grab a couple of twenties from her wallet to cover the bill, the other woman slid a credit card across the bar. "Let me get this."

Simone opened her mouth to protest, but the woman silenced her with a raised eyebrow and a slight shake of her head. "I insist. Consider it my appreciation for discovering that chivalry isn't quite as dead as I assumed." She winked.

The kind of saucy, flirty wink that sent a jolt of electricity through Simone's body. Talk about smooth. As pickup lines went, the stranger's was way better than the high school level shit Simone had come up with. But it clearly hadn't been intended as a pickup line, because before Simone could even process what had happened enough to respond, the knockout grabbed her drink and headed outside to the deck alone.

What to do? Follow?

Simone hesitated, her drink in hand, watching the woman's retreating form. The logical part of her brain urged her to stay put, to remember her original plan for one drink and then retreating home. Erica needed her, after all.

But the sway of the woman's hips as she walked was mesmerizing. Hypnotic. Before Simone could overthink it, she found her feet moving of their own accord. Erica wasn't really all that sick, and this was what she would've wanted anyway.

Simone's eyes found their target. It was hard to miss a towering woman with hair the color of a fire engine, even in a crowd. She'd set her drink on the railing and was looking out over the water. The setting sun painted the sky in shades of purple as it inched toward the horizon. But Simone was too busy admiring the woman's profile—her high cheekbones and elegant neck illuminated by the fading light—to appreciate any other view.

You'll be up to your ears in cases of cholera and dengue fever by this time next week, Simone reminded herself. In other words, it wouldn't be the end of the world if she asked the woman to dance. She could almost hear Erica screaming a raucous, *"Hell yeah! Go for it!"*

Determined, Simone tucked the small clutch she carried under her arm, took her drink with her free hand, and headed for the railing. But before she could close in and make her move, a man in a loud Hawaiian shirt cut in and blocked her path. Frustrated, Simone kept watch from a safe distance.

"Hey there, beautiful," the man slurred, and the woman's nose wrinkled at what was likely a strong whiff of alcohol on his breath. "Buy you a drink?"

"I have a drink," she informed him with a haughty expression that could have turned a bubbling hot spring into an ice rink.

"You can never have too many, right?" The man laughed at his own joke.

"I'm not interested. Please leave me alone."

The man's face darkened. "Come on. Don't be like that. I'm just trying to be friendly."

As he leaned in closer, there was no mistaking the look of panic that flashed in the woman's gorgeous green eyes. A red wave of anger surged through Simone's veins. Without thinking, she strode forward, positioning herself between the man and the woman.

"There you are, darling." Simone wrapped an arm around the beautiful stranger's trim waist. "Sorry I'm late. Traffic was a nightmare."

The woman tensed for the briefest moment before relaxing into Simone's embrace, her arm sliding around Simone's shoulders as she caught on to what Simone was trying to do.

"No worries, love." The woman's voice warmed with such genuine affection that even Simone forgot for a second that it wasn't real. "I'm just glad you made it."

The man blinked, confusion evident on his ruddy face. "Is this your sister?"

Simone expected the woman to give the man a verbal dressing down or maybe another icy stare to chill him to the core. What she wasn't anticipating, never in a million years, was for the woman to turn to Simone, cup her face gently with one hand, and press their mouths together in a searing kiss.

Simone's mind went blank as soft lips pressed against hers. The kiss was gentle but insistent, and despite her shock, Simone found herself responding with immediate intoxication that eclipsed the effects of the alcohol in her glass.

The man raised a hand, uttering, "Lesbians," before stumbling away.

As quickly as it had begun, the kiss ended. The woman pulled back, amusement in her eyes as she gazed down at Simone, whose mind hovered on the brink of short-circuiting.

"Aren't men so charming?" the woman observed.

Simone let out a snort. "Are you really a lesbian?" she surprised herself by asking. "Or was that just a ploy to get rid of him?"

The woman's lips curved into a mischievous smile. "What do you think?"

"I think... I'd like to find out for myself." Simone barely

recognized her own voice, the huskiness betraying the desire ignited by their kiss.

The woman's eyebrow arched, her smile widening. "Is that so?"

Simone's heart raced. She was never this bold. But this woman's magnetic presence and that earth-shattering kiss had upended all of Simone's carefully laid plans.

Besides, hadn't Erica basically begged her to go out and enjoy one of her last nights of freedom? It seemed almost rude not to respect her friend's wishes.

Simone found herself nodding, unable to form words as her gaze locked with those mesmerizing eyes. No matter what else happened tonight, she was pretty sure she'd be seeing them in her sleep for years to come.

"Well then," the woman purred, her fingers trailing lightly along Simone's arm. "Perhaps we should find someplace a little more private."

The last bit of rational thought Simone possessed managed one final objection. "But I don't even know your name."

"It's Rowan." Though they'd already shared a kiss, the woman held out a hand.

Simone clasped it in hers, giving it a shake. "I'm Simone."

"Nice to meet you." Rowan grinned in a way that turned Simone's insides to jelly. "Do you want to get out of here?"

Simone touched the tip of her tongue to her lips before swallowing. "I thought you'd never ask."

CHAPTER TWO

Rowan attempted to insert the key into her front door as her hand shook out of control. What the hell was going on? She was as steady as they came. Nerves of steel, everyone always said that about her. Yet here she was, a quivering mess, and all because she'd taken her best friend's challenge seriously and invited a woman she didn't know to come back to her house for sex.

A woman who was younger than her, to boot. By how much, Rowan wasn't sure, but at least five years. What could they possibly have in common, aside from being horny on a Saturday night? Of course, if Candace were here, she would probably say that was the only commonality that mattered. But Candace wasn't here. She'd bailed on Rowan at the last minute, leaving her to her own devices after putting crazy ideas into her head.

Yes, this was one hundred percent Candace's fault.

Rowan wasn't the type to succumb to reckless impulses. Ever since she'd finalized her divorce from Lance six months ago, she'd basically lived as a nun, despite having initiated the split from her ex-husband in part because it pained her to hide her true sexuality any longer.

But it was one thing to realize she was exclusively attracted to women after years of considering herself bisexual, and quite another to act on it. Especially with a stranger she'd met at a bar. If Candace hadn't goaded her into promising to get laid during her week-long vacation on the Cape, this would not be happening.

"Are you sure this is your house?" asked the woman, whose name was... *oh, shit*. Rowan struggled to recall the name the woman had offered minutes before in the pulsating club. Was it Sarah? Sadie? No, those weren't right.

Shit, shit, and triple shit.

"Of course, this is my house," Rowan all but growled, attempting to jam the key into the lock again but failing miserably.

She hadn't wanted the damn place, but it was all hers, bought and paid for with every penny from her divorce settlement. Because she'd let guilt win instead of refusing to bail Lance out of his money troubles when he had pleaded with her.

Always the fixer, that's what she was. Not anymore, dammit. Tonight was about her needs, for once.

She cursed under her breath as she attempted to stab the lock with the key one more time, her frustration mounting with each failed attempt. The woman beside her shifted, and Rowan could sense the intensity of her discomfort.

"Perhaps I should go," the woman said hesitantly.

"No—" Fuck, why couldn't Rowan remember her name? "I just need to jiggle it a little, and then I'm sure it will slip right in."

The laugh that accompanied Rowan's statement bordered on hysterical. Could that have come out sounding any more ridiculously sexual? Considering her total display of ineptitude, she wouldn't blame the woman for skipping out as quickly as possible.

"Um, or maybe... I think the key's upside down."

Rowan stopped and stared at the key in her hand. The woman was right. How could she have been so distracted not to notice? With the heat of embarrassment surging in her cheeks, Rowan flipped the key and easily slid it into the lock. The door clicked open without even a hint of a struggle.

"Thanks—" Susan? Sandra? "Simone!"

Yikes. That exclamation point had probably been audible all the way in Provincetown.

Simone arched an eyebrow, a hint of a smile playing at the corners of her mouth. "You forgot my name, didn't you?"

"I most certainly did not." After all, Rowan was on track to become the chair of internal medicine at Boston General Hospital. Her memory was impeccable, even if her nerves were currently shot to hell.

She stepped inside, flicking on the lights and gesturing for Simone to follow. "Please, come in. *Simone.*" Overemphasizing Simone's name likely did nothing to disprove a memory lapse, but it was too late to change it.

A stack of cardboard moving boxes still cluttered the entryway, a stark reminder that Rowan had yet to finish packing up all the crap Lance had left behind for her to deal with now that the sale had gone through. Why would he care how much extra work that created for her to get the place ready for the short-term rental market? But she would have to power through as quickly as she could. It wasn't like she planned to live on the Cape, despite having grown up here. Her life was in Boston, in a dingy apartment she paid far too much to rent and rarely saw anyway thanks to the long hours she put in at work.

Simone stepped inside, her gaze sweeping over the cluttered entryway. "Just moving in?" she asked, her tone light and conversational. "Unless cardboard chic is the latest decorating trend."

"Uh—" The woman's lingering perfume proved too distracting for Rowan to compose a coherent sentence. What was that scent? Jasmine, maybe? Or was it gardenia? The fragrance teased at Rowan's senses, subtle yet alluring, much like the woman herself. She shook her head, trying to clear the fog from her brain before Simone began to question Rowan's sanity. Or worse, changed her mind about their plans for the evening.

"Would you like a glass of wine?" Rowan offered, sidestepping an answer. She could have launched into a long diatribe about how Lance always left his messes for her to clean up, but bringing up her ex-husband and his money woes was hardly the best way to seduce a woman. Rowan might be out of practice, but even she knew that. "If you like white, I should have something decent in the fridge."

Simone smiled, dazzling Rowan with a flash of perfect white teeth against her honeyed skin. "Wine would be lovely, thanks. If you don't mind, I need to send a quick text to let a friend know I'm going to be out later than I anticipated."

Rowan frowned. "If you have plans, I understand."

"Even if I did, I would change them." Simone looked at Rowan with hooded eyes that left little doubt about what the woman envisioned happening between the two of them that night.

A jolt of lust shot through Rowan's body from the heady combination of Simone's words and the heat in her gaze. She swallowed hard, suddenly parched. Nothing like that had ever happened with Lance. Not even in the beginning, when Rowan had been so flattered to have an older, distinguished doctor pursuing her that she'd convinced herself she was attracted to him. Everyone had gushed over how lucky she'd been to hook such a handsome guy. It had never occurred to her at the time to question the lack of zing, just as she'd never suspected how much of his put-together appearance was merely a façade.

This was different. Electric. Intoxicating. On a certain level, it terrified her. She knew exactly what she wanted to do with Simone, but was she too out of practice to get it right?

"Right. Wine. I'll just..." Rowan gestured vaguely toward the kitchen and turned on her heel, nearly tripping over a box in her haste to escape the overwhelming intensity of Simone's presence.

She stumbled into the kitchen, grateful for a moment alone to collect herself. With the fridge ajar, Rowan grabbed the first bottle of white she spotted, not even bothering to check the label. Whatever it was would be good. At least Lance had left some bottles behind along with all the junk, and one thing her ex-husband reliably did was spend far too much money on high-quality wine. And just about everything else. The way he used to—

Stop thinking about Lance! Talk about the quickest way to kill the mood.

Rowan poured two generous glasses of the chilled Chardonnay, hoping the wine would help settle her nerves. This was supposed to be fun, not stress-inducing. She was a grown woman, more than capable of handling a casual hookup. So what if it had been a while since she'd been intimate with anyone —and way longer if she was only counting women? That didn't mean she'd forgotten how to do this. It was like riding a bike, right?

Simone appeared in the kitchen doorway, startling Rowan from her thoughts. She leaned against the frame, her posture relaxed and effortlessly sensual. "Need any help?"

"No, thanks. I've got it." Rowan grabbed the wine glasses and handed one to Simone with what she hoped was a confident, flirtatious smile. Their fingers brushed as the glass exchanged hands, sending a tingle of awareness up Rowan's arm.

"Much appreciated." Simone took a sip, her full lips caressing the rim of the glass in a way that made Rowan's mouth go dry. Imagining those lips caressing her body turned the tingling into a flush of heat that shot straight to Rowan's core.

Simone took another sip of wine, her eyes never leaving Rowan's. "This is excellent. You have good taste."

"Glad you like it," Rowan managed, her voice sounding unnaturally high to her own ears. Holy fuck, she needed to pull herself together, or she was going to blow this whole thing before it even started. She took a large gulp of wine, hoping the alcohol would help soothe her frazzled nerves. Instead, it burned half of the way down, and it was all Rowan could do not to choke. "Let's take our wine out to the deck. There's supposed to be a full moon tonight."

"Sure, the deck sounds nice," Simone replied, the hint of amusement in her eyes suggesting she wasn't taken in by Rowan's attempt at playing it cool. She followed Rowan to the sliding door beyond the dining room, the clicking of her heels against the hardwood floor making Rowan's pulse race.

It was all Rowan could do to stay upright as she slid open the glass door and stepped out onto the weathered wooden deck. The salty night air hit her flushed skin, providing relief from the heat that had been building inside her since she'd first laid eyes on Simone at the bar.

The deck overlooked a small stretch of private beach where the rhythmic crash of waves echoed in the otherwise silent night. Despite being only minutes from the center of town, this house was tucked away, offering a sense of privacy that Rowan had always appreciated. She flicked on the string of patio lights with a practiced motion, smiling as the dim glow of illumination created the perfect intimate atmosphere.

"You seem pretty at home for having just moved in," Simone commented as she stepped out onto the deck, her keen observation skills catching Rowan off guard.

"I've, uh, been here before," Rowan explained, crossing to lean against the railing before taking another sip of wine to buy herself a moment to think. The truth was, for over thirteen years, this had been her marital home. But that wasn't really something she wanted to delve into tonight, so a little white lie would have to do. "It was a summer rental." She forced a casual shrug and hoped Simone wouldn't press further.

Simone joined her at the railing, standing close enough that Rowan could sense the warmth emanating from her body. "A summer rental, huh? Lucky for you it went on the market. Did you move to the Cape for a job or something?"

"No. I work in Boston."

"Oh, so this is a vacation place. I'm assuming you don't commute."

"Not a chance." Rowan let out a laugh at the thought of commuting over the Sagamore Bridge every day. "The traffic is brutal. I'm actually just here for a week while I get the house settled. Plus, I needed to get away from the city for a bit."

Simone nodded, taking another sip of her wine before setting the glass down on the railing. "What do you do in the city? For work, I mean."

It was a perfectly reasonable question to ask, but not one that Rowan was in the mood to answer. This was supposed to be a no-strings-attached encounter, not a getting-to-know-you session. Rowan drained half of her glass before setting it down. She turned to face Simone, summoning every ounce of confidence she could muster and flashing a flirtatious grin. "What do you think I do?"

Simone's eyes narrowed slightly as she studied Rowan, a playful smirk tugging at her lips. "Hmm... let me think." She took a step closer, her gaze roaming over Rowan's body in a way that made Rowan's skin tingle. "You carry yourself with confidence, even when you're nervous."

"What makes you think I'm nervous?" Rowan interrupted, feeling her cheeks grow warm.

Simone's smirk widened. "The key incident was a pretty big

tell. Not to mention how you were fidgeting with your wine glass."

Rowan's face flushed even hotter. Was she really that transparent? She prided herself on her composure, especially at work, where lives literally hung in the balance. But something about this woman stripped away her usual cool façade. "You're very observant."

"I am. So, anyway, you're clearly intelligent and successful. You have a place on the Cape but you live in Boston. That takes some—" Simone rubbed her thumb over her fingertips to imply money. "I'm guessing finance."

"Finance?" Rowan folded her arms across her chest. She might not have wanted to tell Simone she was a doctor, but it was possible she'd hoped the woman would guess it on her own. Rowan was strangely disappointed. And *finance*? "That's the type of job people with no imagination do when they can't think of anything better."

"And yet, that wasn't a denial." Simone's mouth twisted into a smile, and all of a sudden, Rowan had the most desperate urge to experience those lips on hers again. If she wasn't careful, she would completely unravel before she got the chance.

"Hmph." Rowan neither confirmed nor denied the woman's guess, too busy trying to regain control of her racing pulse. "Now it's my turn to figure out what you do."

"We're playing it like that, are we?" Simone pursed her lips, and Rowan nearly swooned.

"We are," Rowan said, her confidence growing as the rhythm of their banter became more familiar. She could handle this. "Let's see. You saved me twice this evening. First by getting me a drink when the bartender kept ignoring me—"

"A drink you wouldn't let me pay for and which you left behind without finishing," Simone pointed out.

"You were going to buy my drink?" Rowan was genuinely surprised. "I didn't realize."

"I was trying to be subtle," Simone said with a wink. "But you beat me to it."

"Oh." Rowan's stomach fluttered at the thought of a beautiful woman like Simone wanting to buy her a drink. That type of thing hadn't happened since her first year of medical school. Even though she'd somehow ended up bringing this woman back to her place for the night, the thought of Simone trying to hit on her made Rowan suddenly shy.

"What was the other time I saved you?" Simone prompted when Rowan stayed quiet a few seconds too long. "The key?"

"No, not that. Don't you remember?"

Simone slanted her head, her eyes playful. "You might have to refresh my memory."

Was she being shy or playing hard to get?

"I was thinking of how you pretended to be my girlfriend to get me away from that obnoxious drunk."

"Girlfriend? How do you know the guy wasn't right and I was trying to pretend to be your sister?" Simone's teasing tone connected with all the right spots, and Rowan had to shift her stance to keep her libido in check a little while longer.

"Because no sister would have kissed me like that."

"True. That was definitely not a sisterly kiss. But for the record, you were the one who kissed me."

"I suppose you're right." Rowan was filled with uncertainty. Had Simone not wanted to kiss her? If that were the case, why had she agreed to come back to Rowan's house? Before Rowan could spiral further into self-doubt, Simone took a step closer, her gaze fixated on Rowan's lips.

"I'm not complaining," Simone murmured. "In fact, I'd very much like to do it again."

Rowan's heart lodged in her throat. This was it. The moment she'd been both anticipating and dreading since they'd left the bar. Her thoughts swirled as she tried to remember how to breathe. Before she could summon the courage to close the distance between them, Simone took another step, her jasmine scent—it was definitely jasmine and not gardenia—swirled in the air, making Rowan dizzy with desire.

"Then what are you waiting for?" Rowan whispered, her voice husky with need. "I believe it's your move."

Simone didn't need any further invitation. She erased the last few inches between them, her hands coming to rest on Rowan's hips as she leaned in. Their lips met, softly at first, then with increasing urgency. Rowan's eyes fluttered closed as she melted into the kiss, her hands instinctively moving to grasp Simone's hair. The soft golden strands slipped through her fingers as Simone's tongue teased the seam of Rowan's lips. Rowan parted them willingly, letting out a soft moan as Simone's tongue slipped into her mouth.

The sound seemed to unleash something primal in Simone, her hands sliding from Rowan's hips to her breasts, grasping them through the thin fabric of Rowan's blouse. Rowan gasped at the sudden contact, arching into Simone's touch. Her nipples hardened instantly, sending jolts of pleasure through her body. It had been so long since anyone had touched her like this—with such passion and urgency.

"How many bedrooms does this place have?" Simone asked, panting for breath between words.

Rowan's mind swam, struggling to process the question through the haze of her desire. "Uh, three," she managed to reply. "But they're all so far away."

Simone's eyes flitted to the nearby patio table. With a quick swipe of her arm, she sent the tablecloth, along with its assortment of seashells and citronella candles, flying to reveal the clean, glass-topped surface beneath. A second later, she hopped up onto it. With a hungry look in her eyes, Simone reached out and grabbed a fistful of Rowan's now very rumpled blouse, drawing her closer until she could snake her arms around Rowan's waist.

"Impressive agility," Rowan commented. "It might have

been better to take off your dress first. Although, I have to admit that dress is amazing. It's almost too fucking hot to take off." Rowan reached around Simone, lowering the zipper as she whispered in her ear, "Almost."

While she was there, she nibbled on Simone's delightfully plump earlobe.

Simone let out a moan.

"You like this?" Rowan gently tugged on the lobe with her teeth.

"Very much."

Rowan slipped Simone's dress from her shoulders, leaving a trail of kisses across the exposed skin as the fabric pooled at her waist. Her breath caught at the sight of Simone's full breasts encased in black lace.

"You're stunning," Rowan murmured, unable to tear her eyes away from Simone's body. Her fingers traced the delicate lace of Simone's bra, marveling at the softness of her skin.

"Hold that thought." Simone hopped off the table, her dress falling to the ground, leaving only the lacy black bra, a pair of matching panties, and those stiletto heels that showed off the perfect shape of her legs. She stepped out of the dress, kicking it aside with one high-heeled foot, before fixing Rowan with an appraising eye. "You're a little overdressed, don't you think?"

Simone set about unbuttoning Rowan's blouse, her knuckles grazing Rowan's skin with each movement. As her blouse fell open to reveal her simple cotton bra beneath, Rowan blushed. Why hadn't she worn something sexier? But Simone didn't seem to mind. Her eyes darkened with desire as she slid the blouse off Rowan's shoulders, letting it fall to the deck a short distance from her own discarded dress.

"Much better," Simone murmured, her hands skimming over Rowan's newly exposed skin. She made a move as if to unclasp Rowan's bra, but Rowan put her hands firmly on

Simone's shoulders and, with a slight shake of her head, gently pushed her back against the table.

"My turn first," she said, her voice low and husky.

Simone's eyes widened in surprise, but she didn't resist as Rowan's hands trailed down Simone's sides, savoring the smooth skin beneath her fingertips. She hooked her fingers into the waistband of Simone's panties, slowly sliding them down her legs. Simone lifted her hips to help, and Rowan tossed the lacy garment aside. She drank in the sight of Simone laid out before her, nearly naked save for her bra and heels.

"God, you're beautiful," Rowan breathed, her eyes roaming over Simone's body.

She could barely believe this was real. It was like something out of a daydream. A really sexy one where Rowan could abandon all her inhibitions and embrace the raw experience of her desires.

With newfound boldness, Rowan captured Simone's lips in a searing kiss as she pressed her thigh against Simone's exposed center. Simone gasped into Rowan's mouth, her hips arching up to increase the pressure. Rowan slid her hands up Simone's sides, cupping her breasts through the lace of her bra before sliding her hands around, deftly unhooking the clasp. She pulled back just long enough to remove the garment completely, tossing it aside to join the growing pile of discarded clothing.

She'd never felt more alive.

Rowan's mouth watered at the sight of Simone's nipples, already hard and begging for attention. She lowered her head, taking one rosy peak into her mouth and swirling her tongue around it. She slid one hand between Simone's legs, letting out a groan when she encountered the hot, searing wetness that awaited her there.

This was better than any fantasy Rowan had dared to entertain during all those years when she'd been so miserable, unhappily married to someone who had never elicited excitement in her like this. She shut that thought down, not wanting the guilt to submerge her like it had so many times before.

Life was too fucking short, and she'd wasted enough of it.

Rowan's fingers glided through Simone's slick folds, exploring and teasing. She circled Simone's clit with light, feathery touches, drawing out soft gasps and moans. Simone's hips rocked against Rowan's hand as her own hands tangled in Rowan's hair. It would take a week to brush out all the knots after this, not that Rowan cared. The way Simone was gripping her hair, pulling her closer, was intoxicating. She increased the pressure on Simone's clit, rubbing tight circles as she continued to lavish attention on her breasts with her mouth.

"Please," Simone gasped. "I need you inside me."

Rowan didn't need to be told twice. She slid two fingers into Simone's wetness, groaning at how tight and hot she felt. She curled her fingers, finding that spot inside Simone that made her cry out in pleasure. She began to pump her fingers in and out, setting a steady rhythm as she continued to circle Simone's clit with her thumb.

Fucking hell, this felt amazing.

Pulling her by the hair until she could reach her lips, Simone kissed Rowan with such need it almost made Rowan's knees buckle. Rowan responded with equal fervor, her fingers never slowing their pace deep inside. She could feel Simone's inner walls beginning to tighten around her fingers, a telltale sign she was close to the edge.

Rowan increased her speed, curling her fingers with each thrust as Simone's breathing got heavier, her moans growing in urgency. Simone wrapped her legs, with high heels still on her feet, around Rowan's leg, her pelvis bucking in time with Rowan's movements.

It was close. So fucking close. All it would take was one final—

"Jesus fucking Christ!" Simone belted out as she succumbed

to her orgasm, her body tensing as waves of pleasure crashed over her.

Rowan kept her fingers moving, drawing out Simone's climax for as long as possible before finally withdrawing her fingers and collapsing against Simone's heaving chest. They remained that way for several moments, both panting heavily as they came down from the high. Rowan could feel Simone's heart racing beneath her cheek, matching the frantic rhythm of her own.

"That was…" Simone bit her lip, seemingly at a loss for words.

"Like riding a bicycle," Rowan blurted out, unable to stop herself from laughing at the confusion on Simone's face. And no wonder. She was babbling like a fool. Fortunately, Simone seemed too blissed-out to be bothered by it.

"It's a shame it's such a dark night." Simone slowly turned her head, the light from inside the house falling just right across her face. "I can hear the ocean, but I can't see it."

"Then stick around until sunrise." Rowan quickly added, "If you want to, that is."

"Of course, I do," Simone said, her voice soft and sincere. "But are you sure that's okay?"

"More than okay," she assured her, reaching out to tuck a stray lock of hair behind Simone's ear. "I'd love for you to stay."

Simone's lips curved into a smile. "In that case, I will. But only if you promise to give me a full tour of the house."

"A tour?" Rowan raised an eyebrow at the unexpected request.

"Yes. I'm curious to see if all the rooms are as accommodating as the deck has been." Simone trailed a finger along Rowan's collarbone. "I mean, if we were this good out here, imagine what we could do if we had a bed."

CHAPTER THREE

A ray of sunshine fell across Simone's face, gently rousing her from sleep. She blinked and stretched, taking in the white shiplap-covered walls and vaguely nautical decor that was visible from her cozy bed. She felt disoriented, unsure of where she was. Then the memories of the day before came trickling back bit by bit. The last-minute call from Global Health Frontiers to say her departure date had been delayed. Meeting up with Erica in Boston. The long drive down the coast to spend the weekend on the Cape.

Was that where she was? The gentle sound of rolling waves somewhere in the distance suggested this was the case, but she wasn't sure. What was more, Simone was surprised to find she was too relaxed to care. She closed her eyes again, savoring the warmth that surrounded her as she snuggled deeper into the bed's snow-white blanket. She hadn't slept so deeply in months. What had changed?

"Knock, knock."

Startled by an unfamiliar voice, Simone bolted upright, clutching the blanket to her chest as she belatedly realized she was completely naked. Her heart raced as she scanned the room, her eyes landing on a short stack of cardboard moving boxes next to the bed.

Rowan.

She was still at Rowan's place.

Her eyes darted to the doorway, where a statuesque woman with a pale complexion and a head of rogue crimson curls stood, her hand resting on the doorframe. Her attire consisted of a silk robe, barely covering her body and tied loosely at her waist. It was clear to Simone's eyes that there was nothing underneath it.

Oh my. This woman was even more alluring in the light of day than she had been the night before. Simone pressed her thighs together, trying to quell the sudden rush of unbridled lust that flooded her body. Memories of the previous night flashed through her mind—the passionate kisses, exploratory touches, and waves of pleasure that had left her breathless and sated.

"Um..." Simone felt her cheeks flush as she struggled to find her voice. "If I'm not mistaken, this is your place. Why are you knocking?"

Technically, Rowan hadn't knocked. She'd only said the words. But Simone was too flustered to insist on complete accuracy. She was also too busy holding herself back from leaping out from the covers, grabbing Rowan by the ties of her robe, and dragging her into the bed.

As if reading Simone's mind, Rowan's lips curled into a mischievous smile. "Just being polite," she purred, her voice low and sultry. "I didn't want to startle you, though it seems I did anyway. I wasn't expecting you to be so wide awake already."

"What time is it?"

"It's barely after five in the morning." Rowan disappeared into the hallway, reappearing with a wooden tray in her hands, on top of which were two steaming coffee mugs. "I made myself coffee, so I brought you some, too, but that doesn't mean you have to get up if you still want to sleep."

Simone let out an involuntary yawn, and the first sniff of

freshly brewed coffee made her mouth water. "Why are you up so early?"

Rowan chuckled. "Occupational hazard, I'm afraid." She entered the bedroom and crossed to the bed.

"Ah, yes. Money never sleeps. I assume you must work on an international trading desk."

"I see you're still convinced I work in finance." Rowan set the tray down on the comforter before lowering herself into a seated position beside it.

"You never specifically denied it, and I'm familiar enough with Boston to know if you throw a stone, more than likely you'll hit someone from the Evil Empire."

"Evil Empire, is it?" Rowan laughed. "I'm not sure if I should be insulted or proud. No one has ever called me evil before. Well, almost no one." A cloud descended over her face. Simone wasn't certain why and didn't want to ask.

"Did you say one of those coffees is for me?" Simone eyed the two cups with unabashed longing. The scent was reminiscent of that super high-end coffee place near the hospital she used to pass every day but could never afford.

"It was, until you insisted I was evil." Rowan curled a protective arm around the cups like a fierce dragon protecting her treasure. "You have to tell me. What about me screams stockbroker to you?"

"How about all this?" Simone pointed to the view. "Not many professions can afford a beachfront vacation home."

"You have a point, but I could be royalty." Rowan's eyes sparkled as she handed Simone one of the mugs.

"Not buying it. You don't have a fancy foreign accent." Simone poured some milk into her coffee from the small jug on the tray, bypassing the sugar bowl. She took a sip and closed her eyes in bliss. "A little more of this and I might start to feel human."

"Not a morning person?"

Simone shook her head, savoring another sip of the rich, hot brew. This stuff was amazing, not like the crap she was accustomed to. "Voluntarily? No. That doesn't mean I don't have to get up early most days, but I'm usually powered by enough coffee to fuel a small city."

"Why don't you try sleeping more?" Rowan picked up her cup and raised it to her lips, puckering them in a way that instantly made Simone's thoughts drift to less innocent places. She forced herself to focus on the conversation.

"Sleep more? I wish," Simone sighed. "Sadly, I have no time."

"Always partying?"

"Sure," Simone answered with a snort, mulling over the last three years of her life as a resident. Routinely working twenty-eight-hour shifts. Catching catnaps whenever she had a spare moment and a flat surface. It was the life she'd chosen, and most days, she loved it. But it was as far from a party as you could get. "What does a princess do all day? Drink gourmet coffee?"

Rowan shrugged. "It's what I had. Do you prefer instant?"

"I wouldn't call it a preference, but it's more what I'm used to."

"Shall I run out and get some?"

"Only if you plan to have it, because I may never be able to drink anything but this again. If I were a princess"—Simone jerked her chin to the window overlooking the water—"I'd sit here all day, drinking this amazing coffee and staring at the view."

"It is rather hypnotic."

When Simone noticed Rowan wasn't looking at the ocean but at her when she said this, she took another sip of coffee to hide the flush of her cheeks. She nearly choked as Rowan's hand came to rest on her knee, the touch electric even through the blanket.

"How long are you in town for?" Rowan asked.

"One more night."

"Then home?"

"Not exactly." Wasn't that just Simone's luck? To come across a woman like this at precisely the worst time.

"Intriguing." Rowan studied her with an intensity that made Simone feel exposed in the best possible way. "I'm starting to wonder if you really exist or if this has been a delightful dream."

"Do you want me to pinch you?" Simone asked, her voice low and teasing. She set her coffee mug on the tray, her eyes never leaving Rowan's.

"Sounds kinky." Rowan leaned in closer, her hand sliding up Simone's thigh. "Have dinner with me tonight."

Why was this happening now? Simone wanted to scream. She had a plane to catch tomorrow, a new life to begin. Now was not the time to get caught up in a long-distance romance.

"I..." Simone wasn't sure what to say, torn between desire and duty. "I really wish I could, but I need to spend time with my friend before I leave the country tomorrow."

"Was that the best excuse you could come up with?" There was genuine hurt in Rowan's eyes as she withdrew her hand from Simone's leg. "I think that's the first time someone has ever said they were leaving the country as a way of letting me down easy."

"It's true, though," Simone protested, reaching out to grasp Rowan's hand before she could pull away completely. "It's not an excuse. I really am leaving tomorrow to go to Logan airport. I was supposed to fly out a few days ago, but my departure was delayed, so I came down to the Cape with a friend to kill some time before—"

Rowan held up a hand, her serious expression stopping Simone's firehose of words mid-stream. "Are you a spy?"

It was difficult to determine if Rowan was fucking with Simone or genuinely asking. But the transition was so unexpected and ludicrous that Simone couldn't help but burst out laughing. "A spy? Yes, you got me. I am an international woman of mystery, known by many names, but you can call me Bond. Simone Bond."

Rowan's lips twitched, fighting a smile. "Well, Ms. Bond, I must say you're doing a terrible job of maintaining your cover. Spies aren't supposed to admit they're spies, you know."

"I never said I was any good at it," Simone quipped, relieved to see the hurt disappearing from Rowan's eyes. "In fact, I'm probably the worst spy in the history of espionage."

"Clearly," Rowan chuckled, her fingers intertwining with Simone's. "Do you have to leave right away? It's not even six."

"I'm sorry." Simone rubbed her ears, uncertain what she'd heard. "Did you say six or sex?"

Rowan arched a brow. "Why do you ask?"

"Because if it's six, I'm pretty sure the friend I mentioned is still asleep."

"And if it was the other thing I said?" Rowan raised an eyebrow.

Simone bit her lip and swallowed hard. "In that case, I guess I'd ask if you want me to stay a little longer?"

To answer the question, Rowan moved the tray with the empty mugs to the floor. Then she pulled the covers back and straddled Simone's naked body, untying her robe and letting it fall open. "Come on, super spy. Rock my world."

BY THE TIME Simone returned to the condo, it was a little after eight, but she was coasting on fumes. That last fuck had been epic, and Simone would be taking the memories—not to mention the scratches on her back—all the way to Haiti with a smile on her face.

Letting herself in with the key Erica had given her, Simone

strained her ears for any signs of stirring from her friend. The condo was quiet, save for the gentle hum of the air conditioning. Simone tiptoed toward the guest room, hoping to slip in unnoticed and grab a quick shower before Erica woke up.

As she passed the kitchen, however, a voice called out. "Look what the cat dragged in." Erica's voice was gravelly with sleep but sounded much more powerful than it had the day before.

Simone froze, caught red-handed. She turned slowly to face her friend, who was leaning against the kitchen counter next to the Keurig machine. "Hey, you're up early. How are you feeling?"

"Not as good as you," Erica said with a smirk.

"What do you mean?" Simone couldn't help but think her friend was looking far too smug for someone who'd been puking her guts out twelve hours ago.

"I know a walk of shame when I see one." Erica made a motion with her hand, calling attention to Simone's attire. "I've always thought it should be called a stride of pride, personally."

Simone's face grew hot as she realized how disheveled she must look. Her hair was tangled, her makeup smudged, and she was pretty sure her dress was on inside out. She'd been in such a daze leaving Rowan's place that she hadn't bothered to check the mirror.

"It's not what you think," Simone stammered, though she knew it was exactly what Erica thought.

Erica rolled her eyes. "Please. Spare me the denials. What I want is details."

"There are no details to share." Simone spoke in a prim tone while avoiding her friend's gaze.

"You've always been such a terrible liar."

"Maybe I've been letting you think that all these years because I'm a super spy." That had not been the wisest thing to say because as soon as she was reminded of Rowan, Simone's clit did a spin, and it was all she could do to keep from squirming.

"A super spy, huh? Is that what you're calling it these days?" Erica laughed wickedly. "I want to know the name of the woman who fucked you senseless."

"And I, as a doctor, want to know why my patient is out of bed and walking around when she is clearly delirious."

"You said you aren't really a doctor. You're a super spy."

Simone tried to give her best stern glare but to no avail.

Erica's grin turned into an exaggerated pout. "I've been on death's doorstep all night. The least you can do is give me some hot gossip. The only person I've had to chat with while you were away is my dad."

"What did he have to say?" Simone asked, hoping to change the subject. "Is he enjoying his conference in Chicago?"

Erica's eyes narrowed. "Nice try, but you're not getting off that easily. Dad's fine, conference is boring, he's worried about me being sick, blah blah blah. Now spill it. Who's the mystery woman?"

"You sure you don't want to go back to bed? You seem a little pale," Simone deflected, though she knew it was futile. Erica was like a dog with a bone when she wanted information.

Erica waved her hand dismissively. "I'm fine. The worst is over. Now stop stalling, and tell me about your night!"

Simone sighed, realizing she wasn't going to escape Erica's interrogation. "Okay, I'll tell you. But tea first. I'd suggest coffee, but I think it will be too harsh for your poor tummy."

"Tea sounds nice. But go change first. I'm getting jealous seeing you all gussied up when I spent the night in this." Erica gestured to her stained T-shirt and yoga pants with a look of distaste.

Simone reluctantly changed in her room, a sadness washing over her as she stripped off the dress and tossed it on a chair. All she could think of was Rowan saying her dress was almost too sexy to remove. Taking it off was akin to discarding the last physical reminder of their night together.

After putting on a pair of leggings and a hoodie, Simone set about making breakfast for Erica, who was camped out on the sofa with her phone in hand, busy documenting her harrowing experience with food poisoning for all of her social media friends.

"I made you something to eat," Simone said, handing Erica a plate with two slices of lightly buttered toast. "And here's your tea," she added, setting down a steaming mug on the coffee table. "Peppermint. It should help settle your stomach."

"Thanks, Mom," Erica said with a playful roll of her eyes. "Speaking of, you know what I wish I had? Chicken soup from Francesca's deli."

"How the heck did you get from Mom to a deli?" Simone asked, amazed once again at the twists and turns of her friend's conversation. Sometimes it seemed like Erica, with her creative brain and artistic temperament, had less a train of thought and more of a roller coaster with a dozen loops.

"Because when I was a sophomore in high school, I got really sick. My mom—I mean, my dad's ex-wife—" Erica flinched a little as she corrected herself. "Anyway, she brought me this amazing chicken soup from Francesca's. It was like magic. I felt better almost instantly."

Simone nodded sympathetically, noting the sadness in her friend's tone. As much as Erica blamed her former stepmother for leaving, there was still clearly a part that missed her. It must be hard to be so angry with someone you obviously still love.

"I could always run out later today and get some for you," Simone offered, settling onto the couch next to Erica.

"I'd rather you tell me all about your hot date last night." Erica flashed a devilish grin before taking a small nibble of toast.

"Not much to tell, really." Simone was only partially lying. Plenty had happened, sure, but there wasn't much she planned to share. "I went to the gig last night. Met a sexy woman. She took me home. And, now I'm here."

"She took you home. Just like that?" Erica's eyes rounded. "Are you sure you went to The Driftwood Lounge and not a sex club or something?"

Simone snorted a laugh. "Not to my knowledge, but it did happen fast."

"Geez. I didn't know you had it in you." Erica took a bite of toast, chasing it down with some tea. "No offense."

"None taken. To be honest, I surprised myself." Simone leaned into the couch cushions, her mind drifting back to the events of the previous night. "It was unexpected. But amazing. This creepy guy was hitting on her, and I pretended to be her girlfriend to get him to back off. She kissed me—only for show. But one thing led to another, and before I knew it, we were leaving together."

"That's so fucking hot." Erica wore a dreamy expression. "Are you seeing her again?"

Deflated, Simone shook her head.

Erica's brow furrowed. "Why not?"

"Because I'm leaving the country tomorrow." Simone cursed her weakness as tears welled up in her eyes. She had no business crying. Going to work for Global Health Frontiers was her dream job.

"Oh shit, I totally forgot about that. Being sick and all, it slipped my mind that you're leaving so soon." Erica's shoulders slumped. "Bummer."

Simone nodded, rubbing at her eyes under the guise of having an itch. "Yeah, it really does suck. I mean, I'm excited about the opportunity with Global Health Frontiers, but..."

"You met someone amazing right before you have to leave," Erica finished for her.

"No one has made me feel like that in a long time," Simone admitted softly. "Maybe ever. It's my rotten luck."

"Did you at least get her number?" Erica asked, hope creeping into her voice.

Simone shook her head, experiencing a pang of regret. "No, I didn't. It all happened so fast, and then this morning..." She left the rest unsaid, not wanting to keep talking about it and make herself feel even worse. "What's the point anyway? It's not like I'm going to be sexting between shifts while I'm caring for earthquake and flood victims around the globe."

Erica reached out and squeezed Simone's hand. "I'm sorry. But hey, look at it this way. You had an amazing night with a gorgeous woman right before embarking on this huge adventure. Maybe it's the universe's way of sending you off in style."

"Sure. Maybe so." Simone knew she didn't sound convinced, but she forced a small smile for Erica's benefit. "I should focus on the positives. It was an incredible night, and I'm grateful for the experience."

"Yeah. Exactly." Erica frowned as she picked up her tea, taking a slow sip. "Unless. Are you sure about this whole humanitarian thing? Haiti is so dangerous tourists aren't even supposed to go there. And who knows where they'll send you after that."

"There are sick people there who need help. I've worked too hard for this opportunity to throw it away on some woman I don't even know." Even as she said it, Simone once again wanted to curl into a ball and cry at how unfair life could be.

"But what if she's the one?" Erica pressed, leaning forward with an earnest expression. "I mean, you said yourself that no one has ever made you feel this way before. Doesn't that count for something?"

"Come on. I met her last night. There's no such thing as *the one* after one night." Simone let out a long breath. "What's the plan for today? Are you feeling up to something this afternoon?"

"I think so, unless you want to see your mysterious lady one last time."

"That would make leaving even harder, I think." Simone straightened her spine, resolute in putting the whole experience behind her. "Nope, the best thing is to cut all ties right here and now."

Erica finished her tea with one final gulp and set the mug down. "You're an idiot. I'm going to hop in the shower."

Alone in the room, Simone slumped back into the couch, her mind a whirlwind of conflicting emotions. Part of her knew Erica was right. She was being an idiot, though probably not for the reasons Erica thought. Why couldn't she stop thinking about her encounter with Rowan? The way her fiery red curls had felt wrapped around Simone's fingers. The taste of her skin, salty and sweet. The sound of her breathy moans when Simone's tongue and fingers had finally worked their magic in the moonlit bedroom.

The doorbell rang, startling Simone from her daydreaming.

Since Erica was still in the shower, Simone heaved herself off the couch with a groan and made her way to the front door. She plastered on a polite smile as she swung the door open.

There stood Rowan, holding a giant paper bag from Francesca's deli.

"What the fuck?" Simone blurted. She blinked rapidly, wondering if she was hallucinating. "What are you doing here?"

"Bringing my sick daughter some soup. What the hell are you doing in my ex-husband's condo?" Rowan countered, looking as though she might hyperventilate or possibly go on a rampage worthy of a raging rhinoceros.

Simone gripped the doorframe to stop the sensation of the floor dropping out from beneath her. "Your ex-husband? Your daughter?" she stammered, certain she must have misheard. "God, no. You're Erica's evil stepmom."

All of a sudden, Simone's flight out of the country couldn't come fast enough.

CHAPTER FOUR

"Did you call me an evil stepmother?" Rowan demanded, all the while trying to stop herself from giving in to the panic attack that threatened to overtake her.

How could this be happening? Less than two hours ago, this gorgeous woman's naked body had been entwined with hers, doing all sorts of things best left unmentioned in polite company. Now her two worlds were colliding like a train wreck in slow motion.

"Of all the things you could be worried about in this situation, that's the one you're going with?" Simone demanded in a harsh whisper.

"Oh my fucking God! Are you the college friend Erica posted about on social media who was visiting this weekend? Dear Jesus, I'm going to hell." Rowan clapped a hand over her mouth, a little late in realizing that her stepdaughter was also somewhere nearby and would hear anything she said.

Simone put a finger to her lips. "Yes, but Erica's in the shower, so no screaming."

A memory of the screams she'd made last night under a very

different set of circumstances didn't help Rowan's mood. It might've been a lovely memory to indulge in, but—"Wait. I thought you were maybe five years younger than me. You're the same age as my daughter?"

"No." Simone shook her head so vigorously Rowan could imagine it snapping right off her neck. Apparently, she wasn't the only one who was freaked out by that particular bit of math. "I was a senior when she was a freshman. I was the RA in her dorm. I'm thirty. And I thought *you* were like five years older than *me*."

"Well, I'm forty. So color me flattered, but that doesn't make me feel all that much better about the situation." The twisted paper handles of the takeout bag dug into Rowan's fingers. But that type of pain was preferable to what her emotions were doing. "This can't be happening. It's too surreal, too absurd."

"How do you think I feel?" Simone angry-whispered. "I just found out I had sex with my friend's mother."

"Stepmother. I'm not really old enough to be Erica's birth mother. Not that it makes this much less scandalous."

No, the word scandalous didn't do this scenario justice. Was there even a word in the English language that covered having sex with your kid's best friend?

"What are we going to do?" Simone hissed.

Rowan's mind raced, searching for a way out of this nightmare. "Okay. Let's just calm down and think about this rationally." She said this more to herself than to Simone. "We're both adults. We made a mistake, but it doesn't have to be a catastrophe. Maybe we can, uh, pretend this never happened?"

Simone's eyes widened in disbelief. "Pretend nothing happened? Are you serious? How am I supposed to look Erica in the eye after... after..."

"After what?"

Rowan and Simone froze, their faces draining of color as

they turned to see Erica standing in the hallway outside the bathroom, a towel wrapped around her body and her wet hair dripping onto the floor.

"What are you doing here?" Erica addressed this question directly to Rowan with an iciness that cut into her heart like a dagger.

Rowan was stunned into silence. Ever since she'd walked out on Erica's father, things had been tense between them, but this open hostility cut deeply. Had Erica really described her as an evil stepmother to her friend?

"Soup," Simone managed to blurt out, gesturing weakly at the bag in Rowan's hand. "Your stepmom brought soup."

Rowan nodded frantically, holding up the bag she'd been clutching. "Yes, soup. Your father texted me to say you were sick. I happened to be... in the area."

Because she'd just bought the house that had been in Erica's family for generations and was preparing to turn it into a rental property. But that was not news Rowan felt prepared to break to her stepdaughter today. Besides, it was supposed to be Lance's job to tell her.

"Is that chicken noodle from Francesca's deli?" Erica's frosty demeanor began to thaw as she took a step closer. "Did Dad ask you to bring it?"

Had Lance asked her to bring the soup? Of course not. He'd sent a three-word text, *Erica is sick*, no doubt expecting Rowan to do the rest of the emotional heavy lifting on her own.

"He was concerned about you," Rowan said, not actually confirming Erica's assumption, but not correcting it either. Just like all those Christmases and birthdays when she'd signed her ex's name on the gift tags of the presents she'd picked out and kept silent while his doting daughter gave him all the credit.

"I guess you should come inside." Erica offered the faintest hint of a smile.

Rowan's heart leapt at this small olive branch, even as her stomach churned with guilt. If Erica ever found out what had happened with Simone—no, Rowan couldn't let herself so much as think it. If that happened, everything would be ruined. Determined to keep her mind a blank slate, she stepped into the condo, hyper-aware of Simone's presence inches away.

"Why don't you go throw on some clothes?" Rowan suggested. "If you're hungry, I can fix you a bowl."

Erica nodded, pulling the towel tighter around her body. "I guess I could try a few bites. Thanks for bringing the soup. That was thoughtful of you."

As soon as Erica had disappeared into her bedroom, Rowan and Simone exchanged panicked glances.

"That was a close call," Simone muttered. "I nearly got caught saying something I could never take back. What do we do now?"

"Simple. We have soup." Rowan headed into the kitchen, setting the bag on the counter before stepping back to survey the cabinets. She opened the one above the fridge, grateful for her considerable height as she reached inside and rummaged around for the item she was certain would be there. "Yep. Here it is."

"Here what is?" Simone asked.

"Erica's favorite bowl." Rowan held out an oversized cereal bowl made of white melamine and printed with a brightly colored cartoon bird inside.

"Toucan Sam? Really?" Simone chuckled despite the recent tension. "I wouldn't have pegged Erica as a Froot Loops fan."

"It's from when she was little," Rowan explained softly, a surge of wistfulness causing her eyes to mist. "Her mother bought it for Erica when they went to the grocery store together one time not long before her mother passed away. Ever since I've known her, Erica's always insisted on using this bowl when she was sick."

Simone's expression softened as she watched Rowan carefully ladle the soup into the cherished bowl. "It's really sweet that you remember that."

"It's one of those things you pick up when you're raising someone, I guess." Rowan shrugged, trying to downplay the emotion threatening to overwhelm her. "Can you get a spoon?"

Simone opened a drawer and pulled out a large spoon, but Rowan shook her head and waved it away.

"That one's too big. She prefers the teaspoons."

Simone swapped out the spoon and handed the smaller one to Rowan, their fingers brushing. The brief contact sent a jolt through Rowan. She quickly pulled her hand away. "Soup's all set. I should get going."

"You're not staying?" Erica stood in the doorway wearing a fuzzy robe, her hair still wet.

"You want me to stay? How are you feeling?" Rowan pressed her hand to Erica's forehead, certain she'd discover a fever was the cause of this sudden goodwill. "Huh. You don't feel warm."

"It was food poisoning. I think I'm on the mend. I should be, considering I have not one but two doctors here to take care of me now."

"You're a doctor?" Rowan's eyes widened in surprise as she turned to look at Simone. "I assumed you were an artist, like Erica."

"No. I just finished my residency in emergency medicine."

"Oh." Rowan's stomach dropped. How could it be that the sexy stranger she'd had a one-night stand with happened to be exactly her type? It was like the universe was taunting her with the perfect woman—one who was completely off-limits. She forced a smile. "That's impressive."

"Let's sit in the living room," Erica said, taking her bowl and spoon and leading the way to the sofa. After quickly dishing out two more bowls, Rowan and Simone followed, exchanging nervous glances but otherwise keeping their cool.

Rowan took a seat as far away as possible from Simone, but considering it was a tiny space befitting a bachelor pad, that was still way too close for comfort. She balanced the bowl on her lap, wishing Erica had opted for the dining room table instead.

"I'm going to go look for some crackers for the soup." Erica jumped up almost as soon as she sat down, putting her bowl directly on the coffee table without so much as a coaster beneath it. "Does anyone else want anything?"

"No, but I can get it for you," Rowan moved to get up, eager to put some distance between Simone and herself.

"That's okay. I've got it," Erica assured her before heading for the kitchen.

"I thought you worked in finance," Simone whispered when the coast was clear.

"I literally told you I didn't." Unable to stand it another second, Rowan leaned toward the coffee table, setting her own bowl on a coaster before grabbing a second one and placing it under Erica's bowl.

"Okay, but you never said you were a doctor," Simone pointed out, her eyes darting toward the kitchen to make sure Erica wasn't returning yet. "I assumed—"

"You know what they say about assumptions," Rowan muttered, picking up her bowl again and giving the soup a stir.

"At least if I'd known you were a doctor, along with that beach house of yours, I might've put the clues together and figured out who you were before the evening got out of hand."

"Or if I'd remembered to lead with 'by the way, I'm somebody's stepmother before I'm a person in my own right' at the bar," Rowan shot back, her body tensing with a sudden surge of rage. After everything she'd sacrificed for her family over the years, bending to the demands of both her father and her husband, it was infuriating that her one night of spontaneity and passion had come back to bite her so spectacularly in the ass.

"Obviously, this whole mess is my fault. It's hardly the first time I've been told that."

"I didn't mean it like that," Simone said, her expression softening. "Honestly, I don't know what I meant, except that I—"

"Found them!" Erica called from the kitchen, cutting off whatever Simone had been about to say. She returned to the living room, a sleeve of saltines in hand, and slid back into the sofa cushions, seemingly oblivious to the tension crackling between the two women.

"Did you tell her about your new job?" Erica asked Simone as she crumbled some crackers over her bowl, sending crumbs all over the place in the process.

"New job?" Rowan froze, her spoon halfway to her mouth. Please God, no. There was only one hospital in this part of Cape Cod, and not only was her ex-husband the chief medical officer, but her brilliant surgeon father was the CEO. If Simone was going to work there, it would make this debacle infinitely more complicated than it already was.

"I'm going on a medical mission with Global Health Frontiers," Simone said, sparking instant relief in Rowan's chest, along with a stab of envy.

"That's the NGO that sends teams of doctors to regions around the world that have been hit by natural disasters, isn't it?" Rowan asked. She already knew the answer. Before life had taken her in a completely different direction, Rowan had longed to work with an organization like that, back when she still believed she could leave her mark on the world. Back when she'd thought her life was hers alone to shape.

Once again, the universe was taunting her with all of the dreams she'd pushed aside for the sake of stability and a marriage that ultimately had crumbled with all the messiness of one of Erica's saltines.

"That's right. I was supposed to leave for Haiti already, but the mission was delayed because of the most recent tropical storm that hit the area."

"You really are leaving the country." Rowan stifled a laugh, knowing it would be impossible to explain to Erica, who already looked a little confused by this statement. But all Rowan could think was at least Simone hadn't lied earlier about the reason they couldn't see each other again.

Ah, those simple times a few hours ago when she'd believed geographical distance was the only impediment to being together, as opposed to a ten-year age difference and the fact this was her stepdaughter's *best friend*.

Rowan let go of her spoon and let it sink into the soup, her appetite gone.

"This soup is really good." Erica took in a painfully tiny spoonful of broth.

Rowan had always found it charmingly childlike that Erica preferred such a tiny spoon, but right now, it was agonizing to wait for every bite; the seconds stretched into small eternities. She would never survive this.

"How did you decide to work for Global Health Frontiers?" Rowan asked, feeling the need to fill the silence with polite conversation.

Simone glanced at Rowan, her face carefully neutral but her words hesitant, as if trying not to say too much or too little. "My family lost everything in Hurricane Katrina when I was young. Including my father, who died during the storm. It made me realize the importance of disaster response and accessible medical care. I knew I wanted to be someone who could help people in their darkest moments."

"That's very admirable." Rowan's words were tinged with genuine respect. "It takes a lot of courage to face that kind of tragedy and decide to turn it into something so meaningful."

Simone shrugged, her gaze dropping to her bowl. "It's not

that special. It's survival. Anyway, why did you get into medicine?"

How Rowan wished she had an inspiring story to match Simone's. Instead of the truth, that her career had been one more example of her bending to her father's will and being the good daughter.

"To be honest, I come from a long line of doctors. My father's a surgeon, my grandfather was a cardiologist. I followed in their footsteps."

Simone nodded politely, though to Rowan's ears, it sounded pathetic.

She hadn't even mentioned how her father had never believed her capable of taking over the hospital for him, instead preferring to elevate Lance at every turn like the son he'd wished he'd had. She wouldn't be mentioning it, either. Not now, and not ever.

It was the single greatest source of shame in her life. Or at least it had been until a few minutes ago. It certainly wasn't something she wanted to lay bare in front of a stepdaughter who already viewed her as inadequate. Nor in front of a woman who, despite everything, Rowan still found herself wanting to impress, even if it was completely inappropriate to feel that way.

"Sounds like you didn't really have much of a choice, huh?" Erica rounded out this observation with a wide-mouthed yawn as she set her bowl on the coffee table again, this time using the coaster.

"You look tired, sweetie," Rowan was quick to say. "Maybe you should get some rest. I ought to be going."

"I think you're right. I could use a nap." Erica stood, reaching for her bowl.

"I've got it," Rowan offered, gathering up the dirty dishes and taking them to the sink. "I'll check on you tomorrow. If you need anything, don't hesitate to ask, okay?"

Erica nodded, her eyelids battling to stay open, before shuffling off to her bedroom. As soon as the door clicked shut, Rowan let out a long, shaky breath.

"That was…" Simone shook her head.

"Yeah." Rowan rubbed her temples, trying to ease the tension that had been building there since she'd walked through the door. "Can I have a word with you outside before I go?"

Simone nodded, following Rowan to the front door.

They had walked a good fifty feet from the condo before Rowan whipped around, pointing a finger toward Simone's chest. "Last night did not happen. Erica can never, ever know."

Simone came to a halt, wearing a startled expression as she ran a hand through her hair. "I wasn't planning on writing about it in my Christmas letter, if that's what you were thinking."

"I'm serious. My relationship with Erica is complicated enough since the divorce, but I care about her. I really do." Rowan clutched her hands, wringing them together so tightly that her knuckles went white. "She's shut me out so much these past months, but maybe, just maybe, she's starting to thaw. If she found out about us, it would destroy any chance of that happening. I can't lose what little connection we have left."

"Relax. I'm leaving tomorrow, and you'll never see me again." Simone's words were meant to be reassuring, but they sent an unexpected pang straight to Rowan's heart.

"Right. Of course." Rowan nodded, forcing a smile.

"It was an unfortunate accident," Simone continued. "We both need to forget it and move on. Simple as that."

The words nearly squeezed all the air from Rowan's lungs. Simone was completely correct, but the way she said it made it seem like the night had meant nothing to her. It probably hadn't. She was in the prime of her life and most likely seduced women at bars all the time.

Whereas Rowan had been so terribly lonely for so long, and last night she'd connected with someone for the first time in forever. It had unlocked something Rowan didn't know she had hidden inside, and before she could explore it even more, it was cruelly being ripped away from her.

It wasn't like Rowan wanted anything more than a fling, but one more night would have been—Rowan caught herself mid-thought. What the hell was she doing? Fantasizing about another night with Simone was exactly the kind of thinking she needed to avoid. She shook her head, trying to clear away the lingering memories of jasmine-scented skin and earth-shattering kisses.

"Well..." Rowan finished with a shrug in lieu of words.

"It was..." Simone didn't finish her thought, either.

Squaring her shoulders, Rowan stuck out her hand as if Simone was a candidate at the end of a job interview. "Best of luck in Haiti. That's really incredible. Be safe."

With a defeated sigh, Rowan turned her back on Simone, practically sprinting away before she could make a bigger fool of herself. Her emotions were in turmoil, tears stinging at the corners of her eyes. During the short drive home, she did everything she could think of to shake off the overwhelming surge of sadness and frustration that weighed her down, but it wouldn't budge.

How embarrassing, crying over someone she barely knew. As she flung herself across the still-rumpled sheets of her bed, she knew she was a fool for caring this much. But the pain was real, and she couldn't escape it. Instead, she buried her face in her pillow, inhaling deeply. The faint scent of jasmine still lingered. Rowan let out a muffled sob, her shoulders shaking as she finally allowed herself to break down.

It wasn't just the loss of Simone she mourned, but the culmination of everything that had unraveled in her life. The fractured relationships with her family, the relentless striving to be what everyone else wanted, the endless sacrifices that seemed to amount to nothing. This cruel little twist of fate—a single night of passion with no future and a secret she must carry to her grave—was just one more bitter pill to swallow in a long line of disappointments.

Rowan cried until her throat was raw and her eyes were swollen, purging years of pent-up emotion in the process. When she was finished, she got up and straightened the covers, determined to put on a brave face as she had done a million times before.

After all, that was what Rowan did best.

CHAPTER FIVE

Simone's heart sank at the mournful sounds coming from somewhere deep within the car's engine as Erica turned the key for the fifth time. After a few sputtering attempts at life, the engine fell silent once more.

"I don't understand," Erica muttered. "It was working fine the other day."

Simone glanced anxiously at her watch, helpless in the passenger's seat of her friend's car. She needed to be at Logan airport for her flight in four hours, and the traffic from the Cape to Boston was notoriously unpredictable.

"Maybe we should call AAA," Simone suggested, trying to keep the panic out of her voice.

"On it." Erica held the phone to her ear, launching into an explanation of their predicament the second an agent answered. "Um, in my driveway. No, not blocking traffic. Uh-huh." Erica's eyes widened, and she squealed, "Five hours?"

The person on the other line continued speaking, but Simone couldn't make out the words, which only caused her heart rate to spike even more. She didn't have five hours to spare. If she missed that flight, her entire future was on the line.

Erica hung up with a frustrated huff, dropping the phone into her lap. "They said it's the earliest they can do. Something about high call volume today." She rubbed her temples, looking as though she might burst into tears. "It seems that, since we're not stuck on the side of the road or blocking traffic, we're a lower priority."

Simone closed her eyes and let out a sharp breath through her nose, willing herself to stay calm. Panic wouldn't solve this. "Okay," she said, "should I rent a car?"

"And do what? Leave it at the airport?" Erica shook her head. "Good luck finding a one-way rental last-minute at the peak of the summer season."

"Valid point. How much do you think an Uber would cost?" Simone reached for her phone in her jeans pocket and attempted to pull up the app, but all she got was a spinning circle of doom. "Damn it. Why is there no service on this godforsaken sandbar?"

Simone shook her phone a few times before holding it up to the sky, as if that might magically summon a stronger signal.

"The reception out here for some mobile carriers is terrible," Erica agreed. "You'd have a better chance sending messages with a carrier pigeon. But don't worry. I already solved the problem."

"How?" Simone stabbed a finger at her phone screen, not trusting that whatever her friend came up with would actually work. Erica was a great person, but when it came to survival skills, she was too much of a pampered princess to be relied on in a crisis. Case in point: Simone was pretty sure the car wouldn't start because Erica had forgotten to fill up the gas tank. Again.

"I texted Rowan," Erica announced, clearly proud of herself. "She may be on my shit list right now, but she's the most reliable person I can think of, and this is an emergency."

"No!" Simone cringed at her over-the-top reaction. Or rather, her totally natural response that would definitely not be seen as such by anyone who didn't know that Erica's stepmom and that hot woman Simone had hooked up with on Saturday night were one and the same person. And if she didn't want Erica to figure it out, Simone had better come up with a plausible excuse for her weird behavior. Like now. "I mean, no, we can't impose on your stepmom like that. It's such a long drive. And she doesn't even know me."

That was one lie that Simone planned to stick with to her dying breath.

Erica waved her hand dismissively. "Don't be silly. I'm sure she's happy to do it."

"She's a doctor. She probably has a dozen more important things to do today than play chauffeur for your stranded friend."

"I doubt it. I don't know what she's doing on the Cape, but since she lives in Boston, I know it isn't work. And if she's not working, she's pretty boring. Now that she's divorced my dad, she's probably living like a hermit. I can't imagine her going on a coffee date, let alone like having a sex life or—"

"I've got a signal," Simone announced loudly, absolutely not wanting to hear the rest of that sentence. "An Uber can be here in ten minutes." Simone was about to push the request through, but Erica snatched the phone from Simone's hand.

"Don't be ridiculous. Rowan's already texted back to say she's on her way. She'll be here—oh, hey!" Erica jerked her thumb over her shoulder. "There she is now. I told you she wouldn't have any plans." Erica hopped out of her car to greet her stepmother as an older model Honda pulled into the driveway.

Of all the things that could have caused Simone to do a double-take, Rowan's car was a surprise. The woman was a doctor in Boston who had a vacation house on Cape Cod. Someone like that was almost required by law to drive a flashier car, maybe a sports car or a big SUV.

Simone barely had time to gather her composure before Rowan's long, lean frame unfolded from the driver's seat. Her outfit was casual, a plain gray T-shirt and a simple denim skirt that was modest-seeming, and yet also somehow short enough to make Simone's mouth go dry. She swallowed hard as memories of those toned legs straddling her flooded her brain. She quickly averted her gaze, pretending to busy herself with something in her bag, as Rowan went over to talk to Erica. Maybe if she kept looking anywhere but at Rowan, the tension coiling in her stomach would dissipate.

Spoiler: it absolutely did not.

A minute later, Simone jumped, startled, as the passenger side door opened. She looked up to see Rowan leaning in, a bemused expression on her face.

"You okay there? You seem rattled." Rowan's voice was every bit as low and husky as Simone remembered, and the effect it had on her body was even more potent than before.

"I'm fine," she managed to squeak out, sounding more like a mouse than a human. Grabbing both of her suitcases at once, she practically fell out of Erica's car in her haste to put some distance between herself and Rowan.

"Let me help you with your bags." Rowan took one from Simone, who stood there like a helpless kitten.

Get your ass moving, Simone urged herself, clutching the remaining suitcase tighter than necessary. "I've got it, really. No need to trouble yourself."

Rowan quirked an eyebrow, the faintest smirk tugging at one corner of her mouth before going back to neutral. "These suitcases are the least of my troubles today."

Rowan's words hung in the air, casual but charged, as if daring Simone to read deeper into them. How could she not? It wasn't like she didn't feel the exact same way. There was nothing but trouble on the horizon with Rowan around.

Soon enough, they transferred everything to Rowan's car, and Simone was hugging Erica goodbye. Simone lingered longer than necessary in the embrace, more out of dread than anything. Three hours alone in a car with Rowan was the last thing Simone wanted. Or maybe it was the only thing she wanted, which was a far more dangerous truth to admit.

Erica, oblivious to Simone's true motivation, patted her back reassuringly. "Don't stress too much about making your flight. Trust me. My stepmom will get you to the airport on time. She drives like a bat out of hell."

Simone managed a weak laugh, which faded quickly as Rowan opened the driver's side door and slid behind the wheel, her skirt riding up enough to reveal a hint of her thigh, including a deep red mark that Simone was almost certain she'd been responsible for putting there. Simone tore her gaze away from the thigh hickey and climbed into the passenger seat, determined to keep her focus on the road, or maybe on the scrubby pine trees blurring past on the side of the highway as they drove, or literally anything that wasn't Rowan.

As they pulled out of the driveway, Rowan broke the silence. "Long time no see, huh?"

"Yes. That *never seeing each other again* thing didn't go quite the way I anticipated." Simone tapped her fingers on the dashboard, trying to channel her nervous energy somewhere other than her racing thoughts.

"The universe does have a sense of humor sometimes." Rowan briefly gave Simone a smile before returning her gaze to the road. "How bad is it?"

"The universe? Fucking awful, as far as I can tell."

"No. I meant how much time do we have to make it to Logan?"

Simone swallowed, consulting the app on her phone. "My flight leaves at 5:35 p.m."

"Plenty of time." Rowan let out a relieved sigh. "Thank goodness you're not like Erica, who has always played fast and loose with deadlines. I can't tell you how often she's nearly missed something important because she underestimated traffic or overestimated how fast her car could go."

"Or if it would go at all," Simone added.

Rowan chuckled, a warm sound that made Simone's stomach flip. "Exactly. That girl would forget her head if it wasn't attached."

"How long have you been in her life?" Simone found herself asking, even though it was dangerous territory to discuss. Or maybe it wasn't. After all, focusing on the primary reason she and Rowan could absolutely never repeat their mistake would remind Simone why she needed to keep things platonic for the next three hours. Three very long, nerve-wracking, unreasonably attractive hours.

"She was not quite fourteen when Lance and I got married."

"Her mom died when she was ten, right?" Simone was fairly certain she had this correct, as it was almost the same age she'd been when her father had died. It was one of the things that had cemented their friendship in college.

"Yes. Even after four years, she was still having nightmares and couldn't stand being alone."

"In college, she always had friends over in her dorm room," Simone recalled, wondering if that had been the reason.

Rowan's fingers tightened on the steering wheel. "The divorce hit her hard. I wish it hadn't needed to come to that, but..." Her knuckles were pure white now. "I think I stayed as long as I did because of Erica."

Simone had to wonder if Erica ever suspected as much. Did she feel some guilt about that fact? That might explain some of the deep resentment Erica carried toward a woman who clearly still cared about her even after the divorce. Erica made it sound like her stepmother had abandoned her when as far as Simone could see, that was not at all the case.

"How long were you—no, never mind." Simone was prying into personal matters. "I'm sorry, that's none of my business."

Rowan glanced at Simone, her expression softening. "It's okay, you can ask. We were married for twelve years when I filed, and the divorce has been final for about six months."

"Did you meet at work?" Simone asked, fully expecting Rowan to shut her down in this line of questioning. To her surprise, Rowan let out a laugh.

"I suppose you could say that. We met when I was in medical school. Lance was the head of surgery at the hospital where I was doing my clinical work. He was well-respected, charming... all the things that make someone seem larger than life when you're twenty-four and working eighty-hour weeks." Rowan's lips quirked into a wry smile, her eyes still focused on the road. "He wasn't my professor, but even so, I know now it was completely inappropriate for us to date. But at the time, it felt exciting and flattering to be pursued by someone in his position."

Simone nodded, understanding all too well how that dynamic could play out. "Power imbalances can be intoxicating when you're young."

"Exactly." Rowan's words hung in the air, heavy with implication. Simone shifted uncomfortably in her seat, suddenly very aware of the age difference between them.

"Good thing we don't work together," Simone joked, eager to lighten the mood. Rowan snorted but didn't say anything in response. "How did you manage having a teenager at home while you were working those crazy hours?"

Rowan sighed. "The way women always seem to in situations like that, by putting everyone else first. I gave up my plan to become a surgeon and pursued internal medicine instead because the hours were more predictable. I allowed my career to take a back seat for a while when Erica needed me at home. It felt like the right choice, but it turns out neglecting your own needs isn't exactly the glue that holds a family together."

Rowan didn't go into detail, but based on the heat of their encounter a few nights before, Simone could guess at least one need that had gone unfulfilled for a very long time.

"Do you regret getting married?" Simone asked, genuinely curious.

"Now there's a loaded question." Rowan laughed nervously. "I'm not sure I believe in regret. Everything happens for a reason."

"Interesting theory." Simone was desperate to know if that applied to Cape Cod hookups with near-strangers who turned out to be their ex-stepdaughter's best friend. But she wisely bit her tongue. "Have you spent a lot of time on the Cape?" Simone asked instead, not wanting to be left alone with her thoughts.

"I grew up here." Rowan's eyes flicked toward Simone briefly before returning to the road. "How about you?"

"This was my first time."

"What'd you think?"

"It's nice, but I have to ask. What the hell is up with all the places selling fried clams and ice cream? Those two things do not go together."

"Blasphemy! That's a Cape Cod tradition," Rowan said with mock outrage, a hand briefly leaving the wheel to clutch her chest as though Simone's comment had wounded her deeply. "Fried clams and ice cream are the backbone of our summer economy!"

"Massholes are weird." Simone couldn't help but laugh.

"Absolutely. We pride ourselves on it." Rowan grinned, and Simone felt another unwelcome pang in her chest.

It was unfair how easily this banter flowed between them, like it was the most natural thing in the world. Under different circumstances, maybe she could have leaned into it, seen where it went. But Simone knew if she stepped wrong, everything would blow up in her face. It was too big a risk.

And yet, every smile from Rowan felt like a slow unraveling of Simone's resolve, one frayed thread at a time. This drive couldn't end soon enough.

ROWAN TOOK THE AIRPORT EXIT, smoothly merging into busy traffic. Simone should have felt relief, but her chest was weighed down by disappointment. The sign for her terminal was up ahead, and after dropping her off at the curb with an awkward goodbye—a handshake, or maybe a hug—Rowan would be out of her life forever.

As Rowan changed lanes again, Simone's phone lit up with a text.

"Huh." Simone read the alert a second time, just to be sure. "My flight has been delayed."

"By how long?"

"Two hours." Simone groaned, slumping back in her seat. "Fucking fantastic."

Without hesitation, Rowan yanked the wheel, following the sign for central parking instead of the departure drop-off area. "We can't have you sitting alone in the airport for hours. Did you want to get coffee or something?"

"I don't know. Coffee might make me more jittery than I already am." Simone wasn't sure coffee could be blamed for the sudden fluttering in her stomach at the prospect of spending more time with Rowan. The rational part of her brain screamed that this was a terrible idea, but a small voice whispered that maybe, just maybe, it would turn into something good.

"Fair enough," Rowan conceded. "Did you have something else in mind? A bite to eat, maybe?"

Simone knew she should politely decline and find a quiet

corner of the airport to wait out the delay alone. But as the car climbed the ramp to the next level of the parking garage, the only ideas racing through Simone's mind were ones she absolutely should not entertain. Like how the back seat of Rowan's Honda looked spacious enough for two people to—

No. Simone shook her head, trying to banish the inappropriate images that flooded her imagination.

"Oh, okay." Clearly, Rowan had mistaken her head shake for a reply. "I can drop you off at the gate if that's what you'd prefer."

"No." This time, Simone said the word aloud, perhaps more emphatically than she'd intended if Rowan's skyrocketing eyebrows were any indication. "No, that wasn't what I meant. I don't want to go to the gate. I'm just not sure what I want."

This was only partly true. Simone knew what she wanted. She also knew she couldn't have it.

Without speaking, Rowan pulled into an empty parking spot. It was in a desolate portion of the garage, with not a soul in sight, and where more of the overhead lights were off than on. She took the time to back in, positioning the car so the rear bumper was flush against the wall, shrouding them in privacy. The silence in the car thickened, broken only by the faint hum of the engine as Rowan turned to face her.

"Simone," Rowan said softly, her voice low but with an intensity that could burn through steel. Her gaze was steady, searching Simone's face for something. Permission? A shred of sanity?

Simone almost burst out laughing. Fat chance of finding something resembling sanity here. "We could stay in the car. Alone."

Rowan's eyes darkened, her breath catching audibly. "Are you sure?"

Every rational part of Simone's brain screamed this was a

terrible idea, but that wasn't the part of her that was in control right now. "I'm sure."

In one fluid motion, Rowan unbuckled her seatbelt and leaned across the center console, her lips finding Simone's before there was time for second-guessing. Their mouths collided, skipping the tender stage completely and going right for *I want you now, or I will fucking die.*

"You have no idea how badly I've wanted this," Rowan murmured against Simone's lips, her voice a low, smoky whisper that snapped the last vestiges of Simone's restraint like an overstretched rubber band.

"Should we—?" Simone jerked her head to the back seat. Every nerve ending went into high alert, and her clit pulsed as if to a disco beat.

Rowan grinned. "I thought you'd never ask."

Simone began to maneuver her way between the seats, prompting laughter from Rowan. She opened the front driver's side door, got out, shut it, and proceeded to open the back door.

"Sure, take the easy way," Simone joked, breathing heavily after her own awkward scramble. She settled into the back seat, pulse racing as Rowan slid in beside her and shut the door.

"Now, where were we?" Rowan purred, her hand finding Simone's thigh, which was mostly bare now that the long sundress she was wearing had been hiked up during her climb.

"I think we were right about here," Simone managed to say, her breath catching as Rowan's fingers traced lazy circles on her inner thigh, inching higher with each pass. She leaned in, capturing Rowan's lips in a searing kiss. As their lips met, Simone melted into Rowan's touch. The kiss deepened, tongues exploring, hands roaming. Rowan's fingers traced higher up Simone's thigh, sending shivers through her body.

Simone slid her hand under Rowan's T-shirt, not bothering to unclasp the bra but simply shoving the fabric down to give her access to a nipple that was already hard and begging for attention. Simone pinched it lightly between her fingers, eliciting a sharp intake of breath from Rowan.

"God, you're incredible. The way you react when I—" Instead of completing the sentence, Simone demonstrated by lowering her head and drawing Rowan's nipple into her mouth, swirling her tongue around the sensitive bud. Rowan gasped, arching her back to press herself more firmly against Simone's lips.

"Fuck," Rowan breathed, her fingers tangling in Simone's hair. "I've been thinking about this non-stop since Saturday night."

Simone lifted her head, meeting Rowan's intense gaze. "Me too," she admitted. "I tried not to, but…"

"It's impossible not to," Rowan finished, her voice strained with longing.

"Come here." Simone's hands moved southward toward Rowan's skirt, fulfilling a fantasy she'd been fighting against since she'd watched that light blue denim start to ride up in Erica's driveway.

Her fingers tugged at the hem, sliding it higher until Rowan shifted closer, guiding Simone's hand with a firm grip. It didn't take any effort at all to slide the edge of Rowan's underwear to one side, giving Simone access to the warm, wet heat she craved. Rowan gasped as Simone's fingers made contact, her hips bucking involuntarily.

"God, you feel amazing," Simone murmured, her thumb circling Rowan's clit. "You're so beautifully wet."

"Constantly since meeting you."

Simone licked her lips as her mouth watered. "I need to taste you."

Without hesitation, Rowan reclined across the back seat, her skirt bunching around her waist as she spread her legs as much as possible in the cramped quarters. Simone wasted no time, positioning herself upside down on top of Rowan's torso, her knees on either side of Rowan's arms and her hands grasping Rowan's thighs.

As Simone lowered her head, the scent of Rowan's arousal was intoxicating. Simone couldn't fight the primal urge to dive in.

"Oh, God, yes," Rowan moaned.

There wasn't much time to waste. Someone could discover them, and that thought should have stopped her in her tracks.

Instead, it only added to the excitement.

Simone lapped eagerly, flicking and swirling her tongue in a steady, urgent rhythm. She felt Rowan's breath on her inner thighs.

"This okay?" Rowan asked.

"More than okay."

It took all Simone's concentration to continue what she was doing as Rowan's hands slid along her thighs, pushing her dress higher. Simone redoubled her efforts, her tongue moving faster against Rowan's clit as two of Rowan's fingers slipped inside her.

Simone cried out, her hips rocking against Rowan's hand as those skilled fingers curled inside her, stroking that sensitive spot that made stars explode behind her eyelids. She ground down, trying to take Rowan's fingers deeper, needing more, all the while working Rowan to the edge with her own tongue.

They moved together, a tangle of limbs and gasps and moans, each driving the other higher. The windows were starting to fog. Not that either of them cared. At one point, the sound of a rolling suitcase in the distance caught Simone's ear, but it faded quickly, and the distraction was fleeting. She was reasonably certain no one could see them in this shadowy corner of the garage. And if they could, Simone didn't care. Nothing else mattered except this moment, this connection, the overwhelming need coursing through her veins.

Rowan's fingers picked up speed, driving Simone closer to

the brink. At the same time, Rowan's thighs began to quiver and tense around Simone's head.

She was close, so close. They both were.

With a final flick of her tongue, Simone sent Rowan over the edge. Rowan's back arched off the seat as a guttural moan tore from her throat. At the same time, Rowan curled her fingers inside Simone, thrusting deeper, the heel of her hand grinding against Simone's clit with each stroke. Just the way she needed it.

The building pressure finally burst, shattering Simone into a million blissful pieces. Her inner walls clenched around Rowan's fingers as wave after wave of pleasure crashed over her. She cried out, the sound muffled against the soft skin of Rowan's thigh as she rode out the most intense orgasm of her life.

As the last tremors faded, Simone shifted her body around and collapsed against Rowan, her head on the older woman's shoulder. Both were breathing heavily in the suddenly too-warm confines of the car. They simply held each other, letting their racing hearts gradually slow. The fogged windows enclosed them in their own private world, reality temporarily held at bay.

Finally, Rowan captured Simone's lips with hers, kissing her with such forcefulness that it seemed as if she wanted to imprint the moment deep in her memory to replay it for the rest of her life.

At least, Simone knew that was what she would be doing.

"You're so amazing," Simone murmured against Rowan's lips. "I don't want this to end."

"Then kiss me again."

Simone was more than happy to oblige. She never wanted to leave this car. Or this woman.

But that was ridiculous. She barely knew Rowan. Aside from how perfectly they felt together. It was madness, what they'd just done. She could hardly believe it had happened.

The sound of a car engine in the distance jolted Simone back to reality. Another vehicle was slowly climbing the ramp to their level of the parking garage.

"Shit." Simone pulled away from Rowan's embrace, straightening her disheveled dress and doing what she could to smooth her hopelessly tangled hair. "Someone's coming."

Rowan nodded, her expression a mix of satisfaction at what they had done and disappointment that they couldn't do it again. At least, that was how Simone interpreted it, perhaps because that was what she was feeling.

After adjusting her own clothing, Rowan reached for the door. "We should get that cup of coffee now."

CHAPTER SIX

Two years later

Rowan steeled her nerves as she pulled into the hospital parking lot and brought her modest little Honda to rest beside her father's gleaming Audi. The contrast between the two vehicles was a stark reminder of how different they were, despite their shared DNA. No matter how hard she had tried her whole life, her father had never seen her as an equal. To him, she would always be his little girl, incapable of filling the shoes of a man, especially one as brilliant as he believed her ex-husband to be.

Which was why accepting the position as interim chief medical officer at Marbury Hospital after Lance's abrupt departure might turn out to be the biggest mistake of her life. Rowan knew taking this job meant subjecting herself to her father's constant scrutiny and inevitable disappointment, but she also knew she couldn't pass up the opportunity to make a real difference in the hospital her great-great grandmother had helped found.

No matter how difficult it might be.

Rowan took a deep breath and stepped out of her car, smoothing her crisp white coat. She wouldn't wear it every day.

After all, her role was strictly administrative now. But on her first day, she wanted to remind the doctors and nurses working under her she was still one of them. That she hadn't forgotten her roots or the importance of patient care.

Before shutting the car door, Rowan grabbed her thermal travel cup filled with coffee she had brewed herself, less out of a desire to save money and more because she had yet to find a shop that could make it with the strength to blast someone into space. Even that might not get her through the day. Her reflection in the tinted windows as she shut the door showed her a confident woman, composed, ready to take on whatever challenges lay ahead. But inside, Rowan's stomach churned with anxiety.

As Rowan approached the hospital entrance, she caught sight of a familiar figure emerging from the automatic sliding doors. A wave of relief washed over her as she recognized her friend Candace. They both had deep roots in Cape Cod and had graduated med school around the same time. They'd become fast friends the first time Rowan had worked at this place, and she knew her friend would have her back this time, too.

"I always knew you'd come back here." Candace wore a lopsided grin, standing outside the sliding glass doors.

"I should have grabbed my ice skates on my way out the door because it seems hell has actually frozen over," Rowan quipped, returning Candace's smile as she drew closer. "You must be psychic, because I never thought I'd move back to Marbury, let alone be working at the hospital again."

"At least you get to see me every day."

Rowan responded with a growl, but it quickly turned into a laugh as Candace pulled her into a tight hug. And her friend was right. Not seeing Candace every day was one of the few things Rowan had disliked while she was at Boston General.

"Just think," Candace said, "now you get to go home to that beautiful beach house of yours every night instead of leaving it for the short-term renters to enjoy."

Rowan pulled back from the hug and sighed. "At least I won't have to worry about covering the mortgage on that place while paying rent for my Boston apartment anymore. Not gonna lie. It was a struggle."

"When you bought it from Lance, I told you it was a mistake. It's a gorgeous house, don't get me wrong, but you didn't want it, and you could barely afford it. You only agreed because he guilted you into it."

Rowan shrugged. "It's not like I had much of a choice. Lance made it clear he needed to sell. I couldn't bear the thought of Erica's mother's house being lost to a total stranger like that. I'm sure he'll buy it back from me when he can."

Although, if she were honest with herself, Rowan was a little less certain of this with each passing day. Especially now that Lance's gambling addiction had cost him his position at the hospital. There was no question the situation was serious, if only because there was no other way her father would have agreed to offer Rowan the job of his second-in-command otherwise.

"And how is your stepdaughter treating you these days? With immense gratitude befitting the woman who saved her family legacy? Oh, wait. No." Candace shot her a pointed look. "She thinks you strong-armed her beloved family home out of her father as part of the divorce settlement. Is she even speaking to you?"

"Not beyond the occasional text equivalent of a monosyllabic grunt," Rowan admitted, her shoulders slumping despite her determination to remain positive where Erica was concerned. "But that's an improvement over the stony silence I got when she first found out I owned the house. I'm hoping once she's back in Marbury after her art program in Italy wraps up, we might have a chance to repair some of the damage."

"Damage, my ass. That girl needs to wake up and realize what an amazing person you are," Candace said, shaking her head. "You've bent over backward trying to build a relationship with her over the past few years despite how things ended with her dad."

"She's been through a lot," Rowan said, feeling the need to defend Erica despite the young woman's chilly treatment. "Losing her mother—"

"Why do you always do that?" Candace demanded, denying Rowan the chance to finish her thought. "Why do you give everyone the benefit of the doubt except yourself? Poor Erica, who can be cruel to you because her mom died before she even met you. Or Lance, who can count on you to bail him out when he gambles away his money or spends beyond his means because you still feel guilty for leaving a loveless marriage. Or your father, whose blatant misogyny you ignore because—"

"Stop, please. I get it." Rowan held up her hands in a gesture of surrender. "And I'm working on it. But this is who I am. Try as I might, guilt is my default factory setting. Besides, when it comes to my marriage ending, I'm far from innocent."

"Stop making it sound like you're the only woman who ever married a man and then realized down the road that she was gay. You didn't even cheat on him. You told him the truth."

"And broke his heart," Rowan countered, although she wasn't completely certain that was the case. Sure, Lance had loved her in his way, but she had always suspected his pride was more wounded than anything when she'd finally called it quits. Even so, it felt more comfortable to blame herself for the demise of her marriage, to convince herself if she had tried harder, been better somehow, she could have made it work.

"You're a lesbian, honey," Candace said gently, almost as if she'd read Rowan's mind. "Staying married to a man was never going to work, no matter how hard you tried. That's no way to live. As a fellow lesbian, I know this is true. Even when my own wife drives me up a goddamn wall."

Rowan sighed. "Logically, I know you're right, but—"

"Good. Then you'll agree to join Christine and me at Roxie's on Friday. The Velvet Sirens are playing and—"

"No." Rowan all but recoiled at the mention of the same band that had been playing at The Driftwood Lounge the night she'd met Simone.

Just the thought of that woman sent a jolt of pain through Rowan's chest. She had tried so hard to put the memory of that night behind her, even succeeded for the most part while she was in Boston. But being back on the Cape brought the tiniest of details rushing back with such intensity, Rowan could almost smell that damn jasmine perfume Simone had worn. Even now, going on two years later, she couldn't so much as hum the melody of one of that band's songs without choking back a lonely sob.

"Please tell me you have a date and that's why you can't come out with us," Candace said, her eyes narrowing with suspicion. "Because if you're still staying celibate to punish yourself—"

"Don't be so dramatic. It's just that I can't stand their music."

Candace frowned. "I don't get it. You used to like them. And they're the number one lesbian group around. If you ever want to meet a woman—"

"Who said I did?" Rowan scowled at her friend, if for no other reason than to get her to drop this conversation before it went places she didn't want it to go.

"Come on," Candace urged. "You didn't leave Lance to stay single the rest of your life."

"I'm doing well. I have a vibrator."

"You know who would be perfect for you? There's a doctor in the emergency department, Dr. Doucette, who is such a—"

"I think we'd better go inside and get to work," Rowan said as sternly as she could. No way was she going to let Candace play matchmaker, and especially not with someone Rowan would have to work with every day. That was a recipe for disaster. "Don't you have patients waiting for you?"

"Not so many right now. Of course, in two weeks, when the summer folks arrive for Memorial Day weekend, we'll be the busiest hospital in all of Massachusetts." Candace actually appeared eager for this turn of events. "Shall I show you the way to the executive offices, in case you've forgotten?"

Rowan rolled her eyes. "I think I can manage to find my way. It hasn't been that long. But I won't turn down your company as long as you lay off lecturing me about my private life."

Candace motioned for Rowan to enter the building ahead of her, and Rowan paused as the doors took a second longer than they should have to slide open. *Someone needs to talk to maintenance about that*, she thought, right before realizing that as a hospital administrator, that someone was probably her.

Maybe she'd bring it up with her father first, if only to gauge his reaction to her taking the initiative. She didn't need to step on anyone's toes on her first day, but she also knew how heavily her father had relied on Lance, far beyond the usual scope of a CMO's job description. It was safe to say that anything needing doing around here would probably end up in her lap.

"So, you and Christine are going out on Friday night? Does that mean things have been getting better between you two?" Rowan asked as they entered the quiet lobby. Candace hadn't been kidding about it being a slow day. If this had been Boston, the waiting room would have been packed, even at this early hour. But in Marbury, there were only a handful of patients scattered about, most of them elderly locals who probably came in more for the social interaction than any pressing medical need.

Candace shrugged. "About the same. I work too much, and when I'm home, she's always got a million things she claims she has to do for the kids. Sometimes I wonder if we even live on the same planet anymore."

Rowan frowned as she pressed the call button for the elevator, noting that one of the three elevator doors had an out-of-order sign taped to it. Another issue to add to her list of things to ask her father about. "Have you tried talking to her? Or maybe talking together to somebody else?"

Candace let out a humorless laugh as they stepped into the elevator. "Sure, if I can catch her between soccer practice and PTA meetings, I'd love to have a chat. But not on date night. I'd rather not kill my chance of getting lucky by pissing her off."

The elevator hitched before climbing to the third floor. Did anything in this hospital run smoothly anymore? Rowan made a mental note to look into the maintenance records as soon as possible.

In the hallway, Rowan started to head to the left before Candace grabbed her arm and pulled her in the opposite direction.

"I knew you needed me. It's this way."

How could Rowan have forgotten? She'd been to her new office hundreds of times before, back when it was still Lance's. Of course, she'd resented the hell out of the way her father had groomed his son-in-law for the job she'd coveted without even considering her for the role, so maybe that had something to do with her memory lapse.

They were halfway down the hallway when Candace got a text. "Sorry," she said after reading the message, "but there's some issue down in the ER. Duty calls."

Rowan nodded, feeling a twinge of envy at Candace's ability to rush off to handle a medical emergency. As much as she'd wanted this position, part of her already missed the hands-on aspect of patient care she'd enjoyed at Boston General.

"Go," she said, waving her friend away. "I can find my way from here."

Alone, Rowan approached the familiar door. A wave of imposter syndrome washed over her. Was she really cut out for this? Her father had made his opinion clear time and time again.

But this was what she wanted. She had the training, along with the experience she needed thanks to her time at Boston General. Even without her family ties to the hospital, she made a strong candidate. She needed to believe in herself.

She took a deep breath and grasped the doorknob, the metal cool against her hand. This was it. Her new office. Her new life. She turned the handle and stepped inside.

Right into the middle of a fucking disaster.

Papers were piled high on the desk. Post-it notes fluttered from about every possible surface where one could stick. Even on the stapler. That note simply read *staples* in her ex's nearly illegible chicken-scratch. The others were harder to make heads or tails of.

Rowan stood frozen in the doorway, stunned by the chaos before her. This wasn't at all what she had expected. Lance had always been meticulous, almost to a fault. His need for order and control had been one of the many things that had driven a wedge between them during their last few years together. This wasn't just messy. It was a complete breakdown of organization. How had Lance been functioning like this? And how had her father allowed it to get to this point?

She took a tentative step inside, careful not to disturb any of the precariously balanced stacks of paperwork.

"There you are." Her father stood in the doorway, his imposing frame filling the space. Even at seventy-eight, he cut an impressive figure in his tailored suit, his silver hair neatly combed. "I was beginning to wonder if you'd changed your mind."

Ah, there it was. One of her father's famously passive-aggressive comments that cut with the precision of a scalpel, but which he could play off as a funny joke that was misinterpreted by an overly sensitive woman. Rowan plastered a smile on her face, choosing to pretend she didn't know how much her father wished she had changed her mind about not only the job but staying in her marriage, too. He'd taken her divorce almost as personally as Lance had.

"Simply getting the lay of the land," she said, gesturing to the chaotic office. "It seems things were left in a bit of disarray."

Her father's eyes swept over the chaos, his expression unreadable. "Yes, well, you've got some big shoes to fill. Lance ran this place like a well-oiled machine."

"I'm sure." Her eyes wandered the detritus scattered around the room as a final testament to her ex's abilities. *A well-oiled machine indeed.* Rowan bit back the sarcastic comment that threatened to escape her lips. Instead, she nodded. "Hopefully, I won't let you down."

Instead of saying something encouraging, perhaps along the lines of how he believed in her and was proud of her for stepping up to take on this challenge, her father simply nodded curtly. "I won't keep you."

Rowan sank into her desk chair, swiping a pile of papers into her hands, doing her best to sort them. They appeared to be bills and honestly, who still had paper bills? How had the hospital finances not been fully automated when Rowan herself had gone paperless the day she'd taken her personal finances back into her own hands?

She opened a drawer full of hanging file folders, at least half of which dangled precariously with hooks that had become dislodged from the side rails. She pulled out the stack and neatened them, but when she went to put them back, the files slipped from her hand and landed with a splat on the floor, their contents going every which way.

"Fuck."

Rowan dropped to her knees and began scooping the errant pages back into, if not their original folders, at least a single pile that could be dealt with later. What was all this stuff? She shuffled through the loose papers, gasping as a dozen black and white spreadsheets gave way to a full-color photo of a naked woman posed in a manner usually reserved for adult magazines.

What the hell?

Rowan's heart raced as she shoved everything, including the photo, back into the drawer and slammed it shut, her mind reeling. What had she just seen? Surely there had to be some explanation. Lance may have been many things, but he had never struck her as the type to keep pornography in his office. Then again, he'd never been the type to forego his obsessively organized day planner in favor of a random collection of sticky notes.

Had Lance developed a pornography addiction on top of the gambling that had sent him to rehab? Rowan felt like she didn't know the depths of depravity her ex was capable of anymore. Maybe she should look at the photo again to see if she could figure out what was going on. She gripped the drawer handle, sucking in a breath as she steadied her nerves enough to open it.

The desk phone rang. Rowan jumped at the shrill sound, her hand jerking away from the drawer handle as if it had burned her. She stared at the phone, not convinced she had the mental capacity to deal with whatever it would turn out to be. But it was her job to deal with shit, so after three rings, she finally reached for the receiver, clearing her throat before answering.

"Dr. Rowan Colchester." Even as she spoke her full name with confidence in her most commanding tone, Rowan's eyes fell to the drawer. Who was the woman in the photo? *Please God, don't let it be someone who worked at the hospital.* That was a complication she didn't need.

"I'm sorry, who?" the man on the other end of the line asked. "I was trying to reach Dr. Donovan."

"I'm afraid he's no longer with the hospital. Can I help you?"

"Oh, that's right. It was so sudden I forgot," the man said, sounding flustered. "I'm sorry about that. This is Dr. Reeves in the emergency department. We've got a situation down here that needs immediate attention."

"Hit me with it." Rowan braced herself for whatever crisis awaited her. This was it, her first real test as CMO. She grabbed a pen and notepad, ready to jot down the details.

"We're out of gowns."

"Gowns?" All Rowan could picture was a sparkly dress like the one she'd worn to prom. That couldn't be right. "You mean for the patients?"

"Yes."

"Um, isn't that more of a question for the head of environmental services?"

"It would be, if we had one. The person who was in charge left back in February, and the hospital hasn't found a replacement yet. Dr. Donovan said he would handle those responsibilities in the meantime."

Rowan pinched the bridge of her nose, fighting off a headache. Of course, Lance had said he'd handle it. Like most surgeons, he believed he was an all-powerful god. But clearly, he had taken on more than he could manage. She reached for a stack of papers where she thought she remembered seeing the logo of a linen supply service. Shit. It was a bill, and it was several months past due.

Rowan held in a sigh. "Okay, Dr. Reeves. I'll look into this right away and get back to you as soon as I have a solution."

"I'm getting off my shift in a few minutes, but you can speak with Dr. Doucette if I'm not around."

There was that name again. Rowan felt a flash of irritation. The last thing she needed was for her first official act in her new role to involve the woman Candace wanted to set her up with. Her friend could be so inappropriate sometimes. "Understood. I'm sure it's just an oversight."

Rowan pressed the button to disconnect the call and then dialed the laundry service's number. "Hello, I'm calling from

Marbury Hospital. You'll have to forgive me. It's my first day on the job, and it seems like we're late with a payment."

"Payments," was the gruff reply from the woman on the other end of the line.

"Pardon?"

"Payments," the woman repeated, each syllable clipped and surly. "As in multiple. Your hospital hasn't paid a single invoice in over six months. We've been more than patient, but at this point, we have no choice but to suspend service until the account is brought current."

Rowan cringed. This was worse than she thought. "I apologize for that oversight. Surely you can deliver one more shipment while we get this sorted out? The hospital is in desperate need of gowns for the patients."

"Yeah, well, you tell Dr. Donovan he should've thought of that before he ignored our repeated attempts to collect what was due. Until we receive payment in full, you'll have to find another supplier." The woman's tone left no room for negotiation, and before Rowan could argue, the line went dead.

Damn it, Lance. What the hell have you done?

Rowan gritted her teeth before she started dialing different departments throughout the hospital to find out if they had any gowns to spare. After several calls and much digging, Rowan was able to round up a mismatched assortment of threadbare gowns from the dark, forgotten recesses of cupboards that probably hadn't been opened in years. It was enough to make it through the day, longer if she figured out a system to wash them in house and reuse them—though that was a whole other headache she would have to face.

Rowan rushed down to the emergency department, her arms loaded with as much as she could carry, silently cursing Lance with each step. How could he have let things get this bad? And more importantly, why had her father allowed it to happen right under his nose?

At the nurse's station, her nostrils still flaring a tiny bit from how worked up she'd become, Rowan asked for Dr. Doucette's whereabouts.

"She's in exam room two," the nurse replied.

Rowan made her way over, standing outside the curtain so as not to disturb the patient. Rowan heard the snap of gloves being removed.

"Let's get him upstairs," a woman's voice said.

Something about the voice seemed familiar, but Rowan couldn't quite place it. She shook her head, attributing the sense of déjà vu to stress and lack of sleep. After the curtain was pulled back and the patient's gurney had been rolled out, Rowan stepped forward and cleared her throat to attract the attention of the woman in scrubs whose back was turned to her as she scribbled notes onto a clipboard.

"Dr. Doucette? I've got your—" Rowan froze, the gowns nearly tumbling from her arms as she stared into the face of the last person she ever expected to see. "Simone?"

CHAPTER SEVEN

This has to be a bad dream.

Simone was vaguely aware she must look like a complete idiot standing in the middle of the exam room with her mouth dangling open. But what else was she supposed to do when the woman she had tried so hard to forget was suddenly standing right in front of her, looking every bit as flabbergasted as Simone felt?

Simone blinked, trying to clear the shock from her brain, but the vision of Rowan didn't disappear. The same red, curly hair Simone had once tangled her fingers through, now pulled back into a messy bun. The same green eyes that had followed her hungrily all the way through the security line at the airport, now looked at her with surprise, and possibly apprehension. The same full lips that Simone couldn't help but remember the taste of, even after all this time, now pressed into a thin line.

This was real.

Rowan was here, in Simone's hospital.

She was clutching a bundle of what looked like patient gowns to her chest. It made no sense. Why was Rowan in Marbury Hospital, and with gowns, no less? Rowan worked in

Boston, not on the Cape. This was Simone's workplace, not Rowan's.

Someone, please help this make sense.

"What are you doing here?" Simone finally managed to ask, the words sounding more accusing than she'd intended.

"Come with me, Dr. Doucette," Rowan barked.

And damned if it wasn't ridiculously hot. Not to mention completely confusing because the woman was acting like she was the boss of this place.

When Simone's feet didn't budge, Rowan added, "Now," in a quiet but firm voice that left no room for refusal.

Simone felt her feet moving before her brain could catch up, following Rowan out of the exam room and down the hallway, slowing only long enough to hand off the bundle of gowns to a startled orderly. Simone trailed slightly behind as her sensible shoes squeaked on the linoleum floor. A far cry from the stilettos she'd been wearing the night they'd first met. The older woman's pace was brisk, her shoulders tense as she led them to the elevator bank in the lobby, slamming her palm against the call button.

"Only one of them works," Simone informed her.

Rowan's eyes flicked to Simone, a hint of irritation flashing across her face. "Seriously? I thought just the one in the middle was broken."

"That one has a sign on it, but I've been here for four months, and I've never seen the one on the right move at all. I've started to suspect the door is a decoy to make people think there are more elevators than there are."

"Add that to the fucking list," Rowan muttered as she let out a frustrated sigh, rubbing her temple. "We'll take the stairs."

As they trekked up the stairwell together with Rowan in the lead, Simone did everything she could not to think about the last time they'd been together. Whatever was going on here, playing back every second of hot car sex in the Boston Logan parking garage would almost certainly not improve the situation. But that was the only thing her brain would focus on. That and the way Rowan's hips swayed as she climbed the stairs ahead of Simone. The younger woman forced her gaze to the floor, counting each step to distract herself.

They emerged onto the third floor, and Rowan strode purposefully down the hall to a corner office, her long legs covering the distance at such a fast clip that Simone had to trot to keep up. Rowan flung open the door, ushered Simone in without a word, and shut the door with a decisive click. Simone's eyes darted around the room, taking in the sparse décor and stacks of papers on the desk. Her gaze landed on a nameplate that made her heart skip: "Dr. Lance Donovan."

What were they doing in Rowan's ex-husband's office?

Rowan flicked her fingers to a chair. "Sit."

Simone wanted to obey. She really did—maybe too much, actually, as she'd never realized how big a turn-on it was to be ordered around by a bossy lady in a white lab coat and high heels. The problem was, there were file boxes stacked on the only chair.

Rowan followed Simone's gaze to the chair, let out an exasperated sigh, and then quickly moved to clear the boxes, stacking them haphazardly in the corner. "Sit," she repeated, her tone softening slightly. "Please."

Simone lowered herself into the now-empty chair, her mind racing. What was happening?

Rowan paced behind the cluttered mahogany desk, running a hand through her hair, which had come completely undone from its bun and now framed her face in wild curls. Simone's fingers twitched with the urge to reach out and smooth them back.

Rowan's gaze flitted around the room, never quite landing on Simone, as if she was afraid to make eye contact. Which seemed unlikely, because Rowan wasn't the type to be afraid of much, but something was definitely eating at her. "This is a disaster."

By disaster, Simone was fairly certain Rowan was referring to their unexpected reunion, but there was a slim chance she meant the state of the office, which was shockingly messy. Not that she knew much about Lance Donovan. She'd only met him once, the day he'd agreed to hire her. If Erica hadn't pulled some strings with her father, she wouldn't have gotten this job at all. Her pride still stung at needing the help, but beggars couldn't be choosers. And right now, she felt very much like a beggar, waiting for Rowan to toss her some crumbs of information about what the hell was going on.

As the silence stretched, Simone couldn't bear it any longer.

"Rowan—" Simone swallowed hard, her throat suddenly dry from having said the woman's name. She cleared her throat and started again. "Why are you here?"

Rowan finally stopped pacing and braced her hands on the desk, leaning forward slightly. "Because I'm the new Chief Medical Officer."

"No you're not. You work in Boston."

"Not anymore." Rowan added, "I thought you were skydiving into disaster zones, saving the world."

Simone folded her arms in front of her chest protectively, not wanting to think about the circumstances that had led her to leave Global Health Frontiers. "Not anymore."

The silence that followed was deafening. Simone's mind raced, trying to process this new information. Rowan wasn't just a doctor at Marbury Hospital, she was basically running the place. Which meant...

"Holy crap. You're my boss." Simone pressed her hand to her forehead in a vain attempt to keep her brain from exploding.

"I had no idea you were working here. If I'd known..." Rowan left the implication hanging in the air.

If she'd known, what? She wouldn't have taken the job?

Unlikely. She would have warned Simone ahead of time? Perhaps. She would've had Simone fired before they'd had a chance to cross paths? That sounded all too likely.

But, no. That couldn't happen. Simone might only have been at Marbury Hospital for a few months, but she'd gotten here first. That gave her seniority. If one of them had to leave because of this massive conflict of interest, it'd be Rowan, right?

Yeah, right. She was the CEO's daughter. One of her ancestors had literally founded the hospital.

"Shit. You brought me in here to fire me."

"Fire you? For what?" To her credit, Rowan seemed genuinely surprised, like the possibility of firing Simone had never occurred to her.

"Do I have to state the obvious?" Simone's face grew hot. The last thing she needed was to deliver a play-by-play of the way they'd passed their last hour together in the back seat of Rowan's car.

Rowan's eyes finally met hers. A flicker of something— desire? regret?—passed through them before she schooled her features. "That never happened. Nothing has changed. I can't fire someone without giving a reason, and I can't very well..." Simone gestured into the air as words seemed to escape her.

"Tell the truth?" Simone suggested, coming to Rowan's rescue.

"There's no truth to tell. I am meeting you for the first time today."

"We didn't meet when you brought soup over to the condo for Erica when she was sick?"

"Fuck." Rowan grimaced. "There's no denying that one since Erica was a witness. And the way she feels about me these days, she'd be more than happy to call me out in a lie. This is the second time, then. No, the third. Erica also knows I took you to the airport."

"The third time," Simone parroted, not feeling overly confident about this plan, if it could be called that. "But we only met in passing. And I was engrossed in my phone the whole way to Logan. You dropped me off at the gate without so much as turning the engine off."

"Exactly. We hardly know each other. Now, I suggest you get back to the emergency department and find that young man who has all the clean gowns."

"Yes, Dr…" Simone realized she didn't even know Rowan's last name. "Er, Dr. Donovan?"

The instant scowl on the other woman's face told her she'd guessed wrong.

"It's Colchester. Dr. Colchester."

"Of course. You don't seem like the type of woman to have taken her husband's last name." This was something Simone definitely understood should have been kept to herself, but that didn't stop her from blurting it out anyway. There was probably some simple yet brilliant way to defuse the awkwardness from a situation such as this, but Simone had no idea what that was. All she could do was forge ahead, hoping her natural tendency to put her foot in her mouth when flustered didn't get her into even hotter water with her new boss.

By the glare Rowan was giving Simone, Dr. Colchester—Simone better get used to calling her that, and only that, right away—was not amused by Simone's overly familiar observation about her last name. The temperature in the room seemed to drop by ten degrees.

Simone quickly rose from the chair, nearly tripping over her own feet in her haste to escape the other woman's icy stare.

"I'll go find that orderly," she mumbled, edging toward the door.

Rowan—that is to say, Dr. Colchester—watched her the entire time, until Simone was finally in the hallway with the door closed between them. Simone would probably see that expression in her dreams for a week.

Which was a problem, because even pissed off, Rowan Colchester was hot as fuck. And seeing her in dreams was a very dangerous thing.

THAT WAS the longest shift of my life.

As Simone pulled her car into the long driveway that led past her landlady's house to the guest cottage in the back that she currently called home, the only thing she wanted to do was close her eyes and go to sleep. The day hadn't even been difficult as far as medical emergencies were concerned. In a way, Simone might've preferred a busy day, as the relative quiet only made each second drag by slower than the previous one.

What had exhausted her was staying on high alert, keeping an eye out for Rowan. The whole day, Simone couldn't shake the feeling that Rowan might appear from around a corner, clipboard in hand, ready to critique her work or, worse, fire her on the spot. Sure, Rowan had said she wouldn't, but that didn't stop Simone from worrying about it all the same. She'd already had one job end badly. Two in one year was more than she could handle.

Simone parked in her usual place, raising an eyebrow as she spotted a vehicle the size of a small RV with cartoon images of cats and dogs painted on the side. She'd never seen it before, although with the number of pets in her landlady's house, it was no surprise the vet was making house calls. Or perhaps this was some new charity project, since Marigold—as wealthy as she was eccentric—was one of the biggest philanthropists in their small Cape Cod community. Just last week, she'd been talking about starting a pet adoption drive, although if it happened, Simone suspected Marigold would end up with most of the animals herself.

Simone removed her keys from the ignition and opened the

door, but before she had a chance to do more than barely get out of the car, Poppy, her landlady's seven-year-old daughter, rushed up and took her by the hand, dragging her toward the porch of the main house.

"Do you want to see Mr. Fuzzy?" Poppy's eyes bulged with anticipation.

Marigold, dressed in a flowing kaftan speckled with what was either floral designs or oil paint from her latest artistic endeavor, grinned at Simone from the porch in a way that telegraphed a warning that Simone was in for a shock. Not that much shocked Simone anymore. Not in this household. Marigold was a force of nature, and Poppy was the type of kid who ran toward the scariest looking creature without a fear in the world. Given the name, Simone expected a caterpillar, or possibly a big, furry moth.

"Is Mr. Fuzzy a new teddy bear?" Simone crossed her fingers so Poppy could see, hamming it up because she knew the kid loved it when Simone played along and acted nervous.

"No." Poppy giggled. "My teddy's name is Mickey. Duh."

"I thought Mickey was a mouse's name." Simone teased, struggling to stop her mouth from twitching.

"No, my mouse is called Donald."

"A stuffed mouse?" Simone guessed, although she already knew the answer because Poppy loved nothing more than to introduce Simone to every single creature, both warm-blooded and plush, in her menagerie.

"No, she's a real mouse!" Poppy clapped her hands with glee as she bounced up and down hard enough to make the porch floorboards rattle. "Don't you remember?"

"I do now that you mention it, although I didn't realize Donald was a girl. But isn't Donald supposed to be a duck?"

"No." Poppy put her hands on her hips and scrunched her face as she sighed dramatically. "I thought doctors were supposed to be smart."

"Not always, kiddo." Simone held back a sigh as she recalled her predicament with Rowan at work. If Simone were really as smart as she was supposed to be, she wouldn't have gotten herself into this mess in the first place. Surely with enough brains, she wouldn't have slept with her best friend's ex-stepmother two years ago, and she certainly wouldn't have taken a job at the hospital where said woman was now her boss. "So, tell me about Mr. Fuzzy. What kind of animal is he?"

"A tarantula!"

Simone's eyes widened for real. "A tarantula?" She glanced at Marigold, who nodded with an amused shrug.

Poppy nodded enthusiastically. "Yep! He's huge! And hairy!"

"Oh my." Simone swallowed hard, trying to mask her apprehension, but even the thought of a spider made her a little jumpy. "That certainly sounds exciting. Where did you get a tarantula?"

"Bobby's family is moving this summer, and his mom doesn't want to bring Mr. Fuzzy. Can you believe I was the only kid in class who wanted to adopt him?"

Yes. Simone could believe that. "Isn't that something?"

"It is," Poppy agreed in a solemn tone. "Do you want to meet him?"

"You mean he's not in your pocket?" Simone laughed, but she was only half-joking, because Poppy was the kind of kid who always had some sort of critter tucked away in her pockets or stuck inside the hood of a sweatshirt.

"I only do that once we're good friends."

"A wise policy." Simone patted the top of Poppy's head. "You're definitely smart enough to become a doctor someday."

"I'm probably smarter," Poppy opined, and Simone couldn't disagree.

"You look like you could use a beer," Marigold said to Simone as Poppy raced to the front door, letting the screen bang shut after she went inside.

"God, yes," Simone replied, grateful for Marigold's perceptiveness. "A beer sounds perfect right about now."

Marigold nodded knowingly as she ushered Simone into the house. "Rough day at work?"

Simone thought for a moment, unsure how much to divulge. "Nothing too exciting."

Not that Simone didn't trust her landlady. In fact, Marigold was one of the few people, other than Erica, in whom Simone could truly confide. Four times married and three times divorced, Marigold had suffered her fair share of life's misfortunes before her final husband, Poppy's father, had left her a fabulously wealthy widow by the age of fifty. She had a knack for providing comfort without pushing the boundaries of privacy, but the less Simone talked about Rowan, the better. It wouldn't do to have rumors spreading all over town about her complicated history with the new boss.

Walking through the foyer, which was littered with pet supplies, painted canvases in various stages of completion, and an odd assortment of items Marigold had collected for some charity auction or another, Simone couldn't help but note how this space alone was almost as big as her whole house. Not that she was envious. If anything, Simone was simply grateful to have a place to live that was affordable and close to work. Housing was one of the biggest issues on the Cape, and she hadn't exactly had a lot of time to plan before leaving Global Health Frontiers earlier that year. Her place even had a partial view of the ocean. Not as impressive as the view from Rowan's bedroom, but that was a memory she most certainly did not need to be replaying right now.

Poppy dashed off toward her room, presumably to get Mr. Fuzzy, whom Simone hoped was in a cage of some sort. Coming face-to-face with a loose tarantula was not something Simone felt equipped to handle. She followed Marigold into the spacious kitchen, grateful for the distraction from her tumultuous day.

As Marigold pulled two beers from the fridge, Simone leaned against the granite countertop, trying to push thoughts of Rowan from her mind.

"Let's sit on the back deck," Marigold said, handing one of the bottles to Simone after popping off the cap. "It's a gorgeous evening. Soon we won't need sweaters."

"I can't believe it's almost summer." Simone sat in one of the Adirondack chairs before taking a much-needed gulp of beer. "Honestly, it's been so quiet the past few weeks, I'm almost bored. Hopefully work picks up."

Especially since the busier she was, the less time she'd have to obsess over Rowan's sudden reappearance in her life.

Marigold chuckled, taking a swig from her own bottle. "Be careful what you wish for. But speaking of work, I have a proposition that will keep you busy."

"Oh?" Simone leaned forward, intrigued. "What kind of proposition?"

Marigold took another sip of her beer before responding. "Did you see that beautiful vehicle parked in the driveway?"

"It was hard to miss. But before you go any further, I should point out I'm a human doctor, not a vet."

"I know that. It's got a little bit of renovation ahead of it, but as soon as it's done, it's going to be the first mobile clinic in this part of Cape Cod. For humans."

Simone's eyebrows shot up in surprise. "A mobile clinic? That's actually pretty amazing. But how did you get your hands on something like that?"

Marigold grinned. "Let's just say I have connections. The important thing is, my foundation has an opportunity to bring healthcare to people who really need it. There are a lot of folks around here who can't easily get to the hospital, or even a regular doctor's appointment, especially in the off-season when public transportation is limited."

Simone nodded, fully in agreement. "The number of

patients coming in to the ER with issues that could have been prevented with regular check-ups is staggering. A mobile clinic could really make a difference."

"Exactly," Marigold said, her eyes lighting up. "I've got the wheels. Now I need some volunteer doctors and nurses."

Simone couldn't help but grin. Marigold was the type of woman who had complete faith that whatever idea she came up with, no matter how ambitious or outlandish, would come to fruition. And somehow, it usually did.

"So you want me to volunteer my time in this mobile clinic of yours?" Simone guessed.

Marigold nodded enthusiastically, her long gray hair swaying with the movement. "Not volunteer, exactly. You'd be compensated for your time, but I'm not sure how steady a gig it will be yet, so I'm not looking to hire more than a few permanent employees until I know what's what. I know you've got a full-time job at the hospital, but even a few hours here and there would make a huge difference to get us up and running. What do you say? Will you at least give it some thought?"

Before Simone could answer, the screen door opened and shut with a bang, and little footsteps rang out across the deck.

"Here he is." Poppy held up a tiny terrarium. "Mom says we need to get him a bigger home. We're going shopping this weekend."

Simone shuddered at the sight of eight thick legs covered in coarse black hair. "He's certainly fuzzy. Lives up to the name."

"Do you want to pet him?"

Simone's eyes widened in alarm. "Oh, um, that's very kind of you to offer, Poppy, but I think I'll pass for now. Maybe once he's more settled in his new home."

She tried to keep her voice steady, not wanting to hurt Poppy's feelings but also really not wanting to be within a hundred feet of that creepy-crawly thing.

"Why don't you let Mr. Fuzzy rest, Poppy?" the girl's

mother directed. "He's had a big day. Did you finish your homework?"

"No." Poppy's shoulders sagged. "I hate math."

"Join the club, kiddo. You still have to do it." Marigold spoke in that special mom tone that brooked no argument.

With the heaviest of sighs, Poppy trudged back inside, the terrarium clutched carefully in her hands. Simone let out her breath in a whoosh, surprised to discover she'd completely stopped breathing for several seconds of mortal terror.

"Sorry about that," Marigold said with a chuckle. "Poppy's always been fascinated by nature."

"I was really hoping Mr. Fuzzy would turn out to be a hamster," Simone admitted with a nervous laugh. "Or at least something with fewer than eight legs. I hate spiders."

"I can't believe how squeamish you can be," Marigold remarked. "You literally have held people's insides in your hands while working in a tent in the middle of the jungle, but a little spider freaks you out?"

"Nothing about Mr. Fuzzy is little," Simone argued. "And about the worst I've faced lately is putting a couple stitches in a skateboarder's forehead."

It was a far cry from what she'd thought she would be doing. Simone had believed she would be making a big difference in some of the hardest hit and most medically needy places in the world. But she couldn't hack it. The nightmares from childhood had started up after living through her first bad storm in the field, long repressed memories of Hurricane Katrina, of watching her father succumb to drowning before anyone could arrive to save him. In the end, Simone had been forced to quit. The nightmares had subsided, but she still hadn't recovered from the sense of failure.

Maybe this idea of Marigold's for a mobile clinic could be exactly what she needed—a way to make a real difference until her mental health had improved enough to go back out in the field. Simone took another long swig of her beer, trying to push away the memories of her failed mission. She didn't want to think about that right now. Or about Rowan. Or about anything, really.

Oscar, a mutt Poppy had brought home last week, bounded out of the house to chase some birds off the lawn.

"Close, Oscar. So close," Marigold shouted to the dog, who in fact hadn't gotten anywhere near the birds.

Simone got to her feet. "I better get home. I have a pile of laundry that's pretty much life-threatening if I don't take care of it."

"One of the universal truths about life. There are always dishes, laundry, and cleaning that need doing. I guess I better take care of dinner. Do you want me to order a sub for you from Pete's?"

"Not tonight, thanks. A salad's calling my name."

"Why would you want that?" This time it was Marigold's turn to shudder.

"Because vegetables are good for you."

"I don't allow that kind of talk in my home." Marigold gave Simone a hug. "Be kind to yourself, okay? You don't always have to do what's good for you twenty-four hours a day."

"I'll try. And I promise to give this mobile clinic idea some real consideration." Simone walked across the lawn, past Oscar, who was chewing on a stick he'd found, and entered the guest house, closing the door behind her with a sigh of relief. As much as she enjoyed Marigold and Poppy's company, right now she craved solitude.

Simone kicked off her shoes and padded through the living room, her eyes searching out the photo she'd taken with the rest of her crew when she'd been in Madagascar last September, right before it had all gone wrong. Maybe it was time to put that photo away. It only served as a painful reminder of her failure. But it was still so hard for her to let go.

After tossing a load of scrubs into the washer and fixing her salad, she sat at the table that overlooked the water. As the sun dipped lower into the sky, turning Cape Cod Bay orange, red, and purple, her mind wandered to Rowan, who also had a water view. Was she watching this sunset, too?

Was she thinking of Simone?

CHAPTER EIGHT

The hospital cafeteria was bustling with activity as Rowan made her way through the line, balancing a tray laden with a wilted salad and what passed for coffee in this place. The subpar food was another point of improvement to add to her list, which had, after two weeks on the job, expanded to such a length that Rowan felt certain she would never get to the end of it if she lived to be a hundred and fifty.

She scanned the room, searching for a quiet corner where she could eat in peace without even a remote chance of running into Simone. She'd been lucky so far with a ten-day streak of not seeing the woman at all since their encounter on Rowan's first day.

Instead, it was Candace who waved enthusiastically from a table near the window, her curly dark hair bouncing as she motioned for Rowan to join her. So much for that solitude Rowan had been craving, but it wasn't like she could turn down her best friend's invitation. With a resigned sigh, she made her way over to Candace's table and slid into the seat opposite her.

"I saw you considering a quick bolt for the door," Candace

joked. "Afraid to be seen fraternizing with me? I know I'm your direct report now, but it's okay for us to be friends."

"It's nothing to do with you. Whenever people see me, they tell me about some fresh problem with something I didn't even know could be an issue." Rowan glugged her coffee, wishing she'd purchased two of them instead of one. She didn't care how bad they were. The only requirement was that they contained enough caffeine to keep her going through the seemingly endless stream of crises that had become her daily routine.

"Would now be a good time to mention we lost two more nurses from the ER?" Candace nibbled on a piece of bacon from a slightly squished BLT sandwich, making Rowan wish she'd chosen that instead.

"Shit." Rowan groaned, massaging her temples. "That's six in a month. At this rate, we'll have no one left to staff the department."

"Yeah. Your ex-hubby really did a number on staff morale and retention."

"It's hard to manage a hospital when you have a busy schedule of day drinking and betting on sports." Rowan stabbed at her limp salad with more force than necessary. "Dad has the nerve to defend that man every time I bring up anything. He won't even admit Lance was essentially ordered to rehab by the board. He insists it's an executive wellness retreat. It's only because divorce has been so hard on him, you know?" Rowan rolled her eyes. "To hear my father tell it, it's like Lance went through the divorce all by himself. I wanted it, ergo it had no impact on me."

"It's been two and a half years," Candace said, shaking her head. "At some point, you've got to pull yourself together and face the music."

"Can you imagine quitting your job to take care of your mental health?" Rowan asked.

Candace let out a whistle. "Is that a thing we're allowed to do?"

"You? Absolutely not. We're already understaffed," Rowan said with a wry smile. "This behavior is reserved for middle-aged man babies with silver spoons in their mouths. The rest of us have to buck the fuck up, buttercup."

Candace scrunched her nose. "Last winter, I broke my leg skiing, and I still reported to work, cast and all."

Rowan nodded, knowing most of the doctors she worked with would take extraordinary measures not to miss a shift. Lives literally depended on it. "You know the worst part? Dad's gaslighting works on me. Deep down, I'm still blaming myself for Lance spiraling the way he has."

"Don't be ridiculous," Candace said, reaching across the table to squeeze Rowan's hand. "You can't blame yourself for that man's choices."

"I know, but I'm sure he wasn't like this before I left. I mean, he wasn't, was he?" Rowan pushed her salad around with her fork, uncertain of anything anymore. "I feel like I would've seen it."

"What was there to see?" Candace asked.

"His office was a disaster when I took over. Files everywhere, half-eaten lunches, sticky notes with incomprehensible scribbles. It was like walking into the mind of a madman." Rowan shook her head, her voice dropping. "And the financial records? A complete mess. I guess I knew he'd taken on more and more of the CEO responsibilities over the years as my father became less able to keep up, but it's clear he was in over his head. I've spent hours trying to untangle the web of mismanagement, and I'm still not sure I understand the full extent of the damage."

Candace leaned back, her eyes widening. "That bad, huh?"

"I feel like things must have gotten progressively worse, but I can't pinpoint when it started." Rowan paused, a memory from her first day flashing through her mind. "Do you know if he was seeing someone?"

"You think Lance was having an affair when you were married?" Candace's face perked up, ready for the gossip.

"No!" Rowan held a finger up to her lips, urging her friend to keep quiet. "I'm talking about recently. I don't care if he's started dating, but I just hadn't heard anything. Have you?"

"No, nothing. Why?"

"I keep finding photos of this same woman tucked into hiding places around his office. Racy ones."

"How racy?"

Rowan pictured the photos in her head, and a flush crept up her neck. "Let's just say they're the kind of photos you'd stash under your mattress and pray your mother wouldn't find."

"From a porn site?" There was a hint of wicked glee in Candace's tone.

"I don't think so." There was more to say, but the discomfort Rowan felt discussing Lance's private life held her back momentarily. "I don't know. Some of them have personal notes to go with them. With his name and everything."

"Like love letters?" Candace's eyebrows shot up as she leaned forward. "This is juicy. Looks like Lance was living quite the double life. Any idea who she is?"

"Not a clue. But here's the thing. This chick is like supermodel gorgeous. She doesn't have one flaw that I can see, and trust me, I've seen all of her, in every position imaginable and some that I hadn't considered."

"Wait—" Candace slammed her coffee onto the table. "Do you think this mental health break is a sham, and he's off fucking a supermodel while you're running around cleaning up all his messes?"

"I wouldn't go that far. But honestly, have you seen the rehab facility the board sent him to? On the hospital's dime, no less. He's basically gone golfing down in Florida with a bunch of other over-privileged douchebags, oblivious to the chaos he's left behind." Rowan clenched her hand around her fork, wishing Lance was there so she could jab it into his forehead. "Why not throw in a floozy or two for good measure?"

"To think, at one point, I had respect for the man."

"Everyone did. Hell, they still do. If I said half this stuff publicly, I'd be labeled the bitter ex-wife trying to tarnish his reputation."

Candace shook her head sympathetically. "That's not fair. You're the one picking up the pieces."

"I keep replaying scenes from our marriage, trying to figure out if he was a raging, incompetent asshole the entire time and I simply didn't see it." Rowan pressed her lips together as a new round of guilt overcame her. "Or is my dad right? Did me leaving make this happen?"

"I see what you mean about your dad's gaslighting working on you," Candace muttered.

Rowan shot her friend a look. "I heard that."

"Well, hear this. You can't beat yourself up over this. Only Lance is responsible for Lance."

Rowan gave a snort. "That sounds great coming from a therapist, but when I have to spend eighteen hours of every day fixing his problems, it's hard not to think I'm responsible and this is karma coming to bite me in the ass."

"How about Erica? Has she come around and started speaking to you again yet?"

"No. She left early to spend the summer in Italy before her art program starts this fall, so it's not like it's hard for her to give me the silent treatment."

Candace leaned back in her chair, a sympathetic expression on her face. "Does she know anything about her dad's situation? The debt, the rehab, and everything?"

Rowan shook her head. "I'm pretty sure she doesn't have a clue, and I don't plan on telling her. She already thinks I'm the villain in this story. She still doesn't know the real reason I bought the beach house from him, either."

"She thinks you stole her childhood home out from under her in the divorce settlement because you're a wicked shrew. No wonder she won't speak to you."

"It breaks my heart, especially when she was starting to get past her resentment over me leaving her father. We had a few good weeks where I really thought we'd get past it. Unfortunately, as soon as she discovered her father wasn't just letting me use the beach house for a vacation but that I owned it, she completely shut me out."

"I still can't believe Lance was willing to sell that house to pay off his gambling debts," Candace said, her brow furrowing. "I mean, it was supposed to be Erica's inheritance, wasn't it?"

"It should've been. It was in her mom's family for generations, though technically it went to him in the will. I don't think Erica's mom ever imagined he would do anything other than keep it safe for her until she was grown. But apparently his addiction trumped any concern for Erica's future." She sighed heavily, the weight of the situation pressing down on her. "She completely idolizes her father. I can't explain why I bought the house without having to tell her a whole lot of stuff about that man that I don't believe should be my place to tell. Do I want to be the one to wreck her image of him? It feels self-serving. And it would most likely backfire, and she'd hate me even more."

"Hm." Candace took a bite of scrambled eggs, as if needing to stop herself from saying what was really going through her mind.

"Oh, excuse me."

At the same time the voice hit her ears, a faint trace of jasmine perfume tickled Rowan's nose. Her head snapped up to find Simone holding a tray.

"The potted palm was hiding my view," Simone explained, looking flushed. "I didn't know this table was taken."

Rowan's stomach clenched, her earlier wish for solitude suddenly seeming prophetic. She forced a polite smile. "No problem, Dr. Doucette. It's a busy cafeteria."

"Why don't you join us?" Candace waved to an empty chair.

Simone shook her head so vigorously that her blond ponytail whipped back and forth. "Oh, no. I couldn't possibly intrude. I'll—"

"Nonsense." Candace pulled out the chair. "There's plenty of room."

But Simone was already backing away, her tray clutched tightly to her chest. "Thank you, but I really should get back to work. Lots of charts to review. Another time, perhaps." She turned abruptly, nearly colliding with the aforementioned potted palm before making her escape.

"I think she likes you," Candace said with a chuckle.

"What?" Rowan's heart pounded against her ribcage. "She does not. Why the fuck would you say that?"

"Relax." Candace regarded Rowan with a bemused expression. "I was being sarcastic. She clearly couldn't get away from us fast enough."

"Oh. Right. Of course." Rowan's face felt like it was on fire. She shoved a forkful of salad into her mouth before remembering it was wilted and nasty.

"Interesting reaction." Candace tapped her fingers on the table as she studied Rowan's face like it was a slide under a microscope. "Could it be that you're the one harboring a little crush?"

Rowan nearly choked on her limp lettuce. "Don't be ridiculous. She's my employee. And besides, I'm not—" She wasn't sure how to finish that sentence.

"You're not what? Ready to date?" Candace crossed her arms, giving Rowan a disgusted once-over. "It's been two and a half years. Why aren't you the one banging a supermodel?"

"Who has time for that?"

"Lance, apparently," Candace said with a smirk. "But seriously, if you're ready to get back out there, she's the perfect candidate."

"Who?" Rowan squeaked, knowing full well who Candace had meant. "The supermodel?"

"Simone. I'm pretty sure she's single. I know she's a little younger than you, but you two—"

"Nope." Rowan pushed the plate away. "No workplace romances. Look how well that turned out the last time I did it."

She'd been a student when she'd met Lance, while he was already an attending physician. The power dynamics had been all wrong from the start, even if she hadn't recognized it at the time.

"Fair point," Candace conceded. "But you can't live like a nun."

"I don't."

"Really? It's Friday. What are your plans tonight?"

"Cozy sweats. Maybe watch a movie. Take a hot bath. Tell me, do nuns do that?" Rowan pointed a finger at her friend's face.

"Yeah, you're living the high life." Candace's tone oozed sarcasm. "You sure showed me."

Rowan blew out a breath. "Look, for now, it's exactly what I want. Me time."

"Does that mean a date with a vibrator?" Candace waggled her eyebrows. "Because I can get onboard with that if it's one of those good ones with the—"

"Stop." Rowan let out a long, anguished sigh. "I swear to God, you are incorrigible. Can we please change the subject?"

"Fine, fine." Candace held up her hands in surrender. "But don't think this conversation is over. I'm just giving you a temporary reprieve."

Rowan tore the plastic film from her pre-made dinner—some sort of chicken and vegetables topped with a sauce that claimed to be "chef inspired." She wasn't entirely sure what that meant, other than a price tag that was triple the cost of a typical frozen meal from the grocery store. Not that it mattered. Anything would be an improvement over hospital cafeteria fare, and as long as it had the proper nutrients, and she didn't have to go shopping for it or cook it herself, she didn't care too much what it tasted like.

Using her knuckle, Rowan punched in four minutes for the microwave. There'd been a time when she'd spent more than an hour each night making dinner from scratch. Lance had expected gourmet meals, even on nights when Rowan had seen patients well into the evening. She'd accommodated him, though for the life of her, she could no longer remember why. Perhaps because her mother had done the same for her father, thereby convincing Rowan it was her wifely duty. Or some such shit.

There were still thirty seconds to go when Rowan's phone rang. Speak of the devil. Her mother's avatar photo smiled at her from the screen.

"RoRo? It's Mom."

As if another single human being on the planet had called her RoRo since she was maybe three years old.

"Hey, what's up?" Rowan asked, trying to keep the weariness out of her voice. She loved her mother, but sometimes that woman's energy was a bit much after a long day.

"I had a meeting with the most wonderful donor," her mom began, presumably referring to one of the many philanthropists who supported Marbury Hospital's charitable foundation, of which she was the head. "She's practically my new best friend."

"Oh?" Rowan murmured, only half-listening as she retrieved her dinner from the microwave. She peeled back the corner of the plastic film, releasing a plume of steam. "That's nice."

"Nice? It's extraordinary! She's offered us the most

marvelous opportunity. You simply must hear about it. Oh, goodness!" Her mother's voice became muffled, as if she'd pulled the phone away from her mouth. "Marigold, dear, do be careful with that turn. We don't want to tip over!"

Rowan frowned, fork poised halfway to her mouth. "Mom?"

"Everything's fine. I'll explain when we get there."

"Wait, what?" Rowan closed her eyes, wishing there was a higher power to intervene, but her mother was a force of nature all on her own. And the call had ended.

Less than a minute later, there was a honk outside.

Rowan looked forlornly at her barely eaten dinner, aware that the next bite she took would be ice cold. Her mom wasn't one to pop by. The woman camped out.

Rowan's jaw dropped as she stepped out her front door to discover some type of RV with dog and cat cartoon figures slathered on the sides sitting in her driveway.

Grace Colchester, the grand maven of Marbury, waved from the passenger side, decked out in a classic Chanel suit and beaming like a game show hostess announcing a grand prize. "Isn't it fantastic?"

"It's something." Rowan paused, completely out of things to say, except, "What is it?"

"The next big thing for Marbury Hospital!" her mother exclaimed, hopping down from the passenger seat with surprising agility for a woman in her seventies, especially while wearing pantyhose and a pair of pumps. "This is going to revolutionize patient care. As soon as you convince your father to sponsor it."

Suddenly, the reason for her mother's visit was all too clear. Before Rowan could protest that she didn't wield that kind of influence over her father, the driver's side door swung open. A willowy woman with silver-streaked hair emerged, her brightly colored maxi dress and array of scarves a stark contrast to her mother's tailored suit. The stranger made her way around the front of the vehicle, stopping in front of Rowan and extending a hand. "Hi, I'm Marigold Brewster."

Shit. That explained it.

Rowan might not have been up-to-date on every donor, but she knew the Brewster name. Their family had been one of Marbury Hospital's biggest benefactors for generations. Grace Colchester would join a drum circle and howl at the moon—two pastimes that, based on her appearance, seemed all too likely to rank on Marigold's top-ten list—if it meant securing the Brewster family's continued support for the hospital's charitable foundation.

"Rowan Colchester." As she shook Marigold's hand, Rowan spied some movement inside the vehicle but couldn't make out what it was. She prayed the RV, which appeared to be a veterinary clinic on wheels, hadn't come with furry patients still inside.

Perhaps picking up on Rowan's skeptical look, Marigold pointed to the vehicle. "It's a little rough right now, but I got it for a song." The woman squinted as a shadow crossed one of the windows. "What are you doing in there?" Marigold shouted into the RV. "Join us!"

Rowan sucked in a breath, wondering if she was about to come face-to-face with a rescue lion. The door swung open, and her heart nearly stopped as Simone Doucette emerged from the RV, looking sheepish and slightly disheveled. A lion would've been so much easier to deal with.

"This is Simone." Marigold wrapped an arm around Simone, pulling her in close for a kiss on top of her head. "We live together."

"We've met," Rowan choked out, her mind reeling. What had the woman meant by them living together? Were they a couple? Candace had said Simone was single, but she may have gotten it wrong. The age difference was striking, but then again, maybe older women was Simone's thing.

"Is that right?" Marigold gave Simone an appraising look.

"She's a doctor at the hospital. Of course, I know her," Rowan said, a touch of ice in her tone. "She also happens to be my daughter's friend from college."

And if Rowan had a daughter close to Simone's age, then Marigold was truly robbing the cradle.

"Lovely!" Marigold clapped her hands, several silver bracelets on each wrist jangling. "I have a daughter, too. She's seven."

Rowan blinked, struggling to process this new information, suddenly feeling ancient to have a kid who was a full-grown adult.

"Isn't it a small world?" Rowan's mother exclaimed. "Of course, here in Marbury, it's even smaller. Everyone knows everything about everyone." Her mother held up a grocery bag. "Now for business. Marigold was kind enough to pack some snacks."

"I really don't have time right now," Rowan argued. "As it happens, my dinner is inside, getting cold."

"Bah. More of that packaged junk," her mother said dismissively. "This will be much healthier. It's such a lovely night. Let's sit on the deck."

Passing through the house with three guests in tow, Rowan's carefully constructed evening plans crumbled around her. She glanced longingly at the kitchen, knowing her sad microwave dinner was sitting abandoned on the counter.

It wasn't until her mother plopped the grocery bag on the patio table and started to unpack plastic containers of food that Rowan experienced a full-body cringe.

Two years ago, she and Simone had had sex. On this very table.

Slowly, Rowan met Simone's eyes. Given how wide they were, Simone was also remembering that night. Was she worried Rowan would say something to her girlfriend? It suddenly struck Rowan that Simone had not uttered a single word since she'd arrived.

As everyone tucked into the stuffed grape leaves, falafel, and hummus that Marigold apparently thought constituted appropriate snack food—as opposed to say, a bag of Cheetos—Simone never looked in Rowan's direction. For her part, Rowan found herself unable to focus on the conversation. Her mind kept drifting back to that night two years ago. All she could see was Simone, naked except for a pair of high heels.

Rowan shook her head, trying to banish the memory. She forced herself to focus on her mother's enthusiastic chatter.

"...which is why the plan is to retro fit the mobile vet unit for people." Her mom ripped off a piece of naan to dip into the hummus.

Rowan pressed a hand to the side of her head to stop it from spinning. "Come again?"

Dear God, considering the memories swimming in her brain right now, that was the worst possible choice of words. Across the table, Simone looked like she'd swallowed a bug.

"To serve the community better. While the clinics we hold are a huge success, not everyone can come to us. We want to go to them." Marigold popped an entire stuffed grape leaf into her mouth, giving Rowan a view of her lips and tongue that conjured nothing but inappropriate thoughts and something that felt oddly like jealousy.

"Wine." Rowan's mother made a move as if to rise from her seat. "We need wine."

"I can get some." Rowan jumped to her feet, eager for any excuse to escape.

"Be a good girl and help." Marigold nudged Simone in the side before pausing with a frown. "Hold on. You got hummus on your lip."

Marigold leaned over and swiped it from Simone's bottom lip. A second later, she sucked the hummus off her finger.

Rowan wanted to look away but found herself transfixed by the intimate gesture between Marigold and Simone. Heat crept up her neck as she remembered her own lips on Simone's, tasting of vodka and cranberry. A confusing mix of emotions churned in her stomach—jealousy, embarrassment, and a hint of arousal she desperately tried to tamp down.

"Right. Wine."

Rowan nearly tripped over her own feet as she hurried into the house, Simone trailing behind her.

As soon as they were out of earshot, Simone began to babble apologetically. "I'm so sorry. I didn't know where we were going until we pulled into your driveway. I didn't mean to barge into your house and—"

"Can you grab the wine glasses from the cabinet behind your head?" Rowan demanded, cutting her off.

"You don't believe me."

"It doesn't matter."

"Okay." Simone's eyes glistened as if on the verge of tears. "No. You're right. It doesn't matter."

Filled with irrational anger she couldn't begin to explain, Rowan grabbed two bottles and a corkscrew. Before Simone could get another word out, she stormed onto the deck. Simone followed with the glasses, expertly carrying four without so much as a clink. Surely that new girlfriend of hers, who had already set to work popping out the corks, would be very impressed.

What a fool Rowan had been, thinking the night she'd spent with Simone had been special. Clearly, the woman had experience wining and dining older ladies. And she'd landed herself a big catch, one of the wealthiest women in town.

Their own time together hadn't meant a thing.

This was ridiculous. Of course it hadn't meant anything. They'd had a fling, thought better of it, and that was that. Rowan had no right to feel jealous or angry. What had happened between her and Simone was in the past and could never happen again even if Simone hadn't moved on. There were way too many reasons—really fucking good reasons, too—why they could never be together. Like Erica. And their professional integrity.

So what was this all about?

As Rowan retook her seat, her mother continued the conversation. "Now that you're in charge, I know things will get done."

"I'm not in charge," Rowan argued, mainly because she felt peevish and in the mood to argue. "Dad is, same as always. Mom, I understand you're excited about this mobile clinic idea, but I'm not sure it's feasible right now. We're already stretched thin as it is."

"Oh, pishposh," Grace waved her hand dismissively. "Talk to your father, and get him on board. It's what Lance always did."

Rowan's jaw clenched at the mention of her ex. "I'm not Lance, and I won't allow you to manipulate me into making rash decisions on a whim."

"Rowan Marie Colchester," Rowan's mother said, her voice taking on a steely edge as she rose to her feet. "I will not be spoken to in that tone. Ladies, I think we should leave now."

Without getting up, Rowan watched in disbelief as her mother stormed off toward the RV, Marigold trailing behind with a sympathetic glance back at Rowan. Simone lingered, looking torn between following the others and staying behind.

"I'm sorry," Simone said softly.

"Just go." Rowan turned her head away so she wouldn't have to watch Simone leave. She listened to the soft footsteps retreating, followed by the slam of the RV door and the rumble of the engine starting up.

Rowan slumped in her chair, letting out a long sigh as she stared at the stupid patio table that was currently the source of so much inner turmoil. All she'd wanted was a quiet night at home with her microwavable dinner. Instead, she'd been blindsided by her mother, faced with painful reminders of her past, and now found herself alone with a table full of half-eaten Mediterranean appetizers and two open bottles of wine.

Rowan reached for one of the wine bottles and contemplated refilling a glass before thinking better of that plan. Instead, she tipped it to her lips and took a long swig directly from the bottle.

What a fucking disaster.

CHAPTER NINE

"It's coming down in sheets out there." Candace pivoted on the ER's tile floor, the soles of her sneakers making a hideous sound.

Looking up from the computer terminal where Simone had been entering notes, she leaned back and stretched her arms over her head, feeling a satisfying pop halfway down her back. "That explains the quiet. It's hard for tourists to get sunburn and heat stroke when it's pouring rain. I'm not complaining, though. After all the firework injuries from last week's Fourth of July celebrations, we could use a breather."

Candace nodded, a couple of droplets of water shaking from her head. "True. Though I bet we'll get a fender bender before the shift's over. As soon as the streets get a little wet, people lose their goddamn minds."

Simone checked the clock. "Two hours to go, and then we both have the weekend off."

"Poor Dr. Reeves is going to have his hands full. Did you hear? Another nurse quit."

"Who?"

"I can't even remember the name. One of the new ones."

"Oh." Simone sat silently, letting the news sink in. She couldn't recall so many staffing issues at any other hospital she'd worked at. Even with Global Health Frontiers, they'd had more stability.

"I'd come in if I could, but I legally can't work any more hours in a row," Candace said.

Simone offered a sympathetic nod. "Got any plans for your time off?"

"Not really. Chris has gone to visit her mother in Maine with the kids, so I might catch up on laundry while I binge-watch that new reality cooking show everyone's been talking about. You?"

Simone shrugged, her eyes drifting back to the computer screen. "I'm helping stock the mobile clinic. It's supposed to get back from being retrofitted this afternoon, and I know Marigold's hoping to roll it out as soon as possible. If she can find enough people to work."

"Marigold still hasn't had any luck convincing Rowan—I mean, Dr. Colchester—to have the hospital become an official partner with the clinic? Not that we have any staff to spare."

Simone shook her head. "The way that meeting with her mother and Marigold went last month, I doubt she even wants to hear the words *mobile clinic* again."

Candace leaned against the counter, her eyebrows raised. "I thought she'd be all for a community outreach initiative. Especially one that could keep some of the less serious cases from clogging the emergency department."

Simone sighed, her fingers hovering over the keyboard. "Trust me. It was the most uncomfortable thing I've ever witnessed. I felt so awkward getting caught in the middle of it."

"Has she talked to you at all about it?"

"Dr. Colchester?" Simone's pulse quickened as she wondered how much her colleague might know about her and Rowan's past. After all, the two of them were friends. Maybe

Rowan had confided in Candace about their fling. "No! I mean why would she have any reason to discuss it with me?"

Candace gave her a strange look. "Because you're on the volunteer coordination committee for the mobile clinic. I thought she might have asked for your input, given your experience with GHF."

"That. Right," Simone's cheeks warmed. "No, she hasn't asked me anything about it. I think she's trying to keep her distance from the whole project."

Candace frowned. "That's a shame. Putting in some shifts at the mobile clinic would be good for her. When we were in medical school, Rowan talked about wanting to do something similar to what you did with your humanitarian mission."

"She did?" Simone tried to picture a younger Rowan, idealistic and passionate about humanitarian work. It was hard to reconcile with the cool, detached administrator. "I had no idea. She seems so corporate now."

"Yeah, well, life has a way of changing things. Once she married Lance—" Candace's expression darkened. "Never mind that. But you two have a lot more in common than you might think. Maybe when Chris gets back from visiting her mom, the four of us could grab dinner or something. I think you'd really hit it off."

Panic fluttered in Simone's chest. Was Candace trying to set up Simone and Rowan on a date?

Simone opened her mouth to respond, but was cut off by the sudden blare of sirens approaching the ER bay. She and Candace exchanged a look before springing into action, moving swiftly down the hallway toward the ambulance entrance. Simone panted as she and Candace rushed to meet the incoming emergency vehicles. The sirens grew louder, piercing through the steady drumming of rain on the pavement.

The first ambulance pulled in, and the doors swung open, revealing paramedics unloading a stretcher.

"What do we have?" Simone called out, holding a hand to her forehead and squinting through the rain.

"Boating accident," the paramedic shouted. "Two victims, father and son. This one's a thirty-two-year-old male, possible spinal injury and severe lacerations to the chest and abdomen. Second ambulance has a boy, age seven. The child wasn't wearing a life jacket and went overboard when the boat nearly capsized in the storm. The father dove in to save him but struggled to reach him. No pulse or respirations on scene."

A drowning? Simone froze, dread coiling in her belly at the news. A car accident she would've been prepared for, but not this. And the kid was so young. The same age as Poppy. The same age as the little boy... Simone's mind raced, memories of Madagascar threatening to overwhelm her. Rain streamed down her face, into her nose and mouth, giving her the sensation of drowning, like someone had plunged her head underwater.

The man on the stretcher groaned in pain. Simone blinked hard, forcing herself to focus on the present. She couldn't afford to freeze up now. Two lives hung in the balance.

"Dr. Doucette?" Candace's voice cut through the fog. "I'll go with the father to Trauma 1."

"I've got the boy," Simone called out, her voice steady despite the pounding of her heart.

She rushed to the second ambulance where the small, motionless body of a child lay on a stretcher as one paramedic did chest compressions.

"How long was he under?" she asked the other paramedic who was bagging the child.

"Uncertain. Bystanders pulled him out and started CPR before we arrived," the paramedic replied grimly, not pausing in his efforts. "We've been working on him for ten minutes en route."

The boy's skin was pale and tinged with blue, his wet clothes clinging to his small frame. The surrounding team zoomed into action, but Simone felt as if she were moving through molasses. She forced herself to take a deep breath, willing her training to kick in. She couldn't let her bad memories paralyze her. This boy needed her.

"Get him inside, now!" Simone ordered, her voice ringing with an authority that surprised her, considering the chaos she felt inside.

She took over the chest compressions, counting the whole time as they wheeled the stretcher inside, racing toward Trauma 2.

"He's so cold," Simone muttered, feeling the chill of the boy's skin through her gloves. "Let's get him on warm saline and start rewarming measures immediately."

After the boy's wet clothes were cut off and blankets were applied, Simone switched with another team member, allowing him to do chest compressions while she checked for a pulse.

"Damn it. No pulse."

The boy's core temperature would be dangerously low. Even if they managed to restart his heart, there was a high risk of neurological damage from oxygen deprivation.

"One, two, three, four, five, six…" The sound of the team counting the chest compressions ticked in Simone's head like a clock. They were rapidly running out of time.

It seemed like Simone was in a bad dream where she had turned to stone, watching helplessly as the boy slipped away. A single rain drop trickled from her forehead and into her eye. The room blurred around her, the sounds of the medical team fading into a distant hum.

She was back beside the swollen river, the flooding from the typhoon obscuring every recognizable landmark. Desperate cries rang in her ears, a small body limp in her arms. Her chest tightened, her breath coming in short gasps.

"Dr. Doucette?"

Someone called her name, but she couldn't respond.

"Dr. Doucette, status report." The voice was sharper now, cutting through the fog like a sharp knife.

Simone looked up to see Rowan entering the trauma room. She'd already flung her suit coat to the floor and was shoving the sleeves of her blouse up as she approached in long strides. Simone felt a flash of relief, followed quickly by shame at her own paralysis. With every ounce of effort, she blocked out all the bad memories and snapped to attention.

"Seven-year-old male, drowning victim," Simone managed to say.

"Have you checked for a pulse?" Rowan prompted, her eyes scanning the monitors and taking in the scene.

Simone nodded, finding her voice. "No pulse. It's been…" She glanced at the clock, shocked to see how much time had passed. "Jesus. At least eighteen minutes since the paramedics reached him. Not sure how long without a pulse, though. We should…uh…"

No matter how hard she tried, Simone couldn't get the thoughts in her brain to turn into words in her mouth.

"Let's get a central line in and push a round of epi," Rowan said when it must have become clear to her that Simone was incapable of speech. "Dr. Doucette, I'll take over compressions. Nurse, page cardiology, and tell them we need the portable ECMO machine in Trauma 2 stat."

What the hell is wrong with me? Simone wondered. She knew what needed to be done every bit as well as Rowan did. Hell, even more so, given that she was the specialist in the room. Why wasn't she able to make the calls?

No matter how mortified Simone was at her own shortcomings, she couldn't help but be impressed with the way Rowan took charge, her presence steadying the chaotic energy in the room. The woman was an amazing doctor, a fact that too easily could get lost when all a person saw was an administrator in an expensive suit.

"Dr. Doucette," Rowan said firmly, her eyes locking with Simone's as her arms moved in perfect time, up and down, on the boy's chest. "Can you handle the central line?"

Simone nodded, grateful for the clear direction. Her hands moved with practiced efficiency as she inserted the catheter into the boy's neck, her muscle memory kicking in even though her mind struggled to keep up.

"Line's in," she reported, her voice steadier now.

She could feel Rowan's eyes on her, assessing her every move. She couldn't afford to falter again. Not with a child's life hanging in the balance.

"Good," Rowan said, her voice low and reassuring. "Let's push a round of epinephrine."

Simone administered the medication, her eyes fixed on the monitor. Still no change.

"My husband!" a woman's voice screeched from the hallway. "Where's my baby?"

Simone's head snapped up, her eyes meeting Rowan's. The anguish in the woman's voice was all too familiar. She'd heard the same sound coming from her mother all those years ago after the storm that had killed Simone's father.

The woman appeared in the doorway, her eyes wild with panic. She was soaking wet, her hair plastered to her face, as though she'd run all the way to the hospital on foot without an umbrella.

"You, take over compressions," Rowan directed one of the nurses. "I'll handle this."

Rowan wrapped an arm around the woman's shoulders, gently guiding her away from the trauma room. "Ma'am, I'm Dr. Colchester. Can you come with me?"

Simone watched as Rowan led the distraught mother away, her voice low and soothing. Simone turned back to the boy, her resolve strengthened. She couldn't let this child become another tragic memory.

"Okay, people, let's keep going," she said, her voice ringing with newfound authority. "We're not giving up on this kid."

"Dr. Doucette, ECMO is here," a different nurse announced, wheeling in the bulky machine.

"Okay, let's—wait." Simone's eyes widened as she noticed a faint flutter on the heart monitor. "Hold on. I think I saw something."

The room fell silent, everyone holding their breath as they watched the monitor. A faint, erratic rhythm appeared on the screen, growing steadier with each passing second.

"We've got sinus rhythm," Simone announced. She pressed her stethoscope to the boy's chest, listening intently. "Breath sounds present bilaterally but diminished. Let's get him intubated and start mechanical ventilation."

The room erupted into a flurry of activity. Simone focused intently on each task, her earlier paralysis forgotten in the rush of adrenaline.

"Dr. Doucette, may I speak with you for a minute?" Rowan asked once the boy was stabilized and being prepped for transfer to the ICU.

Simone nodded, her heart sinking. This was it. Rowan had seen how badly she'd frozen up in there, and now Simone was going to be reprimanded, maybe even fired.

No, there was no maybe about it. She deserved to be fired.

"Let's go somewhere more private," Rowan said, leading the way.

Simone followed Rowan out of the trauma room, her legs unsteady. The adrenaline was wearing off, leaving her exhausted and shaky. As they walked down the hallway, she noticed for the first time that Rowan's silk blouse was soaked through from the embrace she'd given the boy's mother. Her fiery curls were damp from sweat. She'd thrown herself entirely into the task of saving the boy with no concern for herself or her designer wardrobe. From her waterlogged appearance, anyone might have thought Rowan was the one who had nearly drowned.

Rowan led Simone to the employee locker room, where no one was in sight. She'd be spared that embarrassment at least. Simone took a breath, preparing herself for the inevitable dressing down. Or worse.

"You okay?" Rowan asked.

Simone nodded, but the movement felt mechanical, disconnected from her spiraling thoughts. She braced herself for the reprimand, the disappointment, the inevitable termination of her position.

"No, seriously. Are you okay?" Rowan's eyes narrowed, scrutinizing Simone's face. "You don't look okay."

Simone's shoulders slumped. "Can we get to the firing so I can go home?"

"What?"

"Aren't you going to fire me?"

Rowan's brow furrowed, her expression softening. "Fire you? Why on earth would I fire you?"

Simone blinked, caught off guard by Rowan's reaction. "Because I froze up in there. If you hadn't come in when you did—"

Rowan shook her head, her wet curls sticking to her cheeks. "Simone, you didn't freeze up. You were there, working on that boy the entire time. I saw you doing compressions and administering medication. You were as present and focused as could be expected."

"I wasn't. I was thousands of miles away." Simone stared helplessly at the floor. "It was like I was right back in Madagascar again."

Rowan's expression softened further. She reached out and gently squeezed Simone's arm. "What happened in Madagascar?"

Simone took a shaky breath, the memories flooding back.

"There was a typhoon that triggered a major flooding disaster. We were trying to evacuate a village when I found a little boy, about the same age as the one today. He'd been swept away by the floodwaters. I managed to reach him, but by the time I got him to shore, it was too late. I tried everything, but I couldn't bring him back. And today, when that boy came in, I was right back there, feeling that same sense of panic and helplessness."

"That's natural. We're not superheroes or robots without emotions."

"You don't understand. In Madagascar, that was when I realized I had PTSD. From my father's death. Today, I could feel it happening all over again." Simone's voice trailed off as she realized what she was revealing. She'd never spoken about her PTSD to anyone at Marbury, not even Candace. And here she was, confessing it to Rowan of all people.

"It was Hurricane Katrina, right?"

"Yes, but you should know I was cleared by a psychiatrist before I started working here," Simone rushed to explain. "I thought I had it under control. I never imagined it would affect my work like this."

Rowan continued as if she hadn't heard a single word. "When your father died, you would've been, what? About twelve?"

"Yes. How did you—"

"I remember," Rowan said quietly. "You told me about losing your father back when we... well, you know."

Another reason Simone was about to get axed. They'd had this conversation two years ago, the same weekend they'd shared that passionate, ill-advised night together. No matter how much time passed, that mistake would always be there between them. A risk. A complication. There was no getting around it.

"That's—" Simone's throat was so tight she could barely speak. "That's why I left GHF and returned to the States. After losing that little boy, I couldn't shake it. Every disaster dredged up the trauma from my childhood. I thought working in a regular ER would be easier, less triggering. I thought I could get better so I could go back into the field. But clearly, I was wrong."

"Are you going to quit again, like you did GHF?"

"Quit?" Simone looked up sharply, meeting Rowan's concerned gaze. "I assumed you were going to fire me."

"You know what they say about assumptions." Rowan shook her head, a small smile playing at her lips. "Simone, you're a good doctor. You had a few seconds of doubt in an extremely stressful situation. I'm not going to fire you over this. Only you can decide if you have it in you to stay."

Simone blinked, stunned. "But I froze. I put that child's life in danger."

The truth was she had faltered, and in their line of work, even a moment's hesitation could mean the difference between life and death. What must Rowan think of her now that she knew? There was no way Rowan would forget. She would see Simone as weak, unfit for the pressures of emergency medicine. She would question Simone's ability to handle the stress and trauma that came with the job.

The thought made Simone's stomach churn, and she found herself fighting back a sudden wave of tears. She had worked so hard to build a reputation as a competent and reliable physician, but all of that had been called into question.

"Simone," Rowan said, her voice cutting through the haze of self-doubt. "Look at me."

Reluctantly, Simone raised her eyes to meet Rowan's, bracing herself for the disappointment she was sure to find there. Instead, she was met with a gaze filled with understanding and compassion.

"We all have our moments," Rowan said, resting her hand on Simone's shoulder as warmth radiated through the damp fabric of her scrubs. "God knows I've had my share. Do you know how many times I've second-guessed myself or felt paralyzed by a difficult decision? But what defines us is how we choose to move forward. From where I'm standing, you've got nothing to be ashamed of."

"He almost died."

"He was dying before he got here. You helped save him."

"You had to rush to my rescue." For some reason, Simone simply couldn't accept Rowan's kindness. It was too generous. Too understanding. Too much at odds with her own desire to beat herself up for her failure.

"I didn't rescue you," Rowan said firmly. "I assisted you. There's a difference. I've had people come to my aid. It's what we do for each other so we can save people's lives. You are not alone. Unless you quit. Then you really will be all alone. Is that what you want? To run off and hide? Beat yourself up for what could have been?"

"He died!" Simone wasn't sure if she was talking about her father, or the little boy in Madagascar, or if every single person she hadn't been able to save had morphed into one collective tragedy. The weight of it all pressed down on her chest, making it hard to catch her breath. Simone balled her fists, squeezing her eyes shut as she fought to regain control. She wanted to scream, to punch the wall, to do something to break the hold her emotions had over her.

"Who died? The boy we just treated is alive. He's in the ICU right now, fighting."

"I'm sorry," Simone choked, her voice barely audible. "I shouldn't be falling apart like this."

Rowan slid her fingers over Simone's fist. "Ten years ago, I wasn't even working, just out for a walk when I saw an accident on the street. One second a little girl was riding her bike, the next a car slammed into her. It would have taken a miracle—no, all the miracles—to save her, but I still tried. Until the EMT literally had to pull me away, kicking and screaming." Rowan took a deep breath. "I can still feel it. They never leave us, Simone.

That's what makes us better at our jobs. If we don't care, we should quit."

"Sometimes I feel like I'm not making a difference. Not like I thought I would." Simone's shoulders slumped, defeat setting in. "Nothing in my life has gone the way I planned."

"You made a difference today. You saved a family from going through unspeakable loss." Rowan lifted Simone's chin with a finger. "You can't beat yourself up for not being able to perform miracles every single time. We can't save every patient we treat, but we save a hell of a lot more than we lose."

"But is it enough? At least you're in charge, making a difference on a larger scale."

Rowan let out a humorless laugh. "Can I tell you something? I miss being a doctor sometimes. Being in charge fucking sucks. I miss helping people. Directly. Not through budgets and board meetings."

Simone blinked in surprise at Rowan's admission. "You do? I thought you were born to be in charge. It's literally your family who founded the hospital."

Rowan sighed, running a hand through her damp hair. "I thought I would love it. But some days, I feel like I'm drowning in paperwork and bullshit. What I wouldn't give to be on the front lines sometimes, doing what we did today."

Simone snorted. "If you really mean that, there's always the mobile clinic. We're still looking for people to help out."

She expected Rowan to brush off the suggestion as a joke—it had mostly been intended as such—but was surprised by a flicker of genuine interest deep in Rowan's eyes.

"Maybe that's not such a bad idea after all," Rowan mused, her expression thoughtful. "I've been so caught up in trying to prove myself in this administrative role I've almost forgotten why I became a doctor in the first place."

Despite herself, Simone felt a flutter of excitement in her chest at the prospect of spending time working side by side with

Rowan as equals, instead of as boss and employee. She quickly tamped down the feeling, reminding herself of the complications that could arise if they crossed the professional boundaries between them.

"I'm sure your expertise would be welcome," Simone said. "But if you're serious, I think there's one thing you'll need to do first. Apologize to your mother."

Rowan's eyebrows shot up, her mouth quirking into a wry smile. "Apologize to my mother? That's a tall order. You met the woman and saw what happened. After the way I spoke to her at that disastrous meeting last month, I can only assume she'll want nothing to do with my help."

"I think there's only one way to find out. You know what they say about assumptions, Dr. Colchester." Before she could stop herself, Simone punctuated her remark with what could only be described as a flirtatious wink. Horrified, Simone waited for Rowan to recoil at her inappropriate behavior.

Instead, Rowan chuckled, shaking her head. "Using my own words against me, I see. Touché, Dr. Doucette."

They stood there, grinning at each other like fools. Simone relaxed for the first time since those two ambulances had arrived. She was still shaken by her experience, but Rowan's unexpected kindness and vulnerability had eased some of the crushing weight of her guilt, even as it seemed to awaken other, more complicated feelings. Standing here together like this, Simone could barely recall a single reason why pursuing anything with Rowan would be a terrible idea.

"I suppose I should get back to work," Simone said, trying and failing to suppress a yawn. Now that the adrenaline was finally wearing off, exhaustion was rapidly seeping into every fiber of her being.

"You look dead on your feet," Rowan observed. "Why don't you go home and get some rest?"

Simone hesitated, torn between her sense of duty and her

body's desperate need for rest. "Are you sure? My shift doesn't end for another hour, and we're short-staffed."

"I'm positive," Rowan said firmly. "You've been through a lot today. Go home. Boss's orders."

And there it was. One really big reason, which Simone had so conveniently forgotten just moments ago, that nothing could ever happen between Rowan and her. No matter how much Simone might wish otherwise, Rowan was her boss. That was a professional line she could never dare to cross.

CHAPTER TEN

Rowan paused in front of her father's office door and straightened the hem of her already perfect suit jacket before raising a fist to knock.

"Enter."

Her father was so predictable, always playing the role of the imperious CEO, even when it was after hours and only the two of them were in the office. Rowan had to shove down the urge to roll her eyes at his pompous tone as she pushed open the heavy oak door.

She popped her head inside, plastering on a polite smile. "Do you have a moment to chat?"

"Ah, yes. I've been expecting this." He closed his laptop, waving her in.

Damn. Mom must've already busted her about their disagreement over the hospital's involvement in the mobile clinic initiative. He was going to have a field day putting Rowan in her place over this one.

"You heard, then?" Rowan recognized the ill-concealed look of glee in his eyes, as if he relished the opportunity to see his daughter struggle so he could swoop in and come to the rescue.

She took a seat opposite him, perching on the edge and steeling herself for the inevitable lecture.

"There's something you should know. I hear everything." He steepled his fingers, resting his chin on them. "But go ahead and tell me. How bad is it?"

Rowan shrugged. "I've texted her four days in a row trying to apologize, but she refuses to acknowledge me. Do you know how humiliating it is to be left on read by your own mother?"

Rowan's father frowned, his white eyebrows furrowing in confusion. "Left on read? I'm not sure I follow."

Rowan sighed, reminding herself her father was from a different generation. "It means she's seen my messages but hasn't responded. She's upset with me for not immediately agreeing to provide unlimited hospital resources to her new pet project."

"Who's that we're talking about?"

Rowan arched an eyebrow. "I'm talking about Mom."

So much for him being Mr. I Know Everything.

Rowan's father leaned back in his chair, a look of dawning comprehension crossing his face. "I see. I thought you were here about the regulatory compliance meeting. I know that information can be a little tricky, so if you need my help—"

"No, Dad. I'm fine for the compliance meeting." Rowan felt a flicker of irritation. Of course, he'd think she was here about hospital business and immediately assume she was in over her head. "I'm here about Mom's mobile clinic project. The one she's been badgering me about for weeks, trying to get me to agree to talk to you about getting the hospital involved."

"Do you need me to go over the numbers?" he said in his women-can't-be-trusted voice.

Rowan bristled at her father's condescending tone. "No. I've gone over the numbers myself. Multiple times. The hospital simply can't afford to allocate resources to an external project right now, no matter how noble the cause."

"I don't see how that's possible. Lance—"

THE ANATOMY OF FOREVER

Rowan's jaw clenched at the mention of her ex-husband's name. "Lance isn't here, Dad. This is my job now, and I'm telling you, the numbers don't add up."

Her father's eyes narrowed. "Are you sure you're looking at them correctly? Perhaps if I—"

"Dad, please. I understand the hospital's finances. With insurance reimbursal rates what they are, we're increasingly operating on razor-thin margins. That's simply an industry-wide fact." One that her ex-husband hadn't grasped, not that she was going to come right out and say so to the man's number-one fan. Talk about the quickest way to shut down a conversation with Dad. Rowan cleared her throat. "Lance seemed to let a lot of things slip through the cracks recently. I can barely keep the hospital in patient gowns now that our usual service won't deal with us anymore, let alone find money to put toward a major unplanned patient outreach initiative."

In fact, supply shortages were almost easy to manage compared to the chronic understaffing that had become the norm during Lance's tenure as CMO. Her father's unwavering faith in her ex had always been a sore spot, and she feared he'd dismiss her concerns outright. But Rowan couldn't shake the nagging feeling that the unpleasant surprises she kept running across were far from over.

Her father puffed out his cheeks, slowly letting the air seep out. "Yes, I'm aware there were a few lapses. But we need to be compassionate right now. Honestly, the poor man is still reeling from what you put him through."

Rowan's temper flared. "What I put him through? Dad, he's the one who—" She caught herself and took a deep breath. This wasn't the time or place to rehash her divorce. "Look, the point is, the hospital's struggling. Lance seemed to think no matter what he did, things would come out all right. But that's not the real world."

"He's a damn fine surgeon."

"If this were the operating room, I'd trust Lance's judgment implicitly. But the role of a CMO is to build a bridge between clinical expertise and executive management. In that arena, he was far less competent."

Her father's eyes narrowed, a familiar stubbornness settling into the lines of his face. "Now, Rowan, I think you're being a bit harsh. Lance always had the hospital's best interests at heart. This is a rough time for him, whether you want to hear it or not."

Rowan bit back a sharp retort, reminding herself that arguing about Lance wouldn't solve anything. "Let's hope he's getting the help he needs right now."

"I hear he's making some progress." He looked out his office window with a forlorn expression, like he'd lost his dog. "Back to your mother. Am I correct in thinking when she proposed this project, you explained it wasn't financially doable, and now you're in the doghouse?"

"That sums it up succinctly."

"I adore your mother, but I do question her real-life skills."

Of course, he did. Because while his wife had run the hospital's charitable trust for forty years and managed millions in donations, Dad still saw her as some kind of flighty socialite. Just like he would never see Rowan as anything other than a young woman who was better suited for domestic life than a prestigious medical career.

Rowan bit her tongue, resisting the urge to defend her mother's considerable accomplishments. It wouldn't change her father's mind.

"Mom's very passionate about this project. She believes it could make a real difference in underserved communities. And she's right. If it were scaled up enough, it could cut back on traffic through the ER. I even think it could improve morale around here, if only our staff weren't already stretched so thin. I can't ask people to take on more hours without compensation, and the Brewster Foundation has already put everything toward the project that they can. They need to expand their donor base to really get it off the ground."

Her father's expression softened slightly. "Your mother's always had a big heart. It's one of the things I love most about her." He paused, drumming his fingers on the desk. "You know, there might be a way to make this work. There's a fund I have access to that could go to this little pet project of hers."

"A fund?" Rowan had poured over all the financials, and she hadn't seen this magical fund.

"It's not tied to the hospital, but one of the charities I'm on the board for. It would allow us to support the mobile clinic in a small way without compromising the hospital's finances." He flipped his laptop open. "Let me get the ball rolling and send some emails."

He made it sound like the simplest thing in the world. And for him, maybe it was. While her father's age had increasingly led him to hand off many of his day-to-day responsibilities to Lance over the past few years, his influence and the connections built over a lifetime remained as strong as ever. It made Rowan wish, not for the first time, that she had inherited even a fraction of her father's effortless ability to make things happen with a few phone calls and handshakes. She felt a familiar pang of inadequacy, quickly followed by frustration at herself for still craving her father's approval after all these years.

"Why didn't Mom come to you about this in the first place?"

"She may have and I wasn't listening." He had the decency to look sheepish over the comment. "It's possible I have a tendency to block out things I don't want to hear."

Like how unhappy Rowan had been in her marriage? She remembered how her father had dismissed her concerns about Lance for years, always quick to defend his son-in-law. Even now, she half expected her father was waiting for her to admit she was in over her head. She wouldn't be surprised if he fully expected Lance to swoop back in and save her from the tedium of doing what in his mind would always be a man's job.

Why stop there? There was no doubt her dad would be delighted for her to take Lance back as her husband, too. Never mind that Rowan could never truly be happy married to a man. God knows she'd given up just about everything in an effort to make it work. But her father would never see it that way. For such a brilliant doctor, he couldn't understand her perspective, no matter how many times she tried to explain. It was better not to dwell on it because it was never going to change.

"I appreciate you looking into this fund," Rowan said, careful to keep her tone neutral. "It would mean a lot to Mom."

Her father nodded, already typing away on his laptop once more. "Of course. I'll let you know once I've sorted out the details."

In other words, their heart-to-heart was over. Rowan recognized the dismissal in her father's tone and body language. She stood, smoothing her skirt.

"Thank you. I'll let Mom know you're working on a solution."

He grunted in acknowledgment, eyes still fixed on his screen.

As she left her father's office, all Rowan could think about was how much she could use a drink and some friendly company. She fired off a text to Candace with two beer emojis and a face emoji with the tongue lolling out that hopefully implied it was time to get sloppy drunk. A wave of relief washed over her as her phone buzzed almost immediately with a response.

"Meet you at The Driftwood Lounge in 20. First round's on me, girl."

THE DRIFTWOOD LOUNGE would not have been Rowan's first choice of location, but it wouldn't be wise to make a fuss. It'd raise questions Rowan didn't want to answer. Besides, her need to unwind far outweighed her discomfort at returning to the bar where she and Simone had hooked up two years ago. Ancient history, and besides, what were the odds of running into Simone here again? The woman had her precious girlfriend to keep her entertained now, and considering Marigold was richer than double chocolate cheesecake, there were way better places for them to spend a random Thursday night if they were so inclined.

Stepping onto the outside patio, Rowan spotted Candace near the railing, seated at a table with three full glasses of beer.

"I was joking when I told you I wanted two drinks." Rowan took a seat. "Granted, a meeting with my father is enough to send a teetotaler on a bender."

"This one's yours." Candace scooted over one of the pint glasses.

"Does that mean you're double fisting it tonight?"

"Chris would sure love it if I tried." Candace gave an exaggerated wink.

"Please, stop." Rowan put a hand up. "I have a feeling we're talking about two very different things right now. I just came from my father's office. My brain can't handle any sex talk."

"How is the old codger?"

"Frustrating as always." Rowan reached for her drink, frowning as she eyed the third glass with suspicion. "Are we expecting company?"

"Hear me out," Candace said with a look of guilt that made Rowan's nerves jangle. "You said you needed some friendly company. As your best friend, it's my job to understand when you're speaking in code."

"I wasn't speaking in code, aside from the emojis," Rowan protested, but her words stopped short as she caught sight of a familiar figure approaching their table, blond ponytail swinging. Her heart skipped a beat, and she silently cursed Candace's meddling.

Simone smiled tentatively as she reached the table, confusion evident in her eyes. "Dr. Colchester, I wasn't expecting to see you here."

"It's after hours," Candace jumped in before Rowan could say a word. "I'm sure it would be fine to drop the formalities. Isn't that right, Rowan?"

Rowan shot Candace a look that clearly said 'we'll discuss this later' before turning to Simone with what she hoped was a neutral smile. "Of course. Please, join us... Simone."

Simone looked at the empty chair warily before finally sliding into it.

Rowan lifted her glass to her lips, needing fortitude to get through whatever Candace had planned. Why did it seem everyone in Rowan's circle had ulterior motives and didn't listen?

"Glad you could make it." Candace beamed, clearly under the impression she'd done something brilliant by ambushing Rowan in this way. As if life hadn't already been complicated enough.

"Thanks for the invitation." Far from appearing grateful, Simone looked as if she wanted to catapult herself over the railing and jump into the ocean.

Rowan could relate.

"Oh no!" Candace grabbed her phone despite it not having made a sound and stared at it with all the dramatic skill of a toddler in an improv class. "I'm afraid I have to run."

"Is it the hospital? I should go with you." Rowan jumped to her feet, knowing full well there was absolutely no emergency at the hospital. Aside from her friend's terrible acting, if there had been anything important going on, her own phone would have buzzed like a swarm of bees with incoming alerts.

"No, no, nothing like that," Candace said, waving her hand dismissively. "It's just I promised Chris I'd pick up some milk on the way home, and you know how she can be. If she has to drink her evening tea black, she'll kill me."

"Not if I kill you first," Rowan muttered through clenched teeth.

Candace laughed, giving a salute to Simone before skedaddling like the traitor she was.

"I take it this was a setup of some kind," Simone said as Rowan sank back into her seat like a condemned prisoner settling into the electric chair.

"Seems so." Rowan tried to flash an easy-breezy smile but feared it came across with more murderous intent. Candace had gone too far with her meddling this time, trying to fix Rowan up with a woman who not only worked for her but who had a girlfriend already. Obviously, Candace must not have known this, but it left Rowan in a real mess.

"I can go." Simone started to slide away from the table.

Rowan, to her own surprise, found herself reaching out, her hand hovering above Simone's arm. "No, please. Stay." She withdrew her hand quickly, realizing how desperate she must seem. "What I mean is don't be silly. Candace bought the drinks. No reason to waste free booze."

Simone remained wary as she picked up the beer. "I suppose you're right. Cheers, then?"

They clinked glasses, an awkward silence settling between them as they both took long sips. Rowan racked her brain for a safe topic of conversation, something to fill the uncomfortable silence. "So, uh, how's Marigold doing?" she finally asked, immediately wincing inwardly at her choice. Bringing up Simone's girlfriend was probably the single stupidest thing she could have done, mainly because, for reasons she didn't fully understand, the very existence of the older woman made Rowan irrationally stabby. On the other hand, it was the right thing to do so

Simone would know that she didn't have the wrong idea about any of this.

Simone blinked, surprised by the question. "Uh, she's doing well. Busy with her various philanthropic projects, as usual." She took another sip of beer, her eyes darting away.

Rowan nodded, feeling a twinge of something uncomfortably close to blind jealousy squeezing her insides. She knew it was ridiculous. She had no claim on Simone, and their brief encounter two years ago hardly justified any lingering feelings. But there was something about this woman that got under Rowan's skin. Like a deep tissue infection. If only she could prescribe herself an antibiotic to knock Simone out of her system for good.

She cleared her throat, determined to steer the conversation in a more neutral direction. "I hear the ER has been particularly busy lately. Any interesting cases come through?"

Simone's eyes lit up, and Rowan could practically see the wheels turning in her mind as she considered the question. "Actually, yes. We had a patient come in yesterday with a rather unusual presentation."

Rowan leaned forward, her curiosity piqued. "Do tell."

"This guy had purposefully swallowed a Scrabble tile to prevent the other person from getting a triple-word score."

"Which tile was it?"

"Q."

"That would be quite the game changer." Rowan gave a snort at the absurdity of it. "Did you tell him it wasn't going to be fun to pass it?"

"I mean, what else could I do for him?" Simone burst into laughter, her face reddening. "I shouldn't laugh, but what do people think will happen when you swallow something?"

"People are idiots. I swear, half of practicing medicine is either waiting for a patient to pass something they swallowed or trying to remove something they've put up the other end."

Rowan laughed, realizing how much she needed to. "Why do people love putting things up their butts so much? I don't get it."

Simone tilted her head slightly to one side as if considering the question. "I don't know. Under the right circumstances, it can be—a totally inappropriate topic of conversation to be having right now."

Rowan nearly choked on her beer, a blush creeping up her neck as Simone's words conjured up all sorts of mental images she had no business entertaining. "Yes, well, I suppose that's best. So, the patient, did he end up, you know..."

"No surgery required, thank goodness. Though I'm sure he'll think twice before attempting to cheat at Scrabble again. Especially since he'd been trying to propose to his girlfriend at the time."

"What? How?"

"By laying out certain words on the board. Only the woman wasn't noticing because she was so focused on winning." Simone took another swig.

"Ouch." Rowan shook her head as she contemplated how foolish people could be when it came to love. "But, if he wasn't trying to win, why was he upset about the triple-word score?"

"Please. Have you ever met a man who could handle losing gracefully to a woman?" Simone rolled her eyes. "Fragile egos, all of them."

Rowan chuckled, raising her glass in a mock toast. "It's a good reminder why it's best to stay single."

"Or date women," Simone said with a wink.

Rowan's eyes widened, and she quickly took a sip of her beer to hide her reaction. Was Simone flirting with her? No, surely not. The woman was in a relationship, for God's sake. Besides, Rowan had no business going down that road. Not even in her imagination.

"I have some good news about the mobile clinic," Rowan said, eager to get this conversation back to safer ground.

Simone's eyebrows shot up in surprise. "Really? That's great! What happened?"

Rowan traced her finger along the condensation on her glass, choosing her words carefully. "My father mentioned he might have access to a fund that could give the project the support it still needs. One that's separate from the hospital, through a charity he works with."

"I can't believe you went to so much trouble, talking to your father about this," Simone said, genuine appreciation shining in her eyes.

Rowan shrugged, trying to downplay her involvement. "It's the least I could do. My mother is nothing if not persuasive when she sets her mind to something. And she's right. A robust mobile clinic operation could do a lot of good for underserved communities in the area."

Simone nodded, her expression thoughtful. "Your mother is an amazing woman."

"Well, so is Marigold." Rowan's heart clenched as she said the name. She downed the rest of her beer in one gulp, as if that might make the reality of the situation easier to swallow.

"Yes, she is." Simone looked down at her drink, her fingers fidgeting with the coaster. "Marigold's great. Really great. She's been so supportive of me since my work with GHF came to an end."

"How fortunate," Rowan said, but what she was really thinking was how something in the way Simone spoke about Marigold didn't seem quite right. There was a flatness to her tone and a distant look in her eyes that made Rowan wonder if there might be trouble in paradise.

"I don't know what I would've done without her help," Simone continued. "And Erica's, too, in getting me the job at the hospital. I'm really very lucky."

Rowan nodded, attempting a smile that felt more like a grimace. The last thing she wanted was a reminder of the many reasons pursuing anything with Simone would be a terrible idea. But judging by the thud she'd felt as she plummeted back to earth, it was exactly what she needed.

In case the existence of Simone's girlfriend wasn't enough to keep Rowan firmly planted in reality, being reminded that this woman was also her stepdaughter's best friend and her own subordinate at work should do the trick.

Simone's relationship was none of her business. Speculating about problems between the woman she was inconveniently attracted to and said woman's partner was the height of self-indulgence. What Rowan needed was to get a grip.

She had a foundering hospital to turn around, an estranged stepdaughter to worry about, and a demanding mother to placate. And that was on top of the problems created by her misogynistic father and her risk-addicted ex-husband. There was no room in her life for entanglements with unavailable women, no matter how tempting.

She needed to focus on the here and now, not indulge in pointless speculation and fantasies. Simone was off-limits, period. End of internal debate.

"I should probably get going," Rowan said abruptly, pushing back from the table. "Early morning tomorrow and all that."

Simone blinked in surprise at the sudden change in Rowan's demeanor but nodded. "Oh, um, of course. Do you think—no, never mind."

"Do I think what?" Rowan prompted, curiosity getting the better of her.

Simone hesitated then shook her head. "It's nothing. I was going to ask if you were still thinking about spending some time working with the mobile clinic. The other day you said you might consider it."

"I'm not really sure that would be a good idea." Rowan shifted uncomfortably, avoiding Simone's gaze. "What I mean is with everything going on at the hospital right now, I'm not sure I can commit to anything extra. You understand."

Simone nodded, but there was a flicker of disappointment in her eyes. "Of course. Have a good night, Dr. Colchester."

Rowan winced at the return to formality, but she supposed she had no one to blame but herself. "You too, Dr. Doucette."

She turned and walked away before she could change her mind. Simone's gaze burned into Rowan's back, or so she suspected, and her thoughts were a jumbled mess. If only she could go home and get some sleep, maybe it would all be fine. But Rowan knew that was a lost cause, that she would replay this evening in her mind all night, analyzing every word and gesture for hidden meanings that probably weren't there.

CHAPTER ELEVEN

Stepping out of her car, Simone squinted against the morning sun as she took in the dozen or so mothers cradling their babies who waited patiently by the mobile clinic RV. Freshly painted with the Brewster Foundation's logo where the dogs and cats had been, it was set up in the parking lot of the local elementary school. Pop-up tents flanked either side, staffed by volunteers from the local food pantry who were preparing to distribute boxes of fresh produce and canned goods to families after their appointments.

Passing by the crowd, Simone climbed the steps and knocked on the RV's door, which swung open to reveal a young man with tousled dark hair and a friendly smile.

"Good morning," he said. "Are you Dr. Doucette?"

"Guilty as charged," Simone replied with a grin, extending her hand.

"Thrilled to meet you." He took her hand and gave it a firm shake. "I'm Pablo Mendoza. I'm the one who drove this beast over here, and I'll also be doing registration."

"Are you a nurse?"

"Sadly, not yet. But I'm taking classes. Hopefully, I'll get some real-world experience with this gig." A smile spread across his face, and Simone couldn't help but return it. His enthusiasm was infectious.

"You've certainly come to the right place for that," she said as she stepped inside the RV. The space had been efficiently transformed into a compact mobile clinic, with an exam table, a few chairs, and shelves stocked with medical supplies and equipment. Simone set her bag down and began familiarizing herself with the layout. She'd been in countless setups like this with Global Health Frontiers, but it always took a few minutes to adjust to the unique challenges of working in such a confined space with limited resources.

"We should be all set to start seeing patients in about fifteen minutes," Pablo said, checking his watch. "The nurse who's supposed to assist you today called out at the last minute, so we're waiting for her replacement to arrive."

Almost as soon as he said this, Simone spotted a car pulling into the parking lot. Her heart leaped into her throat at the sight of the familiar Honda. She'd only been in it once, more than two years ago, but she would never forget that day no matter how hard she tried.

Sure enough, once the car was parked, Rowan got out. She wore dark navy-blue scrubs and a white lab coat, her hair pulled back in a riot of fiery curls that refused to be contained in a bun. The wardrobe choice threw Simone off guard. At the hospital, Rowan was always impeccably put together in tailored pantsuits and silk blouses, hair smoothed and plastered with hairspray—which was sexy, for sure. But this more relaxed look was captivating in a whole new way. And much more dangerous. It was like seeing Rowan stripped of her armor, more vulnerable and real, and it stirred something deep within Simone, the type of feeling she desperately needed to suppress.

Rowan strode toward the RV with purpose, a stethoscope slung around her neck. When she entered the clinic and caught sight of who would be working with her that day, Simone was almost certain Rowan flinched.

"Hey," Simone said. "We were expecting a nurse."

"Yes, I know. Unfortunately, she's putting in an extra shift at the hospital today because of staffing issues. I'm here in her place." Rowan turned to Pablo and introduced herself. "Rowan Colchester, Chief Medical Officer at Marbury Hospital. Thank you for having me today."

Pablo's eyes widened as he shook her hand eagerly. "It's an honor to meet you, Dr. Colchester. I'm Pablo, the driver."

"And a nursing student," Simone added, not wanting the young man to sell himself short.

Rowan smiled warmly at Pablo. "Wonderful. We certainly need more nurses. I'm sure you'll learn a great deal today." She turned her attention to Simone, and the two women simply looked at each other. Rowan's gaze remained cool and distant, revealing nothing.

Why was she always so difficult to read? Simone wished she could forget the history between them. It would make it so much easier if every encounter didn't lead to countless hours spent trying to decipher the enigmatic woman's every expression and gesture. One minute, Rowan was her boss and nothing more. Other times, it seemed they were on the verge of something almost like friendship. And constantly under the surface was the undeniable hum of attraction that had never gone quiet since that night two years ago when they'd first met. It was enough to make Simone's head spin.

Simone cleared her throat, breaking the charged silence. "We better get started. Pablo, you ready to send in the first patient?"

He looked eagerly at the line of people waiting to register. "Don't you just love babies?"

Pablo stepped out of the RV to begin the patient registration process, leaving Simone and Rowan alone together in the small space. Simone busied herself with organizing the medical supplies, trying to ignore the way her heart raced at the other woman's close proximity.

"I'm sorry you're stuck with me," Rowan said, her eyes focused on the exam table as she adjusted the paper covering.

Simone glanced over at Rowan, surprised by the apologetic note in her voice. "Stuck with you? I don't see it that way."

Rowan raised an eyebrow. "No? I got the distinct impression you weren't thrilled to see me."

"Nonsense. We're happy to have you." Simone busied herself with setting up the infant scale, trying to keep her tone light and breezy. "I was surprised; that's all. I didn't expect the Chief Medical Officer herself to fill in for a nurse. Especially since you went out of your way to make it clear you had no time for it."

Rowan sighed, rubbing her temples. "I'm sorry if I came across as dismissive before. It's not that I don't believe in the importance of this work. Quite the opposite, actually. In fact, I think I need to see firsthand what's really happening in the hospital and the community if I can hope to fix the problems we're facing."

Simone paused in her preparations and studied Rowan thoughtfully. She hadn't expected such candor from the usually guarded woman. "I think that's wise. It's important for leadership to be connected to the day-to-day realities of the struggles we're up against. For example, most of the moms out there would never miss their baby's appointment, but they find it hard to prioritize their own care. Seeing mothers and babies at the same time makes it easier for them to access the care they need on their terms."

"And keeps minor problems from turning into emergencies," Rowan added.

Pablo returned with the first patient, a young mother cradling a fussy infant. "This is Maia and her five-month-old daughter, Layla," he announced. "The mom is sometimes more comfortable speaking Spanish, so I'll stay to translate as needed."

Simone and Rowan instantly switched gears, their personal dynamic set aside as they shifted into work mode. Pablo made a funny face at the baby, eliciting laughter from both mother and child.

Simone greeted the mother with a warm smile. "Good morning, Maia. I'm Dr. Doucette, and this is Dr. Colchester. We're going to take a look at Layla today and make sure she's growing and developing well. Would you mind if I get a weight for the baby?"

After some hesitation on the part of the mother, Pablo repeated the question in Spanish. Maia nodded and carefully transferred Layla into Simone's waiting arms. The baby gurgled and waved her tiny fists, her dark eyes wide and curious as she studied the doctor's face. Simone cooed at her softly as she placed the squirming infant on the scale.

Rowan looked over the forms before asking the mother, "Would you mind if I take your blood pressure?"

The woman frowned, seeming uncertain of the question, but when Rowan gestured to the blood pressure cuff, the patient nodded. Rowan slipped the cuff on, pumping air into it, and adjusted the stethoscope to get a reading.

"You're playing with your toes." Simone noted the milestone in the baby's chart as she spoke to the little one in a singsong voice. "I bet everyone tells you how beautiful your eyes are. Isn't that right, Layla?"

The mother offered Simone a shy smile.

While Rowan listened to the mother's breathing, Simone measured the baby's length and head circumference, noting the results on the chart. "She's growing well," Simone said, smiling at Maia reassuringly. "Right on track."

"Your blood pressure is good," Rowan said gently to Maia as she removed the cuff. "Now for vaccines. Pablo, can you give

Maia the Spanish information sheets for the five-month vaccines?" She turned her attention back to the mother. "*¿Le gustaría vacunarse contra la gripe?*"

Simone raised an eyebrow at the unexpected Spanish phrase. "I didn't realize you spoke Spanish."

"Not as much as I'd like," Rowan admitted. "I picked up a few key phrases years ago when I was in medical school. I guess they're coming back to me."

The mother accepted the flu shot, only wincing slightly as the needle went in. The baby didn't like her vaccinations one bit, but Simone and Rowan made so many funny faces that the crying was soon over, replaced by happy spit bubbles.

As she was preparing to leave, Maia turned to Pablo, speaking in an urgent tone. After listening intently, Pablo translated. "She says she wants to know if we make appointments for pregnant women at the clinic, or if it's only for mothers with babies. She works with a woman, Fabienne, who needs to see a doctor but only speaks a small amount of English and is afraid no one will understand her."

Simone nodded reassuringly at Maia. "Of course, we can see your friend. Please let her know she's welcome here, and we'll do our best to communicate with her. As you can see, our Spanish isn't great, but—"

Maia said something else to Pablo, who nodded before explaining. "She says her friend doesn't speak Spanish. She's from Haiti."

"Oh!" Simone exclaimed with delight. "*Mwen pale kreyòl ayisyen tou. M ap kontan ede zanmi ou a.*" Simone laughed as the three adults in the room stared at her in shock, though baby Layla seemed perfectly content to kick her chubby legs without a care in the world. "Sorry, I got a little carried away. I basically said I'd be happy to help her." Simone jotted down her upcoming volunteer shifts for the next few weeks on a piece of

THE ANATOMY OF FOREVER

paper and handed it to Maia. "Let your friend know it's important for her to see a doctor as soon as she can."

Maia nodded gratefully, thanking Simone and Rowan in Spanish before gathering up Layla and heading out of the RV. Pablo escorted her out, leaving the two doctors alone once again.

Rowan tilted her head, a thoughtful expression on her face. "You know Creole? That's impressive."

Simone shrugged, trying to downplay the compliment even though a blush crept up her neck. "I'm hardly fluent."

"From what I could hear, you're better in Creole than I am in Spanish. Did you learn it growing up in Louisiana? I assume from your name that your father was French. They speak Creole there, right?"

"Yes, my father's family was French. Actually, what they speak in Louisiana is Cajun. It's related to Creole, but it's not the same language. Knowing a little Cajun, plus high school and college French, probably made it easier for me to pick up Creole when I was in Haiti with GHF, though."

"You really are full of surprises. I keep trying to learn Spanish, but aside from some medical phrases, I've only mastered ordering a beer and saying I don't understand."

"Does the not understanding happen before or after you get your beer?" Simone teased, causing Rowan to let out a humorous snort. Simone's heart did a little flip at the sound of Rowan's laughter, so uncharacteristically free and uninhibited. Before she could dwell on it, though, Pablo returned with the next patient.

"It's starting to rain," Pablo mentioned as he ushered in a mother holding a sleeping infant. "Hopefully, it doesn't get too bad out there."

Simone glanced out the small window and saw fat raindrops beginning to splatter against the glass. Rain could be a major deterrent for their patients, many of whom walked or relied on public transportation.

The morning passed in a blur of babies and mothers. Simone and Rowan fell into an easy rhythm, working seamlessly together as they examined patients, administered vaccines, and offered advice. Despite their initial awkwardness, they made an excellent team, complementing each other's skills and knowledge. It made Simone wonder what it would be like to work with Rowan on a regular basis, not just during these fleeting moments of collaboration. How different might things be between them if they were on the same level, rather than boss and employee?

Of course, it was useless to dwell on such thoughts. There was no changing reality, meaning the less time she spent around Rowan, the easier it was to ignore the persistent attraction that was proving impossible to squelch. Fortunately, except for that one day in the ER, their professional paths rarely intersected. Simone knew it was for the best, just like she knew it would be better if Rowan kept her clinic volunteering to a minimum. That didn't stop her from secretly hoping Rowan would come back to work at the clinic again.

As the last patient of the morning left, Simone glanced out the window to see the rain had intensified. Heavy drops pelted the RV, creating a steady drumming sound on the metal roof.

Just before lunch, Pablo came in from outside, his hair plastered to his forehead and his shirt clinging to his chest. "It's really coming down out there," he said, shaking water from his hair. "Most of the people who were waiting have left, and the food bank folks are soaked to the bone. I think they might be calling it a day."

Simone sighed, disappointment weighing her down. "That's a shame. We still had quite a few appointments scheduled for this afternoon, but we might need to do the same."

Rowan nodded, her brow furrowed as she peered out the window at the downpour. "It's unfortunate, but safety first."

"True. I just hate to turn anyone away who's really in need,"

Simone said. "Maybe we could wait it out for a bit. Sometimes these summer storms pass quickly."

Rowan's eyes still fixed on the rain-streaked window. "I'm willing to give it another hour and reassess."

"Yeah, of course. I can stick around for a while longer if you want." Pablo glanced between the two doctors, the expression on his face making it clear that, despite his offer, he was hoping they'd send him home. Simone couldn't blame him; the poor kid looked like a drowned rat.

"Why don't you head out, Pablo?" Simone suggested. "We can stay and make sure everything's wrapped up properly. You've done more than enough today."

Pablo's relief was palpable. "Are you sure? I can get a ride home with one of the food bank ladies who lives in my neighborhood. But what about the clinic? Someone needs to drive it back tonight."

"Don't worry about that," Simone assured him. "As it happens, this clinic currently lives in my driveway. Marigold won't mind if I drive it home."

Pablo's face lit up with a grateful smile. "Thanks, Dr. Doucette. I really appreciate it."

As Pablo gathered his things and said his goodbyes, Simone and Rowan were left alone in the suddenly quiet RV. The steady drumming of rain on the roof seemed to amplify the silence between them. With no patients to distract them, Simone found herself acutely aware of Rowan's presence, the small space suddenly feeling much more intimate. She busied herself tidying up the exam area, hyper-conscious of every movement.

Finally, Rowan cleared her throat. "So, Marigold. I take it that's going well?"

Simone paused, her hand hovering over a stack of patient charts. "Marigold?" she repeated, confused.

"Your partner," Rowan clarified, her tone carefully neutral. "The one whose driveway you share."

Simone couldn't help but laugh, the tension in her shoulders easing slightly. "Oh, no." She waved her arms as if warding off the thought. "Marigold's not my partner. She's my landlady."

"It's okay. I wasn't born yesterday, Simone."

Simone's laughter faded as she realized Rowan was serious. "No, really," she insisted, meeting Rowan's eyes. "Marigold is a sweet older woman who rents me the cottage on her property. There's nothing romantic going on between us."

"You two aren't—?" Rowan pinched her thumb and index finger together as if somehow the hand gesture was meant to illustrate the concept.

"Not like that." Simone pointed to Rowan's hand with a frown. "Assuming by that you mean dating."

Rowan's cheeks flushed slightly as she dropped her hand. "I'm sorry, I shouldn't have assumed. It's just with the way you talked about her, I sort of assumed."

Simone's stomach fluttered at Rowan's flustered expression. It was rare to see the normally composed woman so off-balance. She found it oddly endearing.

"Marigold's more like family to me," Simone explained gently. "She's been incredibly kind and supportive since I moved here. But there's definitely nothing else between us. For one thing, she's not my type."

Rowan nodded slowly, a thoughtful expression crossing her face. "I see."

An awkward silence fell between them, broken only by the steady patter of rain against the RV windows. Simone cleared her throat, desperate to break the tension. "So, um, how about you? Are you seeing anyone?"

As soon as the words left her mouth, Simone regretted them. It was none of her business, and she wasn't sure she actually wanted to know the answer.

Rowan's eyes widened slightly at the unexpected question. "No. Not since my divorce. I mean, except…"

Rowan left the rest unsaid, her eyes meeting Simone's for a brief, intense moment before quickly looking away. Simone's heart raced as she realized what Rowan was referring to. That night two years ago. The memory of it hung between them, electric and unspoken. Simone's breath caught in her throat as she recalled the heat of Rowan's skin, the softness of her lips, the way Simone's fingers had tangled in all that brilliant red hair.

"Except?" Simone's voice wavered slightly as she echoed Rowan's unfinished sentence.

"There was a woman I met at a bar one night when the Velvet Sirens were playing," Rowan's tone brimmed with caution. "It was unforgettable. But it was destined not to work out."

"Why was that?" Simone's voice was faint.

"There were reasons." Rowan swallowed as her eyes met Simone's, the vulnerability and longing in them making Simone's knees weaken. "Funny, though. I can't really remember what they were."

"I see."

"What about you?"

"No. I can't recall the reasons, either."

The tension in the RV was palpable, as thick and heavy as the humid summer air outside. Simone's heart raced as she met Rowan's gaze, seeing her own desire reflected back at her. It seemed as if the world had narrowed to the two of them, until they were brought back to reality by a loud crack of thunder that shook the RV. Simone jumped, startled by the sudden noise, and Rowan instinctively reached out to steady her.

"You okay?" Rowan asked softly, her hand lingering on Simone's arm for only a second but long enough to almost completely undo Simone's resolve.

God, it felt so good to be touched. But there were reasons this couldn't happen, even if neither of them could recall what they were. Simone couldn't let herself get swept away, no matter how tempting it was.

"I'm fine," Simone said, taking a step back. "But I'm not sure it's such a good idea to stay out here in this tin can during an electrical storm. Maybe it would be better if we called it a day."

Rowan nodded, a flicker of disappointment crossing her face before she quickly masked it. "You're probably right. This has been a very rewarding experience, though. Perhaps it's something I should do again."

Simone's heart skipped a beat at Rowan's words. The idea of working alongside her, of spending more time in her intoxicating presence, was both thrilling and terrifying. She knew she should probably discourage it, for both their sakes. But the selfish part—the reckless part of her that couldn't be trusted to make good decisions—replied, "Perhaps you should."

CHAPTER TWELVE

Simone is single.
This was not the thought Rowan should be caught up on right now.

To begin with, Rowan reminded herself as she speed-walked her way down Marbury's main street on her way to brunch with her mother, it changed nothing. The woman was still so much younger—ten whole years—and Rowan was still her boss. And that didn't even touch on the potential repercussions of Simone and Erica being friends.

One simply did not indulge in dirty fantasies about their stepdaughter's friends.

End of story.

Learning Simone wasn't dating Marigold shouldn't have made a difference. It should have been a blip in her life, like learning that some people in the world use the word aubergine instead of eggplant. A weird and interesting fact, but not earth shattering in any way.

Yet the knowledge lingered in Rowan's mind, refusing to be dismissed so easily. Something fundamental had shifted inside her, and it showed no signs of falling back into its proper place. This was going to be a problem.

As she approached the bustling cafe, Rowan tried to push thoughts of Simone from her mind. She needed to focus on the task at hand: surviving a meal with her mother. Grace Colchester was a force to be reckoned with, and Rowan's brain power would be better suited to prepare for the battle of wills that was sure to come.

Straining against the heavy wood and glass door, Rowan stepped inside and breathed in the warm aroma of fresh coffee and about a thousand delicious breakfast smells all at once. To her left was the take-out counter, with a line of patrons already snaking out the door. To the right, the dining room bustled with the chatter of friends catching up over mimosas and families enjoying a leisurely Sunday meal together. As she approached the hostess station, she overheard someone being told the wait would be over an hour for a table.

"Darling." Her mom waved to her from a prime booth by the sunny front window. Naturally, her mother had already been seated. Grace Colchester did not wait for tables.

As Rowan approached, her mother stood and greeted her with air kisses on both cheeks. "Lovely to see you."

"Likewise," Rowan said, the response so generic it made it sound like she might be talking to a member of the hospital's board of directors instead of her own mother. Rowan plastered on a smile, trying to get her head in the game. At this rate, her mother would eat her alive before the server came by with a fresh pot of coffee.

"You're late," her mother admonished, smiling in a way that was meant to take most of, but not necessarily all, the sting out of the words.

Rowan's smile tightened. "I'm sorry. I got caught up with something at the hospital."

"Of course, you did," Grace said with a knowing look.

"You're always so busy these days. I do hope your father isn't working you too hard."

"No more than should be expected," Rowan replied, taking her seat in the booth across from her mother. She unfolded her napkin and placed it on her lap, smoothing out the wrinkles with more attention than was necessary. "It's busy in here today. I'm surprised you got seated so quickly."

"You know I always bribe Fay to get us our favorite table right away." Her mother grinned like a child who had not only been caught with her hand in the cookie jar but had been handed a giant candy bar as a reward. "It pays to be a loyal customer."

As Rowan fell silent to peruse her menu, she reflected that one good thing to be said for meeting up with her mother was that for the past four minutes, Rowan hadn't thought of Simone a single time.

"Simone!" her mother called out, causing Rowan to jump in alarm.

"What the fuck?" Rowan blurted out. Rowan was certain she hadn't said the woman's name out loud. Had her mother added mind reading to her repertoire of skills?

Rowan's head whipped around to follow her mother's gaze, her heart pounding. Sure enough, there was Simone, standing in the entryway of the cafe, looking as surprised as Rowan.

"Come join us. We're about to order." Her mother eagerly motioned for Simone to take a seat at their table.

"I'm just here for a coffee," Simone glanced between Rowan and her mother with a hint of uncertainty. "I wouldn't want to intrude on your brunch."

"Nonsense. Join us," Rowan's mother insisted. "Please. The more the merrier. Isn't that right, Rowan?"

"Absolutely," Rowan responded. More like absolutely not. This was the last thing she needed right now—to be trapped at a table with her mother and the woman who had been occupying her thoughts far too often lately. But there was no graceful way to refuse without raising suspicion.

Simone returned Rowan's smile with a tentative one of her own as she approached the table. "If you're sure I'm not intruding."

"Not at all, dear. Please, have a seat." Rowan's mother gestured not to the empty space beside her but to the bench where Rowan sat.

Simone slid into the booth next to Rowan, their thighs brushing for the briefest of moments. Rowan's breath caught in her throat at the unexpected contact. She shifted slightly, trying to put a respectable distance between them without being too obvious. The last thing she needed was for her mother to pick up on any sexual tension between them.

For the past week, Rowan had successfully avoided bumping into Simone—both literally and figuratively—by never venturing near the ER and taking the most circuitous paths possible to both her office and cafeteria. One brunch with her mother and all that hard work was flushed down the toilet.

"So, Simone," Grace began, her piercing eyes fixed on the younger woman, "tell me, how are you finding your work with the mobile clinic?"

Simone's smile was warm and genuine as she replied, "It's been wonderful, Mrs. Colchester. I'm really enjoying getting to know the community."

"Now, now. It's Grace, remember?" Rowan's mother insisted with a wave of her hand. "I'm so glad to hear it's going well. I wish my daughter here could spare some time to volunteer like you do."

"As a matter of fact, Rowan joined us at the clinic last Saturday." Simone's tone seemed unusually warm with approval. Most likely it stemmed from pity over seeing a grown woman in her forties wilting under her mother's criticism like a hot house flower. "She was a tremendous help. She was even able to communicate a little bit in Spanish with some of the patients."

"Is that so?" Grace's eyes narrowed slightly as she turned her attention to Rowan. "Why didn't you mention it sooner?"

"It was nothing," Rowan said, trying to downplay the whole thing. "Just a last-minute fill-in when a nurse was called into the hospital because we were short-staffed."

"Again?" Her mother tsked, shaking her head. "Rowan, darling, you really need to address this staffing issue. You can't keep covering for everyone else's shortcomings. It's not sustainable."

Rowan's jaw clenched as irritation burned through her. "We're working on it. If Lance hadn't—"

"Ah," her mother interrupted. "Here comes Fay to take our orders. Simone, please get whatever you'd like. This is my treat, and I simply won't hear of it if all you get is a coffee."

Simone dutifully scanned the menu while Rowan's mother rattled off her usual order of eggs benedict.

Next, Fay looked to Rowan and Simone's side of the table. "What can I get you ladies?"

"Huevos Rancheros," they both answered in unison.

Rowan and Simone exchanged surprised glances, a hint of a smile playing at the corners of their mouths. Rowan felt a flicker of warmth in her chest at the unexpected connection. It also alarmed her. Why did this always seem to happen when what she needed were more things she and Simone did not have in common?

"Great minds think alike," Grace commented with a laugh, though Rowan detected the glint of something more calculating behind her gaze. "And bottomless coffee, please, Fay."

As Fay bustled away with their orders, an awkward silence settled over the table. Rowan fidgeted with her napkin, hyper-aware of Simone's presence beside her. The warmth radiating from the younger woman's body was a constant distraction, making it difficult for her to focus on anything else. She desperately searched for a neutral topic of conversation to break the tension but came up short, succeeding in doing nothing more than smacking her lips together several times without any sound coming out.

"Simone," Grace began, saving Rowan from her mental floundering, "I seem to remember you mentioning you're friends with my granddaughter."

Oh, perfect. That was exactly what Rowan did not need to be reminded of right now as she struggled to keep her pulse from racing at the scent of jasmine wafting off Simone's supple flesh. Or rather, she very much did need the reminder. She just didn't appreciate it.

"Yes, I am," Simone replied, her tone warm but cautious. "Erica and I met in college."

"How lovely," Grace's eyes lit up with interest. "How is dear Erica doing these days? I haven't heard from her in ages. Is she enjoying her time in Italy?"

Rowan tensed as her mother's eyes bore into her, bracing herself for what was sure to be an uncomfortable turn in the conversation. "I have no idea. She never responds to my texts."

"Still pissed, I see." Her mother tutted. "After what you did for her with—"

"I'm sure she's too busy working in the gallery and having fun to pay attention to texts," Rowan said quickly, her cheeks flushing. She didn't want to air her family's dirty laundry in front of Simone.

"Have you heard from her?" Rowan's mom asked Simone.

Simone shifted slightly in her seat, clearly uncomfortable being put in the middle. "We've texted a bit. Actually, she sent me this photo." Simone pulled up an image on her phone, sharing it with the table.

"Look at her!" Rowan's mother flushed with pride. "My

goodness, and that view of Florence in the background is amazing. Maybe I should visit her this fall."

"I'm sure she'll be too busy with her graduate studies," Rowan said quickly, her tone sharper than she intended. She immediately regretted her words when Simone's eyes widen slightly.

"That's right. I recall her father made quite a sizable donation to secure her spot in that program," Grace mused, seemingly oblivious to the tension her words had created. "Though I'm sure Erica would have gotten in on her own merits. She's such a talented girl."

Rowan's grip tightened on her coffee mug. "You're mistaken, Mom. She did get in on merit alone. I'm not sure why you would think Lance could afford to make a donation in his current circumstances." She refrained from elaborating with Simone present, though she knew the hospital rumor mill had likely filled her in on the details of Lance's personal troubles.

Grace waved her hand dismissively. "You know Lance. He always finds a way when it comes to Erica. Besides, I hear he's finished his rehab and might have an offer to work at a hospital in Pensacola, so maybe his fortunes are finally looking up."

"He has?" Rowan couldn't hide her shock. This was the first she'd heard of it. "Will he be staying in Florida?"

"Considering he told your father he's putting his condo on the market, I'd say yes." Grace smiled as Fay came by to refresh the coffees. "You're not going to buy this one, too, to save his ass, are you?"

Rowan nearly choked on her coffee. That was one detail she wished Simone hadn't heard.

"Rowan bought the beach house to keep it in the family when Lance was struggling," her mother not-so-helpfully added. "It belonged to Erica's mother. It would have been criminal to let it slip away, but it was quite a hardship, nonetheless."

"Does Erica know that?" Simone's question hung in the air,

causing Rowan to tense even further. She could feel Simone's eyes on her, waiting for an answer.

"No," Rowan admitted quietly. "She doesn't know. And I'd appreciate it if we could keep it that way."

"He's running out of things to sell," Grace commented as she added milk to her coffee. "So hopefully this new job goes well for him. Have you picked out your outfit for the gala?"

"I told you I can't make it," Rowan said through gritted teeth as she lifted her mug to her lips. "The last thing I want to do on an August night is schmooze outside with a bunch of strangers while being feasted on by mosquitoes."

"Nonsense. The sea breeze in Marigold's yard will keep them at bay. Isn't that right, Simone?"

"We don't get too many bugs," Simone agreed, looking a little guilty, like she knew Rowan would consider it a betrayal. "The breeze does seem to keep them away most nights."

"You see? It's our biggest fundraiser of the year," Rowan's mother went on, "and now that you're in administration, you no longer have the luxury to avoid these events."

"I won't know anyone." Rowan knew she sounded like a two-year-old but was unable to rein it in. "I hated going to these things as Lance's plus-one, let alone on my own."

"You'll know Simone." Rowan's mom beamed as though she'd solved world hunger.

"What?" Simone had a deer in headlights expression. "When is this gala?"

"Friday night," Grace said. "And don't worry about an invitation. It's literally being held in your backyard, thanks to Marigold's generosity."

"Sadly, I'm working Friday night," Simone said.

"I know someone who can fix that." Rowan's mother gave her a pointed look that sent flames rushing to Rowan's cheeks.

"Mother, I can't demand to rearrange the staffing schedules

on a whim. That wouldn't be fair to the other doctors. Plus, we're chronically short-staffed."

"You can't work everyone 24/7. It's illegal. People still get to take days off. As for which days they take, you're in charge. You get to decide." She set her napkin on the table. "If you two will excuse me, I need to go powder my nose before the food arrives."

After Grace left, Simone let out a nervous chuckle. "She's really something."

"Oh, yes. World-class problem solver. I'm sure she's convinced herself she's one step closer to winning a Nobel Peace Prize with this latest idea of hers." Rowan took a cleansing breath. "You don't have to come."

"I know she says you're in charge, but I have a feeling your mother won't let me out of it."

Rowan wished she could say that wasn't true, but she knew better. Her mother was like a dog with a bone when she set her mind to something.

"I'm sorry," Rowan said, turning to face Simone. "I'll talk to her. Make it clear you have other commitments."

Simone's expression softened. "It's okay, really. I don't mind going if it would help you out. Besides, it's not like I actually have anything else to do on a Friday night, other than work."

That's right, a voice in Rowan's head chimed in. Because Simone was single. We wouldn't want to forget that little detail.

A MASSIVE TENT was set up in the sprawling backyard of the Brewster estate, white fabric billowing gently in a light breeze. Fairy lights twinkled overhead against a purple and pink sky as the sun made its way to the horizon. Rowan stood to one side, nervously smoothing down her full-skirted, emerald green cocktail dress with a retro vibe. It was the type of outfit she loathed.

It was one thing to put on a suit jacket, skirt, and sensible heels at work. That made her feel powerful and in control. This dress, with its plunging neckline and ultra-feminine silhouette, made her feel exposed and vulnerable. She tugged at the hemline, wishing she'd chosen something less revealing.

She scanned the crowd, searching for a familiar face. She wasn't sure if she wanted to find one or preferred to remain anonymous among the sea of Marbury's elite. Unfortunately for her, she was spotted by Marigold, who motioned to her from the other side of the lawn.

As she strode toward the woman, trying to exude more confidence than she felt, Rowan's heel snagged on a rough patch of lawn, nearly causing her to face-plant. As she steadied herself, she scoped the area to see who might have witnessed her humiliation.

Naturally, Simone stood ten feet away, doing her best to fight a smile.

Could life get harder for Rowan? Actually, scratch that, she implored the universe. With Simone standing there looking like a goddess in a floor-length sapphire gown that made her eyes shine like stars, Rowan realized that yes, life could indeed get harder.

"Rowan!" Marigold approached. "Just the person I'm looking for. Well, one of two. Where's your date?"

"My what?"

"Simone. Where's Simone?"

Rowan's head began to spin. Had Simone actually referred to herself as Rowan's date? The thought sent a thrill through her that she quickly tried to suppress. "I was on my way to—"

"I'm here," Simone said, appearing at Rowan's side with a warm smile. "Sorry I'm late. I got caught up chatting with some of the other guests."

Rowan's breath caught as she took in Simone's radiant presence up close. The velvet gown hugged her curves in all the right places, and her golden hair cascaded over her shoulders in soft waves. Rowan found herself struggling to form coherent thoughts. Everything about this woman begged for Rowan to put her hands all over her, to explore every single inch.

"You look nice." Though there were only three words in that sentence, Rowan managed to stumble over each and every one. Could she act any more like an awkward teenager on prom night?

"You both are adorable," Marigold teased, looping an arm through Rowan's and then Simone's, putting herself in the middle. "Girls, I'm going to need your help. We've got one of the hottest bands on the Cape playing tonight, but no one is dancing. Get out there and dance." Marigold stopped at the edge of a wooden dance floor that had been set up on top of the grass beneath the tent.

"I don't dance." Rowan took a step back from the wooden platform as if Marigold had invited her to play a championship round of the game The Floor is Lava.

"Everyone dances." Marigold gave her a playful nudge toward Simone.

"Clearly, you didn't see me nearly wipe out in my heels mere moments ago," Rowan argued, scowling at her shoes. "Besides, the band isn't playing right now."

"They're about to start. Go on," Marigold urged. "Show these stuffy donors how it's done."

Before Rowan could protest further, Marigold had vanished into the crowd, leaving her alone with Simone.

"You can take them off if you'd like," Simone said. "Your shoes, that is. You know, the night we first met, I had so much trouble with my shoes, I nearly wore sneakers."

"Really?" Even after two years, Rowan could still picture those stiletto heels and the way Simone's legs had looked wrapped around Rowan's waist. Rowan squeezed her eyes shut to clear the image from her mind as best as she could, even while admitting, "I'm kind of glad you didn't."

As if the memory was playing from her own mind, the first strains of "Echoes of Her Smile" began to play. It was the song that had been playing that night at The Driftwood Lounge when she and Simone first met.

"Oh my God." Simone's hand flew to her mouth. "Marigold hired the Velvet Sirens."

"And they're playing your favorite song," Rowan said before she could stop herself.

"They are." Simone seemed taken off guard, searching Rowan's face like a detective. "How do you even remember that?"

Rowan's pulse raced as her cheeks burned. She hadn't meant to reveal that she remembered such an intimate detail from their encounter two years ago. "I, uh… it was a lucky guess," she stammered, avoiding Simone's gaze.

"Not buying that. I want to know the truth." Simone's voice was soft but insistent as she stepped closer to Rowan. "How did you remember?"

"Fine. It was an important night for me." Rowan let out a strangled laugh. "It was the first time in a very long time that I experienced… something. You know, for another person. And that I felt attractive myself. Like I knew who I was and was comfortable in my own skin. The details stayed with me. Is that a good enough explanation?"

"It'll do. For now." Simone's eyes softened, a small smile playing at the corners of her lips. "Since they're playing my favorite song, we have to dance."

Rowan's heart raced. "I don't know."

"Come on," Simone encouraged gently, holding out her hand. "One dance."

Against her better judgment, Rowan nodded and took Simone's outstretched hand. As they stepped onto the dance floor, Rowan was acutely aware of every point of contact between them—Simone's hand on her waist, her own hand resting lightly on Simone's shoulder, their fingers intertwined. The warmth of Simone's body so close to hers sent shivers down Rowan's spine. She nearly forgot how to breathe as Simone pulled her closer, their bodies swaying gently to the music.

"See? Not so bad," Simone murmured, her breath warm against Rowan's ear.

"Not bad? It's torture," Rowan confessed.

Just not in the way she'd expected.

Instead of feeling awkward and out of place, she found herself melting into Simone's embrace, their bodies moving in perfect synchronicity. The rest of the world seemed to fade away, leaving the two of them lost in a romantic melody about women in love.

"Don't be hard on yourself," Simone murmured. "You're a natural."

"I don't mean it like that." Why was Rowan talking? It would've been so easy to keep quiet until the song was over, and she could go on her way.

"How do you mean it, then?" Simone asked, pulling away enough to look into Rowan's eyes.

Rowan swallowed hard, unable to break eye contact with Simone. She knew she should step back, put some distance between them before she said or did something she'd regret. But Simone's arms felt so right around her. The intensity in the younger woman's gaze threatened to undo her completely.

"I mean, being here with you, like this." Rowan gestured vaguely to their intertwined bodies. "It's torture because I want this so badly, but I know I can't have it. It's like a dream I don't want to wake up from. I know I'm not allowed to feel this way."

Simone's eyes widened slightly at Rowan's confession. Her grip on Rowan's waist tightened. "Can I tell you something? I think about that night we met, too. All the time."

"Why?"

"Turning the tables, are you?" Simone let out a low, breathy laugh that tickled Rowan to her core.

"Seems only fair after what I told you."

"I guess you're right. I think about it because I felt that same connection, that same spark between us that you described. I know it's complicated with our positions, but there's something about you, Rowan." Simone's voice was thick with emotion. "You made me feel seen, desired, in a way I never had before. Working together the way we have, getting to know you... It's only made me want you more."

Rowan's heart pounded as Simone's words washed over her. The admission hung in the air between them, and Rowan was scarcely able to believe what she'd heard. She needed to put a stop to this, pull away and remind Simone of all the reasons they couldn't be together. But how could she when the younger woman's words echoed her own deepest desires, the longing she had been trying so hard to suppress?

"Simone, I..." Rowan's words ended in a strangled whisper that was completely obscured by the music from the band.

"Look." Simone's eyes sparkled with amusement. "Everyone's dancing now."

"I guess our job here is done," Rowan joked, laughing nervously. She hadn't expected to get out of this conversation so easily but wasn't about to question her luck.

Simone glanced over her shoulder, taking in the crowd of guests on the dance floor before quirking an eyebrow. "Do you want to get out of here?"

"And go where?" Rowan's breath hitched. The implication behind Simone's words was clear.

But just in case there was any doubt, Simone grinned and said, "Where do you think? We're literally dancing in my backyard."

CHAPTER THIRTEEN

Simone ushered Rowan into the guest house, both of them glancing over their shoulders to spy anyone catching their great escape. They stepped through the back door into the small pantry off Simone's kitchen, where she took off her shoes, placing them beside the door. Rowan did the same, letting out an exaggerated sigh of relief.

"I think we're in the clear," Rowan announced as the door clicked shut behind them.

Simone turned to face Rowan, her heart racing. "Good. I want you all to myself tonight." She reached out, her fingertips grazing Rowan's cheek with the lightest of touches, watching intently as Rowan's eyes fluttered closed. "What are you thinking right now?"

A faint blush crept into Rowan's cheeks as she leaned into Simone's touch, her voice a mere whisper. "I'm thinking I want this more than I should. That being here with you feels so right, even though my head keeps telling me it's wrong." Rowan opened her eyes, her gaze locking with Simone's with a raw intensity that seemed to lay bare her soul. "I shouldn't want you this much, Simone. But I do. God, I do."

As if pulled by a magnetic force, their bodies crashed into each other, their mouths fusing in a hungry, desperate kiss. Rowan's hands slid into Simone's hair, pulling her closer as their tongues danced and explored. Simone moaned into Rowan's mouth as her hands roamed over Rowan's back, finding the zipper of her dress and tugging it down with deliberate slowness. She broke the kiss just long enough to whisper, "I want you, too. How long do you think we have before we're missed?"

Rowan let out a groan. "If my mother needs me for something, about five minutes."

"Not nearly long enough. I have an idea." Releasing Rowan from her embrace, Simone walked from the pantry to the kitchen and grabbed her phone from the countertop. "I'm going to tell Marigold that Poppy's babysitter couldn't find Mr. Fuzzy and that you're helping me look for him. That'll buy us an hour, at least."

"Who or what is a Poppy or a Mr. Fuzzy?" Rowan asked, joining Simone in the kitchen, a bemused smile playing on her lips.

"Poppy is Marigold's daughter and the very definition of a modern-day flower child." Simone grinned as she fired off the text to Marigold. "Mr. Fuzzy is Poppy's pet tarantula."

"Jesus." Rowan jumped back, her eyes glued to the floor as if expecting an eight-legged monster to emerge from the shadows at any minute. "He wouldn't actually be in here, would he?"

Simone laughed, setting her phone down and reaching for Rowan's hand. "No, don't worry. Mr. Fuzzy is safely in his terrarium in the main house. If there was any chance he wasn't, I'd be freaking out right along with you. But that excuse should give us plenty of uninterrupted time together."

"What if Marigold asks Poppy about it later?"

"She won't. Not with a backyard full of top donors to keep her attention. Marigold has many great qualities, but a solid long-term memory is not one of them. She'll forget all about it before morning."

Rowan visibly relaxed at Simone's reassurances, a mischievous glint returning to her eyes. "In that case, now that we have some guaranteed alone time, what exactly did you have in mind?"

Simone stepped closer.

"I think you know exactly what I have in mind," Simone murmured, her lips grazing Rowan's ear. She pressed her body flush against Rowan's, pinning her to the wall as her hands roamed over the smooth fabric of Rowan's dress. "We'll need to get this off right away."

Simone turned Rowan's body around to face the wall so that her fingers could find the zipper at the back of the dress once more. Slowly, she dragged it the rest of the way down, revealing pale, freckled skin inch by tantalizing inch. Simone's lips followed the path of newly exposed flesh down Rowan's spine, her hands skimming Rowan's sides, pushing the dress off her shoulders. Rowan let out a shaky breath as Simone dragged her tongue along the curve of her shoulder, tasting the saltiness of her skin.

God, how she had missed this. The intimacy of skin against skin. The quiet sounds of pleasure. The heady rush of desire. Had it really been two years? In all that time, she hadn't been with anyone else.

Simone's mouth journeyed down the inside of Rowan's arm. Once out of real estate, Simone continued lowering the fabric, exposing Rowan's body as the dress pooled on the floor. More kisses, exploring Rowan's right leg all the way down to the toes and then back up the left side until she reached Rowan's neck. Simone's hands slid around Rowan's body to cup her breasts through the thin lace of her bra, thumbs grazing over hardened nipples.

Rowan let out a gasp. "The deck. The back seat of a car. We seem to have a thing against beds, but maybe now would be a good time to change that before adding *up against the kitchen wall* to our list?"

"Spoil sport." Laughter rumbled through Simone. "I can't help being impatient."

"Whereas I'd like to savor every second with you," Rowan said softly, turning in Simone's arms to face her. She cradled Simone's face in her hands, her thumbs brushing over Simone's cheekbones with reverent gentleness. Slowly, she traced a path back up to Simone's left eyebrow. "How'd you get this scar?"

"I fell off my bike when I was little." Simone had gotten it from a tree branch that hit her during the hurricane that had killed her father. But that wasn't something she wanted to talk about now. Maybe another time.

"Poor baby." Rowan placed a tender kiss on the faint line of scar tissue, her lips lingering before she pulled back, her eyes searching Simone's face. "I bet you were a fearless little thing, weren't you?"

"I don't know about that. I think I was more reckless than fearless," Simone mused, her fingers tracing lazy patterns on Rowan's bare back. "Always chasing the next thrill, the next adventure. It's a wonder I made it out of childhood in one piece."

Rowan's hands slid down Simone's sides to grip her hips, pulling their bodies flush together once more. "I like a little recklessness," she whispered against Simone's lips before capturing them with her own in a kiss hot enough to melt steel. Simone moaned into the kiss, her hands roaming over Rowan's body with renewed urgency.

"Are you going to take me to your bed?" Rowan asked when they finally broke apart, both breathless and flushed with desire.

"An excellent suggestion." Grinning, Simone took Rowan's

hand and led her down the hallway to the bedroom, desire thrumming through her veins with each step. Once inside, she turned to face Rowan, admiring her slightly mussed hair and flushed cheeks.

"You are stunning. Truly stunning," Simone breathed, her voice thick with desire.

"You make me feel beautiful, and I think that shines when you're near me." Rowan smiled, a slow, seductive curve of her lips as she reached behind her back to unclasp her bra. It fell away, revealing full, perfect breasts that made Simone's mouth go dry. If she'd been mesmerized by the sight of Rowan before, Simone was utterly captivated now. She drank in every detail—the rosy peaks of Rowan's nipples, the creamy swell of her breasts, the constellation of freckles dotting her skin.

"You have a bad habit," Rowan declared once they were at the foot of the bed.

"Just one? I can hardly wait to find out what it is."

"You keep wearing dresses that are so fucking hot it's almost a shame to take them off."

Simone laughed, the sound low and sultry in the intimate space of the bedroom. "If it's such a shame, maybe you should leave it on." She stepped closer to Rowan, her hands sliding along the smooth, bare skin of Rowan's waist.

"Not a chance." Rowan undid Simone's dress, letting the garment drop unceremoniously to the bedroom floor.

"What about this?" Simone ran her thumb under one of the bra straps. "Another tough choice?"

"Nope." Rowan unhooked Simone's bra and stripped it off, along with her underwear, before removing her own bra and tossing it aside. "Easiest decision ever."

Simone leaned forward, taking a nipple into her mouth. Gently. Letting it burst to life, giving her teeth something to sink into, while Rowan shimmied out of her underwear.

They moved together, climbing into bed, Simone on top of Rowan. Her hips pushed against Rowan's legs while they embraced and kissed. The moments stretched out between them as if they had all the time in the world to savor one another entirely.

Simone let her lips trail a fiery path down the column of Rowan's throat. She paused to suck gently at the hollow of Rowan's collarbone. Rowan arched beneath her, a breathy moan escaping her lips as she tangled her fingers in Simone's hair.

Simone's lips continued their journey down Rowan's body, mapping every curve and plane with worshipful attention. She took her time, savoring the taste of her skin, the smell of her arousal, and the small gasps and moans that spilled from Rowan's lips with each caress. She wanted to touch Rowan everywhere at once, to drink in every inch of her.

But Simone took her time, pressing soft, open-mouthed kisses along the inside of Rowan's thighs, teasing her with fleeting touches that promised so much more.

"Simone, please…" Rowan's voice was strained, her fingers tightening in Simone's hair.

She glanced up at Rowan through hooded eyes, a wicked grin tugging at her lips. "Tell me what you want, Rowan." Her voice was low and rough with desire. "I want to hear you say it."

Rowan's chest heaved as she struggled to form words, her body trembling with need. "I want your mouth on me. Please. Before I go out of my mind."

That plea was all Simone needed. She dipped her head, running her tongue along Rowan's slit in one long, slow lick. Rowan cried out, her hips bucking off the bed as Simone began to devour her in earnest, lapping and sucking at her most sensitive places until Rowan was writhing beneath her, lost in a haze of pleasure. Simone reveled in every gasp and moan, spurred on by the knowledge that she was the one unraveling Rowan so completely.

Simone varied her rhythm, alternating between long, slow licks and quick flicks of her tongue against Rowan's clit. She slid two fingers inside Rowan's slick heat, curling them just so, building her higher and higher. Rowan's thighs trembled on either side of Simone's head, her fingers tangling almost painfully in Simone's hair as she ground against her mouth, chasing her release.

"Oh, God, Simone, I'm... I'm so close," Rowan panted, her words dissolving into a cry as her orgasm crashed over her.

There was a time when Simone thought she would never have this opportunity again. But now, Rowan belonged to her. At least for the time being. They hadn't discussed any specifics yet, so Simone knew she shouldn't waste a single moment and should cherish every second they spent together.

Simone kept her mouth on Rowan, licking and stroking her through the aftershocks until Rowan collapsed back against the pillows, spent and sated.

Simone pressed a final, gentle kiss to Rowan's center before crawling back up her body, trailing kisses along her stomach and between her breasts. She stretched out beside Rowan, propping herself up on one elbow to gaze down at her flushed face. Rowan's eyes fluttered open, hazy and unfocused in the aftermath of her climax. A slow, lazy smile spread across her face as she met Simone's gaze.

"That was incredible," Rowan murmured, her voice low and slightly hoarse. She reached up to tuck a strand of hair behind Simone's ear, her fingertips lingering.

"Just think. We still have another thirty minutes." Simone's grin turned mischievous as she trailed a finger down the valley between Rowan's breasts.

Rowan's lips found the sensitive spot just below her ear, teeth grazing the tender skin. "I like the way you think, except for one thing."

"Oh? What's that?"

"I don't think thirty minutes is going to be nearly enough time."

Simone strolled into the hospital Monday morning, whistling a little tune. After a weekend spent tangled up in Rowan's arms, she felt lighter than she had in ages, a giddy sort of happiness bubbling inside her. Even the prospect of a long shift in the ER couldn't dampen her spirits.

After changing into her scrubs, Simone made her way to the lockers, a secret smile playing on her lips. The memory of Rowan's touch, her kisses, her breathy moans, was still fresh in Simone's mind, making her skin tingle with pleasure. While they would have to keep the intimate nature of their relationship under wraps at work, and there was still a lot between them they had yet to define, Simone felt confident in predicting she'd be seeing a lot more of Rowan going forward. Neither of them seemed able to get enough of the other, and Simone found herself already anticipating their next encounter.

As she pulled her hair back into a ponytail, Dr. Reeves, the senior ER doctor who had filled in for her over the weekend, walked in looking haggard and drained.

"Good morning," Simone chirped.

"Looks like someone had a much better weekend than we did," Dr. Reeves commented in response to Simone's cheerful greeting. "I hope you're well-rested, because it's been absolute chaos here."

Simone's smile faltered. "What happened? Don't take this the wrong way, but you look like shit."

"I'll take that as a compliment, considering." Dr. Reeves ran a hand through his thinning hair, his expression grim. His forehead glistened with sweat. "It's hot. Is the AC on the fritz again?"

"I wouldn't be surprised." Silently, Simone weighed whether she should mention this to Rowan when they met up for dinner that night. Would it be crossing a line to allow their work and personal lives to intersect? They'd agreed to interact as little as possible at the hospital. "If the weekend was that bad, you should have called me in."

"There was nothing one extra doctor could've done, compared to the twenty nurses we were down," Dr. Reeves said in a matter-of-fact tone that belied the sheer enormity of the number he'd just said.

"Hold on, twenty nurses called in sick?" Simone was aghast.

"They didn't call in. They don't exist." Dr. Reeves slammed his locker door, the echo reverberating through the room. "This fucking place. We're critically understaffed. Have been for months. Strike that—years. This weekend, it finally caught up with us. Fingers crossed we don't get sued."

"Sued?" Simone gasped.

"I think we're in the clear. The dead guy doesn't seem to have any family."

A chill ran down Simone's spine, her earlier happiness evaporating. "What the hell happened here this weekend?"

"Where do I even begin?" He took out a cloth to wipe the back of his neck. Simone was sweating now, too, so his observation about the AC was right on the money. "Long story short? An old guy came in with chest pains. He should have been pushed to the front of the line, but he didn't even have his vitals checked by a nurse because we didn't have anyone available."

Simone's stomach dropped. "How long was he waiting?"

"Over four hours." Dr. Reeves' expression was grim. "By the time someone realized he was unresponsive, it was too late. He'd had a massive heart attack right there in the waiting area. We tried to resuscitate him, but it was no good." Dr. Reeves shook his head.

Simone felt sick. "Jesus Christ," she whispered, leaning

against the lockers for support. "That's unacceptable. How could this happen?"

Dr. Reeves gave a derisive snort. "How could it not? By state law, we should've had at least six nurses on duty in the ER alone. We had two. Two nurses for a packed waiting room on a Friday night. Understaffing in every other department, too, so no one could spare any nurses to fill in. It was a disaster waiting to happen."

"That's awful." Simone felt her chest tighten as the gravity of the situation sank in.

Dr. Reeves shrugged with the demeanor of a seasoned veteran who had seen it all. "It's more than awful. It's negligent. But what can we do? On the bright side, the deceased was old and poor. No next of kin. Talk about dodging a bullet."

Simone swallowed, not sharing in Dr. Reeves's grim relief. "That doesn't make it any better. We need to report this. The hospital administration needs to know how serious the situation is."

Dr. Reeves let out a humorless laugh. "Report it? To whom? Administration is already well aware of the potential for such disasters, yet they keep cutting corners to save money, and we're the ones left holding the bag when things go wrong. Personally, I'd rather keep my head down, my mouth shut, and avoid trouble."

Simone's anger rose to form a hot knot in her chest. "This isn't right. We can't let this slide. There has to be something we can do."

Dr. Reeves sighed, his shoulders sagging. "You're new, so let me give you some free advice. If you don't have to report things around here, don't. Our former CMO was the type to gun down the messenger. You'd get the worst shifts, passed over for raises, critical performance reviews. I learned quickly enough not to stick my head out of the foxhole or—" He mimed having it chopped off.

"But there's a new CMO now," Simone pointed out, certain Rowan would never react that way.

"Yeah, we've gone from the CEO's son-in-law to his daughter running the place. Talk about nepotism. Until that old son-of-a-bitch retires, nothing will change."

Simone's jaw clenched at Dr. Reeves's dismissive words about Rowan. She knew Rowan was nothing like her ex-husband, but she couldn't explain that to Dr. Reeves without revealing more about their personal relationship than she could afford. Still, the idea of staying silent about such a serious incident didn't sit well. "I understand what you're saying, but surely Dr. Colchester would want to know about something this serious."

"I only have one more year until retirement. I don't have the energy to fight anymore." With that, he shuffled away.

Simone stood in the locker room, her mind reeling. The giddy happiness she'd felt earlier had evaporated, replaced by a heavy weight of responsibility. She sucked in a deep breath as she weighed her options. Should she follow Dr. Reeves's advice and keep her head down?

That might be the wisest course of action, but it wasn't the right one.

She couldn't ignore what had happened. A man had died because of the hospital's systemic failures, and she refused to be complicit in covering it up. Hell, if she'd been there like she was supposed to, maybe she could have saved him. Rowan needed to know about this, regardless of the potential complications it might create in their personal relationship.

"Fuck it," she muttered under her breath as she dashed toward the stairwell. If she hurried, there was enough time before her shift started to drop in and speak with Rowan.

Simone came to a stop outside the door, her hand poised to knock. This might cross a line, waltzing in like she expected special access to a hospital administrator without an appointment, but the urgency of the situation overrode her hesitation. She rapped sharply on the door.

"Come in," Rowan called out.

Simone entered Rowan's office. Rowan looked up from her desk, surprise flickering across her face.

"Dr. Doucette? Is everything alright?" Rowan asked, her professional demeanor firmly in place despite the intimate moments they'd shared over the past few days.

"Do you mind if I close the door?"

"O-kay." Rowan dragged out the word as a warning, clearly fearing Simone had less than professional motivations in mind.

"I'm sorry to barge in like this, but there's something urgent I need to discuss with you," Simone began, her voice low and serious. "To be clear, I'm not making an official report. And don't even ask me how I learned about this."

Rowan capped her pen, setting it down on her desk. "You have my attention. What's going on?"

Simone recounted what she'd learned.

Rowan's eyes widened, her professional mask slipping to reveal genuine shock. "My God. That's unacceptable. Why was I not informed?"

"Because in the past, people who reported unpleasant information faced retaliation," Simone told her. "It gets worse. Apparently, these kinds of dangerous conditions have been going on for a long time, but no one feels they can report concerns without becoming a scapegoat, so they're getting swept under the rug."

Rowan leaned back in her chair, processing the information with a scowl. "I see. And you're telling me this in confidence because you're afraid of the potential backlash as well?"

"Not from you," Simone clarified, meeting Rowan's gaze directly. "But the staff here are clearly used to operating under a culture of fear. Apparently, reporting issues under the previous CMO was as good as painting a target on your back."

"That certainly sounds like Lance's management style," Rowan muttered, shaking her head in disgust. She sighed heavily, pinching the bridge of her nose. "I knew I'd have my work cut out for me cleaning up his messes, but this is beyond the pale."

"I'm sorry to be the bearer of bad news," Simone said softly, her heart aching at the weariness in Rowan's voice. "I debated whether I should even bring this to you, given our personal connection. I wasn't even on duty when this happened—"

"I don't want you feeling guilty about attending the gala," Rowan interjected, her voice gentle but firm. "You've been working as much as you legally can for months now. You can't be on the clock every second. Even if you had been working Friday night, nothing you did would have changed the outcome. We doctors like to think we're superhuman, but any nurse will tell you we usually don't know the first thing about what they actually do, and one doctor sure as hell can't do the job of twenty nurses. Deep down, you must know that. You were right to come to me with this information. Why do you think I accepted this position in the first place? To continue on with business as usual?"

"That would be out of character for you." A small smile tugged at the corner of Simone's mouth. "I know we said we'd keep our distance at work, but I couldn't in good conscience let this go on without saying anything."

"I know," Rowan replied with a weary chuckle. "That's one of the reasons I... care about you as much as I do."

Despite the gravity of the situation, Simone's pulse raced at Rowan's words. "I care about you, too. A lot."

Rowan trained her eyes on her desk, though she allowed a small, tender smile to cross her face at Simone's admission before quickly composing herself. "Thank you for bringing this information to my attention, Dr. Doucette. I assure you I'll look into the matter with the utmost discretion."

"I appreciate that, Dr. Colchester," Simone replied, taking her cue from Rowan and using her most professional tone. "I'll see myself out."

"Oh, and Simone?"

Simone paused at the door, her hand on the knob. "Yes?"

"I'll see you tonight."

CHAPTER FOURTEEN

As she reached for Simone's hand, Rowan thought the Saturday after Labor Day was the perfect time to visit Provincetown. There were so many reasons to love the small seaside town at the tip of Cape Cod, starting with it being one of the most queer-friendly destinations in the country. Not to mention it was far enough away from Marbury they were unlikely to bump into anyone they knew while strolling along Commercial Street, where all the shops and restaurants were.

A bicycle with a chihuahua in the front basket breezed past them.

"That dog's wearing a rainbow bandanna," Simone gushed.

"I think it's actually legally required here to have a spoiled dog with queer clothing," Rowan said with a laugh. After weeks of hiding their relationship at every turn, she loved the simple feeling of Simone's fingers intertwining with hers as they walked. "I probably should have asked you before planning this little getaway, but have you ever been to P-town before?"

Simone shook her head. "No, never. Before moving here, the only thing I knew about Cape Cod was it was a place rich people went for the summer."

"It definitely has that reputation, although I would like it noted we're not as snooty as Nantucket or Martha's Vineyard." Rowan chuckled, relaxing into the easy rhythm of their stroll, her thumb absently caressing Simone's hand.

The late summer sun warmed their faces, and a salty breeze carried the scent of the nearby ocean as they edged closer to the buildings along a stretch of road where the sidewalk suddenly disappeared. Traffic was light on the one-way street, and there was only a fraction of the people who would've been clogging the sidewalks a week ago.

"I'm pretty sure I wouldn't be able to board the ferry to either of those places," Simone joked. "They'd smell my working-class upbringing a mile away and turn me away at the dock."

"Oh, me too," Rowan confessed. "Minus the working-class background, but I certainly wouldn't pass muster if they did a spot inspection of my bank account balance."

Simone's eyebrows arched in surprise. "Really? I thought... I mean, given your family's prominence and everything..."

Rowan sighed, her grip on Simone's hand tightening slightly. "It's a common misconception."

"I hope this isn't too personal, but can I ask why?" Simone gave Rowan's hand a gentle squeeze. "I'll admit when we first met, I sort of assumed you were rolling in the dough—not that it matters to me one way or another. That isn't what motivates me. But I mean, with the beach house and your position at the hospital..."

Rowan's gaze drifted to the colorful storefronts lining the street. She'd never discussed her financial situation with anyone outside her immediate family, except for Candace, but something about Simone's open, non-judgmental expression made her want to share.

"It's complicated," Rowan began. "With the divorce, things got messy. I could have pushed for more, but I didn't. In the end, all I got, besides my freedom, is a whole lot of debt."

THE ANATOMY OF FOREVER

Simone's eyes widened, her steps slowing as she processed Rowan's words. "I had no idea. What about the beach house? I remember your mom saying you bought it from Lance."

"Spent pretty much every penny of the divorce settlement to do so," Rowan admitted, her voice lowering. "It wasn't the smartest financial decision, but Lance had to sell it, and I didn't want a stranger to end up with it. It's going to take me years, if not decades to recover."

"You did it for Erica's sake. Why don't you want her to know?"

"She's always idolized her father. While I've lost all respect for the man through all this, I never wanted to make her feel that way about him. I know she's pissed at me and believes I stole the house from Lance. Yet, if I tell her the truth, it'll damage their relationship. I'm between a rock and a fucking impossible hard spot." Rowan's voice caught in her throat, and she blinked rapidly, fighting back the sudden sting of tears.

"I wish Erica knew instead of taking everything out on you." Simone squeezed Rowan's hand, offering silent support as they paused to look into a shop with a window full of silly T-shirts on display. "Shall we go in?"

Rowan nodded, grateful for the distraction. As they stepped into the shop, a bell tinkled overhead. Racks of colorful T-shirts and shelves lined with quirky knickknacks filled the cramped space.

"Oh, here's one for you." Simone pulled a T-shirt from the rack and held it up. It was printed with the words 'wicked' and 'stepmother' in huge letters, with the word 'awesome' in much smaller letters sandwiched in between.

Rowan let out a startled laugh, her eyes crinkling at the corners. "God, that's terrible. And hilarious."

"Probably a bit too on the nose right now." Simone slipped the hanger back on the metal rod.

"It's so easy to put all the blame on an ex-stepmother."

Rowan swallowed, not wanting to let on how deeply it hurt. Her eyes were drawn to a small display of seashell necklaces near the register. She ran her fingers over one of the strands, remembering beach days with Erica when she was a teenager. How different things were now.

"I still don't think it's fair the way Lance and Erica treat you," Simone said softly, stepping closer to Rowan. "You've sacrificed so much."

"I've let both of them do it, and I know I shouldn't." Rowan's fingers stilled on the necklace. "But I felt so guilty about the divorce. I still do. I was the one who chose to break up my family."

Simone reached out, gently brushing a stray curl from Rowan's face. "I don't know how to break it to you, but your ex has some issues."

Rowan snorted. "Obviously. His addiction struggles landed him in rehab, and he left the hospital a frigging disaster."

"Thank God we've survived the summer," Simone said. "At least now you can have some breathing room to figure out the staffing issues. It's no wonder you couldn't stay with a man like that."

"It wouldn't have mattered what kind of man he was." Rowan paused, pointing to a shirt that proclaimed: *No One Knows I'm a Lesbian*. "That was the issue right there."

"No one knew—including you?"

Rowan nodded, a wry smile tugging at her lips. "Don't get me wrong. I knew I was attracted to women early on. But there was so much societal pressure around needing to find a boyfriend, I never stopped to question whether I actually wanted one. Was I attracted to men? It's what everyone told me I should be, and I accepted it at face value. I had this image in my head of what people told me my life was supposed to look like— a husband, kids—and when I met Lance, he—"

"Fit the mold perfectly?" Simone suggested.

"Exactly. I convinced myself the awe and professional admiration I felt for him was love, that it was enough. But deep down, I always knew something was missing. It took me a long time to realize I was a lesbian. Once I did, I couldn't undo the knowledge in my—" Choking up, she completed the sentence by covering her heart.

"How did Lance react when you told him this and asked for a divorce?"

Rowan kept her gaze on the T-shirt, her fingers tracing the letters as she spoke. "He asked me to stay anyway. To him, it was all about sunk cost. We'd already been married for over a decade, so why not stay that way? After all, he had a mother for his kid and a father-in-law who had anointed him as successor. It was all working fine for him."

"What about your happiness?"

Rowan's fingers stilled on the shirt, her eyes meeting Simone's. "That's exactly what I asked myself. For the first time in my life, I put my own happiness above everyone else's. It was terrifying and liberating all at once. But it came with a mountain of guilt."

"It sounds like, as far as Lance is concerned, only his happiness matters. Not yours, and not Erica's."

"I'm sure he loves his daughter but maybe not as much as he loves himself." Rowan rolled her head from side to side. "I'm sorry. I didn't mean to get so serious."

"You don't have to do that, ya know," Simone said as she placed a few trinkets on the counter and waited for the cashier to ring them up. "I want you to be able to talk to me. I imagine it's been lonely. Do your parents know about you being a lesbian? Or should we grab that T-shirt you keep fondling and add it to my purchase?"

"Um..." Contemplating her complicated family dynamics, Rowan made a face. "They don't not know."

Simone laughed. "What does that mean?"

"I haven't lied about it. Maybe Lance told them. Who knows? My parents are..." Rowan searched for a word to describe them but gave up with a shrug. "They're my parents. We talk, but we're not the kind of family that discusses personal matters."

"They do know you're not with Lance anymore, right?" Simone asked—probably jokingly, though Rowan wasn't a hundred percent certain—as she handed over her credit card to the cashier.

Rowan let out a soft chuckle. "Yes, they know about the divorce. But we've never explicitly discussed my sexuality. I mean, hell, I never told them I was straight, either. I only brought them into the loop when marrying Lance because my dad would've been gutted if he couldn't throw a big wedding for all his friends and give the bride away."

"Do you think they've figured it out, the whole lesbian thing?" Simone asked as they stepped out of the shop, the bell tinkling behind them.

Rowan paused, considering. "Honestly? I have no idea. I think they've guessed I have no interest in dating men anymore. It's possible they figured out some of the girls I dated in college were more than friends. But it's all very unspoken." They continued walking along Commercial Street, the afternoon sun glinting off the shop windows, causing Rowan to squint until she found her sunglasses and put them on.

"Let me see if I'm understanding everything." Simone spoke quietly, making it difficult to hear her. "You've been dealing with realizing you're a lesbian, getting a divorce, money worries, a stepdaughter who barely talks to you, the hospital issues. Is there anything else?"

"That pretty much covers it, unless you want to toss in having to hide our relationship from everyone at work for fear of inviting accusations of favoritism or worse." Despite all that, Rowan felt like a weight had lifted from her chest thanks to

Simone's understanding and simple acceptance of her complicated past.

Simone stopped walking, pulling Rowan to the side and looking earnestly into her eyes. "Do you ever just want to cry?"

"Yes." Even as she answered, Rowan fought a lump that formed in her throat at Simone's obvious concern for her. "Yes, I do. Especially at three in the morning when I wake and everything you listed seems so hard to overcome. By the time the sun rises, it's not so scary, but between the hours of three to five in the morning, it's fucking terrifying in my head."

Simone pulled Rowan into her arms. "The next time you wake up scared, if I'm not there, call me. You don't have to go through all this alone."

"You aren't going to run for the hills now that you know the full truth?" Rowan asked. "I might not blame you. Especially now that you know I'm not rich."

Simone pulled back slightly, her blue eyes shining with intensity. "Run for the hills? Rowan, I'm not going anywhere. I've never cared about that shit. If anything, knowing all this makes me admire you even more."

"Lucky for me." Rowan felt a surge of excitement as she recognized the building they were in front of. "This is my favorite store. We have to go in."

"Marine Specialties?" Simone read the sign above the door in a questioning tone.

"Trust me on this," Rowan said, tugging Simone's hand as they entered the store.

The moment they stepped inside, Simone's eyes widened. "Wow," she breathed, taking in the eclectic mix of items crammed into every available space.

Nautical antiques hung from the ceiling, while shelves overflowed with an assortment of oddities, ranging from vintage postcards to military surplus gear. Browsing the front, Simone stopped at the fridge magnets, selecting the one that read *I prefer girls.* "You could buy this and put it up in your kitchen. If you're parents still don't get the memo, then it's really on them."

"I might do that. There's also the rainbow hoodie. It's not subtle." Rowan patted the pile of sweatshirts.

"Maybe one of those used license plates on the wall that reads *I'm a lezzie.*"

"Now you're really thinking." Rowan grabbed a dress with cats on it off a nearby rack. "Do you think the cats are supposed to be symbolic?"

"Are you asking me if that's a pussy dress? Sadly, I don't think it gets the message across with as much clarity as some of the other options." Simone laughed as she grabbed the price tag and took a look. "It's actually really affordable, though."

"A lot of the stuff here is, but don't even look at the wool sweaters," Rowan cautioned. "They cost a fortune. That's part of the fun here. You can find bargains but also things that will cause your credit card to go up in smoke."

Simone pointed to a mermaid figurehead like the type that went on the front of a boat. "Now, I've always wanted one of those."

"You see? You never know what you'll find in here."

"It's a good place to get gifts for Marigold and Poppy," Simone said. She selected a knitted rainbow turtle that was not much larger than a quarter. "This is perfect for Poppy."

Meanwhile, Rowan perused the packages of novelty cocktail napkins. "I don't know Marigold very well, but this one speaks to me." The selection in question had a woman with a glass of wine along with the words 'If drinking on the porch counts, then yes, call me outdoorsy.'

Simone clapped her hands together. "That's perfect!"

While Simone paid, Rowan stood off to the side where she couldn't help admiring this woman who had burst into her life like a ray of sunshine. Simone's easy laughter and genuine interest in every aspect of Rowan's life, even the messiest parts that would have turned most people away, made her heart burst with affection. Or maybe something even deeper. Was it possible Rowan was falling in love?

Outside, Rowan reached to brush away a speck of lint that had clung to Simone's eyebrow. She frowned as her fingertips skimmed the scar she'd noticed before. "This was deep. It really must have hurt when you fell off your bike."

"Yeah, about that..." There was an almost guilty look on Simone's face that caught Rowan by surprise.

"What is it?"

Simone took a deep breath, her eyes darting away from Rowan's gaze. "I wasn't entirely truthful about how I got this scar."

Rowan's brow furrowed. "What do you mean?"

"It's kind of a long story. What would you say to grabbing a bite to eat and a beer to go along with my confession?"

"How could I turn down such an intriguing offer? I know the perfect place." Rowan led the way to a little covered walkway where a selection of food vendors lined the walls. Beyond it was an open seating area with a view of the ocean.

"I'm leaning toward Chinese," Rowan announced after weighing all the options. "Is that okay with you?"

"You're a woman after my own heart," Simone said with a grin. "Here I thought you would make me eat at a place that would issue a fine if I dropped my linen napkin or used the wrong fork."

"Have you seen the way I live?" Rowan scoffed. "I know how to play the game and act the part when I must, but I'm infinitely more comfortable in sweats with a meal from the microwave. This"—she pointed to the Chinese joint—"is my idea of the perfect night out."

After gathering their food and ordering beers from the bar, they settled at a weathered wooden table overlooking the water and dug into steaming containers of lo mein and sesame chicken. Rowan couldn't help but notice the nervous energy radiating from Simone.

"So, about that scar..." She reached across the table and squeezed Simone's hand reassuringly. "What's the confession?"

"That night, when you asked me how I got it, I told you it was from a bike accident. It wasn't. I didn't want to ruin the mood, so that's why I lied about it. I got it—" Simone ran a finger over the faint line. "During Hurricane Katrina, we had to evacuate our house. We were trying to get to higher ground, but the water was rising so fast. My dad was carrying me through the floodwaters when a broken tree limb hit us. It sliced my face, and I was bleeding everywhere."

"Head wounds will do that," Rowan commented, blinking back tears as she forked in a bite of sesame chicken.

"My dad was so worried about finding help for me he completely ignored the chest pains he was having. When we finally reached a makeshift medical tent, my dad insisted they treat my wound before letting them check on him. He died of a heart attack while I was being stitched up."

Rowan's heart clenched at the pain in Simone's voice. She reached across the table, taking Simone's hand in both of hers. "Oh, my God. What a horrible thing to go through. You were just a kid."

"Yeah, but guilt works in mysterious ways. When I replay that terrible day, I keep thinking if I hadn't gotten hurt, maybe my dad would have gotten help in time. Maybe he'd still be alive. And I have this stupid scar staring at me every time I look in the mirror to remind me."

"Jesus, we're a fine pair, aren't we? Wracked with guilt and beating ourselves up over things that we can't change."

"Maybe that's part of the attraction. Seeing ourselves in the other." Simone shook her head. "No, that didn't come out right because I think that means we're in love with ourselves instead of each other."

Rowan's heart beat so fast and loud she was sure Simone could hear it. "In love?"

"What?" Simone's cheeks flushed a deep pink. "Oh! I didn't mean... I mean, I wasn't implying we're..." Her sentence stopped short with a flustered raspberry.

Rowan felt a surge of warmth spread through her chest. "It's okay," she breathed. "I think I know what you mean. We've both been through things that have shaped us, left us with scars, inside and out. Maybe this thing with us is about recognizing a kindred spirit. Someone who understands what it's like to survive carrying that weight."

Simone nodded thoughtfully before raising her bottle. "To surviving. It's not easy, but some of us have to do it."

"Maybe that should be the new motto for the hospital staff," Rowan quipped, causing them both to laugh.

They sat in comfortable silence, the gentle lapping of waves against the shore providing a soothing backdrop. Rowan found herself mesmerized by the way the setting sun intensified the youthful glow of Simone's face and made her blue eyes sparkle. She felt an overwhelming urge to lean across the table and kiss her, public setting be damned. Only the thought of accidentally getting caught by utter recklessness stopped her from acting on that impulse.

"I know we've talked about a lot of difficult things, but this day has been perfect," Rowan whispered.

"It's not over yet." Simone gave a seductive wink.

"I'm taking that wink as a promise." Rowan said.

"It absolutely is."

"In that case, maybe we should look into a hotel for the night. I know it's only a short drive home, but there's this one place here that has—" Rowan's phone suddenly started to ring, causing her heart to jump. "I swear to God, if this is the hospital —huh, it's an unknown number."

"Maybe you shouldn't answer," Simone suggested, though her tone suggested she wasn't sold on her own advice.

Rowan's thumb hovered over the screen. "It could be important," she said, more to herself than to Simone. With a quick, apologetic glance, she answered the call. "Hello?"

"Mom?" Erica's voice came through, sounding shaky and distressed.

Rowan's heart leapt into her throat at the sound of Erica's voice, not to mention the use of the word mom, which she hadn't heard from the young woman since the day she'd filed for divorce. "Erica? What's wrong? Are you okay?"

There was a pause on the other end of the line, filled with muffled background noise. When Erica spoke again, she seemed barely able to hold back a sob. "I need your help. I've been arrested."

CHAPTER FIFTEEN

Simone checked her reflection in the car window, mussing her hair to give it that *just rushed over at the end of my shift* look. She'd donned a pair of scrubs from her trunk, too, after Rowan had dropped her off at her car, which she'd parked in Rowan's driveway before heading to Provincetown that morning. It was the perfect cover story. Erica would never suspect that Simone had spent the day on a date with her stepmom.

Why did everything about her and Rowan have to be so damned complicated?

Simone glanced at the entrance of the police station where Rowan was already working to bail out Erica. She knew this because she'd received a call from Erica shortly after Rowan did, begging her to come help.

Thanks to Erica's unexpected return to Marbury, things were only going to get harder.

Simone took a deep breath and pushed open the heavy glass doors of the police station. Between the fluorescent lights and the smell of stale coffee that permeated the air, it wasn't much different from the ER. She scanned the lobby, quickly spotting Rowan's distinctive red curls at the front desk.

Rowan turned, her eyes widening slightly at Simone's appearance. A flicker of understanding passed between them before Rowan's face settled into a mask of cool professionalism.

"Dr. Doucette, I assume my daughter must've called you?" Rowan said, knowing full well that was the case since she'd been sitting next to Simone in the car, one hand on her knee, when it had happened. In a barely audible voice, she added, "Good thinking with the scrubs."

"Yes, she did," Simone replied, playing along while glowing a little inside from the compliment. "I came as soon as my shift ended. How is she?"

Before Rowan could answer, Erica emerged from a side door, her eyes red-rimmed and her shoulders slumped.

"Simone!" Erica ran in for a hug, almost knocking Simone off her feet. "You came. Thank God. This place is horrendous."

"What happened?" Simone asked, noticing Erica hadn't given Rowan the time of day, not even a thank you for the bail money, which Simone now knew was something Rowan couldn't quite afford. "You're supposed to be studying art in Florence right now."

"I don't even know where to start." Erica pulled away from Simone, her eyes darting between her and Rowan. "I got kicked out of school."

Simone's brow furrowed. "Kicked out? Why?"

"It wasn't my fault. The day before classes started, my school told me my tuition hadn't been paid. I tried calling Dad several times, but I couldn't reach him, so they unceremoniously booted my ass."

"Oh, Erica," Simone sighed, her heart aching for her friend. "I'm so sorry. That must have been awful."

Erica nodded, her eyes welling up with fresh tears. "I didn't know what to do. It wasn't just classes, but student housing, too. Can you believe it? I couldn't even afford a hotel. My credit card is practically maxed."

"I thought your father paid your credit card each month," Rowan commented, her mouth set in a thin line. Simone could see the wheels turning in Rowan's head, piecing together the puzzle of Lance's financial mismanagement.

Erica shot Rowan a withering glare. "Yeah, well, apparently, he's only been paying the minimum on it, which I did not know, or I never would've charged so much." She blew a breath out, ruffling the hairs on her forehead. "It really is at the limit now since I had to pay for a flight home."

"But how did you end up here?" Simone asked, gesturing at the police station around them.

Erica's cheeks flushed, and her eyes shifted toward the ground. "I went to Dad's condo. I thought I could crash there until I figured things out. But when I tried to use my key, it didn't work, so I skirted around to the back and climbed in through that one window that never closes all the way."

"You broke in?" Simone's eyebrows shot up to her hairline.

"It's my dad's place. Except the cops seem to think he doesn't own it anymore. Total incompetence." Erica crossed her arms, her face the picture of defiance. "I'm dealing with idiots all around me. I'm sure the thing with the school is a huge mix up, too. If I can just get a hold of my dad, it'll be squared away."

"Uh..." Rowan stepped closer. "I don't know about the tuition, but your dad did sell the condo."

"What?" Erica blinked several times before taking a step away from Rowan. "I don't believe you."

"That doesn't change the facts," Rowan said in a quiet tone.

"No," Erica whispered, shaking her head. "No, he would've told me."

Simone watched as Erica's face crumpled, defiance melting into confusion and hurt. Simone wanted to reach out and comfort her, but she knew that right now, Erica needed the truth more than anything else.

"I'm really sorry," Rowan began, but Erica cut her off with a sharp wave of her hand.

"What did you do this time? Chase him out of town? Have someone kidnap him or something? Every single thing has gone to shit since you divorced him. He's miserable, and it's all your fault," she hissed.

"Erica," Simone started to say, but it was clear her friend wasn't listening.

"Can you take me to your place, Simone?" Erica begged. She gave the surroundings a dirty glare, doing a full-body shudder. "I want a shower."

Simone glanced at Rowan. The hurt in her eyes was palpable, but she gave a slight nod.

"Of course, you can stay with me tonight," Simone said, wrapping an arm around Erica's shoulders. "Let's get you out of here."

Erica immediately headed for the door, but Simone hung back long enough to offer Rowan a sympathetic smile. "Let me calm her down, and then you can come over for a heart-to-heart."

"She won't like that." Rowan's jaw clenched as she wrestled with a storm of emotions Simone could only guess at.

"Probably not," Simone agreed. "It doesn't change the fact that she needs to learn some hard truths."

Rowan looked like Simone had asked her to babysit Mr. Fuzzy.

"It's going to be okay." Simone put a hand on Rowan's shoulder, wishing she could pull her in for a hug. But under the circumstances, that was impossible.

As Simone went to join Erica outside the police station, she couldn't help but feel a twinge of guilt. She was caught between her loyalty to her friend and her growing feelings for Rowan, the weight of their secret relationship pressing down on her and making each step feel heavier than the last.

How was she going to navigate this minefield without hurting either of them?

The drive to Simone's was deadly silent. Erica stared out the window, her face a mask of anger and hurt. Simone gripped the steering wheel, her mind racing with all the complications that had arisen in a few brief hours. How was it possible that earlier in the day, she and Rowan had been strolling hand in hand along the beach in Provincetown, their biggest worry whether to get ice cream?

The weight of Erica's crisis hung heavily in the air. The poor woman's life had spiraled into chaos. Simone wanted to comfort her friend, but she also knew Erica needed time to process what had happened.

"Home sweet home," Simone said, trying to inject some lightness into her voice as she pulled into her driveway.

Erica finally broke the silence. "I can't believe this is happening," she muttered, her voice thick with emotion. "It's like my whole life just imploded."

Simone killed the engine and turned to face her friend. "I know it feels that way right now." She squeezed Erica's shoulder. "But we're going to figure it out, okay? You're not alone in this."

Erica nodded weakly, her eyes glistening with unshed tears. "Thanks for letting me stay. I don't know what I'd do without you. I really can't face Rowan right now."

"No problem." She forced a smile even though her heart clenched at Erica's words. "What are friends for?"

If only Erica knew about Simone's relationship with Rowan, she'd probably never speak to either of them again. Even bringing Erica here felt like false pretenses, knowing she would push for a reconciliation between her friend and her... girlfriend? Honestly, Simone didn't even know what to call Rowan, other than the woman she was rapidly falling head over heels for.

God, what a mess.

As they climbed out of the car, Poppy came rushing over

from the main house with an infectious enthusiasm that lifted Simone's spirits. The child wore a bright yellow raincoat despite the clear night sky, her pigtails bouncing as she ran.

"Simone! Simone!"

Simone couldn't help but smile at Poppy's exuberance. "Change of plans, kiddo. Turns out I didn't have to work all weekend after all."

Did Simone feel guilty for lying to a child? Yes. But it couldn't be helped. The last thing she wanted to explain to Erica was that, up until her friend's unexpected arrival in Marbury, her weekend plans had mostly consisted of a lot of naked time with said friend's stepmother.

"Who is this?" Poppy asked, pointing to Erica.

"This is my friend Erica," Simone explained, ruffling Poppy's hair. "She's going to be staying with us for a little while."

Erica managed a weak smile and a small wave at the child. "Hi there."

Poppy's eyes lit up. "Come see Mrs. Squeakers." Poppy tugged on both Simone's and Erica's hands at the same time. "She's the classroom hamster, and it's my weekend to watch her. Isn't that fantastic?"

"It is," Simone said, gently extricating her hand from Poppy's iron-like grip. "And I'll come over tomorrow to say hello, okay? It's late and right now, Erica needs to go inside and take a shower."

"You should ask if you can have a bath instead," Poppy advised, her tone serious. "You look sad, and baths are way better than showers when you're sad. My mom always lets me have a bubble bath if I have a bad day. My favorite type is strawberry."

Erica let out a small laugh, the first genuine smile Simone had seen on her face since the police station. "You know what? I just might do that."

Simone laughed as she gave Poppy another pat on the head. "Why don't you head back home now and give Mrs. Squeakers a little treat for me? I'm sure she'd love that. Tell her I can't wait to meet her."

"Okay!" Poppy agreed cheerfully. She skipped off with all the boundless energy of a child with a mission, her yellow raincoat flapping behind her like a cape.

It'd be a lie to say Simone wasn't a little jealous of Poppy, who so easily could escape Erica's foul mood.

Although Erica did at least concede, "Cute kid," as they entered Simone's house.

"She's one of a kind; that's for sure." Simone set her key on the hook inside the front door. "The bathroom's down the hall. There should be some clean towels in the cabinet above the toilet."

"I think I need a glass of water first," Erica replied, wearing a troubled expression that Simone was certain had little to do with thirst. "Did my dad really sell his condo?"

"Yes." Simone saw no reason to sugarcoat it.

"Why?"

"You'll have to ask him that question." Simone walked to the kitchen, filling a water glass.

"I guess I'll head over to his office at the hospital in the morning."

Simone drew in a surprised breath as she handed over the glass. "He won't be there."

"He's always working."

"He doesn't work there anymore," Simone explained, carefully skirting the part about rehab. Best to tackle one thing at a time. "He took a job in Pensacola."

"What's going on?" Erica's hand shook as she raised the glass to her lips.

"Why don't we sit." Simone motioned to the couch in the living room.

Erica didn't so much sit as collapse onto the cushions. "This is all Rowan's fault. He was happy—"

"No one ever knows what's going on in a marriage, aside from the two people involved," Simone said, knowing she was walking a fine line between conversation and scolding.

Erica frowned, clearly sensing the same thing. "Why do you keep coming to her rescue?"

Simone's heart rate kicked up a hundred notches as she scrambled for any answer other than the truth. "Probably because I'm jealous," she said, which was at least partially true.

"Jealous of Rowan?"

"No. Jealous of you," Simone clarified. "Pretty much the day I left for college, my mom met a guy and fell head over heels in love. Got married within a year and moved to Oregon before I'd even finished my freshman year."

"I didn't know you had a stepfather," Erica said.

"Probably because I've only met him a handful of times. I understand my mother is dealing with her trauma in her own way, by moving on and putting her old life behind her. But you have no idea how lucky you have it."

"Yeah, right," Erica scoffed. "My dad's MIA, I got kicked out of school, and my evil stepmother—"

"Dropped everything to bail you out of jail," Simone finished, her voice firm but gentle. "Jail. No questions asked. I know you're hurting right now, but Rowan isn't the enemy here. She's trying to help you."

Erica's eyes flashed with anger. "Stop defending her! You're supposed to be on my side. She's the reason my dad is... well, whatever it is my dad is doing."

Simone took a deep breath, trying to find the right words to navigate this delicate situation. "He was asked to leave. By the hospital's board of directors."

Erica's eyes widened in shock. "What? Why?"

Simone hesitated, unsure how much to reveal. "Things there haven't been running smoothly. For a while."

"That can't be true. He loves that place."

Simone sighed, knowing she had to tread carefully. "I know this is hard to hear, but your dad hasn't been himself lately. I can't even imagine how you're feeling, given everything. But the person you should be talking to for real answers is your stepmom."

"No. I need to speak with my father." Erica retrieved her phone from her back pocket and pulled up her contacts, making a call. After several seconds of it ringing, she glanced up with tear-streaked eyes. "Why isn't he answering?"

"When's the last time you talked to him?"

Erica's brow furrowed. "I'm not sure. He texted me happy birthday last month, but we haven't talked for real in a long time because I was working at the gallery in Italy the last several months leading up to my grad program. And he said he was busy with a big project at the hospital." She looked up at Simone, her eyes wide with dawning realization. "But that wasn't true, was it?"

"Talk to Rowan." Simone patted Erica's hand. "She might have some answers."

Erica tucked her chin to her chest. "Fine, but I'm not going over to her house. It's too hard to be there, knowing it's not my home anymore."

"That's fine," Simone said softly. "Text and ask her to come here."

"You're okay with that?"

"Absolutely," Simone reassured her, squeezing Erica's hand. "I'll be around if you need me, but I think it's important for you two to have some time alone to talk things through."

Erica nodded, her fingers trembling slightly as she typed out a message to Rowan. It only took a few seconds to get a response. Erica stared at her phone, her brow furrowed.

"She says she'll be here in fifteen minutes. I don't know if I'm ready for this."

Simone gave her friend's shoulder a reassuring squeeze. "You can do this. Just try to keep an open mind and an open heart."

"None of this is making sense." Erica paced the living room, scrubbing her face with her hands. "I just don't understand."

Simone watched Erica anxiously, wanting to comfort her friend but knowing she needed to process this information on her own. The last hour had been a whirlwind of revelations as Rowan carefully explained Lance's history of addiction, the financial irregularities at the hospital, and his recent departure for rehab at the board's request.

"I wish I had more answers for you." Rowan's voice brimmed with sadness for Erica and an underlying anger toward Lance. "I didn't want you to find any of this out this way. But I was wrong not to have told you everything before—"

"Before I ended up in the slammer?" Erica sniffled.

Rowan winced at Erica's words. "I'm so sorry, sweetheart. I truly thought your father would have told you about selling the condo. I never imagined–"

"That he'd completely abandon me?" Erica's voice cracked. "God, I feel so stupid. All this time, I thought he was busy with work." Erica's eyes welled with fresh tears. "I still haven't taken a shower. I need to do that and then sleep."

"That sounds like a good idea," Rowan encouraged. "Have you eaten?"

Simone recognized Rowan's behavior toward Erica as going into *mother hen* mode, the same as she had two years ago when Erica had food poisoning. It was an endearing trait, especially since the woman could be so intimidating at work. Maternal instincts weren't necessarily something most people would have associated with Rowan the hospital administrator, but seeing her concern for Erica now, even in the face of hostility, warmed Simone's heart.

"I can't. My stomach—" Erica swirled a hand in the air. "Sleep. I'm so tired."

Simone showed Erica to the bathroom, setting out clean towels and a shirt and shorts to sleep in since the police had not yet returned Erica's luggage.

Back in the living room, Simone was relieved to see Rowan sitting on the couch.

"You're still here." Simone sat next to Rowan but not too close. It was better to be cautious in case Erica emerged unexpectedly. The sound of running water from the bathroom provided a temporary sense of privacy.

"Yep, I'm still here," Rowan said softly. "I couldn't leave without making sure you're okay with everything that's going on."

"I'm not sure if okay is the right word for it, but I'm adjusting," Simone answered. "How are you holding up?"

Rowan let out a long, shaky breath. "I don't even know. Overwhelmed, I suppose. Angry at Lance for putting Erica through this with all his lies. Worried about what other surprises might be waiting for us." She ran a hand through her red curls.

Simone nearly groaned at the realization that, no matter how much she longed to do so, reaching out and running her fingers through those luxurious tresses was not an option right now. Not with Erica down the hall.

Since comforting Rowan with a touch was out of the question, Simone settled for words. "We'll figure this out. I know it's complicated, but I'm here for you. For both of you."

"This is all my fault—"

"No. Don't do that. This is on Lance. You can't keep covering for that asshole."

"He's not answering my calls, either," Rowan said, anger giving her voice a hard edge. "I've been ringing him nonstop since leaving the police station. I even left a message that Erica had been kicked out of school in Italy and got arrested. Nothing."

Simone inhaled deeply. "Nothing?" Simone's mouth settled into a deep frown. "That's concerning. Even at his worst, I can't imagine Lance not responding to news about Erica."

Rowan nodded, her eyes clouded with worry. "There's more. Do you remember when my mother mentioned Lance making a huge donation to the school in Italy to get Erica into their elite art program?"

Simone's body tensed against whatever Rowan was about to reveal.

"I'll be honest. I'd forgotten all about it or conveniently pushed it out of my head. My mother has a tenuous grasp on facts sometimes. But the other day, I remembered and did some digging. There was a donation, but it didn't come from Lance. It came from the hospital."

"The hospital?" Simone covered her mouth, having spoken too loudly. "Why would the hospital make a donation to an art school in Italy?"

"Why indeed?" Rowan fell against the couch. "The more I find out, the more I'm afraid of what I'll discover next. What else has Lance done? Where's the bottom of this shit storm?"

Simone wanted to pull Rowan into an embrace, but any second, Erica could stroll out of the bathroom. She settled for placing her hand next to Rowan's on the couch, their pinkies barely touching. She had no doubt the anguish and desire that gripped her heart showed plainly on her face. She could see it reflected in Rowan's eyes, too.

"What are we going to do?" Rowan whispered, jerking her head in Erica's direction. "About us?"

"She can't find out. Not now."

"You're right," Rowan whispered back. "It would devastate her. But where does that leave us? We already have to hide at work. Having Erica back on the Cape is only going to complicate things."

"Especially if she's living in my house," Simone added. "Or yours."

"Fuck." Rowan looked as though she was on the verge of tears.

"I don't have all the answers right now." Simone moved closer, willing to risk it to feel Rowan's warmth for a second. "But I know this. I'm not going to lose you, Rowan. We'll figure things out together."

The shower turned off, causing Simone and Rowan to pull apart.

"Together?" Rowan asked in a hushed voice, hope and fear battling for dominance over her expression.

"One hundred percent together."

"I wish we could go back to P-town," Rowan murmured, her eyes filled with longing. "Everything was so much simpler."

Simone nodded, feeling a pang of nostalgia for their brief escape. It had only been hours, but it felt like a lifetime ago. "We will. Soon."

Rowan stood. "I better go. I'll keep trying Lance. I don't know what he's up to, but keeping my head buried in the sand isn't the solution."

Simone watched as Rowan gathered her things, her heart aching with the desire to embrace her, to offer comfort and reassurance. But it was too risky. Simone feared it might always be. What would happen then?

CHAPTER SIXTEEN

"Look what you've reduced me to." Rowan rested her forehead against Simone's, breathing in the faint smell of cleaning supplies in the dark, enclosed space. "Making out in the janitor's closet like a naughty teenager." Rowan leaned in for another kiss, savoring the softness of Simone's lips against hers.

"I never did this when I was a teenager," Simone confessed. "I was much too serious. Maybe because I knew I needed a scholarship if I was going to become a doctor."

"You've come so far."

Simone nudged a water bucket on the floor with her foot. "Oh yes. So far."

Rowan quietly chuckled. "You know what I mean. Here you are, saving lives and stealing hearts. In supply closets."

"Just one heart."

They kissed again, lingering before Rowan let out a sigh. "You better sneak out of here first. I'll wait a couple of minutes so no one spots me."

Simone heaved an anguished breath. "Fine, but we need to find a way to have more than a few minutes together. I love

Erica, but sharing my house with her makes privacy a thing of the past."

"Agreed." Rowan sealed the promise with a kiss before giving Simone a light nudge toward the door. "Go on, now. Miss you already."

"Ditto." Simone gave a half-smile that was just visible as she cracked the door open, but the sadness in her eyes was clear to see.

After the door closed, Rowan leaned against the shelving unit behind her, closing her eyes to savor the lingering warmth of Simone's touch and the faint scent of jasmine that hung in the air. The thrill of their stolen moment was tempered by a twinge of guilt over the secrecy of their relationship. Rowan knew they couldn't keep sneaking around like this forever, but the thought of going public sent a shiver of anxiety through her. There was so much at stake. Her position at the hospital, her fragile relationship with Erica, even her newfound sense of identity, could be impacted in ways that were impossible to predict.

Rowan began to count silently to one hundred. She'd reached thirty-two when the closet door suddenly swung open, flooding the small space with harsh fluorescent light. Rowan's eyes flew open, her heart leaping into her throat as she jumped into action, pretending to look for... *something*.

"I knew it!" Candace stood in the doorway, wearing a triumphant grin that didn't bode well for Rowan. "Exactly what do you think you're doing in here, Dr. Colchester?"

"Looking for bleach."

Candace stared her down with a look that said she wasn't buying it for a second. "Bleach? In your suit and heels? Try again, honey."

Rowan's face flushed hot with embarrassment. She straightened her spine, attempting to regain some composure and maybe a shred of dignity. "Yes, bleach. For my toilet, if you must know."

"The toilet at your home?" Candace crossed her arms, leaning her shoulder against the doorframe.

"No. The bathroom next to my office. It's disgusting."

"Uh-huh. Since when did it become the job of hospital administration to scrub the toilets?"

"We're short-staffed. You may have heard." Rowan picked up a random bottle of bleach, having no clue what she was going to do with it but determined to keep her ruse going as long as possible.

Candace rolled her eyes and lowered her voice. "Girl, please. I saw Simone come out of here looking all flushed and guilty. You can drop the act."

Rowan was about to deny it, but it was pointless. Defeat was inevitable. "My office," she snapped. "Now."

"Don't forget your bleach. You want me to help you clean that nasty toilet on the way?"

"Watch it, or I will assign you to scrub every toilet in this hospital, Dr. Mitchell," Rowan muttered as she brushed past Candace, still clutching the bottle of bleach.

"Yes, ma'am." Candace touched her fingers to her forehead in a salute that dripped with sarcasm.

They walked in tense silence to Rowan's office, Candace's knowing smirk a sharp contrast to Rowan's tight-lipped frown. She'd always imagined the walk of shame coming home from a one-night stand was the most humiliating thing a person could experience, but that was before one of her closest friends and colleagues had caught her red-handed in a supply closet. Thank God it had been Candace and not someone else who had discovered her. Rowan still felt like a kid being marched to the principal's office. Her cheeks burned as she strode down the hallway, painfully aware of every curious glance from passing staff members.

Once safely inside Rowan's office with the door closed, Candace pumped a fist in the air. "Hell yeah. Who's the best matchmaker on the planet? I'm expecting a big Christmas gift from you this year, just so you know."

"As a bribe to keep you quiet?"

"As a thank you for setting you and Simone up on that blind date at the bar over the summer." Candace waited a beat before breaking into a grin. "Ha. You're not denying it."

"Why bother? I know when I'm beat. Besides, what I really need is to focus on damage control." Rowan sank into her chair, setting the bottle of bleach on her desk with a thud. She rubbed her temples, feeling a headache coming on. "This can't get out. Not yet."

Candace's playful demeanor softened as she took a seat across from Rowan. "Hey, I get it. Your secret's safe with me. But can I ask why you're so worried about people finding out? It's not the lesbian thing, is it? Because in my experience, Marbury Hospital has been a fairly welcoming environment."

"No, it's not that," Rowan said, shaking her head. "I mean, yes, I'm apprehensive about my private affairs becoming fodder for public gossip. But it's more complicated than that. The power imbalance, for one thing."

"Simone's a thirty-two-year-old woman, not some first-year resident. And she's not even your direct report. There are plenty of layers of bureaucracy between the two of you to insulate you from any real ethics concerns."

"That might be true, but it won't stop the gossips, will it? What if Simone gets a promotion?"

"She should get a promotion. She's damn good at her job. But," Candace blew out a breath, "I see your point. Doesn't help that she's a woman, either. Everyone takes so much more glee from tearing women apart than they do men."

"Exactly."

"Still, you're in charge. Meaning you set the rules."

"Yes, but you're missing the biggest issue."

Candace leaned closer. "Your dad? I know he's pretty set in his ways."

"He won't be happy, of course. But only because no one can ever replace his precious Lance. I was thinking of Erica."

"Why would Erica care? She barely speaks to you. Even though you got her a job at the hospital gift shop."

"I had nothing to do with that," Rowan said automatically, even though it was untrue.

"Yeah, right. The kid who got arrested for breaking into her father's old condo managed to land a job here at the hospital less than a week later, all on her own."

"Miracles do happen," Rowan said with a shrug. "As for the arrest, once the new condo owners understood everything, they opted to drop the charges without even needing to be persuaded. There won't be any repercussions for Erica, thankfully."

"Just once in my life, I'd like to be a spoiled rich kid and have all my troubles disappear like that." Candace snapped her fingers. "But back to the issue at hand, you're probably overthinking it. I can't imagine Erica's homophobic."

"You're forgetting Erica and Simone are college friends."

"Shit. I did forget that detail." Candace had the decency to look properly horrified, which Rowan appreciated. "That's actually how Simone ended up here—not that we wouldn't have hired her, anyway, but Lance kinda strong-armed us into taking her on, sight unseen." Her shoulders fell. "I'm starting to see why you're worried. Erica might feel betrayed if she finds out her friend is dating her ex-stepmother."

"I divorced Lance, not her. Erica will always be family to me." Rowan massaged her forehead. "How did my life get so complicated? And what do you mean Lance strong-armed you into hiring Simone?"

Candace shifted uncomfortably in her seat. "You know how Lance can be when he sets his mind to something. He called in every favor he had, pulled every string. Said Simone was this brilliant doctor who'd save our ER. Which, to be fair, she is. But he ran this place like it was his own personal fiefdom, and your father never said a word."

Rowan's jaw clenched at the mention of Lance's mismanagement. "That's not even the half of it. Did you know Lance had the hospital rent him a luxury apartment in Boston for those times he attended conferences and meetings in the city? Not on a short-term basis, like an Airbnb, but an actual lease. In fact, the hospital is still paying rent on it that we can ill-afford."

"How many times did he have to go to Boston on business?"

"Not nearly enough to justify it. Also..." Rowan hesitated before asking, "You know about that man who died of a heart attack in the lobby back in August, right?"

"Of course," Candace shifted in her chair, her brow furrowed. "That was an unthinkable tragedy."

"And, unfortunately, not an isolated one." Rowan's lips tightened into a thin line. "I've been digging into the records of patient deaths for the past five years, and there was a sharp uptick in preventable deaths and adverse outcomes in the last three years."

"Three years?" Candace's eyes widened as she made the connection. "Right around the time you told him you wanted a divorce."

Rowan nodded grimly. "That didn't escape my thoughts, either. I'm not saying there's a direct correlation, but the timing is hard to ignore. It's almost as if Lance stopped caring about anything once our marriage fell apart. I feel so—"

Candace held her hand up to stop Rowan. "Don't even think about blaming yourself for Lance's actions. The man is a grown adult, and you are not responsible for his choices or behavior."

Rowan sighed heavily, her shoulders sagging. "Logically, I get that. But emotionally, it's a different story. Can I ask you to do something for me?"

"Hunt down Lance and smother him with a pillow in his sleep?" Candace volunteered. "Consider it done."

Rowan laughed despite herself. "As tempting as that is, no. I need you to take a closer look at a few of the files from the preventable deaths I identified. I'm trying to determine if the hospital could be vulnerable, but a lot of the doctors and nurses involved are no longer here. I could really use the perspective of someone I trust, who was here when it happened and knows the people involved."

Candace lifted her chin, taking in the gravity of Rowan's request. "Yes, I can do that. But you do realize if there's a pattern of negligence or malpractice, it could open up the hospital to some serious liability issues, right? Are you sure you want to open this can of worms? It could get ugly fast."

Rowan's gaze remained steady as she met Candace's concerned eyes. "I know the risks, but I can't in good conscience sweep this under the rug. If there's a systemic problem at this hospital that's putting patients at risk, we have an ethical and moral obligation to identify it and correct it. No matter how painful it is."

"I don't envy your position."

"Are you talking about my professional life or my personal one?"

"Honestly? Both," Candace said with a sympathetic smile. "But I've got your back, no matter what. I'll take a look at those files and let you know what I find out." She stood up to leave but paused at the door. "Don't beat yourself up over this. You have a tendency to take too much responsibility for things. Guilt is overrated."

Rowan gave Candace a grateful nod as she left the office, then fell back in her chair with a heavy sigh. She glanced at the bottle of bleach still sitting on her desk and shook her head ruefully. If only this were the type of mess she could clean up with a scrub brush and some elbow grease.

"Holy shit." Rowan tilted her head upward to take in the glass skyscraper in which Lance had apparently been staying on his trips to Boston for the past several years.

Simone whistled. "This is definitely not the kind of place I'd expect the hospital to be renting."

"No kidding," Rowan agreed. "This is prime city real estate. You should've seen the dump I lived in when I was working at Boston General. Even as CMO, no way would I be able to rent a place like this."

"Are you saying your glamorous title isn't all it's cracked up to be?" Simone teased, her sparkling laughter putting Rowan more at ease than she had been in weeks.

They entered the building and proceeded to the desk near the elevator, where a uniformed concierge greeted them with a polite smile.

"Good afternoon, ladies. How may I assist you today?"

Rowan stepped forward, projecting an air of confidence far exceeding what she actually felt. "We're here to access apartment 1407. I'm Dr. Rowan Colchester, Chief Medical Officer at Marbury Hospital. We're conducting an internal audit and need to inspect the property. I called ahead."

"Yes, of course," the concierge said with a nod, his polite smile never wavering. "Please sign here, and I'll provide you with the key."

Rowan's signature came out a shaky scrawl. She could blame it on being a doctor—bad penmanship being almost a requirement in her line of work—but the truth was, her mind was racing with possibilities of what they might find in Lance's apartment. Drugs? Evidence he'd had a secret mistress?

What if Lance was staying in the apartment right now, and they walked in on him in his underwear?

The elevator doors slid open, and Rowan stepped inside,

Simone close behind. As she pressed the button for the fourteenth floor, Rowan's stomach churned with anxiety.

"Have I ever told you what a turn on it is when you use your sexy boss voice?" Simone asked, her eyes glued to the floor numbers above the door as they lit up one by one.

"Boss voice?"

"You know, like you did when talking to that concierge. All authoritative and in charge," Simone clarified, a sly smile playing on her lips. "It's hot."

A flush crept up Rowan's neck. "I'm glad someone appreciates my professional demeanor. Most people find it cold and intimidating."

"You're anything but cold," Simone murmured. The elevator door opened, and they stepped out onto plush carpeting that muffled the sound of their footsteps. "1407 is down that way. Come on."

Simone held Rowan's hand as they walked down the long hallway. Rowan's heart pounded as they approached the door. She paused before inserting the key into the lock.

"Do you remember that first night when we met at The Driftwood Lounge and you took me back to your place?" Simone's voice was low and seductive with a sultry quality that sent a shiver down Rowan's spine.

Rowan slanted her head toward Simone, the attraction so palpable between them she almost forgot why they were there. "How could I forget?"

"This feels a bit like that night. The anticipation, the nervousness..." Simone's finger traced along Rowan's arm from elbow to wrist, leaving goose bumps in its wake. "The fact you're trying to put the key into the lock upside down right now." Simone took the key and flipped it round, easily inserting it into the lock. "Doors are hard," she said with a giggle.

"I guess I'm not exactly nailing the sexy boss lady vibe right now." Rowan chuckled softly, grateful for Simone's attempt to lighten the mood.

"I don't know. I'd still fuck you."

"Simone!" Rowan sent furtive glances down the hallway in both directions, as if expecting to see someone they knew. "We're supposed to be here on official business."

"Sorry," Simone said, not looking sorry at all. "But it's been weeks since I've seen you naked. If this keeps up, I'm going to lose my mind."

Rowan smiled despite herself. "I know, I know. We'll figure something out soon. I promise. But right now, we need to focus."

With a deep breath, Rowan turned the key and pushed the door inward. The apartment was dark and silent, the air stale with disuse. Rowan fumbled for a light switch. "Ugh, we should open some windows."

Simone nodded, her eyes scanning the open space. "Doesn't look like anyone has been here for a while."

"It's surprisingly clean," Simone commented. "Given the state of Lance's office when you first took over, I expected the worst. It was pretty clear he was falling apart."

"The lease includes professional cleaning and maintenance," Rowan said, unable to keep the anger out of her voice. "Can you believe that?"

"Must be nice," Simone commented, her eyes scanning the space. She opened a cupboard in the kitchen, revealing a set of neatly stacked dishes in utilitarian white. "What exactly are we looking for? Because it's pretty bare in here."

"I think I see a laptop on the desk over there. He must have left a spare to use when he was here." Rowan crossed the room to the sleek glass desk tucked in the corner. A slim silver laptop sat closed on its surface. Her hand hovered over the lid, hesitating. "I'm not sure I want to know what's on it."

"Porn?" Simone suggested with a grin. "Maybe he has the good stuff."

Rowan shot Simone a withering look, even as her clit began to tap out signals in Morse code. Simone wasn't the only one who was feeling the effects of their prolonged separation. But now was not the moment to indulge those impulses. One of them was going to have to be grown-up about this, hard as it would be.

"I was thinking more along the lines of financial records or correspondence that might explain why he felt the need to squander so much of the hospital's money."

"That makes more sense than porn, I guess," Simone said, her wide grin not faltering in the slightest.

Rowan opened the laptop, plugging in the charger before powering it on. The screen flickered to life, revealing a login prompt. "Damn. It's password protected. He'd become so lax with everything, I was almost hoping he'd forgotten about security."

Simone peered over Rowan's shoulder. "Any ideas what it might be?"

Rowan thought for a moment. "Wanna bet he uses the same password as the one we shared years ago?"

"He's not that stupid, is he?"

Rowan sat down at the desk and started typing. "It's Erica's name and her birthday, only he uses an exclamation point for the letter I, and her name is spelled with a K instead of a C."

"Yes, that will fool the criminal masterminds," Simone scoffed.

Rowan's fingers hovered over the keyboard as she entered the familiar password, instantly unlocking the screen.

"Unbelievable," Simone muttered, shaking her head. "He really didn't change it after all these years."

"He can be very predictable about some things," Rowan said, "even while being completely inscrutable in others."

There were only a few apps installed, including a popular messaging app Rowan recognized but hadn't realized Lance used. She clicked on the icon, revealing a long list of conversations. Most were innocuous work-related exchanges, but one thread caught her eye. The contact was simply labeled *Honey*.

Simone stood behind her, head resting on Rowan's shoulder as she hovered over the thread with the mouse.

"Is it weird that the one and only place where I'm not worried about anyone discovering us is in your ex-husband's apartment?" Simone asked with a snort.

"Our lives are interesting these days."

"Understatement."

Rowan's finger hovered over the mouse button, her heart pounding. "I'm not sure I want to read this."

"We came here for answers," Simone pointed out. "The messages are right there. They might be important."

Rowan steeled her nerve, clicking on the message thread. As soon as she saw Honey's profile photo, she knew they were onto something. "It's her. Look at that photo. It's the same woman who's in all the photos in his office."

"So he was dating someone?"

"Apparently." As if compelled to start reading from the very beginning, Rowan scrolled all the way to the top of the messages, rolling her eyes when she saw the first line. "You've gotta be kidding me. She literally started the conversation by saying *hello handsome*. How cliche."

Rowan scrolled through the messages, her brow furrowing deeper with each exchange. The conversation started innocently enough, with flirtatious banter and compliments. It quickly escalated to include many of the racy photos she'd found in his office. But as she read on, a disturbing pattern emerged.

"Oh, Lance," Rowan sighed, shaking her head. "She's telling him she has a sick grandmother who needs an expensive surgery."

Simone leaned in closer, her eyes scanning the messages. "Let me guess. She needs money for it?"

"Huh." Rowan read the passage in question a second time. "No. He even offers, the fool, but she turns him down. A little bit later, she claims she came into some money."

"Oh shit. It's textbook."

Rowan's heart clenched at Simone's tone, even though she didn't understand. "What do you mean?"

"He's being catfished. More than likely by some man halfway around the world who's using stock photos of a model and passing them off as real. I read an article about this not too long ago. The scammer starts off with the sex angle and then builds trust by bringing up some story about needing money, knowing the mark will expect them to ask for a loan or something. But they don't ask."

"I don't get it. What's the point if they don't ask for money?"

"Keep reading. Does she say how she got the money for the surgery?"

Rowan's eyes scanned quickly before landing on the answer. "Right here. She mentions it was an investment that paid off."

"Yep." Simone gave a cynical laugh. "A magical investment that not only saved her dear, old grandmother from certain death but also made her fabulously rich in the process."

"Still not understanding."

"People will only part with so much money in the name of charity, but when it comes to personal enrichment, the sky's the limit. Here." Simone tapped the laptop screen. "She's saying she can't tell him about the investment because the people in charge don't want to invite anyone unless they trust them. Keep scrolling. I bet he trips all over himself as he tells her personal information that makes it clear exactly how much money he has access to."

"You're absolutely right. The idiot." Rowan ran her finger

down the screen like she had in medical school, speed reading. "Here it is. She finally invites him into the inner circle. He, too, can be fabulously wealthy if he just so happens to have ten thousand dollars to buy into the next round. Which she had to have known was chump change for him."

Simone exhaled. "Gotta start gentle."

Rowan's heart sank. "Oh my God. He fell for it, didn't he?"

Simone nodded grimly. "Hook, line, and sinker, from the looks of it. Keep going. I bet it gets worse. From what I read, these crooks set up a fake account where the marks can see how much they're supposedly earning on their investment. It looks totally legit, and the returns are beyond what even the best investment firms can achieve. They get looped into investing more and more because they're greedy little fuckers, and they think they're winning the lottery. It's not until they go to make a withdrawal that they realize it's all fake."

Rowan's stomach churned as she scrolled through more messages. The pattern became painfully clear—Lance investing larger and larger sums, his excitement growing with each supposed return. In reality, it was the picture of a man spiraling deeper and deeper into financial ruin.

"Jesus Christ, this is bad," Rowan muttered. "Really bad. Look at these amounts. This is beyond even the worst of his gambling debts."

"Look at this." Simone pointed to a message dating back to the beginning of the year. "She says, 'I can explain but only in person. Meet me tomorrow at the ferry.' I bet she didn't show."

"You're right. Here's an apology and an excuse, followed by another proposed meetup. This goes on for months." Rowan continued scrolling through the messages, her heart sinking further with each exchange. "There are dozens of meetings that never materialized and increasingly desperate pleas from Lance to give him access to his supposed investment returns."

The last message—written all in caps—nearly stopped Rowan's heart.

WHERE'S MY MONEY, BITCH?!?!?!?!

Rowan shut the laptop, muttering, "Lance, you imbecile."

"How much do you think they took?" Simone's quivering voice matched Rowan's worry.

"Everything, I'm guessing."

"This is why he hasn't told Erica anything."

"He's humiliated." Rowan sucked in a deep breath. "And desperate. I'm afraid he's dragged the hospital into his mess, too."

Simone wrapped her arms around Rowan. "It's going to be okay."

Rowan wanted to believe her, but a gnawing in the pit of her stomach wouldn't go away. She needed to speak with Lance, which would be bad enough, given their history. But even worse, she was going to have to talk to her father.

CHAPTER SEVENTEEN

"All I want is a cup of tea and some quiet," Simone said to no one in particular as she unlocked her door after a particularly grueling shift. One hour of nothingness—no sick patients, no screaming family members, no harried coworkers—none of that for sixty minutes. After that, she could go to Rowan's house for dinner a completely new woman.

As soon as she stepped inside, Simone's heart plummeted.

Next to the couch where Erica slept, a pile of bedding had been tossed on the floor. Clothing was haphazardly placed on all available surfaces, including a few stray pieces that had made their way into a vase. Not Simone's vase, but Marigold's, which meant it was probably worth more than Simone's beater of a car.

Simone carefully extricated the items—three socks, the fourth of which was nowhere in sight—from the vase before taking it to her bedroom. It had been almost three weeks since Erica had arrived back in Marbury, and Simone had yet to adjust to sharing the already cramped space with another person. She'd known letting Erica stay would be challenging, but she hadn't anticipated quite this level of disruption. She loved Erica like a sister, but the chaos of her extended stay was wearing thin.

Returning to the kitchen, Simone filled the kettle, putting it on its electric base and flipping the on switch. She opened the cupboard only to discover another issue. All the mugs were either in the sink or scattered, dirty, around the room. Simone's blood reached its boiling point faster than her tea.

Had Erica grown up with servants? It was like the woman had never seen the inside of a dishwasher.

"Don't lose it. Don't lose it. Don't lose it," Simone chanted.

"Who are you talking to?" Erica appeared as if by magic, nearly making Simone jump out of her skin.

"Jesus!" Simone exclaimed, clutching her chest.

"Cool. Tell him I said hi." Erica grinned, but Simone couldn't muster a smile in return. Erica's grin faded as she took in Simone's expression. "Tough day?" At least there was genuine concern etched into the crinkles around Erica's eyes, which partially made up for the state of the house.

"You could say that." Simone grabbed a mug and swiped the inside with a soapy sponge. "I thought you were apartment hunting."

"I was." Erica's eyes fell to the ground. "Turns out not many landlords want to take a chance on a kid who works part-time without any money socked away in savings."

Should Simone point out that, at the age of twenty-eight, Erica hardly qualified as a kid anymore? Probably not. Even though she was personally irked by the situation, Simone understood Erica's entire life had been tossed upside down by her father's irresponsible behavior.

And Erica didn't even know the half of it.

Simone softened her expression and gestured toward the kettle. "Want some tea? I plan to have a cup outside. It's a beautiful evening."

"That sounds nice. Let me get a mug."

Instead of going toward the cupboard, Erica picked up a dirty mug from the far end of the counter, handing it to Simone.

On the one hand, at least she'd known there weren't any clean ones in the cupboard, which showed some basic awareness of the state of the kitchen. On the other hand, it meant she'd been aware of the mess and done nothing about it. Simone bit her tongue and washed the second mug. Honestly, she was too tired to try to correct Erica's behavior. Simone would have to find a way to address the issue later, when she was rested and better able to do so without screaming or breaking down in tears. Probably both would happen if she attempted now.

As Simone settled onto the porch swing, steaming tea in hand, she felt some of her tension dissipate. The evening air held the crisp hint of fall, and though it wasn't overly late, only a hair past six o'clock, the sun was almost gone. In another few weeks, the days would be noticeably shorter, most of the shops would close for the season, and the Cape would start to feel truly deserted. For now, though, it was perfect.

Simone took a sip of her tea, letting the warmth spread through her. She glanced at Erica, who was staring pensively into her mug. The younger woman's usual vibrant energy seemed subdued, and it was clear there was more on Erica's mind than the frustration of looking for a place to live.

"You know," Erica began hesitantly, "I've been thinking a lot about Rowan lately."

Simone's pulse quickened at the mention of Rowan's name. She took another sip of tea to hide her reaction. "Oh?" she said, aiming for a casual tone.

Erica nodded, her gaze still fixed on her mug. "I've been... I don't know, reevaluating, I guess. The way I've treated her, the assumptions I've made."

Simone's eyebrows rose in surprise. This was unexpected, considering how vehemently Erica had railed against Rowan for the past three years, ever since the divorce. She waited, giving Erica space to continue.

Erica set the cup down on the arm of the Adirondack chair.

"Do you think Rowan really bought the beach house because of me?"

"That's what she said." Of course, Simone knew for a fact that was the case. Rowan had told Simone all about it when they'd gone to Provincetown together. But she couldn't really explain how she'd come to have a heart-to-heart talk with Erica's stepmother without revealing the true nature of their relationship. "Why do you ask?"

Erica sighed, running a hand through her hair. "I've been thinking about how quick I was to blame her for everything. I immediately sided with Dad without even considering Rowan's perspective. But now, with what I'm discovering about my dad, I don't know. I keep replaying the things I've said to Rowan and how I've acted." Erica turned to look Simone in the eyes, her expression troubled. "Be honest with me. Am I the jerk in this situation?"

Yes, Simone wanted to shout, or at least the part of her that was loyal to Rowan. But Simone also cared about Erica and knew the situation was far more complex than some random post in an *Am I the Asshole* Reddit thread.

Simone inhaled, weighing her words carefully. "I don't know if it's that simple. I think you've been told selective things by your father, and that may have tainted your impression of your stepmom." Simone refrained from stating unequivocally that Lance Donovan had lied to his daughter for the purpose of turning her against her stepmother, but she knew in her heart it was true.

"I'm so angry with him." Erica's voice came out in a sob. "He's ruined everything."

Simone set down her mug, reaching out to put an arm on Erica's shoulder. "I know. It's okay to be angry."

Erica leaned into Simone, her body shaking with quiet sobs. "I feel so stupid. I believed everything he ever told me without question."

"He's your father." Simone rubbed Erica's back. "It's natural to want to believe him."

Erica sniffled, dabbing her eyes with the sleeve of her shirt. "But I should have known better. How much of what he said to me about Rowan was a lie? I mean, she always treated me like I was her own flesh and blood. Meanwhile, he let me head off to Italy without breathing a word that there might be trouble with my tuition payment. How could he do that to me?"

"I have absolutely no idea." Simone wanted to tell Erica everything she knew about Lance's deception and Rowan's true character, but it wasn't her place. This was something Erica needed to work through on her own.

"I'm scared." Eric's voice trembled. "I'm completely on my own. I've been applying for jobs at some of the art galleries, but they keep telling me to come back in the summer. No one's hiring for the off season. Not even for the upcoming holidays. I don't know when I'll be able to get my shit together."

Simone offered a sympathetic smile, not knowing what to say. By the time Simone had been Erica's age, she'd finished medical school and was well into her residency. But comparing their paths wouldn't be helpful. While Erica was a grown woman, she had been sheltered from many of life's harsher realities. This sudden upheaval in her world was clearly taking its toll.

"You'll figure it out." Simone gave Erica's shoulder a squeeze. "These things take time. And you're not alone. You've got me, and I'm sure Rowan would be there for you, too, if you reached out to her."

"I'm not sure I'm ready for that," Erica said, her voice steadier now. "I know having me here isn't ideal, but I really am trying."

"I understand—" Before Simone could say anything else, Poppy zipped across the shadow-filled lawn.

"I'm a fairy cowgirl!" the little girl called out.

Simone took in Poppy's dress, fairy wings, and red cowgirl boots with delight. "You sure are!"

Running beside her, Oscar the puppy yapped at Poppy as the two turned in circles on the grass.

Marigold came across from her house, taking a seat in a chair next to Simone. "Poppy's trying on Halloween costumes," she explained. "This is the fourth one today. She'll go through another fifty before the big day arrives."

"She takes the holiday seriously," Erica commented.

"It's basically her religion." Marigold laughed, watching Poppy roll on the grass with Oscar kissing her face. "Little girls and their dogs. Is there anything more special in the world."

"It'd make a great painting." Erica pulled out her phone, snapping a photo. Sheepishly, she added, "I'm an artist."

"Is that right? What kind of art do you do?" Marigold asked, her interest piqued.

Erica tucked a strand of hair behind her ear, suddenly looking shy. "Mostly mixed media and collage. I love working with texture and layers."

"She's been trying to land a job at a gallery," Simone explained. "But she's been striking out."

Marigold's eyes lit up. "This might be your lucky day. I've been meaning to organize my art collection for ages. It's quite extensive, and it's gotten completely out of hand. I could use someone with a keen eye and artistic knowledge to help catalog and arrange everything.

Erica sat upright in her seat. "I worked at a gallery in Italy over the summer and have experience with cataloging collections. I know my life's a mess in a lot of ways, but there's one thing I know, and that's art."

"Honey, my life has been a mess since the day I popped into this world. That's simply life. Everyone I've met has a story." Marigold spoke like a woman who'd not only been through the wars and made it out successfully but had helped many others along the way.

The two chatted about Erica's time in Italy. As the minutes ticked by, Simone stole glances at her watch, her agitation growing. She was already past due at Rowan's for dinner, but how to extricate herself without having to offer an explanation? Each second pressed down on Simone, increasing the anxiety in her chest like an inflating balloon.

Just as Simone was about to make up an excuse about needing to run errands, Marigold stood up. "We should get some dinner. How about I place a call for Chinese?"

"Sounds great. I'm starving," Erica said in agreement.

"Simone?" Marigold boosted her eyebrows.

"Wish I could, but I promised I'd swing by the hospital to complete some paperwork." As she jumped to her feet, the lie curdled inside Simone.

"You work too much," Marigold admonished, making Simone feel even guiltier. She hated not being honest with Erica and Marigold, but the thought of seeing Rowan pushed all other concerns aside.

OUT OF AN ABUNDANCE OF CAUTION, Simone parked her car two blocks over from Rowan's place. It was a plan they'd discussed and agreed on to avoid Simone's car being spotted in the driveway by a nosy neighbor or unexpected visitor dropping by. It was a smart move, but it only made Simone feel like a criminal sneaking around. Unfortunately, the alternative—being open about their relationship—simply wasn't an option. Neither their work situation nor Erica made it possible at the moment. But would there ever come a time when they could be?

Simone hurried down the quiet street, the evening shadows making her feel even more furtive. As she approached Rowan's house, she felt a familiar flutter of excitement and apprehension in her stomach. Before she had a chance to knock on the door, Rowan opened it, a look of relief washing over her face.

"There you are," Rowan breathed, pulling Simone inside and into her arms. "I was starting to worry."

Simone melted into the embrace, inhaling Rowan's familiar scent. "I'm so, so sorry. Erica and I got to talking, and then Marigold joined. It turned into a thing, but Marigold might be hiring Erica to help with an art collection. She's beating herself up—"

Rowan stopped Simone mid-sentence by capturing her lips in a tender kiss. Simone's worries melted away as she sank into the warmth of Rowan's embrace. When they finally parted, Rowan's eyes sparkled with affection. "Sorry, but I needed to do that."

"I'm glad you did." Simone pressed her forehead to Rowan's, feeling the tension of the day finally begin to dissipate. "I've been looking forward to this all day."

"Me too," Rowan replied, her fingers tracing gentle patterns on Simone's back. "We finally have some us time."

"Dinner isn't ruined, is it?"

"Not at all," Rowan reassured her, leading Simone toward the kitchen. "I kept everything warm. We can eat whenever you're ready."

"It smells wonderful."

"It's nothing fancy," Rowan said with modesty, though Simone couldn't help noticing the kitchen table had been set with real china and a bottle of wine sat out along with a corkscrew and two wineglasses.

"Anything that doesn't involve a takeout container on my sofa might as well be a gourmet meal," Simone pointed out with a laugh.

"While I don't have much time to cook, I enjoy it when I can," Rowan said. "Do you want a glass of wine?"

"Probably not," Simone answered with regret. "I'll have to drive home later. Work in the ER long enough and you see too many results of bad choices to be willing to make them yourself."

"Wise decision." There was a hint of melancholy in Rowan's tone, as if the thought of Simone leaving made her sad. At least, Simone hoped that was the case, because she certainly felt that way. "How was your day?" Rowan busied herself with serving the food, placing a tender fillet of salmon on each plate along with a spoonful of roasted vegetables.

"Long, but it's getting better." Simone pushed up her sleeves. "What can I help with?"

"Everything's taken care of," Rowan assured her. "Have a seat at the table."

"Okay, but I'm in charge of the dishes." Even as she said this, Simone sank into the chair, grateful to be off her feet.

"I won't argue with that." Rowan winked at Simone as she joined her at the table.

"This is nice, isn't it?" The aroma of the perfectly cooked salmon made Simone's mouth water, and as she lifted the fork, a wave of contentment overcame her. This was what she'd been craving all day.

Rowan picked up her fork and knife. "It is. Not that I miss living with Lance in the slightest, but I do miss the act of eating dinner with another person instead of staring at a screen."

"It's the little things in life." Simone forked in the bite, letting out a moan as the flavors burst in her mouth. "You might never get rid of me—"

"Rowan?" The unmistakable sound of Erica's voice calling out from the entryway caused Simone's heart to leap into her throat.

Simone froze, fork suspended in midair, as panic gripped her. Rowan's eyes widened in alarm.

"Quick," Rowan whispered with urgency. "Hide!"

Without hesitation, Simone jumped to her feet, ready to bolt. Only the lack of an obvious escape route kept her rooted in place. Her eyes darted around the kitchen, searching for a hiding spot.

"The pantry," Rowan whispered. "Grab your plate and silverware."

Simone took everything, making it into the tight space right before she heard Erica's voice say, "There you are. Am I interrupting?"

"Not at all," Rowan replied, her tone even and not betraying any hint of being flustered. "Are you hungry?"

"No, I just ate."

There was silence, bringing Simone's own loud breathing to her attention. Could they hear her in the other room?

"Sorry for barging in," Erica said, sounding hesitant. Simone could only imagine how awkward the situation must be for her. Of course, that awkwardness would increase exponentially if Erica had any idea that her best friend was hiding a few feet away.

"This is your home, Erica," Rowan said in a gentle tone. "It always has been."

Simone held her breath, straining to hear the conversation between Rowan and Erica. She felt a twinge of guilt for eavesdropping, but there was little else she could do trapped in the pantry.

"I... I wanted to talk to you," Erica said, tripping over her words. "I don't know how to say this, so I'm going to jump right in. I'm sorry I've been such an asshole."

"Don't say that." Rowan's voice was thick with emotion. "You don't need—"

"Yes, I do." The rawness of Erica's tone was impossible to miss. "I've been so unfair to you."

Part of Simone wished she could see both women's faces as they inched toward a possible reconciliation. But mostly, she wished she had the magical ability to poof herself out of this pantry. Not simply to avoid detection, but because this was a private conversation between two people she cared about deeply.

"Maybe we should go out to the deck," Rowan suggested, perhaps sensing how uncomfortable Simone was getting in her hiding spot. "It's such a lovely evening."

"Okay," Erica agreed.

"You head out. I'll be right with you. I need to make sure I turned off the oven."

There were retreating footfalls. A moment later, the pantry door opened. Rowan reached for the plate in Simone's hands, her expression apologetic. "If you hurry, you can skirt around to the front door."

Simone nodded, unable to think of a response. What could she possibly say that would make this turn of events okay?

Rowan gave Simone a quick kiss goodbye before retrieving the bottle of wine and two glasses to take with her to the deck.

As Simone crept out of the pantry, her racing heart left her breathless. She tiptoed across the kitchen, acutely aware of every creak beneath her feet. In the living room, she jammed her foot into the leg of the coffee table. She began hopping on one foot, shoving her fist into her mouth to muffle a scream.

It wasn't until she rounded the street and her car came into view that Simone finally allowed herself to breathe. She slumped against the driver's side door, her legs shaky beneath her. The adrenaline that had propelled her through her stealthy escape was fading, leaving her drained and conflicted. She slid into the driver's seat, resting her forehead against the steering wheel.

What had started as a promising, intimate dinner with Rowan had turned into a disaster, spiraling from romantic passion to frantic escape so quickly that Simone's head was still spinning. She sat there for several long moments, trying to process everything.

The irony wasn't lost on Simone that she had fled from the

very conversation she'd been hoping Erica and Rowan would have. She should have been happy Erica was finally reaching out to make amends. Instead, she felt hollow and conflicted. If Rowan and Erica were able to reconcile, it would be wonderful for them. But where would that leave Simone? The complicated dynamics between the three suddenly felt even more tangled and precarious.

Were all the signs pointing to Simone and Rowan calling it quits?

CHAPTER EIGHTEEN

Rowan's thoughts were far away as she pulled her car into the empty parking space next to the mobile clinic. It had been twelve hours since her conversation with Erica had brought about the first real thaw in their relationship in ages. Rowan should have been ecstatic, but the thought of seeing Simone this morning sent her emotions on a roller coaster of dread and anticipation. So much remained uncertain, but there was one thing Rowan knew.

Last night's failed attempt at a date had been a disaster.

All Rowan could see when she closed her eyes was the look of panic on Simone's face, the hasty scramble to hide all traces of her presence before Erica walked in on them and guessed what was going on. It was a stark reminder of the precarious nature of their relationship, always looking over their shoulders, terrified of being discovered.

Rowan knew they needed to talk, to figure out where they stood and what this latest wrinkle meant for their future, but she feared she wouldn't like what Simone had to say. For that matter, Rowan wasn't even sure what she wanted to say about it herself.

Rowan sighed and reached for her bag on the passenger seat. As much as she cared for Simone, as much as she craved those intimate moments together, the constant fear and secrecy were taking their toll. On the one hand, Rowan had never felt so alive as she did when she was with Simone. But they were putting everything on the line for every stolen moment—their careers, their reputations, Rowan's already fragile relationship with Erica.

The situation was impossibly complicated, and Rowan felt like she was being pulled in a dozen different directions at once. Just when she was on the verge of a breakthrough with Erica, it felt like any misstep could spell catastrophe. Rowan wasn't sure her nerves could handle the strain much longer.

With a sigh, she stepped out of her car and made her way up the steps to the mobile clinic. Pablo waited inside at the reception desk, his cheerful smile a welcome sight after her long night of soul-searching.

"Good morning, Dr. Colchester," he said brightly.

"Good morning, Pablo. You seem to be in a good mood."

"That makes one of us in here this morning." He sent a furtive glance toward the closed door of the exam room. "Dr. Doucette arrived about fifteen minutes ago with her own personal storm cloud over her head."

"Really?" Rowan's stomach clenched. She had a feeling she knew exactly what had put Simone in a bad mood. But she bluffed her way through by saying, "Maybe she had a tough night at the hospital."

"Or, like my mom says, maybe she woke up on the wrong side of the bed." Pablo leaned forward, his expression earnest. "When I wake up in a bad mood, you know what I do? I make myself get back under the covers, and then I get out of bed on the other side. It always works."

"It's hard to picture you in a bad mood," Rowan confessed, unable to hold back a laugh at the thought of Pablo's literal interpretation of the expression. "I'll have to remember that trick."

"Maybe you can suggest it to Dr. Doucette, have her give it a try. Life's too short to be grumpy. Ya know what I mean?"

"I do. Let me go talk to her and see if I can improve the situation."

"You're a brave lady." Pablo flashed an encouraging smile.

Rowan did her best to return the gesture before heading toward the exam room. After a pause to steel herself for the conversation to come, she knocked softly on the door.

"Come in," Simone called out, her voice tight.

Rowan stepped inside, closing the door behind her. Simone was standing with her back to the door as she flipped through a patient chart. Her shoulders appeared tense, and she didn't turn around at the sound of Rowan's arrival.

"Good morning," Rowan began, her voice tentative and hard to hear, even in the small space.

"Morning," Simone said curtly, setting the patient chart aside but not turning around.

An uncomfortable silence stretched between them. Rowan's heart ached at the distance, both physical and emotional, that had sprung up seemingly overnight. She took a step closer, wishing Simone would turn around, if only so she could search the woman's face for any hint of warmth or encouragement.

"Look, about last night..." Rowan struggled to figure out where to go from there.

Simone finally turned to face Rowan, her expression guarded. "I don't think now is the time to discuss it, do you?"

"That wasn't how I wanted the night to end." Rowan offered.

"No. It wasn't ideal." Simone's voice was clipped, her blue eyes cool as they met Rowan's.

Rowan swallowed hard, taken aback by Simone's icy

demeanor. She had never seen her like this. "I thought we should talk about what happened. Clear the air."

"There's nothing to clear." Simone turned back to the counter, busying herself with organizing the already tidy supplies. "We both knew the risks we were taking going into this. Last night was a wake-up call."

"A wake-up call?" Rowan didn't like the sound of that one bit. "I know it didn't go as planned. Erica showing up like that caught us both off guard. But I don't want one setback to ruin what we have."

Simone's jaw tightened. "What exactly do we have, Dr. Colchester?"

Rowan flinched at Simone's formality. "Simone, please. Don't do this. Don't shut me out."

"I'm not trying to shut you out," Simone insisted as she crossed her arms defensively over her chest. "I'm trying to be realistic. We were careless last night, and it almost cost us everything."

"But it didn't. We handled it. And it wasn't carelessness, just bad timing."

"Okay, maybe it was bad timing. What about next time? Because there will be a next time, and a time after that." Simone sighed, her shoulders slumping.

Acting on impulse, Rowan came closer, resting a hand on Simone's arm, resisting the urge to hold on for dear life. "I know you're scared. I am, too. But what we have is worth fighting for."

Her icy facade slipping, Simone blinked back tears. "I care about you, Rowan. More than I probably should. But we have to face reality. This—us—it's too risky. For both of our careers, our reputations. And what about Erica? How do you think she would react if she—"

Before Simone could finish her thought, a knock sounded at the door. Rowan's heart leaped into her throat as she took a step away from Simone, panic seizing her at the thought of being caught in another compromising situation. But it was Pablo, poking his head into the room with an apologetic smile.

"Sorry to interrupt, but your first patient is here."

"Thank you, Pablo. You can send her in." Simone's professional mask slipped effortlessly into place. She turned to Rowan, her expression unreadable. "We'll have to finish this conversation later."

"I'll hold you to that," Rowan said, trying to keep her voice light despite the dread settling in the pit of her stomach.

A young woman with a pronounced baby bump came into the exam room. She smiled warmly at Simone and Rowan as she entered.

"Good morning, Fabienne," Simone greeted her. "This is Dr. Colchester. She'll be assisting me today."

"A pleasure to meet you." Rowan shook the young woman's hand, noting the calluses on her palm. Like so many of the patients who visited the mobile clinic, Rowan knew Fabienne likely worked long hours at a physically demanding job to make ends meet.

This was the side of Cape Cod that went unseen, the nearly invisible army of migrant workers and service industry employees whose labor kept the region's tourism economy afloat. It was a side Rowan had rarely glimpsed growing up, insulated by her family's wealth and status. But becoming a doctor had opened her eyes to the struggles and inequalities bubbling under the surface of a place known to most as a vacation paradise for wealthy summer visitors. These were the people Rowan felt most called to serve in her role at Marbury Hospital, and it filled her with pride to be able to provide care to patients like Fabienne, who might otherwise fall through the ever-widening cracks of the healthcare system.

As Simone and the patient switched to conversing in Creole, Rowan hung back, observing their easy rapport with a twinge of envy. Immersed in her job, Simone was the picture of cheerfulness as she guided Fabienne through the standard prenatal check-up, her earlier distress forgotten. Was Simone truly so good at compartmentalizing—a skill every doctor needed to some degree—or was it that the connection between them wasn't meaningful enough to Simone to cause her lasting distress?

Rowan tried to push the troubling thought aside as she took Fabienne's vitals and measurements while Simone reviewed the woman's medical history. Despite the language barrier, Rowan could tell Fabienne had grown to trust Simone over the course of her pregnancy. The young woman visibly relaxed under Simone's care, making Rowan wish for some of the warmth Simone showed her patients instead of the coolness she'd directed at Rowan earlier.

How could so much have changed in a day? Yesterday morning, Rowan had woken up on cloud nine, lost in a haze of love and looking forward to a quiet dinner with Simone, followed by a night spent in each other's arms. It had been the best feeling in the world.

Had been.

"Dr. Colchester, would you mind taking the patient's blood pressure?" Simone's tone was pleasant and professional, the personal issues between them fully compartmentalized. "I'd like to compare your reading to what I'm getting."

Rowan pumped up the blood pressure cuff, listening intently through her stethoscope. "140 over 90. A bit high." She glanced at Simone, who nodded in agreement, her brow furrowed. "Is she seeing an OBGYN? I'd like to see her blood work and urinalysis."

"Fabienne doesn't have a regular doctor," Simone said. "And we're not able to order anything beyond the most basic blood tests through the mobile clinic."

"She really needs proper prenatal care, including an ultra-

THE ANATOMY OF FOREVER

sound. Can you please impress upon her how important it is? She's at risk for preeclampsia, among other things."

Simone turned to Fabienne and switched to Creole to explain the situation, keeping her tone calm and reassuring despite the undercurrent of concern. Fabienne listened intently, her hands folded protectively over her belly.

After a few moments, Simone turned back to Rowan. "I'm going to recommend that Fabienne increase her fluid intake, rest as much as possible, and start a low-dose daily aspirin. We'll need to monitor her closely for the remainder of her pregnancy. Maybe we can source a portable ultrasound machine to keep on hand."

Rowan nodded. "Agreed, but under the circumstances, I would still feel better if she were under the care of one of our maternity specialists at the hospital."

Simone translated for Fabienne, who looked uncertain. After a brief exchange, Simone turned back to Rowan with a sigh. "Fabienne is worried about the cost. And as an undocumented immigrant, she's afraid to go to the hospital, even for check-ups. She knows this clinic is a safe space."

Rowan's heart clenched at the fear in Fabienne's eyes. Having to choose between adequate healthcare, financial security, and personal safety was an impossible situation no one should have to face.

"Please assure her we will do everything in our power to keep her information confidential," Rowan said. "And let her know Marbury has funds set aside to help cover the costs of care for patients in need. We won't turn her away."

Unfortunately, with the precarious state of Marbury Hospital's finances, Rowan wasn't sure how much longer they'd be able to provide free and low-cost services to the community. But that was for her to worry about.

Simone relayed Rowan's assurances to the pregnant woman, her voice soothing and encouraging. Gradually, the apprehension on the patient's face eased into a tentative smile. She nodded and grasped Simone's hand in gratitude.

After finishing up with Fabienne and seeing her out, Simone turned to Rowan, her expression unreadable. "Thank you for backing me up there. I've been concerned about Fabienne since her last visit. She knows you're my boss, and I think hearing everything from you made a difference."

"Of course. It's what we're here for." Rowan added softly, "Simone, about earlier—"

But Simone held up a hand. "Did you hear what I said? You're my boss. And Erica told me last night when she got home that you two are on better footing after your talk. Probably for the first time since you've known her. Do you really want to put that at risk?"

"What are you saying?" Rowan stepped back as if the implication of what Simone was about to express held the pent-up force of a tsunami waiting to be unleashed.

"I can't get a certain thought out of my head." Simone closed her eyes, shutting Rowan out like she was drawing the curtains.

"What thought?" Rowan's entire body tensed, every muscle burning.

"That Erica showing up last night was a sign that we shouldn't..." Simone took a deep, shaky breath. "Maybe it would be best if we ended things now. Before anyone gets hurt."

"No, no, no." Rowan sliced the air with one hand, stating, "No," one more time. "This can't be what you want."

"Of course, it isn't. But I also don't want to be the reason Erica hates you. I can't do that to the two of you."

"What about me?" Rowan added, "How do I factor into all of this?"

"You aren't listening to me."

"I am, but I'm also done shoving all sense of happiness out of my life so I don't rock the boat. When do I matter?"

"Don't you get it? You matter so much to me I can't be the reason why you lose everything. It's not just Erica. It's your job. It's my job. It's my friendship with Erica. This isn't easy."

"Nothing in life is easy."

Before Simone had a chance to respond, Pablo announced the next patient. Both Simone and Rowan put on brave faces, focusing on the mother and child who walked through the exam room door.

But Rowan couldn't deny the feeling that she was dying inside.

AS SOON AS the clinic hours were over, Simone bolted before Rowan could get in another word about the status of their relationship.

Not that they still had one, apparently, other than boss and employee.

On the drive to her home, Rowan's eyes brimmed with tears that nearly blinded her. She needed to get home, after which she could break down properly. Maybe she would run a bath and open a bottle of wine. Or break out a pint of ice cream. Was wine ice cream a thing? Because if it wasn't, someone needed to invent it for moments like this, when everything in life went to shit all at once.

By the time Rowan pulled into her driveway, her hands were shaking on the steering wheel and tears were pouring down her cheeks. Normally, the sight of the ocean behind her home brought her peace, but today it only riled her up more, reminding her of the first night she and Simone had met. How they'd devoured one another to the sound of crashing waves like they would never be satiated.

Rowan desperately wished it was only the physical connection she craved, but somewhere along the line, Simone had burrowed deep into her heart. Now, with the prospect of losing her for good, Rowan felt as if a vital part of herself had been ripped away, leaving behind a ragged, gaping hole.

She stumbled out of the car, her vision still blurred by tears, and made her way up the front walk. Forget about the hot bath. All she wanted was to collapse into bed and shut out the world for a while. But as she approached the front door, Rowan pulled up short, noticing for the first time that her father's Audi was parked in the driveway.

What was he doing here? He almost never came to see her, and especially not unannounced and without it being a major holiday. Either Rowan had somehow blacked out for several weeks and today was already Thanksgiving, or the universe was determined to ruin Rowan's life for good. The crazy urge to scream and kick him in the shins threatened to overpower her. Not that he was at fault for her current predicament, but all reason had left her brain. She hurt inside, and she wanted everyone around her to feel it, too.

"Dad? What are you doing here?" Rowan hastily wiped at her eyes as her father got out of the car. The last thing she needed was for him to see her falling apart.

"I'm sorry to drop in unannounced, but we need to talk."

A chill ran down Rowan's spine at his serious tone. "We'd better go inside. I have some things to talk to you about, too." She still had not worked up the courage to present her father with all the financial irregularities she'd dug up on Lance, but now was as good a time as any. After all, the day could hardly get any worse. "This sounds like a wine conversation. You don't know if they make wine ice cream, do you?"

"What?" Her father looked thoroughly befuddled as he followed her into the living room. "I have no idea, but I'll take a whiskey if you have it."

Rowan poured them each a generous glass of whiskey before settling onto the couch, bracing herself for whatever bombshell her father was about to drop. She couldn't imagine what would bring him all the way out here without so much as a phone call first. It couldn't be good.

Her father took a long sip of his drink, his expression grave as he met her eyes. "I'm afraid we've had to make some difficult decisions at the hospital."

Rowan's stomach plummeted. As if this day couldn't get any worse. "What is it?"

He cleared his throat and took a sip of whiskey before saying, "We're closing down the maternity ward."

"What? You're getting rid of the labor and delivery unit?" Rowan asked, using the more modern term for the department, which somehow her father never seemed to remember.

"We simply can't afford to keep it open."

"What about our patients?"

"They'll get excellent care in Hyannis. They have the best maternity ward on the Cape."

"That's not hard, considering if we close down, they'll be the only one on the Cape."

"Now, pumpkin." Her father adopted the patronizing tone he might have used on her when she was a toddler begging for a pony. "I know this is difficult to hear—"

"The difficulty of me hearing it is nothing, Dad. Telling the community will be the difficult part."

"I'm sure you'll do an excellent job of it at the press conference tomorrow."

Rowan stared at her father in disbelief. "You want me to give the press conference? You can't be serious. I'm supposed to get up there and tell the whole community we're abandoning them? What about all the high-risk pregnancies, the women who can't afford to travel for care?"

"You're being dramatic. It's only a twenty-minute drive to Hyannis from here."

"Twenty fucking long minutes if there's an emergency. Not

to mention, you're assuming everyone has access to reliable transportation and the money to pay for gas." Rowan balled her fists at her sides, her breathing growing rapid. "Do you have any idea how this is going to impact the community? The L&D unit isn't just a line item on a budget. It's a lifeline."

"Would you rather close down the ER?" The expression on her father's face was so smug Rowan half wished she could slap it off him. "When you took this job, I warned you there would be tough choices ahead. Running a hospital isn't all cutting ribbons and kissing babies. Lance understood that."

Rowan bristled at the mention of her ex-husband, especially given what she knew about his unscrupulous actions. "Don't bring him into this. Lance is the reason the hospital is in this mess to begin with. In fact, I need to tell you—"

"I know you're upset." Her father sighed heavily, making it clear he was not in a listening mood. "But this decision is final. The board voted unanimously."

"Unanimously?" Rowan's voice rose an octave. "You didn't even fight to stop this?"

"Rowan, be reasonable. We're hemorrhaging money. Something had to give."

"Sure. Why not let the most vulnerable members of our community pay the price for gross incompetence?"

"It's not that simple, and you know it." Her father drained the rest of his whiskey and set the glass down with a *thunk*.

"Do I? Because from where I'm sitting, it looks like you're putting profits over patients." Rowan could barely contain the bitterness and disappointment welling up inside her.

"That's not fair. I've dedicated my life to this hospital, to this community. But we're in an impossible situation. There's something else you need to know. We're in danger of losing our contract with HarborCare Health.

The breath left her lungs as if she'd been punched in the gut. HarborCare was the most widely used insurance provider on the

Cape. Losing that contract would be catastrophic for the hospital and for the entire community that depended on it for care.

"How is that even possible?" Rowan demanded, her mind reeling. "HarborCare has been our biggest partner for decades. What happened?"

"The bastards are playing hardball. They don't want to reimburse us at the current levels, which are already criminal. We can't afford to reduce our fees any more. HarborCare isn't negotiating in good faith. If we don't solve it by the end of the year, we won't be able to accept HarborCare plans in the new year."

"It's the most popular insurance on the Cape."

He nodded but didn't bother to comment.

"Can they do that? Abandon their members like that?" Despair and incredulity warred within Rowan.

"Of course, they can. It's all about the bottom line for them. Unless we give in to their demands, they'll happily direct all their customers to Hyannis or even off-Cape."

Rowan pressed her fingers to her temples, trying to stave off the stress headache building behind her eyes. "So that's it then? We won't be helping pregnant people or anyone with HarborCare anymore?"

"Obviously, if it's an emergency, we can deliver a baby."

"Hopefully they have insurance we take, or they'll have to declare bankruptcy."

He didn't speak, the crinkles around his eyes tightening.

"This day keeps getting better and better."

"What else happened?"

"Nothing."

Rowan closed her eyes, feeling the weight of an impossible decision bearing down on her. Every option felt like a dead end, a path that would only lead to further hardship for the hospital and the community it served. What Rowan wouldn't give to crawl into Simone's arms right now, but apparently that would never be happening again. What was she going to do?

When she opened her eyes again, her father was watching her closely, his expression unreadable. "I know this is a lot to take in all at once, but you need to rally. Before the press conference, you'll need to call a staff meeting. This is our chance to get out in front of this, to control the narrative."

Rowan let out a humorless laugh. "Control the narrative? Is that what we're calling it? Because from where I'm sitting, it looks like you've placed a giant, steaming turd in my lap and expect me to clean it up for you. No wonder you're telling me this here, in my home, instead of at the hospital."

Her father's jaw tightened. "I didn't come here to argue with you. I came to give you a heads-up and ask for your support. Can I count on you, or do I need to tell the board I was mistaken in advocating for you to fill Lance's position when he left?"

Rowan sighed, her shoulders slumping in defeat. As much as she wanted to rail against the injustice of it all, she had no choice but to go along with her father's plan, at least for now. The hospital was already in a risky position. If she refused to cooperate, it would only make things worse.

"Yes, you can count on me," Rowan said, hating the words as they left her mouth. "I'll call the staff meeting first thing in the morning and handle the press conference after that."

Her father nodded, looking relieved. "Good. That's good, pumpkin."

The childhood nickname grated on Rowan's nerves. She wasn't a little girl anymore, blindly following her father's lead. She was a grown woman, a doctor, and now the head of a hospital facing the fight of its life.

Had it been a mistake coming back here?

Nothing was working out.

If only her father's precious Lance hadn't fucked up his life spectacularly, she wouldn't be dealing with any of this.

Maybe she wouldn't have met Simone. On the one hand, that sounded awful, but it might mean one less hole threatening to sink her heart into oblivion.

"Is there anything else?" Rowan wanted nothing more than for her father to leave so she could process everything that had happened today in peace.

"No, that about covers it." Her father stood, straightening his suit jacket. "Oh, your mother wants to do dinner this Saturday. You free?"

It was only after her father left that Rowan realized she still hadn't told her father about Lance's apartment in Boston, the woman who had catfished him, the unusual donation the hospital had given to Erica's art school in Italy, or the uptick in preventable deaths that left the hospital vulnerable to legal action. The more she thought about it, the less she was convinced telling him would change anything. For all she knew, her father was complicit and would do nothing to right the situation.

It was up to Rowan to figure it out, but she felt lost and overwhelmed by an impossible task. The burden was too heavy. And now that Simone was out of her life, she was truly carrying it alone.

CHAPTER NINETEEN

Simone stared at Rowan in shock as angry grumbling from the rest of the staff filled the surrounding cafeteria. Had she actually said they were going to close Marbury's labor and delivery unit?

There had to be a mistake.

"How can you close an entire department?" a doctor Simone recognized as an OBGYN from the department in question shouted through cupped hands. At least half a dozen other people made similar demands all at once.

Rowan stood at the makeshift podium, her face an impassive mask as she weathered the outraged cries from the assembled doctors and nurses. "I understand your frustration," she said, her voice carrying across the room with no need for a microphone, "but this decision was not made lightly. The L&D unit has been operating at a significant loss for years, and births in the area are declining. We simply cannot sustain it any longer."

Simone shook her head in disbelief. While the birthrate may be in decline, the pregnant patients who relied on the hospital were more in need of their services than ever. Simone had poured all her free time for months into volunteering with the mobile clinic specifically to improve outcomes for the most vulnerable women and children. Now, with a few words, Rowan was threatening to upend all the good they'd done. The worst part was, Rowan knew it. She had to. She'd been to the mobile clinic and seen it firsthand.

"What if there's an emergency?" asked one nurse from Simone's own department.

"Then we'll deliver the baby here in the emergency department. Patient safety is still our top concern, as always." Rowan's voice shook as she spoke, making Simone wonder if it was out of anger over being questioned or distress over the disasters that were certainly looming on the horizon as a result of this shortsighted policy.

From the table beside her, Candace met Simone's eye, clearly unhappy with the news and as surprised by it as Simone had been. Their department was already overworked and understaffed. Adding emergency deliveries to their workload would only make things worse.

"One other thing you should be aware of," Rowan continued, projecting her voice even louder to be heard over the din. "While we hope this will be straightened out before our contract expires, there is a possibility we will not be accepting HarborCare insurance in the coming year."

Another flurry of shouted questions was nearly drowned out by groans and cursing.

"I understand your concerns," Rowan said, her expression betraying a hint of the weariness she must be feeling.

"Yeah, sure you do," someone shouted from the back of the room. "You suits never know or care what we're up against. It's all bottom-line and bonuses for you."

A chair banged against a table, followed by the sound of someone stomping out of the room. Though she sympathized with Rowan as the bearer of bad news, Simone couldn't blame the person for being angry. These changes would make everyone's job harder while hitting their most vulnerable patients the hardest. It was enough to make anyone livid.

She turned back to Rowan, who was gathering her notes with shaky hands while being peppered with rapid-fire questions. Simone's heart sank as more staff members stormed out, their anger palpable. She watched Rowan closely, trying to gauge her reaction, but the hospital administrator remained stoic, her shoulders squared and her chin held high. Nonetheless, Simone could see the pain behind her eyes.

"Did she tell you about this ahead of time?" Candace asked, lowering her voice and leaning in close so as not to be overheard.

Simone shook her head, her voice barely audible over the cacophony of outrage. "No, I had no idea. This is as much of a shock to me as it is to everyone else."

Candace's brow furrowed. "But you two are..." She let the sentence trail off, glancing around to make sure no one was listening. "I thought she would have discussed it with you first."

Frankly, Simone would've thought the same thing. Her relationship with Rowan had grown increasingly complex in recent weeks. And yes, they'd hit a rocky patch after Erica nearly walked in on their romantic dinner. Despite all that, with such sweeping changes being announced and not a single word about it to her, Simone couldn't help but feel betrayed.

"Well, she didn't." Simone's jaw tightened. "But there's no way she's on board with all of this. Rowan is too good a doctor, and too dedicated to furthering the legacy of this hospital, to want to see changes like this."

Privately, given what Simone knew about the cards stacked against the hospital, she blamed Lance. That didn't mean Simone wasn't pissed. Why hadn't Rowan confided about any of this?

The meeting concluded with no actual solutions being reached, leaving all the staff members fuming with frustration. If Simone was inclined to make bets, she would guess that at least half of them were already searching for new job opportunities the second they left the room.

Simone tried to catch Rowan's eye as the meeting broke up, but she was trapped at the front of the room, dealing with at least a dozen staff members who were brave enough to tell her exactly what they thought of the hospital's plan.

This wasn't the time or place for Simone to lay into Rowan, so she slipped out of the cafeteria and headed for the staircase. She made her way to Rowan's office and leaned against the wall beside the door, her arms crossed, eyes shut, and mind reeling. After not sleeping very well and working a ten-hour shift, she was wiped. But she had too many concerns to head home before getting them off her chest.

"You here to yell at me?" Rowan asked, having approached so quietly Simone hadn't heard.

Simone's eyes snapped open at the sound of Rowan's voice. She turned to see the other woman standing a few feet away, her shoulders slumped and her face drawn with exhaustion.

"I'm here to understand what the hell is going on," Simone said, pushing off the wall. "I've got questions."

"You and everyone else." Rowan unlocked her office door and gestured for Simone to enter. "Come in. We can discuss this privately."

"How could you drop a bombshell like that without even giving me a heads-up?" Simone demanded the second Rowan had stepped foot in the office and shut the door.

"That's not how a hospital operates," Rowan responded with defiance in her tone. "I didn't tell Candace ahead of time, either."

Simone crossed her arms. "I'm not the same as Candace, and you know it."

"True." Rowan's expression hardened. "Unlike you, she's the head of her department."

"That's not what I meant. Why are you acting like this?"

Simone scratched her upper lip as she searched Rowan's gaze. "Is this some sort of retaliation because we had a minor disagreement?"

"Minor?" Rowan scoffed. "You unceremoniously dumped me. I wouldn't call that minor."

"Dumped you? I did not!" Simone stiffened her spine. "I simply raised some points I thought we needed to address."

"You told me you didn't want to be the reason my relationship with Erica became strained," Rowan said, her voice catching slightly. She turned away, bracing her hands on the desk. "What was I supposed to think?"

"I don't know. Not that I was ending things. I was rambling, trying to talk it out."

Rowan's eyes flashed with anger. "Talk it out? You shut me down and dashed away before I could say a word. I got the message loud and clear."

Simone took a deep breath, trying to calm the frustration rising within her. She hadn't meant to hurt Rowan, but clearly her words had cut deeper than she'd realized. "Rowan, I'm sorry. I never meant to make you feel like I was ending things between us. I was scared. Scared of what it would mean for your relationship with Erica if she found out about us. Scared of how it might impact our work here at the hospital."

Rowan turned back to face Simone, some of the fight seeming to drain out of her. "I understand that fear. Believe me, I do. But shutting me out isn't the answer. We need to be able to talk about these things."

"I wanted to. I just needed time to let things marinate."

"I wish you'd told me that. I would have respected it. Instead, I was left reeling, thinking you had called it quits and wondering if I'd totally misread everything between us."

Simone stepped closer, her hand reaching out to touch Rowan's arm. "You didn't misread anything. But before we talk about any of that, I need to know. Are you on board with these changes at the hospital?"

"How could you even think that?" Rowan sat down on the edge of her desk. "I was informed by my father last night that the board had already voted unanimously to shut the L&D unit. I don't have a say in the matter."

"What about HarborCare?" Simone pressed. "Are you really going to let the hospital drop their coverage without saying a word?"

Rowan sighed heavily, running a hand through her hair. "It's not that simple. HarborCare has been underpaying claims for months. We can't keep hemorrhaging money like this. Something has to give."

"But those are some of our most vulnerable patients," Simone argued, her voice rising with emotion. "Many of them have nowhere else to go for care. We can't abandon them. Patients could die as a result of our actions. More than already have."

"You think I don't know that?" Rowan's voice cracked as she met Simone's gaze, her eyes shining with unshed tears. "Do you honestly believe I want any of this? That I want to see the hospital my family has poured our hearts and souls into for years fall apart like this?"

Simone could see the pain and frustration etched on Rowan's face. She softened her tone. "No, of course not. I'm sorry. I know you're in an impossible position."

"It is impossible, and it's tearing me apart. But my hands are tied. The hospital is in dire financial straits. If we don't make some tough choices now, we may not have a hospital left to serve anyone." Rowan cradled her forehead with a palm. "But I'm not giving up. I'm trying to come up with a solution. Got any ideas?"

Simone shook her head. "The only thought that keeps

running through my head is kicking Lance in the nuts. Do you think that would help?"

Rowan let out a laugh, but it sounded more like a choked sob. "As satisfying as that sounds, I'm not sure it would solve our problems Though I'd be lying if I said I haven't entertained similar thoughts myself." She took a deep breath, seeming to collect herself. "I know things are a mess right now, but I need you to know I'm doing everything in my power to find a way through this. I won't let Marbury fall without a fight. And I don't want to let us go without a fight, either."

Simone's heart ached seeing Rowan so distraught. She moved closer, gently grasping Rowan's shoulders. "I'm sorry I jumped to conclusions. I should have trusted you were on our side. And I'm sorry for the way I acted yesterday. I've never done anything like this, and I don't know how to handle it, I guess."

"I don't either. You work for me. You're best friends with my stepdaughter. The issues feel pretty insurmountable. Although, if the hospital goes under, I guess that solves one of our problems."

"Don't you dare talk like that. This is your family's legacy."

"Family curse is more like it."

Simone nodded slowly. "I know it must feel like that, but if anyone can fix it, it's you."

"I wish I believed that was true. I don't—"

"Be patient, Rowan. Don't be like those idiot board members who can only focus on what's directly in front of them. People like you, the ones who make it through the hard things, are the ones who can see beyond the problems and find a path to success. You may not know exactly how to get there right now, but you are patient enough to search for the right direction."

"I won't give up. I can't. This is my community. I can't let them down."

"I know." Simone cleared her throat. "That's why I think I

should apply for a position at the hospital in Hyannis. Not that I'm likely to have a shot now that half the hospital is probably polishing up their résumés."

"Yeah, I'll bet even Candace is tempted to bail on this place. But you shouldn't have to find another job. I need you here, and I don't want you to leave. Not because of this mess and certainly not because of me."

Simone sighed, her shoulders sagging. "I don't want to leave either. But I also don't want our relationship to cause problems for you or the hospital. If Erica found out, or if rumors started spreading..."

"Then we'll deal with it like the adults we are," Rowan said firmly, reaching out to take Simone's hand. "I'm not going to let you sacrifice your career or your happiness for my sake. I've done that already in my past, and it isn't something I would ever ask of anyone else."

Simone squeezed Rowan's hand, finding strength in her touch. "If I have to choose between a job and you, you're going to win every time. I care about you, Rowan. No, it's more than that. I love you."

"You love me?" Rowan's breath caught in her throat. "Simone, I..."

"It's okay." Simone stepped closer, her hands coming up to gently cradle Rowan's face. "I don't expect you to say it just because I did."

"No, that's not it. I do. I love you, too, Simone," Rowan said, her voice filled with emotion. "I've been holding back from saying it, worried it was too soon and I might scare you away. But I've felt it for a while now. And I want so badly to kiss you right now, but the hospital is about the worst possible place for me to do that."

Simone's heart soared at Rowan's words, a bright smile spreading across her face despite the gravity of their situation. She leaned in, resting her forehead against Rowan's, savoring the closeness and intimacy of the moment. "I want to kiss you, too," she whispered. "But you're right. We can't. Not here."

Rowan sighed, her breath warm against Simone's skin. "We need to be careful. More careful than we've been. If anyone found out about us..."

"I know." Simone pulled back to meet Rowan's gaze with a determined expression. "That's why I'm going to start looking for a new job. I'm not going to let anything come between us. Not this hospital crisis, not my fears, and not even your stepdaughter, if I can find any way around it."

"Erica is my responsibility, not yours," Rowan said softly. "She's an adult now, and while I want to protect her, I can't let her feelings dictate my life. Not anymore."

"Okay, but what are we going to do?" Simone whispered.

"About what?"

It took Simone a second to register that the question hadn't come from Rowan but from a voice behind her. Slowly, she turned around, aware of how inappropriately close she and Rowan were standing. Not exactly a smoking gun, but definitely incriminating given the context. Especially to someone as perceptive as Erica. Simone's stomach dropped as she saw Rowan's stepdaughter standing in the doorway, holding a plate with a slice of cake on it.

"I heard the news about the hospital closing the labor and delivery unit." Erica's voice was oddly hesitant. "And I thought you could use a pick me up, so I grabbed some cake from the cafeteria. Red velvet. Your favorite."

For a second, Simone was confused. She couldn't stand red velvet cake, and Erica knew it. But then she realized Erica must be talking to her stepmom.

"That's very sweet of you," Rowan said, trying to sound casual.

Erica's eyes darted between Simone and Rowan, her brow furrowing. "What's going on here?" she asked, her voice tinged with suspicion. "I'm missing something. As I was coming in, I heard you ask what are we going to do. What did you mean by that?"

"The h-hospital," Simone stammered. "I was talking about this whole mess with the hospital."

Erica blinked. "I don't think that's what you meant. I'm not an idiot. Something else is going on here. Oh my God. Are you two—?" She clapped one hand over her mouth, her other hand letting go of the plate. The cake fell to the floor, splattering in an explosion of red and white mush.

Rowan stepped forward, her hands held out in a placating gesture. "Erica, sweetheart, let me explain."

But Erica was already shaking her head, her eyes wide with shock and betrayal. "No! You don't get to call me that."

"Erica—"

"How long has this been going on?" she demanded, her voice rising in pitch. "Simone is my best friend! She's way younger than you. This is so messed up!"

Simone's heart sank as she saw the pain etched on Erica's face. "Erica, please, let us explain."

"Explain what? That you've been sneaking around behind my back? That you've been lying to me this whole time? I can't believe this. My life is a disaster. First Italy, then getting arrested, and now this." She pointed her finger at Simone's chest. "I thought you were my friend."

"I am your friend."

"If that were true, you wouldn't be fucking my stepmom."

"We're not—" Simone stopped short of a denial. Erica was right, after all. But the word she had used was so crass. Simone was madly in love with Rowan. What they had between them was beautiful. Complicated as hell but beautifully so. She couldn't allow it to be made ugly just because it was hard to understand.

"Don't lie to me," Erica shrieked. "I'm tired of everyone in my life keeping secrets. You're as bad as my father." Tears pooled in the corners of Erica's eyes, threatening to spill over at any moment. "I can't believe I thought I could trust you." This accusation was hurled squarely at Rowan, though Simone felt it land just as hard.

Rowan took a tentative step forward, her hand outstretched. "Erica, please, give us a chance to—"

Erica recoiled as if Rowan's touch would burn her. "No! I don't want to hear any more lies or excuses. I can't even look at you right now."

Erica turned on her heel and bolted out of the office, slamming the door behind her with a resounding bang that seemed to echo in the stunned silence that followed.

Rowan stared at the closed door for a moment, her face a mask of anguish. Then, without a word, she hurried after Erica, leaving Simone alone in the office, the remnants of the red velvet cake still splattered on the floor at her feet.

CHAPTER TWENTY

Rowan glanced at the time as she approached the guest house's front door. It had been eighteen hours since Erica had stormed out of her office, disappearing before Rowan could catch up. Since then, not a single one of Rowan's texts had been opened or answered. No matter how angry Erica was at her, Rowan needed to make sure she was okay.

Rowan banged on the door, her heart pounding. When there was no answer, she tried again, harder this time.

"Erica?" she called out, trying to keep the desperation from her voice. "Erica, are you in there? Please, we need to talk."

The door swung open, but instead of Erica's face, Rowan found herself staring at Simone. The blond doctor looked as tired as Rowan felt, wearing only a robe and a towel wrapped around her head. "What's with all the racket?"

"I'm sorry." Only now did it occur to Rowan that it was still early in the morning, and this was Simone's day off. "Were you in the shower?"

"No. I was in the oven."

"What?" Rowan blinked in confusion.

"Sorry. I get snarky when I haven't slept." Simone gave a

shaky laugh that sounded more like a whimper. "Yes, I was in the shower. Did you want to come in?"

Rowan nodded, stepping past Simone. "I was hoping to talk to Erica about yesterday."

"She isn't here. When I got home last night, all of her stuff was gone. I haven't heard from her." Simone went to the kitchen sink and filled a glass of water. "Drink this."

"Why?" Rowan put up a hand and pushed the glass away.

"Doctor's orders." Simone pressed the glass into Rowan's still-raised hand.

"I am a doctor," Rowan argued, though she continued to hold on to the glass.

"You look like you haven't slept a wink, and dehydration won't help the situation. Everyone knows doctors make the worst patients. Drink."

Rowan reluctantly accepted the water and took a teensy sip, realizing how parched she was. The cool liquid soothed her throat but did little to ease the worry gnawing at her insides. "I've been trying to reach Erica all night. She's not answering any of my messages. We need to find her."

Instead of instantly agreeing, Simone pressed her lips together, remaining silent for a few moments before asking. "Are you sure she wants to be found?"

"Who knows? But I'm the only parent she's got right now. I can't not look for her."

"I get it, Rowan." Simone's brow furrowed. "From your perspective, I really do understand. But if I were Erica, I think I would need some space. I would want to process everything that's happened. Pushing too hard might only make things worse."

"But she isn't checking her phone at all. The texts haven't even been read." Rowan set the glass down on the kitchen counter with more force than intended, water sloshing over the rim. "I can't sit around and wait, hoping she's just mad at me and not in the back of some kidnapper's van. What if something happens to her? It's my job to protect her."

"Even if she doesn't want your protection?" Simone asked gently, placing a hand on Rowan's shoulder. "I know you probably still see her the same as she was the first time you met her, with pigtails and braces. But she's only a few years younger than me."

Rowan nearly flinched at this reminder. What she wouldn't do to forget that complicated reality. There was no doubt in Rowan's mind that Simone was her intellectual and emotional equal, despite the years between them. But when it came to Erica, Rowan struggled to see past the little girl she'd watched grow up. How could she reconcile that image with the woman Erica had become? A woman who hated Rowan's guts.

Rowan shrugged off Simone's hand, not wanting to concede the point, even though Simone was right. "I'm not saying we need to form a search party and call in the hounds. But at least we can get in my car and drive around."

"She's not a lost dog. Or even a small child who's trying to run away from home. She's a twenty-eight-year-old woman who, yes, quite frankly, is used to being treated like a princess and getting her way." Simone picked up Rowan's discarded glass and finished off the water in one big gulp. "I love Erica, but she can be very immature and spoiled sometimes. Maybe she needs to learn to deal with her emotions in a healthy way, instead of running away from them and expecting everyone to chase after her."

Rowan bristled at those words, even though she knew there was truth in them. "That's not fair. Erica has been through a lot, with the divorce and all the stuff with her dad. She's hurting and confused."

"I get it. And I feel terrible for my role in that." Simone's voice softened. "But constantly chasing after her and trying to fix things for her isn't the way to make her more resilient.

Marbury is a really small town. It's unlikely she's gotten into any real trouble."

"So, what? I'm supposed to let her disappear and hope nothing bad—" Rowan squeezed her eyes, not wanting to picture all the dangers that might befall a young woman with questionable judgement. "I don't know what to do. What do you suggest?"

"Okay. There's a time for being rational, but clearly this isn't it." Simone let out a long, anguished sigh. "We can drive around if it will make you feel better. Let's go." Simone unraveled the towel from her head and headed toward the door.

"Aren't you going to change?" Rowan asked incredulously.

"No, I'm good. Let's roll."

Rowan was about to argue but couldn't muster the energy to do so.

Just as Rowan and Simone headed out the door, a strange figure in red and white zipped past them, causing Rowan to stop in her tracks. "I think I'm seeing..." She squinted. "Is that an angel with a halo but also wearing a red tail and holding a pitchfork?"

Simone let out a laugh. "Another one of Poppy's Halloween costumes. She's getting bored with wearing them the way they come, so she's started to mix and match the pieces."

"Is it Halloween? I thought it was still a couple of weeks away." Rowan felt even more off balance than she had when the child whizzed past her, suddenly unsure of something as basic as the date on the calendar. If she had a patient present with these symptoms, she'd probably diagnose acute stress and prescribe a sedative.

God, wouldn't that be nice? A sedative sounded like pure bliss.

"Don't panic," Simone reassured her. "Poppy's been living in costumes for ages now. She tries on one costume after another, all day. I have a feeling this one won't be the last."

Simone tightened her robe, and Rowan shot her a quizzical look.

"You sure you don't want to go back in and change?"

Simone hesitated. "Honestly, I think I forgot there were other people out in the—"

"There you are!" Marigold hollered from her deck, waving frantically. "Don't move!"

Rowan met Simone's eyes with a sinking feeling in her chest. What was this about? While Rowan liked Simone's eccentric landlady a lot better ever since establishing she was not, in fact, Simone's girlfriend, that didn't mean Rowan wanted to stop and chitchat when she had something more important to do.

Scrambling down the stairs, Marigold huffed as she approached. "I really need to use my gym membership instead of simply paying the bills."

"Everything okay?" Simone asked with way more patience than Rowan was inclined to extend.

"With me? Yes. But Erica is an entirely different story."

"Erica? Have you seen her?" Rowan demanded, her heart pounding in her throat. "Do you know where she's gone?"

Instead of answering Rowan's question, Marigold gave her a scolding look. "You two didn't handle things as delicately as you could have, you know."

Rowan's eyes dropped to the grass below her feet. "Uh..." What could she say? The woman had a point.

"I take it you've talked to her," Simone pressed, apparently much better at keeping her head under pressure than Rowan was.

"Oh yes." Marigold shook her head disapprovingly. "Poor thing was in tears, trying to drag those heavy suitcases down the driveway. She could barely talk through all her sobs. I set her down with a nice cup of herbal tea and got the whole story before sending her off to bed with a hot water bottle and some lavender oil on her pillow."

Rowan's head snapped up. "Wait. Erica's with you?"

Marigold nodded. "In my guest room. I couldn't very well let the poor girl wander off into the night in that state."

Relief washed over Rowan like a tidal wave, nearly making her sway on her feet. She placed a hand on Simone's shoulder to stay upright. "Thank God. I've been worried sick."

"As you should be." Marigold wagged a finger at both of them. "That girl is hurting something fierce. What were you two thinking, carrying on like that right under her nose?"

Rowan's mouth opened and closed a few times, but before she could force any words to come out, a car pulled into Marigold's driveway. One that was painfully familiar.

"Is that my mother?" Rowan punctuated her question with a groan as none other than Grace Colchester got out of the car, grasping a plate covered with plastic wrap.

"Grace!" Marigold waved Rowan's mother over with enthusiasm usually reserved for a long-lost friend. "You got my message. She's not up yet, but—"

"Hold on," Rowan interrupted, earning her matching scowls from both older women. "You called my mother?"

"So we're clear, I'm not speaking to you right now," Grace informed Rowan before turning a sweet smile toward Marigold. "I baked her some cookies, like you suggested."

"Well, that's good," Marigold said. "But don't be that way with Rowan."

"How can I not?" Grace screeched, or as close to a screech as her dignity would allow. "After what *they* did?"

Maybe it was mean, but Rowan was a little vindicated to see Simone shrink as much under her mother's accusatory tone as she had. At least she wasn't facing it alone. Meanwhile, Simone shifted uncomfortably, tugging her robe tightly around herself and clearly wishing she had taken the time to change.

"What did they do, really," Marigold clucked like a hen. "Other than fall in love. When did that become a crime?"

"Love? Who said anything about love?" Rowan's mother snapped. "This is some kind of experiment. An identity crisis, like when she was young. Rowan's not even gay. She married Lance!"

"Actually, Mom—" Rowan began, regretting she hadn't had the courage to discuss this with her mother before now. But her mom wouldn't even look at her.

"Think about it, Grace," Marigold said in a tone that was equal parts stern but kind. "No one blows up their life for anything less than true love. At least, women usually don't. As for sexuality, it can be more complicated than we'd like to think."

Rowan's mom tutted, though her expression softened enough that it appeared her friend's words might be getting through. For the first time since Erica had stormed out of her office, Rowan allowed herself to believe that maybe she wasn't such a horrible monster, after all.

"It really is love, Mom," Rowan said. "I should've told you before, but I didn't know how."

"Huh." Grace looked at her daughter, still clutching the plate of cookies. Her expression remained stern, but she wasn't completely flipping her lid, so that was a good sign. "Okay. Well, I'm not doubting your feelings. I guess I can get used to the idea. But don't think for a minute I'm letting you have any of these cookies."

"I didn't even ask," Rowan defended against the absurd statement. She was about to argue she didn't even want cookies when another car pulled into the driveway. This one was even more familiar than her mother's—and exponentially more unwelcome.

"You've got to be kidding me," Rowan muttered under her breath as her father climbed out from the driver's side of his Audi while Lance, looking every bit as polished and pompous as ever in his designer suit, exited the passenger's side.

What fresh hell was this?

"Who's next? My third-grade teacher?" Rowan gritted her teeth.

"You better hope not," her mother commented. "Mrs. Butler hated you."

"I'm aware. I can only assume she would welcome the chance to get in on the action, maybe criticize me for my handwriting like the good ol' days."

"Look who's back!" Rowan's dad announced, beaming with pride as if Lance had returned a hero from the front lines instead of completing an overpriced rehab program in Boca Raton.

"Hello." Lance gave a curt head nod, his eyes bouncing off everyone, hesitating for a moment when he got to Simone and her bathrobe.

"Lance has a plan to save the hospital," Rowan's father began, but he stopped speaking as the screen door opened and Erica came out of the house.

"What's going on?" Erica stepped out onto the porch, her eyes red and puffy from crying. She glanced around at the assembled group, her expression shifting from hurt to confusion to anger. "What is this, an intervention?"

Rowan stepped forward, her hands raised placatingly. "Erica, sweetie, we were worried about you. You didn't answer any of my messages, and I didn't know where you were."

"Now you know. Mystery solved." Erica crossed her arms, her voice sharp. "You can all go home now."

"Hey, now, kiddo," Lance said in a forced jovial tone. "Is that any way to say hi to your old man?"

"You mean the old man"—Erica made air quotes with her fingers—"who left me to die in Italy?"

"What happened in Italy?" Rowan's father demanded.

"Your boy Lance here failed to pay Erica's tuition," Rowan supplied, grateful to have the negative attention focused somewhere other than on her for a minute. "She was left with nowhere to live and a maxed-out credit card after she bought a ticket home."

"Then I got arrested for trying to use my key to open the door on Dad's condo because no one bothered to tell me he'd sold the place," Erica added, clearly not objecting to helping Rowan make a point if it furthered her own aim.

"Erica got arrested?" Lance blinked excessively. "Jesus, Rowan. Did you let everything fall apart?"

"How is that my fault?" Rowan spluttered. "I'm the one who bailed her out."

"I'm so sorry, Erica," Lance said, his voice as smooth as whipped cream and with about as much substance. "I had no idea that was going to happen. I was... indisposed at the time. But it's all better now."

Erica scoffed, rolling her eyes. "Sure, it's all better now. For you, maybe. But what about me? What about all the promises you broke? All the times you let me down? You've been lying to me about everything for months."

Lance's smile faltered for a moment before he recovered. "I know I've made mistakes, sweetheart. But I'm here now, and I'm going to make it up to you. I've got big plans for Marbury Hospital. Your grandfather is bringing me back on as CMO."

"What?" Rowan whirled to face her father, shock and betrayal warring for prominence in her heart.

"Isn't that good news?" her father had the audacity to say, looking as if he actually believed it. "You're off the hook and can return to Boston now. When do you think you can clear your things out of Lance's office?"

"You're firing me?" Rowan gasped. "Is this because of Simone?"

"Who's Simone?" Her father's face twisted in confusion, at which point it dawned on Rowan that her mother hadn't said a word to her husband about what had transpired before rushing to Erica's aid with her plate of cookies.

"Shit," Rowan muttered under her breath.

"Serves you right," Erica said.

"Simone, of course." Lance plastered on an even faker smile than the one he'd been wearing for Erica as he turned toward the bathrobe-clad woman. "Erica's friend. I knew I recognized you, but I couldn't place you out of context. How are you liking Marbury Hospital?"

"Uh, it's good," Simone gulped, looking like she wanted to disappear into the folds of her robe. "Marbury Hospital is, uh, great. Really great."

"What's going on?" Rowan's father growled. Rowan could see the gears turning in his head as he glanced between her and Simone, putting the pieces together. His eyes narrowed. "What does this young doctor have to do with anything?"

"Dad, I can explain," Rowan began, but Erica cut her off with a harsh laugh.

"Please do explain, Rowan," Erica said, her voice dripping with sarcasm. "Explain how you've been screwing my best friend, your employee, behind my back this whole time."

Lance let out a bark of laughter, but when the truth sunk in and he realized it wasn't a joke, he swallowed hard, his Adam's apple bobbing up and down. A stunned silence fell over the group.

Rowan's father looked from Erica to Simone and then to his wife. "Who is she talking about? I didn't know Erica had any male friends at the hospital."

"I'm talking about Simone!" Erica shrieked.

"We'll talk about this at home, Harold," Grace implored in a hushed but urgent tone.

Rowan's father's face turned an alarming shade of purple as he sputtered, "Is this true, Rowan?"

"I don't know. Is it true you're firing me?" Rowan demanded, shaking from head to toe but doing everything she could to hold her ground. "If so, I guess she's not my employee anymore. Still a woman, though."

"I'm not firing you," her father shouted. "I gave Lance his old job back. There's a difference."

"You gave him *my* job, Dad," Rowan yelled back. "Explain how that isn't firing me."

"That's it? That's all anyone's going to say about Rowan having an affair with my best friend? I don't know who I can trust anymore," Erica wailed.

As if suddenly becoming reanimated from stone, Grace shoved the plate of cookies into Rowan's hand and enveloped Erica.

"There, there," Rowan's mother soothed. "You can trust Grandma."

"Remember what we talked about, Erica." Marigold wasn't exactly scolding, but there was a sternness to her voice that stood in contrast to Grace's honey-smothered tones. "Yes, this is a shock, and you need time to absorb and accept it."

"How can I accept it?" Erica blubbered against Grace's tweed jacket, because she was wearing a tweed jacket when everyone else was dressed for a casual morning. Except for Poppy, who chose that moment to gallop past in a witch costume but wearing a cowboy hat and riding on a hobby horse instead of a broom.

"Because you don't want to be that person who denies people happiness, right?" Marigold asked, using that particular tone that made it clear there was only one acceptable answer. "You can stay in your PJs for the rest of the day. Eat cookies. Wallow. But not forever. Okay?"

"Okay," Erica said with a slight hiccup, reaching out to lift the plastic wrap and swipe a cookie from the plate in Rowan's hand.

Rowan's mother reclaimed the plate from Rowan with a steely-eyed glare.

"I wasn't going to take a cookie," Rowan muttered.

"I'd like one." Marigold grabbed a cookie before anyone could tell her otherwise. "Chocolate chip. My fave."

Those were Rowan's favorite, too. Not that she would make a move on them now.

"I think every single one of you has lost your damn mind." Rowan's father shook his head, the very picture of disbelief. "I can't believe what I'm hearing. My own daughter, carrying on with some young female doctor, right under our noses. And you!" He pointed an accusing finger at Lance. "You're supposed to be getting your life back on track, not enabling this nonsense."

Lance held up his hands defensively. "Hey, don't look at me. I had no idea about any of this. I'm as shocked as you are."

"Oh, please," Erica scoffed, wiping tears from her eyes. "Thanks to you, I don't even have a place to live anymore. I've been bunking with Simone since I got back from Italy, but clearly that isn't an option now."

Rowan felt a pang of guilt at Erica's words. Despite everything, she still cared deeply for her stepdaughter and hated to see her hurting like this. "Erica, I'm so sorry. I never meant for any of this to happen."

"Well, it did happen," Erica snapped. "And now I have to deal with the fallout. As usual."

"You can stay with us, sweetheart," Grace offered, rubbing Erica's back soothingly. "For as long as you need."

"No, I have a better idea." Lance took a step forward with all the confidence of a man who was about to announce a new cure for cancer. "The beach house is Erica's rightful home. You said so yourself when I sold it to you."

"She's welcome to live there now," Rowan offered, uncertain what Lance intended by bringing this up now.

"Not while you're there," Erica sniped before burying her face into her grandmother's shoulder.

"No, she's quite right," Lance said. He turned to face Rowan. "My lawyer will be in touch to arrange payment and transfer the deed. It's time for me to buy the beach house back from Rowan, like I always said I would."

"Buy it back?" Rowan's father glanced at his wife, his expression even more confused than it had been at previous times during the conversation. "Would someone tell me what's going on?"

"You didn't know I had to buy the beach house from Lance?" Rowan spluttered. "I used every penny I had to save it for Erica, just so Lance could pay off his debts."

"Nonsense. You got it in the divorce," her father said with an obstinance that infuriated Rowan past her breaking point.

"You don't know a fucking thing that's going on in this family, do you, Dad?" she shouted, her voice cracking with emotion. "You're so oblivious to everything that doesn't directly impact you or your precious hospital. Well, guess what? I'm done being your puppet. I'm done cleaning up everyone else's messes."

"Don't you dare talk to me like that!" her father shot back.

"Or what? You'll fire me? You already did that." Rowan's chest heaved as she stared down her father, years of pent-up resentment and frustration finally boiling over. The stunned silence that followed her outburst was broken only by the sound of Poppy galloping by yet again, this time wearing a sparkly mermaid tail.

Lance cleared his throat uncomfortably. "This is all very dramatic, but I think it's time we go and leave Rowan to calm down."

"I'm not the one who needs to calm down," Rowan snapped, her eyes flashing with anger. But her father and Lance were already heading toward their car, while her mother was hugging Erica goodbye.

"Maybe we should go back to my place," Simone said quietly, holding out her hand.

Rowan was torn between her desire to stay and scream at everyone within earshot and her desperate need to escape this entire disastrous scene. With a heavy sigh, she took Simone's outstretched hand, allowing her to lead them back toward the guest house.

As soon as they were inside with the door closed behind them, Rowan collapsed onto the couch, burying her face in her hands. "I can't believe all of that just happened," she groaned.

"It could have gone better," Simone admitted, sitting down beside Rowan and placing a tentative hand on her back. "But it could have gone a lot worse, too."

Rowan lifted her head, cocking it to one side. "How? How could that have possibly gone any worse?"

"Well, for one, no one threw any punches. That's always a plus in my book." Simone tried for a smile, but it fell flat in the face of Rowan's obvious distress.

"I lost my job, and in another few weeks, I'll be out of a house, too. I'm forty-two years old, and I'm homeless and unemployed."

"You can live here with me," Simone said softly. "For as long as you need to figure things out. Or even longer. Maybe forever, even."

"What?"

"Maybe not like actually forever. Or, I don't know..." Simone shrugged, clearly having reached the end of her ability to articulate whatever it was she was trying to convey.

Rowan swallowed hard, uncertain whether to laugh or cry. "Simone, I can't ask you to do that. It wouldn't be fair to you, especially after everything that's happened."

"You're not asking. I'm offering." Simone took Rowan's hands in hers, her touch warm and reassuring. "I know this isn't how either of us imagined things going, but on the other hand, it kind of feels right. I want to be with you, Rowan.

Rowan looked into Simone's clear blue eyes, overwhelmed by the sincerity and love reflected there. Despite the chaos swirling around them, in that moment, everything else seemed to fall away. It was just the two of them, and nothing else mattered.

"I want to be with you, too," Rowan whispered, her voice thick with emotion. "More than anything. But are you sure about this? About us? It's not going to be easy, especially with my family and Erica. Hell, when all of this comes out, the whole town will probably be judging us."

"Let 'em judge." Simone laughed. "I know what I want. And apparently, it's to be the sugar mama to an unemployed, homeless doctor. Who knew?"

Rowan couldn't help but laugh at that as tears pricked at the corners of her eyes. "You're ridiculous. You know that?"

"Maybe so, but you love me anyway." Simone grinned, leaning in to press a soft kiss to Rowan's lips.

"The heart wants what it wants," Rowan agreed. And then she melted into the kiss, allowing herself this one perfect moment amidst the chaos.

CHAPTER TWENTY-ONE

As Simone passed through the sliding doors and into the hospital parking lot, she couldn't wait to get home. Today was Rowan's official move-in day. The past two weeks had been a whirlwind of activity, but now that the last boxes were out of the beach house, they could finally start this new adventure.

She and Rowan were going to live together. Just the thought gave Simone goose bumps as a swarm of butterflies beat their wings ecstatically in her belly. She smiled to herself as she walked to her car, thinking about all the little moments they would share—lazy Sunday mornings in bed, cooking dinner side by side in their cozy kitchen, falling asleep in each other's arms every night. It was the next chapter in their relationship, and Simone couldn't be more excited to turn the page.

As she drove from the hospital, past the charming shopping district in Marbury's downtown, it was hard to believe how much her life had changed. This time last year, she'd been struggling with her mental health, unable to handle the pressures of working with Global Health Frontiers but unwilling to admit defeat. Now, peace and contentment settled over her as she

THE ANATOMY OF FOREVER

contemplated her future. She'd never dreamed her life could be this good.

If only the falling-out with Erica could've been avoided, everything would be perfect. But surely, in time, Erica would come around. Simone sighed, pushing the thought aside as she pulled into her driveway. There would be time to mend that bridge later. For now, she wanted to focus on the joy of this moment without worrying about things that were out of her control.

She grabbed her bag and headed up the walkway, eager to see Rowan and help her start unpacking the last of her belongings.

"Honey, I'm home!" Simone called out playfully as she walked through the front door. But instead of Rowan's warm embrace, she was greeted by silence.

The swarm of butterflies in Simone's stomach didn't exactly die, but their wings certainly stopped flapping.

It wasn't like Simone expected Rowan to be waiting at the door for her at the end of the workday with a martini in one hand and a pair of slippers in the other. That would be awesome but not realistic. Still, the idea played in her head, bringing a silly grin to her face. In her imagination, Rowan was suddenly wearing fishnet stockings, high heels, and an apron, looking like a 1950s housewife gone wild.

Was Rowan into role-playing?

The fluttering in her belly returned, but this time it was caused by nerves. Wasn't that something Simone should know about Rowan already? After all, they were living together now. Shouldn't she know everything about Rowan before taking such a major step?

As her thoughts spiraled, Simone was approaching full panic mode. She was going to fuck this up, one hundred and fifty percent. She'd always been an overachiever, and in this situation, that trait would probably bite her in the ass.

Simone took a deep breath, trying to calm her racing

thoughts. She was being ridiculous. Of course, she didn't know everything about Rowan yet. That was part of the excitement of living together, discovering new things about each other every day. Despite her pep-talk, her doubts lingered.

A sound at the door startled Simone out of her thoughts, which was probably for the best. She hesitated for a moment, wondering if it was Rowan. Maybe she'd bumped into the door while searching for her key.

Simone's heart leaped as she hurried to the door, eager to greet Rowan and push aside her anxious thoughts. But as she swung it open, she found herself face-to-face, not with her girlfriend, but with Marigold and Poppy, a large plastic animal carrier sitting on the ground between them.

"Hey there!" Marigold greeted her with a cheerful smile.

"A new family member?" Simone asked, pointing to the carrier.

"Actually, what are your thoughts on kittens?" Marigold asked in a coy tone that instantly made Simone suspicious.

She peered into the carrier and saw not one, but two tiny balls of fluff curled up together. "Oh my," Simone breathed, her heart melting at the sight. "They're adorable. Hello, sweeties. I'm Simone. What are your names?"

Naturally, neither responded.

"As it happens, they don't have names yet, which means you can do the honors yourself. You're not allergic, are you?" There was an overeager quality to Marigold's rush of words that made Simone raise an eyebrow.

"No, I'm not allergic," Simone replied cautiously. "But Rowan and I haven't really discussed pets yet. She's only officially moving in today. Why can't you keep them?" After all, it wasn't like there was such a thing as too many pets as far as Marigold was concerned.

"Oscar doesn't like them," Poppy supplied with a pout.

"Let's just say some stereotypes, like dogs and cats not getting along, are based on reality," Marigold added.

"How'd you end up with them?"

"One of the patients at the mobile clinic mentioned they couldn't keep them. Poor thing was in tears, but her baby is highly allergic. Pablo called me—"

"Because everyone in town knows you're a sucker," Simone said with a grin.

"I prefer bighearted. The thing is I need a place for them to stay, at least for the night. Oscar really is being a pest about it." Marigold's tone was pleading.

Simone struggled to choose between her desire to help and her uncertainty about saying yes before Rowan got home. She glanced at the carrier again. One of the kittens had woken up and was peering at her with big, curious eyes.

"Well..." Simone began, her heart melting at the sight of that innocent, furry face. "I suppose we could take them in for the night. But I'll need to talk to Rowan about anything longer term."

Marigold's face lit up. "Oh, thank you, Simone! You're a lifesaver." She turned to the little girl and said, "Poppy, grab the litter box and food from the house and bring it on over like we talked about."

Poppy snapped a salute and got to work while Simone chuckled at what an easy mark she must've been if these two had already worked out their plan ahead of time, assuming she would say yes.

"Does anyone know how to say no to you?" Simone picked up the crate, carrying it inside the guest house with Marigold following behind.

"My first two husbands sure did," Marigold said with a laugh. "Hence why neither of those marriages lasted, I suppose."

Poppy returned, lugging a bag of litter and a plastic box. As soon as she'd deposited the items inside, she dashed back out to get the food.

"Let's get these two settled in the bathroom," Marigold directed, clearly a pro at helping stray animals get settled in new homes. Simone followed her lead, watching as Marigold efficiently set up the litter box on the bathroom's tile floor.

"So, big day for you and Rowan, huh?" Marigold asked as she worked, her tone casual but her eyes twinkling with interest.

Simone felt a blush creep up her cheeks. "I mean it's only temporary, I guess, but..." Simone's voice trailed off as a tiny meow sounded from inside the carrier.

"But you don't want it to be," Marigold guessed, hitting a bull's-eye.

Simone's eyes were fixed on the kittens as they explored their new surroundings. "I don't know," she admitted softly. "I mean, I love Rowan. But what if we're not ready? We've only been dating a few months. Are we crazy to think this will work?"

Marigold's eyes softened as she looked at Simone. "Honey, when it comes to love, I've seen it all. And let me tell you, there's no such thing as a perfect timeline. Some people date for years before moving in together, and they still crash and burn. Others jump in headfirst, and it's magical. Just because you two moved in together in a hurry, doesn't mean it won't last."

"Here's the food, plus some dishes," Poppy said, coming into the bathroom with her arms full.

"Good job, sweetie," Marigold said, patting her on the head. "How about you get them their kibble and water, and then you can play with them while Simone and I go have a little chat."

Simone nodded, following Marigold out of the bathroom while Poppy eagerly set about her task. They settled onto the couch in the living room, and Simone found herself fidgeting with a throw pillow, unable to meet Marigold's gaze.

"We'll have to get them a fountain," Marigold remarked, perhaps picking up on Simone's discomfort and trying to give her a little space. "Cats are notorious for not drinking enough water from a dish."

"Good to know."

"Now that we've got that out of the way, why don't you tell me what's really bothering you about Rowan moving in?"

Simone sighed, twisting the pillow in her hands. "Honestly? I'm scared. In my experience, relationships end badly."

"Experience, huh?" Marigold said this with a hint of humor, as if implying that however much experience Simone might have, it paled in comparison to her own. "Have you ever lived with someone?"

"Not like this." Simone admitted. All at once, she felt impossibly young and immature, despite being thirty-two with years of professional experience under her belt. But in the romance department, she was almost completely lacking when it came to long-term relationships. "Back in college, I had a roommate that turned into sort of a friends with benefits situation."

Marigold nodded thoughtfully. "How did that end?"

Simone winced, remembering. "Not well. Did you know if you chuck a shoe at someone's head, it packs a wallop?"

"High heel or boot?" Marigold let out a hearty laugh as Simone's jaw dropped. "Oh honey, you have no idea some of the shit I've seen. I may be a philanthropist now, but I grew up in a trailer park, and not the nice kind. So, were you the chucker or the chuckee?"

"I'll give you one guess." Simone rubbed the back of her head, still smarting from the blow after ten years, though it had probably hurt her pride more than it had caused any lasting physical damage. "So, you see, I don't have a great track record when it comes to love."

"None of us do. Not until we meet someone we're actually in love with. That changes everything." Marigold stretched her arms above her head before settling back against the cushions again. "I went through a string of men in my youth. I haven't thrown any shoes that I can recall, but I did hurl an ashtray at my second husband. It was his favorite, despite it being hideous. It literally had breasts on it. Can you believe that?"

Simone couldn't help but chuckle at the mental image. "That does sound pretty awful. What happened?"

"Sadly, not only did I miss hitting the bastard, but the stupid thing didn't even break. He served me with divorce papers the next day, though, claiming I was a crazy bitch. At least something good came out of it."

"That's one way to find a silver lining." Simone laughed despite the situation. "You're a character, you know that?"

"Oh, sure. I'm well aware the people in this town only humor me because I have more money than all of them combined. But you know what? I don't give a damn." Marigold's eyes grew misty. "Not about them or about the money. People thought I was a gold digger, but I married Poppy's father because I loved him, plain and simple. He was the kindest, gentlest soul I've ever encountered. And he saw me for who I really am. What more could you ask for?"

"That sounds lovely," Simone agreed. "But right now, I'm more focused on never making Rowan want to throw anything at me."

"She doesn't seem the type. Although, as a doctor, she can also stitch you up. It could be worse."

"There you go with those silver linings again." Simone laughed, feeling some of the tension leave her shoulders. Marigold had a way of putting things into perspective like no one else Simone had ever met.

"You know," Marigold said, her tone turning thoughtful, "living together isn't about avoiding conflicts. It's about learning how to navigate them together. Now, I have a sixth sense about this kind of thing—only with other people, mind you. Could never see the writing on the wall for myself. But I think you two are in it for the long term."

"How do you know?" Simone's heart beat a little faster.

"The way you look at each other. That's the type of communication couples can't hide." Marigold gave Simone's arm a reassuring pat. "You love her, and she adores you. Nurture that every single day, and it'll work out the way you want."

"Hello?" Rowan called out as she opened the front door. Simone had been so engrossed in Marigold's conversation she hadn't even heard the key in the lock.

"We're in here," Simone called back. "And I have something to show you."

"As a doctor, that worries me," Rowan joked as she entered the room. "Hi, Marigold."

Marigold stood quickly. "Follow me to the bathroom."

"Now I'm even more intrigued," Rowan said. "Or should I be horrified?"

"Trust me; you'll love this." Marigold cracked the bathroom door open to reveal Poppy sitting on the floor with two balls of fur scaling her like a skyscraper. "Meet your new kittens."

"Our new what?" Rowan's eyes widened as she took in the slightly chaotic scene. In only a few minutes, the kittens had managed to scatter litter all over the floor and pile most of the contents of their food bowl into a corner.

"Just for tonight," Simone interjected before Rowan had a chance to get too mad. "It's sort of an emergency situation."

"Oh my goodness." Rowan's face softened as one of the kittens, the one with ginger fur, rubbed its tiny head against her ankle. "They're adorable."

A surge of relief washed over Simone. She'd been worried about Rowan's reaction, but seeing her girlfriend's face light up at the sight of the kittens made her heart inflate to nearly bursting levels.

"They are pretty cute, aren't they?" Simone said, bending down to pet the other one, which was black with a white star on its forehead.

"Look how tiny she is," Rowan whispered. "Or is it a he?"

"It's a little hard to tell," Marigold said with a shrug. "Won't know for sure until the vet visit, which is scheduled for tomorrow. Poppy and I had better get going, but I'll check in tomorrow to see how they did and get them to the appointment."

After Marigold and Poppy said their goodbyes, Simone and Rowan found themselves alone with their new furry houseguests. The kittens had settled down, curled up together in a makeshift bed of towels Poppy had arranged.

"So," Simone began, her throat a little dry. "You're really okay with them staying tonight? I mean, I know it's your first night here, and this probably isn't what you were expecting. "

"Of course, I'm okay with it," Rowan said softly, her eyes still fixed on the sleeping kittens. "How could I say no to these little faces?"

"I'm not sure. But Marigold wants us to keep them, so if we're saying no, you'll have to be the one to do it because I already failed the second I opened the door and saw them."

"I don't think we'll need to say no."

"Really?" A smile spread across Simone's face as she watched Rowan gently stroke the ginger kitten's head. "I wasn't sure if you'd want pets. We never really talked about it. Or, well, a lot of things."

Rowan looked up, her brow furrowing slightly as she met Simone's gaze. "What do you mean? You sound concerned."

Simone struggled to express her jumbled thoughts. "It's just this is a big step, you know? Moving in together. Even temporarily. I realized there's still so much we don't know about each other."

Rowan stood up slowly, her eyes never leaving Simone's. "Are you having second thoughts?"

"No, not second thoughts exactly. I want this to work so badly, Rowan. Not badly. You know what I mean. And I'm scared I'll mess it up somehow." Simone's heart raced as she saw the flicker of uncertainty in Rowan's eyes. "Oh, God, I'm already messing it up. I shouldn't have said anything."

Rowan stepped closer, taking Simone's hands in hers. "Hey, it's okay. I'm glad you're telling me this. I'd much rather you be honest about your fears than try to hide them."

"Really?" Simone's voice could barely be heard over the whir of the bathroom fan.

"Yes, really." Rowan put an arm around Simone's waist. "Come on. Let's sit down and talk about what's bothering you."

Simone nodded, letting Rowan lead her to the living room couch. They settled in, Rowan's arm draped comfortably around Simone's shoulders.

"Okay," Rowan said gently, "tell me what's going on in that beautiful head of yours."

Simone took a deep breath, leaning into the warmth of Rowan's embrace. "I don't think I ever pictured my life like this. I mean, from the time I was a teenager, I knew I wanted to be a doctor, and I thought I would be working in disaster zones around the globe. Not exactly the environment for settling down with kittens, you know?"

Rowan nodded, her fingers gently tracing patterns on Simone's arm. "I understand. Do you miss it?"

Simone paused, considering Rowan's question. "I miss the sense of purpose, the feeling that I was making a real difference in people's lives. But I don't miss the constant stress, the nightmares, the feeling that I was always one step away from breaking down completely."

"I can only imagine how intense that must have been. But you're still making a difference here, Simone. Every patient you help at Marbury matters."

"I know," Simone sighed. "It's just different. And then there's us. This relationship. It's so much more than I ever thought I'd have, and sometimes I worry I don't know how to do this. How to be a good partner, how to build a life together. Part of me is terrified that one day you'll wake up and realize you made a terrible mistake."

"Like I did with Lance, you mean?"

Simone winced at Rowan's words, realizing how her fears might have sounded. "I'm sorry, I didn't mean to imply—"

"No, it's okay," Rowan interjected, her voice soft. "I understand where you're coming from. But you have to know that when I married Lance, I was young and naive. I thought I knew what I wanted, but I was actually following a path that had been laid out for me. The experience taught me a lot about what I don't want in a relationship. But it also showed me what I do want."

"What's that?" Simone breathed.

Rowan turned to face Simone fully, her expression earnest and intense. "I want this. I want us to come home after a long day at work, and curl up together on the couch, and eat dinner while watching trashy TV."

Warmth spread through Simone's chest at Rowan's words. "I love trashy TV."

Rowan chuckled, pulling Simone close. "See? I didn't know that before, but now I do."

Simone nuzzled Rowan's neck. "There's something I was wondering about earlier."

"Oh?"

"Yeah. I was thinking..." Simone fought back the nerves that threatened to choke her words. "Are you into role-playing?"

"Role playing?" Rowan's eyebrows shot up. "Like, in the bedroom?"

Simone's face flushed hot. "Yeah. I mean, it's fine if you're not. It's just, when I got home today, I kind of got this image of you greeting me at the door in fishnets and an apron, like some 1950s housewife fantasy. It's silly—"

"I don't think it's silly at all," Rowan admitted, a mischievous glint in her eyes that set Simone's heart racing. "What were you thinking, I'd greet you holding a pipe and slippers?"

"A martini, actually. I'm not a fan of smoking."

Rowan laughed, her eyes crinkling at the corners. "A martini, huh? I do make a mean cocktail. We should keep this in mind." She leaned in close, her breath warm against Simone's ear. "But for now, how about we skip the costumes and get naked?"

A shiver ran down Simone's spine. "I like the sound of that," she murmured, tilting her head to capture Rowan's lips in a kiss.

As they kissed, slow and deep, Simone felt the last of her doubts melt away. Whatever the future held, she knew this was right.

A tiny meow interrupted them. They broke apart, laughing, to see the ginger kitten padding into the living room, looking up at them expectantly.

"I think someone's feeling left out," Rowan said, reaching down to scoop up the tiny ball of fur.

"We can't have that," Simone said, smiling as she watched Rowan cradle the kitten against her chest. "I think we'll have to hold off on that getting naked idea long enough to get the little ones settled in the bathroom for the night."

"I suppose I can go along with that," Rowan agreed. "But only if you promise to put on a pair of stilettos like the ones you wore the first night we met."

"You still remember those?" Simone grinned, her cheeks flushing as she recalled them, too. "If you play your cards right, I'm pretty sure that can be arranged."

CHAPTER TWENTY-TWO

The throbbing beat of a Velvet Sirens' song blasted from inside The Driftwood Lounge as a patron exited. Walking beside Rowan, Simone rushed ahead to grab the door before it could close.

"After you," Simone said with a sweep of her arm.

"Aren't you sweet?" Rowan patted Simone's cheek as she stepped into the crowded bar, which was draped with artificial pine and twinkle lights for the holiday season. Now that the cold weather had arrived and the outside deck was closed, the place was packed, and the warmth inside was a stark contrast to the chilly December air.

"They're playing our song," Simone said, or rather yelled, though Rowan could barely hear her. The music enveloped them fully, pulsing through air that was thick with the scent of beer and fried food.

Rowan raised an eyebrow at Simone, a playful smile tugging at her lips. "I didn't know we had a song," she shouted back, leaning in close to be heard over the music. "I think you're making that up."

"All the Velvet Sirens' songs belong to us," Simone declared with a wink, grabbing Rowan's hand and pulling her toward the bar. "Come on. Let's find Candace."

They weaved through the crowd, dodging elbows and narrowly avoiding spilled drinks, until Rowan spotted Candace on the far side of the room. She was dressed in the tackiest Christmas sweater Rowan had ever seen and waving them down like they were an airplane in distress and wouldn't be able to find their way on their own.

"Woo-hoo! Lovebirds! Over here!" Candace screamed as the music was coming to an end. Her voice echoed through the suddenly quiet bar. Several heads turned to look at them, and Rowan's cheeks went up in flames.

"Subtle as always," Simone joked, her face having gone several shades of pink.

"How in the world did she not bust us before we busted ourselves?" Rowan whispered in Simone's ear, taking the liberty of nibbling on the lobe for the briefest second.

Simone let out a tiny moan that made Rowan wish they were back in the privacy of their own home, where she could explore those little sounds like a symphony. But they were here for drinks with Candace, and Rowan knew she'd have to rein in her desires for now.

"I'm just glad I can hold your hand in public without any fear," Simone said, giving Rowan's hand a gentle squeeze as they approached Candace's table.

"If it isn't the hottest couple in Marbury," Candace greeted them with a mischievous grin. "I was beginning to think you two would ditch me. I know Rowan isn't a fan of the Velvet Sirens."

"What?" Simone appeared genuinely shocked and possibly a little hurt. "But they're how we met."

"I like them just fine now," Rowan said, shooting Candace a scowl for ratting her out. "It was a little harder to listen to them when I was trying not to think of you every time a song came on."

Simone's face softened at Rowan's words, and she leaned in to plant a quick kiss on her cheek. "I'm glad you've come around," she said, her voice warm with affection. "Not liking the Velvet Sirens would be a total deal breaker."

"Is that right?" Rowan challenged.

Candace rolled her eyes playfully. "Alright, you two. Time for drinks. The first round is on me." She flagged down a server, and they put in their orders.

"I'll have to treat sometime in the future, after I find a new job." Rowan perched on one of the high chairs.

"No luck on the job front yet?" Candace asked.

"Not a one. The first couple of weeks, I didn't mind. It was like being on vacation. The longer it goes, though..." Rowan's eyes swept the holiday lights in the bar, making her even more acutely aware of the passage of time. "The more I panic. It doesn't help that I'm trying to find an administration role, and all the hospitals that are hiring are in Boston or beyond."

"What about going back into the doctoring business?" Candace suggested, flashing a smile as the server set down their drinks. She lifted her glass in the air and waited for Rowan and Simone to do the same. "Cheers!"

Rowan clinked her glass against the others, the sound barely audible over the renewed thrum of music. She took a sip, savoring the dark porter, before answering Candace's question.

"Going back to practicing medicine? I don't know," she said, her voice tinged with uncertainty. "It's been so long since I've been in the thick of it every day."

"That's not true," Simone interjected. "You've been putting in so many shifts with the mobile clinic these past few weeks you're basically working full-time. Just, you know, for free."

Rowan nodded, acknowledging Simone's point. "True, but that's different. It's volunteer work, not a full-time career. And honestly, I'm not sure I want to go back to that level of intensity." She sighed, tracing a star shape into the condensation on her glass. "Speaking of intense, how has staffing been at the hospital?" Rowan lifted her drink to her lips.

Candace's eyes lit up with excitement. "You wouldn't believe it! I'm getting a full week off this Christmas."

Rowan nearly choked on her beer. "What? How is that possible?"

"Things have actually improved dramatically," Candace continued, her enthusiasm making her words turn into a song. "We've got a full staff now, and the turnover rate has plummeted."

"But the labor and delivery unit is set to close next week." Simone nervously cleared her throat while giving Candace a warning look. "It's far from perfect since you left."

"Right, no," Candace said, finally seeming to catch onto Simone's meaning. "The pizza in the cafeteria is awful, as a matter of fact. Crust like cardboard."

"You don't have to try to spare my feelings," Rowan told them, nearly adding that if that was the intent, it was much too late. After all, nobody wanted to hear how their ex had swooped in to save the day. "What I want to know is how did Lance turn things around so quickly?"

Candace glanced at Simone before responding. "To be honest, it's a bit of a mystery. Lance brought in this new staffing agency, and the next thing we knew, we had a full roster of experienced nurses and doctors to fill in the gaps."

Rowan's brow furrowed as she processed this information. "A new staffing agency? Do you know which one?"

Candace shook her head. "I'm not sure of the name. Something with an H, I think? But they've been great. Hey, maybe you could look into signing on with them until something permanent comes through."

"I don't think so." A knot formed in Rowan's stomach at

the thought of working under Lance's new management, even indirectly. "I'm not sure I want to step back into Marbury Hospital just yet."

"That makes sense." Candace took an extra-large sip of her beer, which Rowan suspected was to buy herself some time to think of a change in topic. "At least you'll have the money from the sale of the beach house coming in to tide you over."

"If only I'd actually heard from that mysterious lawyer Lance told me to watch out for. Or had any idea when this supposed sale was happening." Rowan sighed.

"Do you think he lied about buying it back from you?" Simone pressed. "Not that I mind living with you, of course, but it would be pretty rotten if he let you move out and Erica move in without any intention of following through."

"I don't think he was lying," Rowan said after considering for a moment. "Not that it would be the first time if he did. But my parents witnessed it, even if my dad always does side with Lance."

"It's so hard not to sock him in that snide face of his whenever our paths cross," Candace said, smacking her fist into her palm for good measure.

"Even though he's turned everything around and given you a week off?" Rowan teased.

Candace chuckled, shaking her head. "Okay, fine. Maybe I won't cause him physical harm. But I'll definitely give him a stern look."

"That'll teach him," Simone said with a grin.

"You're really getting into the Lance-bashing spirit now," Rowan agreed. "We might be able to stay friends."

"Come on," Candace pleaded. "You can't really think I would take his side just because of a few days off, do you? The dude donated our hospital's money to some Italian art school. Not cool."

"Nobody else knows that," Rowan reminded her, recalling how little discretion her friend sometimes had.

"It does raise an interesting question." Simone took a sip of her drink and then said, "How does a hospital that was struggling financially only a few months ago pay for so many new staff?"

A chill ran down Rowan's spine at the question. She had been so caught up in her own job search and adjusting to her new life with Simone that she hadn't given much thought to the hospital's finances or Lance's unscrupulous actions since she'd left. But now that Simone mentioned it, the sudden influx of funds was beyond suspicious.

"That's a good point," Rowan said. "Where is all this money coming from?"

"Maybe Lance found a secret stash of cash hidden in the walls," Candace joked, wiggling her fingers dramatically. "Maybe he found enough to pay you for the house so you two can buy a bigger place. You must be going stir-crazy in that little cottage."

"Actually, we passed our first major test," Rowan said with complete seriousness. "Simone's an over."

"Thank God," Candace declared. "Only sociopaths are unders."

"W-what are you talking about?" Simone sputtered. "Is this something sexual? Am I going to die from embarrassment? What is an over?"

"The toilet paper," both Rowan and Candace answered in unison.

"Oh, totally. There's only one correct direction for toilet paper. Was Lance an under?" Simone asked in a deadly serious tone.

"Please. That man never replaced a toilet paper roll in his life," Rowan scoffed.

"Are there any other tests I should watch out for?" Simone

laughed like she was joking, but Rowan detected a hint of genuine curiosity in her voice.

"Depends. Have you come up with names for those kittens yet?" Candace's eyes darted from Simone to Rowan. "In my experience, that's the biggest challenge a couple can face, other than maybe naming an actual baby."

Rowan chuckled, remembering the intense debate she and Simone had over naming their new feline additions. "We managed to compromise. I got to name the orange tabby Ginger, and Simone chose Pepper for the black one."

"Pepper and Ginger," Candace repeated, nodding approvingly. "Cute and complementary. You two are definitely relationship goals."

"Another test down. Who knew I was passing with flying colors?" Simone playfully wiped imaginary sweat off her brow.

Rowan was about to respond when her phone buzzed in her pocket. She pulled it out, expecting a text from her mother or maybe even Erica but instead saw a notification from her banking app. Her eyes widened as she read the message.

"Oh my God," she gasped. "Someone deposited $750,000 into my bank account."

"If you don't want it, I'll take it," Candace offered.

"Are you sure it's not some kind of scam?" Simone asked.

Rowan clicked on the text from her bank, her heart pounding. "It's from Lance. That was the purchase price of the beach house when I bought it from him. I can only assume that's what this is for."

Simone leaned in, putting her hand on Rowan's arm. "That's good news, right? I mean, you were certain you'd be waiting forever to get the money."

Rowan stared at her phone, her mind reeling as she tried to process the sudden influx of money. "I guess it's good. But it doesn't make sense. I assumed there would be lawyers involved, paperwork to sign. He'd need a mortgage, for sure.

This feels too easy. Where the hell did Lance get this kind of cash?"

ROWAN STOOD at the door with a to-go mug of coffee in her outstretched hand. "Have a lovely day at the hospital, darling. I'm sure you will since apparently my ex is running it all perfectly."

Simone winced like Rowan had tossed freezing water into her face. "You know I'll never defend that man, right? I think everything he's doing is fishy, and I trust him less than I trust oysters that have been sitting out in the blazing sun for a week."

"I'm sorry. Ever since we had drinks with Candace, I can't get Lance out of my head."

Simone grimaced. "Doesn't say much for my bedroom skills."

Rowan couldn't help laughing. "I promise that is the one time I don't think about anything else. Especially Lance."

"I should hope not." Simone took the mug before placing a kiss on Rowan's cheek. "Try to have a good day, and good luck on the job search. I'm sure something will come through soon."

Rowan watched Simone's car disappear down the street before closing the door with a sigh. The house seemed emptier than usual, the silence amplified by the thoughts swirling in her head. She made her way to the living room, where her laptop sat on the coffee table, surrounded by scribbled notes and coffee mugs in varying degrees of emptiness.

Rowan glanced down at the kitten circling her ankles. "I don't know about you, Pepper, but I'm going to get to work. After another cup of coffee."

Once she had fixed herself a cup, Rowan settled onto the couch, pulling the computer onto her lap. Her fingers hovered over the keyboard as she debated her next move. Technically, she was no longer an employee of Marbury Hospital and had no right to access their systems. What were the chances her login credentials still worked? Everyone had been in such a rush to put Lance back on his throne, it would hardly be a surprise if some details had fallen through the cracks.

Rowan took a deep breath and typed in her old username and password. To her relief, the system accepted her credentials without hesitation. She was in.

"I guess Lance isn't as on the ball as everyone thinks." Rowan scratched behind Ginger's ear as the kitten jumped up beside her.

It didn't take too many clicks to find the name of the staffing agency Lance was using: Hydra. Oddly, that rang a bell.

Closing her eyes, Rowan tapped a pencil against the blank notebook. Where had she heard that name before? Not at the hospital in Boston, of that she was sure. She tightened her lids as if trying to zoom in on a memory.

The bill in Lance's office, the one for his rehab stay. Hadn't that been Hydra, too? She remembered because the whole thing had irritated her so. It still chapped her hide that Marbury Hospital had paid for his time at the cushy executive resort after all the harm he'd caused the organization.

But why would a rehab center have a staffing agency?

Rowan typed the company's name into her browser's search bar, landing on a website that was all business-speak that said absolutely nothing about who they were, but nevertheless claimed to be the solution to every problem a busy hospital administrator might face. Rowan frowned at the screen, her suspicion growing.

Rowan had fallen deep down the rabbit hole by the time a knock at the door startled her back into awareness of her surroundings.

"Are we getting a turtle this time?" Rowan asked the kittens, who were playing on their post. She got up from the couch, already practicing turning down another stray pet. But when she opened the door, she was surprised to find her mother instead. "You're not Marigold."

"Not last time I checked." Her mother held up a cardboard drink carrier with two cups. "I have your favorite coffee and some pastries, too."

"This is a surprise. A pleasant one," Rowan quickly added, stepping aside so her mother could enter. "Thank you."

"I wanted to see how you're doing," her mother said, setting the coffee and pastries on the kitchen counter.

"Since Dad booted me to the curb for the world's best CMO?"

"I don't know what he was thinking. Aside from you having every qualification, if your father thinks letting you go won't damage your relationship with him, he's delusional."

Rowan's bottom lip trembled as she reached for two plates to put the pastries on. "I really appreciate you saying that."

"I've been working on him behind the scenes. I want you to know that."

"And?" Rowan handed a coffee and pastry to her mom before waving her to the living room.

"He's a stubborn oaf, but I won't let that deter me. Meanwhile, I'm sorry to report that Lance has been over to the house almost every night for dinner since he got back to town." Her mother's mouth puckered like she'd tasted a lemon. "Was that man always so insufferable?"

"Which one? My father or my ex?"

"Rowan, you should show more respect for your father. Although, I'm tempted to say both," her mother confessed. "You know what he said the other night? Don't do one percent better, but one hundred. Who talks like that?"

Rowan frowned. "Actually, I just read that exact quote on this website." Rowan swiveled the laptop for her mom to see.

Rowan's mother peered at the laptop screen, her brow

furrowing. "Hydra Capital Management? I hate that company." Her mom angrily took a bite out of her pastry.

Rowan turned to her mother, surprised by her vehement reaction. "You know about Hydra Capital Management?"

Her mother nodded, swallowing her bite of pastry. "They've been sponsoring these CEO retreats your father has been attending lately. I don't know exactly what they do there, but if you ask me, it's a golf outing the company gets to write off on its taxes."

"That's why you don't like them?" Rowan suspected there was more. Her mother had never seemed to care much about tax loopholes.

Her mother shook her head, setting down her coffee cup with a little more force than necessary. "No. It's more the way they seem to be influencing your father lately. Ever since he started attending those retreats, he's started sounding like... well, like Lance. All this motivational mumbo-jumbo and business speak. If I didn't know better, I'd think your father had joined a cult."

"They also run the rehab facility Lance went to."

"That's odd, isn't it?"

"Lance is using one of the Hydra off-shoots as a source for temporary employees. Which is probably saving Marbury a boatload because you don't have to pay them any benefits, and they're easy to get rid of. It goes against everything the hospital stands for."

Rowan's mother sighed, looking troubled. "It sounds like this Hydra company has their tentacles in everything these days. And not in a good way."

"I agree. There's something very off about all of this." Rowan tapped her fingers against her coffee. "Just out of curiosity, have you heard from Erica at all?"

Grace's expression softened at the mention of Erica. "I have, actually. She called me a few days ago."

Rowan tried to keep her tone neutral, despite the pang in her chest. "How is she doing?"

"She seems to be adjusting to living in that big house all alone. If it makes you feel better, she's completely livid with her father."

"Why?" Rowan was genuinely surprised at this news. "He bought her the house and everything."

"Everything is right. He's gotten her a new car, and he keeps sending over clothes. He even gave her a diamond necklace. The people at his credit card company probably think he has a mistress."

"How the hell is he affording all of this?" Coldness overtook Rowan, settling in the pit of her stomach. "You don't think he could be gambling again, do you?"

Grace hesitated before responding. "I don't think it's gambling this time. I overheard him on the phone the other day, talking about a big investment deal he'd made. Something about undervalued real estate and maximizing returns."

Rowan rolled her eyes, sure whatever scheme her ex had gotten involved in was shady but not wanting to know the details. "At least it's not crypto, I guess. I have to say, I'm surprised Erica isn't enjoying being Daddy's spoiled princess."

"Honestly, I think she's starting to realize he's always used gifts as a stand-in for actual affection. You were the one who went to all her events. He would apologize after with a gift." Her mother took a drink of coffee as Rowan sat in stunned silence, pondering what she'd just heard.

"Did Erica actually say that?" A lump formed in Rowan's throat. Despite the strain in their relationship, she still cared deeply for Erica. The thought that her stepdaughter might come around filled her with a bittersweet hope.

"Not in so many words, but I could read between the lines. She misses you, Rowan. And Simone, too. I think she's starting to understand how much you were there for her, even when

Lance wasn't." Grace reached out and patted her hand. "She's sad. She's angry. Give her space. Let her work through this. I think all of you will come out stronger for it."

"I hope so, because right now, I feel weak." Rowan tried to blink away some tears, but failed.

Grace pulled her into a tight hug. "Oh, sweetheart. You are one of the strongest people I know. Don't ever forget that."

Rowan let herself sink into the embrace, the tears flowing freely now. She hadn't realized how much she needed this comfort, this reassurance that she wasn't alone in her struggles. For a few precious moments, Rowan allowed herself to be vulnerable, to let go of the weight she'd been carrying.

"Thanks, Mom." Rowan wiped the tears from her cheeks with the back of her hand and took a shaky breath, trying to regain her composure. "Sometimes I still feel like I'm the bad guy, that I should carry around so much guilt and shame for leaving Lance and disappointing Erica. But I'm finally happy with where I am in my life, and I'm tired of blaming myself."

Her mom gave her a reassuring smile. "You have nothing to feel guilty about. You made the right choice for yourself, and that's what matters most. Erica will come around in time. She's a smart girl, and deep down, she knows how much you care about her."

All Rowan could do was nod and pray her mother was right.

CHAPTER TWENTY-THREE

"Let me help you with those." Simone rushed to grab one of the heavy bags from Rowan's arms as she entered the mobile clinic, a light dusting of snow following her inside. "Where's Pablo? I thought Marigold put him on present duty."

"Unfortunately, he texted right before I met up with my mom to say he was going to be out sick today." Rowan set her two bags down next to the reception desk, a brightly wrapped gift spilling out onto the floor.

"Oh no! Poor Pablo." Simone set her bag down beside Rowan's. "He was really looking forward to passing out holiday gifts to the families today."

"I know. At least he got a hold of me in time to grab up everything my mom had. I'd feel terrible if we ran out of presents before everyone got one."

Surveying the three bulging sacks, Simone laughed. "I can't see that happening with all of this. Look." She held up a box wrapped in striped paper with a shiny silver ribbon. "This ribbon is perfection."

"Why, thank you." Rowan's cheeks flushed, and she busied herself arranging the garland that had been draped across the reception desk for decoration. "I may have gone a bit overboard."

Simone smiled, her heart warming at Rowan's modesty. "They're amazing. If it had been left up to me, we would've been lucky if they had paper on them."

"I've had a lot of practice. When I was a teenager, my mom and I used to wrap gifts for Santa to give to every patient who was in the hospital on Christmas morning."

"Did your dad play Santa?"

Rowan let out a hearty laugh. "Hell no. My dad would never allow himself to do something so frivolous in front of his staff. I think he was afraid they wouldn't respect him if they ever saw him let loose. But he hired a Santa to come in and make the rounds, not just for the kids but the adults, too."

"That's so nice. It sucks to be in the hospital on a holiday, no matter what your age."

"Yeah. It might sound strange, but the Christmas season at Marbury Hospital is one of my happiest memories growing up." Rowan re-centered a bow on a gift. "We'd bring in cookies for the staff, and the high school choir would come and sing carols. It was really special."

"Do you have a big family celebration?" Simone asked, realizing that even though the holidays were approaching, she and Rowan hadn't really talked about any plans.

"No, it was just me and my mom and dad on Christmas morning. But we'd host a big dinner later in the day. One thing my parents were always good at was inviting people who didn't have anywhere else to be."

Simone nodded, knowing how seriously Grace Colchester took her role as a pillar of Marbury society. "When I was a kid in New Orleans, my dad had a huge extended family. My grandmother's house would be completely packed."

"What was that like?" Rowan sounded a little awestruck at the thought.

"Loud." Simone chuckled at the memory. "I remember it being really loud. One year, there were so many presents in the living room you couldn't even walk from the door to the tree." Her eyes misted. "I had no idea we'd never do it again."

"Because of the hurricane?"

"Yes. A lot of my relatives were displaced with all the damage, and they ended up settling in so many different places. My mom and I included. My grandmother really made an effort to stay active in my life, but she died a few years after my dad did and..." Simone finished with a shrug. "Nothing was ever the same. She was the rock of that family. Always making sure everyone knew it was someone's birthday or gathering the family together for holidays."

"What about your mother?" Rowan began emptying the bags she'd brought in, placing wrapped gifts under the small tree in the corner.

Simone knelt down to help. "She's like me. Quiet. I think my dad's big family terrified her. Now that she's out west, I hardly see her. We'll have a video call on Christmas, but between the distance and my erratic work schedule, we haven't been able to coordinate spending the holiday together in person for several years. I miss it."

Rowan placed her hand on Simone's shoulder. "I'm sorry. It must be hard to not have any family around, especially during the holidays."

Simone gave Rowan's hand a grateful squeeze. "It is. But this year feels different. Being here, helping with the clinic, spending time with you." She met Rowan's gaze, her heart fluttering at the tenderness reflecting therein. "I know it's probably hard for you, too, missing Erica this year."

Rowan sighed, averting her gaze as she adjusted an ornament on the tree. "It is. I know I didn't come into her life until after the Santa Claus days were done, but I did everything I could to make it a special season. Every year, Erica and I would bake a gingerbread house and decorate it together. On Christmas morning, I'd wake up really early to turn on the tree lights, fill the stockings, and put cinnamon rolls in the oven."

"That sounds really—" Simone stopped talking as her phone buzzed with an incoming text. "Good news. Marigold found someone to sub for Pablo today. They should be here soon."

"Just in time," Rowan said, checking her watch. "We're supposed to open in fifteen minutes. I was starting to think I was going to be adding receptionist to my resume."

"With the amount of time you're putting in with the clinic, Marigold's likely to have you adding the title of director to your accomplishments pretty soon."

"If only it came with a paycheck," Rowan said with a wistful sigh. "You don't mind that I'm spending so much time doing this instead of looking for a full-time job?"

"Of course not." Simone paused, considering her words carefully. "Rowan, I've seen how passionate you are about this clinic. And the way you've thrown yourself into organizing the holiday donations. It's inspiring."

"This is what happens when Marigold and I go for coffee together. We come up with ideas."

"They're good ideas. Very good." Simone wrapped her arms around Rowan's waist. Simone leaned in, her lips brushing Rowan's cheek. "You're amazing, you know that?"

Just then, the door of the mobile clinic burst open, letting in a gust of cold air and a flurry of snowflakes. Erica stumbled inside, her cheeks flushed from the cold and her arms laden with bags.

Instantly, Simone and Rowan sprang apart. Between their exaggerated reaction and the shellshocked expression on Erica's face, one would have thought the two of them had been caught in the middle of performing a satanic ritual in the clinic lobby.

"Erica!" Rowan exclaimed, her voice a pitch higher than usual. "What are you doing here?"

"Hi." Erica swallowed, and for a moment Simone feared she would turn around and bolt. But instead, Erica took a deep breath and squared her shoulders. "I'm here to fill in at the reception desk. Marigold called me about Pablo being out sick."

"Oh," Rowan said, her voice still strained. "That's... That's great. You're volunteering now?"

"I have been," Erica said, not making eye contact. "A few times."

"Do you like it?" Simone asked, uncertain what else to say other than addressing the elephant in the room that no one seemed quite ready to tackle yet. Also, it was hard not to put two and two together to realize Erica had arranged her volunteering when Rowan and Simone weren't on the schedule.

"It's been eye-opening," Erica said, her cheeks turning slightly pink. "I had no idea how much poverty there was in Marbury. It was overwhelming at first, seeing the need up close like this."

An awkward silence settled over the cramped space of the mobile clinic. Erica shifted from foot to foot, her eyes darting between Simone and Rowan.

"Did Marigold tell you we were working today?" Simone finally asked, keeping her tone as casual as she could. Knowing Marigold, it wouldn't surprise her to learn this little reunion had come as a total shock to Erica, too.

"Yeah. I knew." Erica set her things down behind the desk and removed her coat. "I won't lie, I'm still weirded out about you two. Marigold is right, though. I don't want to be that person who impedes other people's happiness. It's going to take some getting used to, but I'm going to try to get past it."

Simone felt giddy as a wave of relief washed over her. She glanced at Rowan, who looked equally moved by Erica's words.

"That means a lot, Erica," Rowan said softly. "I've missed you."

Erica's eyes glistened as she whispered. "I've missed you, too. Both of you."

The moment was interrupted by a sharp knock on the clinic door. Simone hurried to open it, revealing a heavily pregnant woman bundled up against the cold.

"Fabienne!" Simone exclaimed, ushering her inside. "Come in out of that wind. How are you feeling?"

Fabienne's words tumbled out in a flurry of Creole as she brushed the snow from her clothing, her dark eyes wide with worry. Simone listened intently, her brow furrowing as she pieced together the woman's rapid speech.

"She says she started noticing contractions this morning at breakfast," Simone said, translating for Erica and Rowan's benefit. "She had them yesterday, too, off and on."

"That sounds like Braxton Hicks contractions," Rowan said with confidence, already heading toward the exam room. "But we should check to be sure."

Simone explained to Fabienne that they would examine her to make sure everything was alright. As they made their way to the exam room, Simone noticed Fabienne wincing and holding her lower back.

"Have you been able to see your obstetrician recently?" Simone asked.

Fabienne shook her head, her expression clouding with worry. "*Non,*" she replied softly in Creole. "I have not been able to. The doctor moved to the hospital in Hyannis. That's too far for me to travel because I have no car."

A knot formed in Simone's stomach as she helped Fabienne onto the exam table. This was exactly the type of scenario she had feared and what Rowan had tried to argue to the board would happen with the closure of Marbury Hospital's Labor and Delivery unit. It had left a gaping hole in prenatal care for women like Fabienne. She exchanged a concerned glance with Rowan, knowing they shared the same anger toward a healthcare system that could so callously disregard the needs of the patients it was supposed to help.

As Rowan set up their new portable ultrasound machine, Simone did a quick physical examination. Fabienne's blood pressure was back to a normal range, but the woman's swollen belly was taut, and Simone could feel the muscles contracting beneath her hands. She glanced at the clock, timing the duration.

"How far along are you now, Fabienne?"

"Thirty-four weeks," Fabienne replied, her voice tight with discomfort. "Is something wrong?"

"You're doing great." Simone kept her tone calm and reassuring. "We're going to check everything out to be sure. These contractions could be normal Braxton Hicks, but we want to make sure you're not going into preterm labor."

Rowan applied the ultrasound gel to Fabienne's belly and began moving the wand across her skin. The rapid whoosh-whoosh of the baby's heartbeat filled the small exam room.

"Heart rate is good," Rowan said, her eyes fixed on the ultrasound screen. "Baby is in the occipito-anterior position."

"That's great news, Fabienne. It means the baby is head down," Simone explained in Creole. "That's what we want to see at this stage. If you do go into labor, that position will make things easier."

"But the contractions," Fabienne said, wincing as another one gripped her. "They hurt. I'm getting scared."

Simone placed a comforting hand on Fabienne's shoulder. "I know it's scary, but we're going to do everything we can to help you and your baby."

Rowan moved the ultrasound wand, studying the screen intently. "The placenta looks good, no signs of abruption. And I'm not seeing any indications of preterm labor yet. But the fundal height is measuring slightly smaller than expected for thirty-four weeks. And I'm noticing some fluid retention in her legs. Did we ever get tests run for liver enzymes, protein in the urine, or platelet count?"

"I don't think so." Simone pressed a hand against Fabienne's abdomen, and the woman sucked in a breath. "Did that feel tender?"

Fabienne nodded. Simone met Rowan's eyes, a silent understanding passing between them as several possible diagnoses sprang to mind, none of which they could confirm or rule out with the resources they had on hand. Their patient needed more advanced care and monitoring than what they could provide here at the mobile clinic.

"Fabienne, I know it's been difficult for you to get to your appointments since the Marbury L&D closed," Simone said gently. "But with your due date getting closer and these concerning symptoms, it's very important that we find a way to get you the care you need."

Fabienne's eyes welled with tears. "I don't know what to do. I can't miss work to take the bus all the way to Hyannis. And taxis are so expensive." She shook her head helplessly.

Before Simone had a chance to translate, Rowan said, "Please tell her we'll make sure the hospital social worker is aware of her situation and can maybe help arrange transportation."

Simone relayed the information, watching as some of the tension eased from Fabienne's shoulders. "*Merci*," the woman whispered, a glimmer of hope returning to her eyes. "Thank you both so much."

"Of course," Rowan said warmly. "We want to do everything we can to make sure you and your baby get the care you need. In the meantime, I'm going to write you a prescription for a medication that can help stop these contractions and prevent you from going into preterm labor."

After finishing up the exam and ensuring Fabienne had the information she needed for the doctor in Hyannis, Simone walked her patient back out to the reception area.

"Since I won't see you again before Christmas, here's a gift for you and the baby." Simone took a present from under the tree.

Fabienne's eyes widened as she accepted the brightly wrapped package. "*Merci*," she whispered, her voice trembling with emotion. "You have already done so much."

"It's our pleasure," Simone said, giving the woman a warm hug. "You take care of yourself, okay? Don't hesitate to call if you have any concerns at all before your next appointment."

"Is everything okay with her and the baby?" Erica asked as soon as Fabienne had bundled up and headed out into the swirling snow.

Simone sighed, leaning against the reception desk. "For now. But it's situations like this that highlight how damaging the closure of Marbury's L&D unit has been. Fabienne needs consistent prenatal care. But without reliable transportation, how can she be expected to follow through?"

Rowan nodded grimly. "It's not just the pregnant women. Elderly patients, people with disabilities, those without reliable transportation—they're all struggling to access care now with the various cost-saving measures the hospital has implemented."

"Is this my dad's fault?" Erica asked, her voice sounding almost timid.

Simone glanced at Rowan, unsure how to respond in a way that wouldn't cause more damage to a relationship that had only just begun to heal.

"It's complicated," Simone began.

Rowan nodded, her expression softening as she looked at Erica. "Your father inherited a lot of problems when he took on the role of CMO."

"He also made some poor decisions in the past," Simone added, unwilling to let Lance off the hook completely. "Decisions that put the hospital's finances in a precarious position."

Erica's brow furrowed as she processed this information.

"But I thought things were going so much better since Dad came back. He's always talking about all the improvements he's making, and how he's turning things around. He said he was on track to get a big bonus this year."

Simone and Rowan exchanged a loaded glance at this revelation. If that was true, it might explain where all the money Lance had been throwing around recently was coming from.

Simone chose her next words carefully. "I'm sure your father is working hard, but—"

"Sometimes the metrics used to measure success in healthcare administration don't always align with what's best for patients," Rowan finished diplomatically.

"Are you trying to say my father makes money from cutting services people need?" Erica asked, her voice rising slightly.

Simone hesitated, not wanting to upset Erica further. "It's not that simple. Healthcare administration involves a lot of difficult decisions about resource allocation."

Erica's eyes flashed with sudden anger. "You don't have to baby me. I can handle the truth. Is my dad profiting while people like Fabienne suffer?"

"That's one way of looking at it." Simone watched Erica's face carefully, seeing the conflict play out in her eyes. She knew this was a delicate moment—one that could either strengthen their newly repaired relationship or shatter it again.

"You two must think I'm a spoiled brat," Erica said quietly, her eyes downcast. "Never holding a real job. Gallivanting to Italy. Letting my dad buy me a house. I... So many people aren't so lucky, and now it seems like all the privileges I've enjoyed came at their expense."

Simone's heart ached at the raw vulnerability in Erica's voice. Reaching out, she gently squeezed her friend's hand. "You're not responsible for your father's decisions."

Erica's face crumpled, tears welling in her eyes. She glanced at Rowan, who looked equally pained by Erica's distress.

"Oh, honey," Rowan said softly, moving around the desk to pull Erica into an embrace. "You're here now, helping at the clinic. That counts for something."

Erica clung to Rowan, her shoulders shaking with silent sobs. Simone's heart ached for them both as she watched the two women embrace. She knew how much Rowan had missed this connection with Erica, but she was sorry it had been rekindled under these circumstances. It was going to take a lot for Erica to fully come to terms with what her father had done, and right now, she didn't know the half of it.

Simone stepped closer, placing a comforting hand on Erica's back. "Rowan's right. You're already taking steps to make a difference by volunteering here. That shows a lot of character."

Erica pulled back from Rowan's embrace, wiping at her eyes. "I want to do something to help. Really help, not just volunteer a few hours here and there at the clinic. I need to do more. All those years, I was so oblivious. I feel like I owe it to this community to try to make things right somehow."

"We'll find a way for you to do that," Rowan assured her. "In the meantime, don't let this ruin your holidays."

Erica nodded, wiping away the last of her tears. "Okay, but can I ask you for something? It's not anything that costs money. I was wondering, can we make a gingerbread house together like we used to?"

Rowan's eyes welled with tears, and she pulled Erica into another tight embrace. "Of course we can, sweetheart. I'd love that."

"Simone, too," Erica added.

Simone had to swallow the lump that had formed in her throat before she could speak. "Me? Are you sure?"

Erica nodded, a small smile breaking through her tears. "Yeah, I'm sure. You're part of this weird-ass family now, right?"

CHAPTER TWENTY-FOUR

"There's a punch bowl in there," Candace said, pointing to the entrance to Marigold's formal dining room. "But I'd be careful if I were you."

Rowan's eyes went from the glass of neon-green concoction in her friend's hand to the room filled to bursting with all the children of the mobile clinic volunteers for whom this party was being held. "Careful of what, the punch or the kids?"

"Probably both," Simone guessed with a laugh.

"I'm heading to the living room," Candace informed them. "I hear there's a bartender and no kids allowed."

"Tempting," Rowan said. "But we need to say hello to Marigold, so we'll have to take our chances."

The minute they stepped into the room, Poppy and several children ran by, blowing into kazoos and nearly ramming into Rowan's legs.

"Whoa, whoa. Go around the adult humans, not through them." Rowan laughed as she side-stepped to avoid impact.

"Sorry," Poppy called over her shoulder, barely slowing down as she and her friends continued their chaotic circuit of the room.

Simone reached out and steadied Rowan with a gentle hand on her elbow. "You okay there?"

"Just fine," Rowan replied, feeling warmth spread through her at Simone's touch. "Though I'm beginning to think we should have worn protective gear to this party. Marigold is one brave woman to host a New Year's Eve party for what has got to be the entire child population of Marbury."

"That's Noon Year's Eve," Marigold corrected, coming up beside them with two glasses in hand. "Here you go. Try some of my famous holiday punch."

Rowan eyed the foamy contents of the glass she was handed with a frown. "Is this safe for consumption? It looks radioactive. And regardless of what miracles Lance has managed to pull off since his return, Marbury's emergency department is notoriously understaffed during the holidays."

Marigold winked. "Perfectly safe, I promise. It's Sprite, sherbet, and food coloring. We call it Grinch punch."

Simone took a sip, nodding with approval. "It's actually quite good. Sweet but refreshing."

Rowan cautiously tasted hers, pleasantly surprised by the creamy, citrusy flavor. "You're right. It's delicious. But I've gotta know; why are you calling this a Noon Year's Eve Party?"

"Oh, it's a brilliant idea I found on the internet. We're counting down to noon instead of midnight." Marigold pointed to the ceiling where a shiny piñata in the shape of a disco ball was hanging from a rope. "At high noon, our ball is dropping. Only, unlike in Times Square, we'll be hitting ours with sticks to get candy. This way, the kids can celebrate without staying up late, and the parents can still have their evening plans."

"Or collapse into bed at a reasonable hour," Rowan added with a chuckle. "Honestly, I'm not sure which I'm more excited about, celebrating with the kids or the prospect of an early night."

Simone nudged her playfully. "Come on. Where's your sense of adventure? The night is young, and so are we."

"Speak for yourself," Rowan joked, though her stomach fluttered at the saucy look in Simone's eyes. They might not be going out for the evening, but she definitely had some plans for how to celebrate, just the two of them, back at the cottage later.

"If you'll excuse me, I need to greet some guests who just came in. The volunteers for the mobile clinic have done so much, and I want them to know I appreciate it." Marigold bustled off, leaving Rowan and Simone alone in the bustling room.

Rowan took another sip of her punch, surveying the chaos around them. Children darted back and forth, their excited shrieks punctuated by the occasional pop of a party favor. Amidst the pandemonium, she caught sight of her father looking like he was trying to press himself into a corner and disappear.

She cringed inwardly as he made eye contact with her and began to make his way over. With the skill of a magician, Simone disappeared from her side, and Rowan would've given anything to slip away, too, but the ingrained sense of duty that had been drilled into her since childhood glued her feet in place.

"Hi, Dad. Where's Mom?"

"Off doing some activity with the children that she got roped into. Does that have any alcohol?" He looked pleadingly at the punch in Rowan's hand.

"I really hope not since Marigold is dishing out cups of it to all the kids."

"I heard there's a full bar in the living room. Care to join me?" he asked.

Rowan glanced around the room and hoping to catch Simone's eye to plead for rescue, but her girlfriend was engrossed in conversation with Candace in the foyer.

"Sure. Lead the way." The second Rowan said this, Poppy

and a full regimen of children marched by like they were hosting their own parade, a little dog Rowan wasn't sure she'd seen before yapping as it followed along. "I have to admit I'm surprised you showed up today."

"No way out of it," her dad responded, weaving his way through the crowd until they reached the much quieter living room. "The Brewster Foundation has always been a major supporter of the hospital, even if I do have my doubts about that new lady-director of theirs."

"It's okay to call them directors now, Dad. You can leave out the lady part."

Rowan's father waved his hand dismissively as they walked up to the bar. "You know what I mean."

"If you mean that Marigold is single-handedly responsible for bringing together all of the volunteers here today to make her dream of a mobile health clinic for the Cape's underserved community a reality, then yes, I know exactly what you mean," Rowan replied, unable to keep the edge out of her voice. Her father's old-fashioned attitudes never failed to irk her.

His eyes narrowed as he ordered a scotch from the bartender. "That's not what I meant, and you know it. I'm talking about her lack of experience running a foundation of the size and scope of the Brewster Foundation."

Rowan sighed, setting down her unfinished punch and accepting a glass of white wine instead. "I guess she's a natural at it, then. Frankly, you should be grateful. The mobile clinic has really picked up the slack and is saving Marbury Hospital a ton in unnecessary ER visits, among other things."

"I don't know about that. Lance has never mentioned—"

"Since when is Lance the CEO? When I was doing that job, you made it very clear to me that the buck stopped with you." Rowan wasn't normally so combative with her father, but it irritated her beyond belief to know that her ex was back to his old ways, running the hospital that had been in the care of her family for generations like it was his personal property.

Her father's expression tightened, clearly not liking her tone. "Things have changed, Rowan. Lance has been instrumental in turning the hospital around. In fact, I have some news I think you'll be interested in."

Rowan tensed, bracing herself. Her father's idea of "interesting news" rarely aligned with her own.

"Oh?" she prompted, taking a sip of her wine.

"We've been in talks with Hydra Capital Management." Her father's voice lowered conspiratorially. "They're interested in acquiring Marbury Hospital."

Rowan nearly choked on her wine. "What? You're selling the hospital?"

Her father's eyes darted around the room, as if checking for eavesdroppers. "Keep your voice down," he hissed. "Nothing's final yet, but yes, we're considering it."

"You can't be serious."

Her father's eyes gleamed with excitement. "Oh, but I am. Hydra has been making waves in the healthcare industry, acquiring and improving struggling hospitals—"

"You said yourself that Marbury Hospital has been turned around under Lance's brilliant leadership. So which is it? Are you making progress, implementing new programs, and expanding services, or are you on the brink of ruin?"

Her father's expression hardened. "It's not that simple. The healthcare landscape is changing rapidly. We need to adapt or risk being left behind."

Rowan couldn't believe what she was hearing. Her father had always been a stubborn man, set in his ways, but this was beyond anything she could have imagined.

Rowan took a deep breath, trying to quell the anger and disbelief rising within her. "You think selling out to some corporate vultures is the answer? Dad, Marbury Hospital has been in our family for generations. It's not just a business; it's a community institution."

Her father set his glass down on the bar with a decisive clink. "I'm well aware of the hospital's legacy, young lady. But sometimes tradition has to make way for progress. Hydra has the resources and the vision to take Marbury Hospital to the next level. This is a good thing, whether you can see it or not."

Rowan shook her head. "I can't believe you're even considering this. After everything we've been through to keep the hospital afloat, to keep it in the family. How can you throw that all away?"

"It's not like that at all. Lance has assured me our family will still have a role in its governance. This isn't the end of an era, Rowan. It's the beginning of a new one."

"Oh my God. Lance again?" Rowan felt like the room was spinning. She couldn't believe what she was hearing. "How can you still trust his instincts so blindly after everything he's put the hospital through?"

Her father looked at her impatiently. "Because he has a keen business sense. Something you never quite grasped."

The barb stung, but Rowan refused to let it show. "That's it then? You've already made up your mind? The hospital is just another asset to be bought and sold to the highest bidder?"

"You're being dramatic," her father said dismissively. "Nothing has been finalized yet. But yes, I believe this is the right move for the hospital's future. And frankly, it's not your decision to make."

Rowan flinched like she'd been slapped across the face. Her father's words cut deep, reopening old wounds she thought had long since healed. She set her wine glass down on the bar, afraid she might crush the delicate stem in her grip.

"You're right," she said tightly. "It's not my decision. Not anymore. But I still care about what happens to Marbury Hospital."

"Then trust what I'm telling you. Hydra's the real deal. They've saved several other struggling hospitals. This is a good thing."

"Then why aren't you telling people about it?" Rowan asked. "Let the community know so they can celebrate if it's really such a great thing. Hell, half the hospital staff is here right now. Why not make an announcement?"

"That's not how they work," he said, motioning with his hand for her to keep her voice down. "They don't want the publicity. They simply want to help small community hospitals. Look what they've done the past month or so. Everything has been changed for the better." He downed the rest of his drink and set his glass on the bar. "Anyway, I better socialize."

Rowan watched her father walk away, her mind reeling from their conversation. She couldn't believe he was considering selling the hospital, let alone to a corporation that came across more like a cult than a business. The fact that Lance was a driving force behind all this made it all the more unsettling.

She needed some air. And Simone.

Rowan scanned the crowd until she spotted her girlfriend chatting with Candace by the front door. She made her way over, dodging rambunctious children as she went.

"There you are," Simone said, her smile fading as she took in Rowan's troubled expression. "Is everything okay?"

"Yeah. Why are you looking so down?" Candace asked.

"No reason at all."

"Are you sure? It looked a little tense with your dad." Candace gave a supportive smile.

"I don't want to talk about it," Rowan grumbled, her eyes narrowing in warning.

"Okay, okay." Candace held her palms in the air. "If it makes you feel any better, I won't be able to give you a hard time much longer."

"What do you mean?" Rowan's chest tightened in anticipation of more bad news. The new year hadn't even arrived yet, but it was already looking like a disaster.

"I've accepted a position at a family practice up in Maine." Candace gave a nervous laugh as she waited for a response, but Rowan was too shocked to say a word. "So, yeah. Christine and I have been talking about it a while now. She's hoping this means I won't be working long, crazy hours all the time."

"That's wonderful," Rowan forced out, hoping her face didn't betray her disappointment.

"Congrats," Simone also seemed conflicted but doing her best to put on a brave face.

"I'm going to recommend you step into my shoes," Candace said to Simone. "I know you haven't been at the hospital for long, but you've got what it takes. I really think you'd be amazing."

Simone's eyes widened in surprise. "Me? As head of emergency medicine? I'm flattered, but I'm not sure I'm ready for that kind of responsibility."

"Nonsense," Candace said firmly. "You're more than capable. Don't you agree, Rowan?"

Rowan's mind still reeled from the bombshell her father had dropped. The idea of Simone taking on such a prominent role at the hospital filled her with conflicting emotions. On one hand, Rowan was immensely proud of her girlfriend and knew she'd excel in the position. On the other hand, the news of the potential sale to Hydra loomed large in her mind. She didn't want Simone caught up in the mess that was sure to unfold if the deal went through.

"Of course, she'd be amazing," Rowan said. "If that's something she really wants to take on."

"Unfortunately, you'd be reporting directly to Dr. Donovan. Don't hate me for that." Candace laughed, but there was some anger in it that made Rowan sense her friend had not been enjoying Lance's return.

Simone shot Rowan a questioning look, clearly picking up on her hesitation. "It's definitely something to think about," Simone said diplomatically. "I appreciate your confidence in me, Candace, but let's not get ahead of ourselves. We should be celebrating your exciting news!"

Candace's smile returned, though it didn't quite reach her eyes. "You're right. And speaking of celebrating, I think I hear the countdown starting. We better get back in there if we want to see the big moment."

"I'm happy for you," Rowan said to Candace, pushing aside her own inner turmoil for the sake of her friend. "It sure looks like the new year is bringing a lot of changes."

THE SUN HAD ALREADY SET when Rowan and Simone returned home. Rowan sat on the bench by the door, easing off her boots, wiggling her toes once they were free.

"Is it just me, or does it seem like it should be midnight already?" Rowan asked.

"It's not even seven," Simone said with a laugh, glancing at her watch. "But I know what you mean. That party was a lot."

"They say the temps are going to dip down overnight. I don't envy the polar plungers." Rowan shivered.

"Let me turn on the fireplace." Walking into the living room, Simone pressed the button on the device, the faux flames providing soft illumination while a steady stream of warm air began to take away the chill.

Rowan stood, stretching her arms overhead. "I feel like I need a nap. Or a stiff drink. Or both."

Simone stepped closer, wrapping her arms around Rowan's waist. "Is this because of your dad? You were distracted ever since you spoke with him, but we were never alone long enough for me to ask what happened."

Rowan leaned into Simone's embrace, resting her forehead against her girlfriend's shoulder. "He dropped a bombshell on me. He's considering selling the hospital. To Hydra Capital Management."

Simone pulled back slightly, brow furrowed. "The company you and your mom are convinced is basically a cult? But why? I thought things were improving under Lance's leadership."

Rowan couldn't suppress the bitter laugh that escaped her lips. "This idea has Lance written all over it. Both he and my father seem to think Hydra is the answer to all the world's problems."

"What do you think?" Simone motioned for Rowan to take a seat on the couch, covering them both with a warm blanket.

"I think it's a disaster waiting to happen. Hydra may talk a good game about saving struggling hospitals, but something about them feels off. My father was talking about the sale like it was some kind of covert operation." Rowan shook her head, pulling the blanket tighter around her shoulders. "None of this sits right with me."

"All of this is happening right when I'm finally getting a shot at becoming a department head." Simone let out a sigh. "I still can't believe Candace is leaving."

"I know," Rowan said softly, reaching out to take Simone's hand. "It's a lot of change all at once. How do you feel about Candace's recommendation? You've never really said if that was something you wanted to do."

"Honestly?" Simone was quiet for a moment as she stared at the orange flames. "I'm flattered and a bit terrified. When I took the job at Marbury Hospital earlier this year, I wasn't thinking beyond finding as soft a landing as possible after total failure with Global Health Frontiers."

"And now?"

"It's a much better fit than I thought it would be. But I never imagined an opportunity to advance my career like this would happen so quickly. With all this uncertainty about the hospital's future..." Simone shook her head.

"You'd be amazing at it," Rowan said softly.

"Maybe," Simone conceded, snuggling closer and resting her head on Rowan's shoulder. "But I can't help thinking I should keep my options open in case I need to look for something in Boston instead."

"Boston?" Rowan's tone registered shock. "You want to leave Marbury?"

Simone lifted her head, meeting Rowan's gaze. "I know it would be much easier for you to find an administrative position in a big city with lots of hospitals."

"No, Simone. I can't ask you to do that." Rowan squeezed Simone's hand as her throat thickened with emotion. "I have firsthand knowledge of what it's like to sacrifice your career in your prime for someone else. I would never want that for you. If I can't find something close enough to commute, I could get a small apartment in the city and still come home on weekends."

"You do have experience with tiny living," Simone joked, gesturing to the room around them. Intrigued by the motion, both Ginger and Pepper jumped on top of the blanket, weighing them down.

"Oof. When these cats get to be full-grown, there might not be enough room for me to live here anyway," Rowan said with a chuckle.

Simone laughed softly, scratching behind Ginger's ears as the cat settled into her lap. "I think we'd find a way to make it work. But let's not get ahead of ourselves. We don't even know for sure if any of this will happen. Even with Candace's recommendation, I might not get the promotion."

"You would if I were still the CMO," Rowan assured her, but as soon as she'd said it, her brow furrowed. "Except, I wouldn't be able to do that. Not with us being a couple. You'd be my direct report. It was one thing for us to bend the rules before when there were several layers of bureaucracy between us, but as head of emergency medicine, you'd be reporting directly to me. It would be a clear conflict of interest."

Simone nodded, a wry smile on her face. "It's probably for the best that you're not in that position anymore. Though I have to admit I find the idea of you being my boss kind of hot."

Rowan laughed, feeling some of the tension from earlier melt away. "Oh really? Should I start calling you Dr. Doucette and giving you stern looks over my reading glasses?"

"Don't tease." Simone bit her lower lip, her expression taking on that familiar look of being very turned on.

"Who says I'm teasing, Dr. Doucette?" Rowan leaned in closer, her voice dropping to a husky whisper. "It's the end of the year. Perhaps we should discuss your performance review."

Simone's breath hitched as Rowan's lips brushed against her ear. "I hope I've been meeting expectations, Dr. Colchester."

"I'd say you've been exceeding expectations," Rowan murmured, trailing kisses along Simone's jaw. "But there's always room for improvement."

Simone shivered at Rowan's touch, her hands sliding under the blanket to grip Rowan's hips, sending both cats scurrying off the blanket in the process. "Is that so? What areas do you think I should focus on?"

Rowan pulled back slightly, desire making her vision narrow. "Well, Dr. Doucette, I think we should start with a thorough examination."

"Yes, ma'am. I know just the thing." Simone motioned for Rowan to turn around with her back to Simone. Digging in with her hands, Simone worked on the knots in Rowan's shoulders. "How's this?"

"I'd say your bedside manner is exemplary." A moan escaped Rowan's lips. "You have amazing hands."

"That's what everyone tells me."

Rowan glanced over her shoulder. "Everyone?"

Simone chuckled softly. "Maybe not everyone. Just my favorite patient."

Rowan relaxed into Simone's touch, feeling the tension from the day's revelations slowly melting away under her skilled hands. "Mmm, lucky patient. Although, wasn't I supposed to be the boss? I don't think I've gotten the hang of this role-playing thing yet."

"It's funny. You're much bossier when you pretend to be a housewife."

"I'm sorry. I can try to be more docile next time."

"Please don't. It's much more fun when you get feisty." Simone pressed a soft kiss to the nape of Rowan's neck, making her shiver. "Are you cold? We can move closer to the fireplace."

"I thought you'd never ask."

"As the boss, you're supposed to be giving the orders," Simone teased, but she was already standing up, offering her hand to Rowan. "How quickly you forget."

They moved to the thick rug in front of the fireplace, settling down among a nest of pillows. The warm glow of the make-believe flames cast dancing shadows across them as they faced each other.

"Better?" Simone asked, her voice soft.

Rowan nodded, reaching out to tuck a strand of hair behind Simone's ear. "Much better. Although I think we're both a little overdressed for fireside activities."

Simone started to take off her sweater, but Rowan stopped her.

"Wait. Let me."

Rowan's fingers traced the hem of Simone's sweater, savoring the softness of the fabric and the warmth of the skin beneath. She slowly lifted the garment, revealing inch by tantalizing inch of Simone's abdomen. Simone raised her arms, allowing Rowan to pull the sweater over her head.

"Beautiful," Rowan murmured, drinking in the sight of

Simone bathed in the flickering firelight. Her hands skimmed along Simone's sides, eliciting a shiver. "I'm glad I'm not your boss anymore. All those times when I was around you and I couldn't do this. Talk about torture."

"For us both," Simone agreed. "Because I wanted to do this." Simone slid her hand up Rowan's turtleneck, lifting it over Rowan's head and dramatically tossing it across the room.

"And I definitely wanted to do this," Rowan unclasped Simone's bra and cast it off, taking a nipple into her mouth.

"Don't forget about this." Simone eased her hand into Rowan's pants and flashed a devilish smile. "My goodness, Dr. Colchester. You're very wet."

Rowan gasped at Simone's touch, her hips instinctively pressing forward. "What can I say? You have that effect on me. Since the moment we met."

Simone's fingers moved in slow, teasing circles. "I think we need to conduct a more thorough examination. For medical purposes, obviously."

"Of course," Rowan agreed breathlessly. She fumbled with the button of her pants, eager to give Simone better access. "I trust your professional opinion completely."

With a wicked grin, Simone helped Rowan shimmy out of her pants and underwear. She trailed kisses down Rowan's body, pausing to lavish attention on her breasts before continuing lower.

Rowan's breath hitched as Simone settled between her thighs. "Oh, God, Simone."

"Shh," Simone murmured against her skin. "Let the doctor work."

At the first touch of Simone's tongue, Rowan's hips bucked involuntarily. Simone gripped her thighs, holding her steady as she explored with slow, deliberate strokes. Rowan tangled her fingers in Simone's hair, gasping and arching into her touch.

"Simone," she moaned, her body trembling. "Please."

She couldn't say anything else, but she didn't need to. By now, Simone knew exactly what to do, what Rowan's body needed, and responded by increasing her pace, her tongue circling Rowan's most sensitive spots with practiced skill. She slipped two fingers inside, curling them, and Rowan's muscles tightened, pulling them in deeper.

Rowan's body tensed, trembling on the edge of release. Simone's talented mouth and fingers worked in perfect harmony, building the pressure until Rowan thought she might burst. With a cry of ecstasy, she came undone, waves of pleasure washing over her as Simone gently eased her through the aftershocks.

Panting, Rowan collapsed back onto the rug, her skin flushed and glistening. Simone crawled up her body, pressing soft kisses along the way before capturing Rowan's lips in a deep, languid kiss.

"How was that for a thorough examination, Dr. Colchester?" Simone murmured against her lips, a hint of playfulness in her voice. She grabbed the edge of the blanket from the nearby couch and yanked it up over them to ward off the chill.

Rowan chuckled breathlessly, wrapping her arms around Simone and pulling her close. "Exemplary work, Dr. Doucette. I'd say you've more than earned that promotion."

They lay there for a moment, basking in the afterglow and the warmth of the fire. Rowan's fingers traced lazy patterns on Simone's back as her heartbeat slowly returned to normal.

"I love you," Rowan whispered, the words falling easily from her lips. No matter how many times she said it, the truth of it never failed to overwhelm her. "I can't imagine my life without you."

Simone propped herself up on an elbow, gazing down at Rowan with such tenderness it made her heart ache. "Lucky for you, you never have to. I love you, too. More than I ever thought possible."

Rowan reached up to cup Simone's cheek, her thumb tracing the curve of her jaw. "Whatever happens with the hospital, with our jobs, we'll figure it out together. Right?"

Simone nodded, leaning into Rowan's touch. "Absolutely. We're a team."

"A damn good one," Rowan agreed with a smile. She glanced at the clock on the mantel. "It's not even nine yet. What do you say we ring in the new year properly?"

"I thought we just did." Despite her protest, Simone's eyes sparkled with mischief and possibly a challenge.

Rowan laughed, pulling Simone down for another kiss. "Oh, no, my dear. We've only begun."

CHAPTER TWENTY-FIVE

"Do I hear bagpipes?" Simone asked, her brow furrowing as she strained to listen over the raucous chatter of the crowd that had gathered on the beach on New Year's Day to watch the annual Polar Plunge. "Is there a funeral today? What a terrible way to start the new year."

"No, it must be the parade," Rowan said. "It's a Marbury tradition. All the people who will be taking the plunge start off by marching through town to the beach."

"That's actually kind of charming," Simone said, breaking into a grin. "I love how this town goes all out for its traditions."

As if on cue, the first marchers came into view, led by a kilted bagpiper whose red face was the same shade as his tartan. Behind him came a crowd of at least a hundred people carrying towels, many of whom were dressed in various costumes.

Simone blew into her frozen hands. "Do you know who's wearing the shark costume?"

Rowan zipped up her jacket as a blast of wind swirled around the tent. "No idea. There's a polar bear, too. And is that Santa Claus?" Rowan squinted, and then her eyes widened in disbelief.

"It is! Complete with red swim trunks." Simone let out a delighted laugh. "This isn't what I was expecting at all. I can't believe how many people are actually doing this today. I thought it'd be a handful of people crazy enough to strip down to their bathing suit and dip their toes in the water and then dash toward The Driftwood Lounge as fast as possible to get drunk."

"That part will happen, for sure," Rowan said with a wry smile. "But first, we have to get through the actual plunge. And make sure no one gets hypothermia in the process."

A gust of icy wind whipped across the beach, causing both women to shiver and pull their coats tightly around themselves. A little distance away, several dogs barked excitedly. As the parade reached the beach, the crowd of spectators cheered and whooped. Simone scanned the faces, spotting several people she knew from the hospital.

"Have you ever taken part?" Simone asked.

"Me? God, no," Rowan laughed, shaking her head. "I prefer my New Year's Day traditions to involve a warm fireplace and hot cocoa. But..." Her eyebrows shot up as she clapped a hand to her mouth. "Am I losing my mind? I swear I see my mother, and she's wearing a bathing cap."

Simone gasped. "Where?"

"There," Rowan pointed, her mouth agape. "With Marigold. I can't believe it."

Grace Colchester stood at the edge of the crowd, wrapped in a heavy robe-like coat, her hair tucked neatly under a bright yellow swim cap that made her look a little like a rubber duckie. Marigold stood beside her wearing a similar coat, but with her hair flying free in the wind. Catching sight of Rowan and Simone, Marigold waved and headed toward the medical tent, dragging Grace along.

"Isn't this a beautiful day for a swim?" Marigold beamed like it was eighty-five degrees outside, instead of a brisk twenty-two with a windchill that made it feel half that.

Grace didn't speak, her face either frozen in dread or just plain frozen. With noticeable effort, she managed a tight smile that threatened to crack her features right down the middle.

"Mother, what on earth are you doing?" Rowan asked, unable to keep the shock from her voice.

"Marigold convinced me it would be good publicity for the hospital charity if I participated today." Grace's lips thinned into a tight line. "Though I'm beginning to regret my decision, if you can call it that. More like blackmail."

Marigold parroted the word blackmail and then blew a raspberry.

"I can't believe you're actually doing this," Simone said with a shaky laugh, directing her comment to both of the women at once.

"Neither can I," Grace muttered, pulling her coat tighter around her. "I must be out of my mind."

"Nonsense!" Marigold chirped, her enthusiasm unaffected by the frigid air. "You'll feel invigorated afterward. No doubt at all that you're alive when your nerve endings feel like they're on fire. And think of all the money we'll have raised for the mobile clinic. We might be able to get that second RV I've been wanting by spring."

"I would simply want to live to see spring," Grace remarked through chattering teeth. "If it's this cold now, what will it be like when we get out of the water?"

"That's why I got us these fancy coats," Marigold explained. "They're like the ones used by the US Olympic swim team. We'll be toasty warm the moment we're out of the water."

Grace looked skeptical, but Simone sensed in her the same determination and competitive spirit she'd come to know so well in Rowan. When a Colchester woman set her mind to do something, she was not willing to accept failure as an option. That didn't mean there wouldn't be any complaining.

Simone couldn't help but smile at the unlikely pair—the

elegant, reserved matriarch and the eccentric, vibrant artist were the last two people she would have chosen to become best friends, but somehow it worked for them. From what Simone could see, Marigold was a good influence on Grace.

"Consider me impressed," Simone said. "Both of you, be careful out there, okay?"

As the time approached for the plunge to begin, people along the beach started removing their jackets and stripping off their sweatpants. Some stood barefoot on the cold sand while others at least wore water shoes. Assorted costume items were tossed aside, though Rowan noticed one couple, a woman in a white wedding dress and a man in a suit, remained fully committed to their characters.

"Look at those two," Rowan nudged Simone, nodding toward the costumed couple. "I hope they realize those outfits are going to be quite heavy when wet."

Simone chuckled. "They say marriage is about supporting each other, which they'll literally have to do to get out of the waves."

"Maybe it's some kind of metaphor," Rowan suggested. "Like diving into the cold, unknown waters of the future together?"

"Maybe," Simone agreed, pausing to tilt her head. "Is that a priest with them?"

Rowan squinted to get a closer look. "That's the minister from the Congregational Church. Oh my God, I think they're actually getting married!"

The crowd near the costumed couple began to hush, and the officiant's voice carried over the wind. "Dearly beloved, we are gathered here today..."

Simone clapped a hand to her mouth, presumably to stifle the giggles that threatened to erupt. "For future reference, that would not be my idea of a perfect wedding."

Rowan gave Simone a funny look that made her realize

exactly what she'd said. Had Rowan caught on that Simone had spent much more than a moment or two picturing that special day? Did Rowan realize she had played a starring role in that fantasy?

"Though I have to admire their commitment," Simone continued, trying to ignore the sudden heat that had rushed to her face. "Nothing says 'til death do us part quite like risking hypothermia together."

Before Rowan could respond, a woman holding a megaphone shouted, "Two minutes."

"I don't know about this, Marigold." Grace took a few steps away from the water, a renewed uneasiness descending upon her as Marigold began unbuttoning her coat.

"Sure you can." Marigold wrapped her arm around Grace. "I don't want to hear that you're too old for this. Age is only a number."

"The temperature is also a number, and it's not one I particularly like," Grace shot back. "I find the water cold when it's the middle of July."

"Come on. Where's your adventurous spirit?" Marigold wasn't going to back down, and Simone had been acquainted with her landlady long enough to know Grace didn't have a chance in this contest of wills. "It's for a good cause. Look how many people are here to support the mobile clinic. The community needs us."

Grace looked first to Rowan and then to Simone. "Fine, but if I die, I'm coming back to haunt your every waking second."

"Don't threaten me with a good time." Marigold winked, finally shrugging her coat off completely, revealing a surprisingly sexy swimsuit that was more string than fabric.

"Wow," Simone said in a low, breathy voice, instantly earning a response from Rowan, who drilled an elbow into Simone's side.

"We're here in a professional capacity, Dr. Doucette." A hint of jealousy in Rowan's tone made Simone flush with pleasure.

"I simply meant I hope I look that good when I'm her age," Simone assured her, returning Rowan's elbow nudge playfully.

A boat went by, pulling someone on water skis dressed in a full wetsuit. The crowd broke out into a cheer.

"Plungers are you ready to get cold and wet?" a woman screamed through a megaphone.

Marigold pulled Grace by the arm, giving her no option for escape.

"Come on, people," the woman continued to shout. "Are you ready to make some noise to encourage all of our brave plungers?"

Everyone, including the usually reserved Rowan, let out a scream.

The countdown began, and the crowd's excitement reached a fever pitch. Simone held in a laugh as Rowan's mother reluctantly shed her coat, revealing a modest one-piece swimsuit that was the polar opposite—pun intended—of her friend's.

The song "Jump Around" by House of Pain started to play over loudspeakers. The DJ clearly had a wicked sense of humor.

"On your mark!" the megaphone woman yelled. "Get set! Plunge!"

Rowan shouted, "You got this, Mom!"

Simone added, "Go, Marigold, go!"

The group of people moved as a mass toward the water, letting out shrieks as their bodies came into contact with the first blasts of icy salt spray.

The bride and groom led the charge, their wedding attire billowing in the wind as they splashed hand-in-hand into the frigid waves. Their officiant followed close behind, still clutching his prayer book as he submerged himself up to his waist with a yelp.

Santa, in full hat and beard, dove in, going completely under the water.

"That's going to be chilly," Rowan observed as Santa bobbed up several yards from where he'd gone in, the sopping hat molded to his head, miraculously still in place.

"The one thing I've learned being an ER doctor is people gotta people, for better or worse."

"In our line of business, it's usually for the worse when we see them," Rowan pointed out. "At least today it's for a good cause."

"Excuse me," a tiny voice spoke behind them. "Are you doctors?"

Simone wheeled about, facing a mom and child. "We are. Do you need help?"

"I cut my finger." The kid held up her hand, a tiny splotch of blood barely visible near the tip.

"Let's get you cleaned up." Simone motioned for the patient and her mom to join them under the tent. "You're being very brave."

"It doesn't hurt," said the little girl. "But I don't want to get blood on my new jacket. It was a present from Santa."

Her mother laughed. "At least she has priorities."

Simone cleaned the wound. "What happened?"

"I picked up a shell," the girl began, "but—"

"It turned out to be a shard of glass," the mom explained.

Simone removed the paper backing from the bandage, adhering it to the child's skin. "There you go. Good as new."

"Thank you. Do I get hot chocolate?"

"You sure do, if your mom says it's okay. Just go up those stairs to The Driftwood Lounge, and they'll warm you right up. I hear there's also chili and some spiked hot chocolate or mulled wine for the grown-ups."

The mother's face lit up like she'd just heard the best news of her life.

A few minutes later, one of the plungers came by with a bloody toe that needed attention. While Rowan focused on patching him up, Simone went back out to the beach to see if anyone else needed help. Miraculously, everyone was already out of the water, laughing and clapping each other on the back as they wrapped themselves in coats and towels. She returned to the tent to see Marigold and Grace walking past.

"Now that's what I call being alive!" Grace's uncharacteristically booming voice proclaimed.

"I knew you could do it, Grace." Marigold wrapped her arms around her friend. "Let's get some booze!" she said as they disappeared into the bar.

"I've never seen my mother quite so exhilarated and full of life," Rowan told Simone, and it was clear the sight warmed her heart.

Soon enough, everyone was off the beach, aside from some dogs with their owners out for a stroll.

"All clear?" Simone asked.

"All clear," Rowan confirmed, scanning the beach one last time. "I think we can pack up."

As they began dismantling the medical tent, Simone couldn't help but smile. "I have to admit this was actually pretty fun. Only a few minor injuries."

"Definitely a success," Rowan agreed, folding up the last of the blankets. "It looks like we raised a good amount for the mobile clinic, too. Shall we go celebrate?"

"Absolutely. The mulled wine is practically calling my name."

The vibe inside The Driftwood Lounge was joyous as many of the plungers regaled their loved ones with tales of their bravery. The participants were generally divided into two camps, those who believed the water was not that cold and the others who maintained it was fucking freezing.

Overhearing their arguments, Simone couldn't help but laugh. She had a feeling it was like this every year.

"I really love seeing the community rally like this for a good cause."

"It's one of things I've always loved about Marbury," Rowan agreed. "The camaraderie is evident, even when people disagree. It's a much friendlier vibe than you get in a big city. If I end up working in Boston again, I'll really miss this."

As Simone and Rowan made their way through the crowded room, Simone spotted Erica sitting at a large table surrounded by a group of children engaged in some kind of craft project. Colorful paper, glitter, and markers were strewn across the table's surface, and each child had what looked like a baby food jar in front of them.

Simone nodded toward the table. "I didn't expect to see Erica here."

"Pablo, too," Rowan added, raising her hand and giving them both a wave.

"Hey, you two!" Erica called out, her face lighting up as she spotted Simone and Rowan. "Come see what we're making."

"What's all this?" Rowan asked, gesturing to the creative chaos that was spilling onto the floor.

"I told Marigold I would do something to keep the kids busy. We're making New Year's wish jars," Erica explained, holding up her finished example. "The kids write down their wishes for the new year and put them inside. Then they decorate the outside of the jars to take home. It's a fun way to set intentions for the year ahead."

"What a clever idea," Rowan said, picking up one of the jars for inspection. "Did you make that up yourself?"

"Pablo helped," Erica said, and though she glanced at the man for barely a second, Simone was certain she'd caught a glimmer of something special in the look that passed between them. "Did you know he's taking a class in psychotherapy as part of his nursing program? We were talking about it when I volunteered at the mobile clinic last week. Apparently, art therapy is a very effective treatment for all sorts of trauma, especially for children."

"That's really interesting," Simone said, though what was even more intriguing was the way Pablo was watching Erica put glitter in a jar with the same intensity one might watch Michelangelo painting a ceiling. "I didn't know you were interested in psychology."

"I didn't either," Erica admitted. "Realistically, it's not like my art is paying the bills, and I've been giving a lot of thought to more practical ways I can use my creativity to help people. Pablo thinks I should consider art therapy as a career path."

Simone noticed Rowan's eyebrows raise slightly at this revelation. It was hard to tell if it was from surprise at her stepdaughter's sudden career aspirations, or if she had also picked up on the charged chemistry between Erica and Pablo.

"What a wonderful idea," Rowan said in the tone Simone had come to think of as her encouraging *mom* voice. "I'm sure there are some online classes you could look into that would be affordable."

As soon as they were out of earshot, Rowan leaned close to Simone and said, "Did you pick up on that?"

"The sparks flying between those two like a New Year's fireworks display?" Simone replied in a low voice. "Hard to miss."

"Did you know about this?"

"No, I had no idea. But it's nice to see Erica looking so content."

Simone couldn't help but feel a pang of sadness, though. While she was thrilled Erica might have found someone she was interested in, it also hurt to realize her friend hadn't let her in on this development from day one. They'd come a long way since Erica had first found out about Simone's relationship with

Rowan, but there was still work to be done to repair their friendship.

Rowan nodded thoughtfully. "I suppose you're right. It's been a while since I've seen her this animated about something. It's good to see her finding real purpose in her life."

They made their way to the bar, where Simone ordered two steaming mugs of mulled wine. As they waited, Simone caught sight of Grace and Marigold at a corner table, surrounded by a group of what could only be described as male admirers. Grace's usually perfectly coiffed hair was wild and damp, but her cheeks were flushed and her expression animated as she described her experience with the Polar Plunge.

"I think your mother might have enjoyed today more than she was expecting," Simone observed, handing Rowan her drink.

Rowan chuckled. "You might be right. Though I'm sure she'll deny it tomorrow and claim Marigold forced her into it."

They found a small table near the bar and settled in, the warmth from a nearby fireplace finally chasing away the last of the chill from the beach. Simone took a slow sip of her spiced wine and sighed in satisfaction.

"So," Rowan said, "what would you put in your New Year's wish jar?"

It was a casual question, yet there was a flutter in Simone's chest as she contemplated how to respond. There were so many things she could say—wishes for the hospital, for her patients, for her friends. But as her mind flitted back to the newlyweds on the beach, the wish that burned brightest for her was one she wasn't sure she was ready to voice.

"You know," Simone said with a shrug, "the usual. Health, happiness, world peace. Maybe a steaming slice of karma being served up to your ex-husband for all the crap he's pulled, but I feel like that might not be in the spirit of the exercise, technically speaking."

"If wishing Lance the fruits of his labor is wrong, I don't

want to be right," Rowan said with a wry smile. "Though I suppose we should be setting a better example. There are kids here, after all."

Simone laughed, grateful for the levity. "You're probably right. What about you? What would you put in your jar?"

Rowan's eyes grew distant as she gazed out the window toward the ocean. "I don't know. This past year has been such a whirlwind of change. I think I'd wish to find my footing."

Simone nodded, understanding all too well. "That's a good wish. Change can be disorienting, even when it's positive."

"Exactly," Rowan agreed. "Don't get me wrong, I'm happier now than I've been in a long time. But there are still moments when—" Rowan frowned as her phone buzzed, the look of concern deepening as she studied the screen. "It's a text from Candace."

Simone was about to ask if anything was wrong when her own phone rang. "It's Candace calling me." A knot formed in Simone's stomach as she answered, knowing that a call from someone who was on duty in the emergency department on a holiday was rarely good news. "What's going on?"

"Simone." Candace's voice was tight, her tone urgent. "You know that patient you told me to be on the lookout for, Fabienne Laurent? She came into the ER in active labor. It's been a total shitshow."

Simone's blood ran cold. "How bad are you talking?"

"Blood pressure was through the roof. She's bleeding heavily and showing signs of organ failure. We don't have the resources here to handle it. She's being airlifted to Boston General."

"Damn it," Simone muttered. This was exactly the kind of situation they'd been worried about when the hospital abruptly closed the labor and delivery unit. "Is she conscious? Does she understand what's happening?"

"We've explained the situation as best we can, but she's terrified. The language barrier isn't helping."

"We're on our way." Simone stood, gathering her things. "How long until the helicopter arrives?"

"It's already here. She's being prepped for transport now."

"Okay, we'll head directly to Boston and meet her at the hospital. She's going to need someone she trusts who can speak to her and help her understand." As soon as Simone said this, Rowan hopped up and started putting on her coat. "I have to know. Do you think she's going to make it?"

There was silence on the other end of the line that filled Simone with dread.

"Candace! Will she and the baby make it?"

Finally, Candace said, "Only time will tell."

With tears stinging her eyes, Simone grabbed Rowan by the hand and raced toward the exit.

CHAPTER TWENTY-SIX

"At least there isn't any traffic," Rowan said as she zipped along the highway, going ten miles over the speed limit. "We should make good time to Boston."

Simone nodded absently, her mind seemingly a million miles away as her eyes remained fixed on the passing scenery. Rowan couldn't blame her. Even though Simone had a closer connection to the patient, Rowan couldn't shake the image of the young mother, alone and frightened, facing a medical emergency that could claim her life and maybe the life of her child, too.

"Fabienne will be in expert hands at Boston General," Rowan said, sensing the direction of Simone's thoughts ran similar to hers. "They have one of the best neonatal intensive care units in the country."

"I know," Simone said, "but that doesn't make it any less terrifying for her. She's in a foreign country, far from her family and support system, and now she's facing this crisis on top of everything else. Not to mention the expense."

Rowan reached over and gave Simone's hand a reassuring squeeze. "She has you. And me. We'll make sure she gets the care and support she needs, no matter what. We'll crowdfund it if we have to. It'll be okay."

Simone managed a grateful smile, but the worry still lingered in her eyes.

Rowan's phone buzzed with an incoming text from Candace. She played it through the robotic voice: "Helicopter has landed. The baby, a little girl, was healthy and in the nursery. Fabienne is being taken to surgery."

"She shouldn't have to go through this," Simone said, her voice tight. "If we'd fought harder to keep the labor and delivery unit open, maybe—"

"Don't go there," Rowan interrupted gently. "Marbury closing the unit was out of our control. We can't change the past, but we can be there for Fabienne now."

Simone sighed, her shoulders sagging. "You're right. I just wish things were different."

They arrived at Boston General, and Rowan pulled up to the main entrance, dropping Simone off and waiting to watch her rush through the revolving door before pulling into the parking garage. Once she had squeezed into a spot that was only half the size of the most compact car—but completely normal by Boston standards—she pulled out her phone and called Candace.

"How is she?" Rowan asked, forgoing any greeting. "Any word?"

"Still in surgery," Candace replied, her voice cutting in and out thanks to a poor connection because of the walls of the parking structure. "The doctors are optimistic, but it's touch and go."

"What the hell happened?" Rowan demanded before stopping to adjust her tone to something more civil. "I'm sorry. This isn't your fault. It's just I know we had some concerns with Fabienne's last appointment, but nothing that should have led to an emergency of this magnitude."

Candace sighed heavily. "We thought it was a placental

abruption. When she arrived, there was so much blood. But an emergency CT scan showed the bleeding was coming from her liver."

Rowan's breath caught in her throat. A bleeding liver during pregnancy was rare and potentially catastrophic. "HELLP syndrome?" she asked, naming one of the few conditions that could cause such a complication.

"Most likely," Candace confirmed. "It might've been detected if she'd been seeing an OBGYN regularly throughout the pregnancy, but—"

"She couldn't get to the appointments because the doctor was in Hyannis." Rowan pressed her lips together tightly to keep from screaming.

"If we could've stopped the bleeding with an embolization coil, airlifting her to Boston might've been avoided," Candace added, "but the hospital didn't have any."

"Didn't have any... How is that possible?" Rowan's grip tightened on her phone as a fresh wave of frustration washed over her. "Marbury is supposed to be a full-service hospital. We should have basic supplies like that on hand."

"You'd have to talk to your ex-husband about that one," Candace said, her tone equally frustrated. "They should've been in a shipment last month, but everything from that supply company was canceled at the last minute and the contract terminated as a cost-saving measure. Clearly, nobody has bothered to find an alternative supplier yet."

"God damn it." Rowan's stomach churned with anger but also guilt. She should have known things would deteriorate under Lance's watch, no matter how good he made everything appear on the surface. He might be able to fool others, but Rowan knew who he really was deep down. She should have fought her father harder instead of letting him bring back Lance. Why could she never stand up to him when it mattered most?

Rowan took a deep breath, trying to calm the storm of

emotions raging inside her. "Alright, I'll deal with that later. For now, let's focus on Fabienne. Is there anything else we can do?"

"Not at the moment," Candace replied. "The surgical team in Boston is top-notch. We have to wait and hope for the best."

"Okay. I'm heading inside now. I'll keep you posted if I hear anything."

Rowan ended the call and made her way into the hospital, her mind racing. The diagnosis of HELLP syndrome was a shocker. It was such a rare condition that neither Rowan nor Simone had seriously considered it. Fabienne's blood pressure had been within the normal range on her last visit, and without a full panel of blood tests, such as the ones that an OBGYN would have ordered, they never had a chance to discover the low platelet count or elevated liver enzymes that might have tipped them off. No matter how thorough they tried to be, the mobile clinic simply wasn't designed to provide comprehensive prenatal care.

Once inside the familiar environment of the hospital, Rowan's pulse began to slow. Boston General looked the same as she remembered, except that, for the first time in her life, she was wandering its halls without a single thing to do to keep her from going stark raving mad.

Rowan made her way down corridors she still remembered well, the antiseptic hospital smell providing an odd sense of comfort. Even if it wasn't exactly pleasant, it was like being home. After more than two months of not working at all, Rowan found herself itching to be useful. She wasn't made for idle unemployment. Would anyone notice if she grabbed a lab coat and stethoscope and went around checking some patient vitals to keep her brain occupied from running every catastrophic outcome?

She shook her head, reminding herself she was here as a visitor, not a doctor. Her job primarily was to support Simone. Still, the urge to help, to heal, to do something useful gnawed at her, making her head throb. She would just about murder someone for a hit of caffeine and should really try to find some before things got out of hand.

Fortunately, the cafeteria was around the corner. In fact, the aroma of—well, it couldn't exactly be classified as delicious food or gourmet coffee so much as generic sustenance, but it would do in a pinch, tickled her nose. Rowan's steps quickened as she sought the source.

As Rowan rounded the corner, she nearly collided with a familiar face.

"Dr. Colchester?" The man's eyes widened in recognition. "It is you. I didn't expect to see you here."

Rowan broke into a grin as she recognized her former colleague. "Dr. Chen. How are you?"

"I'm good, thanks. Grabbing a quick bite before my shift starts." Dr. Chen glanced questioningly at Rowan's civilian attire, which must have looked odd after years of only seeing her in scrubs. "Are you here as a patient?"

"No, no," Rowan chuckled. "Just accompanying a friend. And desperately in need of coffee."

"You're thinking of getting it here? I see you're still a risk taker. The stuff they serve may have the molecular structure of coffee, but the taste is more akin to motor oil."

Instead of a defense, Rowan offered a shrug. "Desperate times call for desperate measures."

Dr. Chen laughed. "If you're willing to risk it, allow me to treat you. It's the least I can do for our former chair of internal medicine."

"I'll take you up on that offer," Rowan said.

They made it through the line quickly, Dr. Chen encouraging Rowan to add a cinnamon bun to her order, claiming it was the only edible item on the menu.

"You have a few minutes to chat, or do you have to rush off?" Rowan asked once they had gone through the checkout.

"I can sit for a bit." Dr. Chen took a seat at a nearby table and removed the lid to his cup, bobbing a tea bag up and down by a string. "I used to be the type who made fun of tea drinkers until I started working here and had to deal with—" He finished the statement by waving to her drink.

"I don't remember it being that bad." She took a tentative sip, regretting it instantly. "No, wait. I do remember now. It's like sludge, but watery at the same time."

"You'd think it'd be criminal for a hospital to serve a beverage that can actually put people in the hospital." He laughed at his joke. "I hope your friend doesn't have anything serious going on. New Year's Day is a hell of a time to be someplace like this. Unless you're earning overtime for it."

"Actually, it's not a friend so much as a patient who was flown in. Complications during delivery, and Marbury couldn't handle it."

"I'm sorry to hear that. I'll say a prayer for her and the baby."

"They're going to need it." Rowan forced down another sip of coffee, growing used to the taste if not exactly fond. She chased it down with a big chunk of cinnamon roll. "How have things been here?"

"Living the dream." His pinched face said otherwise. "I shouldn't complain. My dad's got it way worse."

Rowan dug into her mental bank, recalling that Dr. Chen's father worked as a hospital administrator. They'd interacted at industry conferences a few times. "He's at St. Mary's in Rhode Island, right?"

"He is," Dr. Chen confirmed.

"His hospital isn't hiring, is it? I'm looking for a new gig."

"I thought you went back to Marbury to be their Chief Medical Officer."

"It didn't quite work out the way I'd planned," Rowan said, hoping she'd managed to keep most of the bitterness out of her tone.

"That's too bad, but you don't want to work at St. Mary's. I doubt it'll last the year."

Rowan sat up a little straighter at this news. "Why? What's happening?"

"They were dealing with staffing shortages and budget problems," Dr. Chen began.

"What hospital isn't these days," Rowan quipped.

"True. But the powers that be made a deal with the devil, and while it's been a while since I read a Greek tragedy, I'm pretty sure it's always a terrible idea."

"The devil?" Rowan raised her cup to her lips, steeling herself for the upcoming onslaught to her taste buds before taking a sip. "Who might that be?"

"Hydra Capital Management."

Rowan's hand let go of the mug, the watery brown substance splattering the table and drenching the rest of the cinnamon roll. "Oh my goodness."

As Rowan flailed helplessly, Dr. Chen jumped up and returned a moment later with a handful of napkins. He quickly mopped up the disaster, eyeing Rowan with concern.

"Are you alright?" he asked, his brow furrowed. "You look like you've seen a ghost."

Rowan took a deep breath, steadying herself. "I'm fine, thank you. Just clumsy. Before I made such a mess, did you happen to say Hydra Capital Management?"

"Yeah, they swooped in about six months ago, promising to solve all of St. Mary's financial woes. But from what my dad tells me, it's been a nightmare." Dr. Chen lowered his voice. "They immediately began slashing budgets left and right, canceling contracts, laying off staff, and pushing for more 'efficiency' at the expense of patient care."

Rowan nodded, mulling this over but not finding the information all that surprising. "That's about what I'd expect, I guess.

Is that all that's going on?" There had to be something else to elevate this bargain to Faustian proportions.

Dr. Chen cast a surreptitious glance around the cafeteria before asking, "Why does it interest you?"

Rowan tensed at the sudden suspicion in his tone but decided she should tell the truth. She would get nothing from lying, but if he knew something useful, he might share it if he knew she had a personal stake. "They're intending to buy Marbury Hospital. My great-grandmother helped to found the hospital over a hundred years ago, and it's been in the care of my family ever since."

Dr. Chen's eyes widened as if he'd reached the really scary part of a horror movie. "Do not let that happen."

Rowan's chest constricted to the point she could barely get air into her lungs. "I've been trying to convince my father not to sell. But he seems determined. What else can you tell me about Hydra's takeover of St. Mary's that might help me convince him?"

Dr. Chen glanced around once before speaking in an even more hushed tone. "It wasn't just budget cuts and layoffs. They systematically dismantled entire departments, particularly those that aren't as profitable. Pediatrics, geriatrics, mental health—all on the chopping block within the first month."

Rowan felt her stomach churn, and it wasn't from the terrible coffee. "Shit. Yeah, we already lost labor and delivery, and that was before any talk of a sale. This could get bad, fast."

"I can send you some articles that explain it in detail, but here's the gist. They waltz in, flashing cash. 'Taking care'"—he made air quotes with his fingers—"of some of the most egregious issues, like staffing, with heroic measures before the deal is done. Everything seems on the up and up, until they get their hooks in and buy the place. Then the cuts start. The bills pile up. And finally, they sell the land right out from under the hospital."

"Are you saying that metaphorically?" Rowan asked, failing

to understand what he could mean. "Like pulling the rug out, or—"

"No, I mean exactly that. They literally sell the land the hospital is built on, and then the hospital leases it back from the new landlord."

Rowan's head spun as she tried to make sense of what Dr. Chen was describing. "Why would they do that? It's stupid. Most hospitals own the land free and clear. Why would they want to pay rent for something they already own?"

"Because it's not about healthcare with Hydra. It's about real estate." Dr. Chen's jaw hardened. "These hospitals are often sitting on prime locations. Hydra comes in, guts the place, runs up the debt in the form of exorbitant rents and bad contracts, and then, when the hospital is hopelessly in arrears, they can close them down."

Rowan felt her blood run cold. Close them down? Marbury Hospital sat on a picturesque stretch of Cape Cod shoreline. The land alone was worth a fortune, or would have been if it hadn't had a hospital sitting on it for the past century.

"What about the patients? The community?" She dreaded the answer.

"That's the tragedy of it all. Once Hydra's done, there's nothing left. Let me show you." Dr. Chen fished his phone out of his shirt pocket, tapping his finger on the screen. Turning the phone to her, he said, "Isn't this a lovely view?"

Rowan took in the photo of bare dirt with the ocean behind it. "I guess so."

"Until earlier this year, that was one of the busiest hospitals in Pensacola." He set the phone on the table, away from the remnants of the spilled coffee.

Rowan stared at the phone, her mind racing. The implications were staggering. If Hydra got their hands on Marbury, it could mean the end of everything her family had built over generations.

"I'm sorry. Did you say Pensacola?" Rowan's breath caught as the detail belatedly sank in. Lance had taken a consulting job at a hospital in Florida right after he finished his program at a rehab facility owned by Hydra. A facility near Pensacola. It was too big a coincidence to ignore. Lance had to know what was going down. "That bastard."

"They're sick fuckers," Dr. Chen agreed, assuming Rowan had been referring to Hydra. "Not only do they put doctors, nurses—hell, everyone—out of a job, they also screw over the community."

"How do they get away with it?" If Rowan was going to put a stop to it, she had to know what she was up against.

"Secrecy. Only the very top of the food chain are involved. By the time the ink has dried, they're richer than they ever imagined. It must help them afford to have their conscience surgically removed."

Rowan remembered her father's whispered voice at the New Year's party. He was certainly at the top of Marbury Hospital's food chain. Was he in the know? Or was Lance using her father's recent frailty and increased reliance on him when it came to decision making to cash in on the Colchester legacy for his own benefit?

"Dr. Chen," she said, her voice tight with urgency, "I can't thank you enough for sharing this with me. Is there any chance you could send me those articles you mentioned? And maybe put me in touch with your father?"

Dr. Chen nodded solemnly. "Of course. I'll email you everything I've got. If you can stop them from buying your family hospital, you have to do it. I hope for your town's sake, you're not too late."

CHAPTER TWENTY-SEVEN

"Aren't you the most beautiful baby in the world," Simone whispered, nuzzling Fabienne's newborn in her arms while standing beside the woman's bed in the recovery area.

It had been a traumatic several hours waiting to hear the outcome of Fabienne's surgery, but now, in the quiet aftermath, Simone was able to relax enough to appreciate the miracle of this new life. The tiny bundle in her arms stirred, and she couldn't help but smile. Despite the seriousness of Fabienne's complications, the medical team at Boston General was cautiously optimistic the woman would make a full recovery.

The curtain that separated Fabienne from the other patients rustled, revealing Rowan's face. "How's the patient?"

"Doing better." Simone glanced at Fabienne, whose eyes made an attempt at opening but almost instantly shut again. "She's still heavily sedated, but there are many reasons to be hopeful. I thought they only allowed one visitor in the recovery area at a time."

"It helps when some of the people enforcing the rules used to work for you." Rowan tiptoed toward Simone, her attention focused on the tiny infant as Simone rearranged the blanket for a better view. "She's gorgeous. Does she have a name yet?"

"Not yet. Candace was able to track down Fabienne's husband at his work and is driving him up to Boston now, so as soon as he arrives and she's had a chance to wake up, I'm sure they'll decide on a name together."

Simone rocked the baby in a gentle back-and-forth motion, a lump forming in her throat. She hadn't expected the rush of emotions that came with holding this new little life. It stirred something deep within her, a longing she hadn't fully acknowledged before. In the future, if circumstances allowed, it might be nice to have a child of her own.

She glanced at Rowan, wondering if her partner had ever harbored similar thoughts. She'd raised Erica, of course, and as a teenager, too—arguably the worst stage for parenting. But doing it all over again, with a baby this time? Simone wasn't sure how that would go over and was almost afraid to ask.

Rowan placed a hand on Simone's shoulder, her touch warm and comforting. "It's amazing, isn't it? How small they are but so perfect?"

Simone cleared her throat before speaking, her approach as cautious as if she were trying to get close to a cobra without getting struck. "Have you ever thought about... I mean, did you and Lance ever consider having more children?"

Rowan's eyes widened slightly, a flicker of surprise crossing her face before she composed herself. "We talked about it, early on. But we had our careers to consider, and after a while, our marriage wasn't exactly in a place where bringing another child into the mix seemed wise."

Simone nodded, sensing the weight of regret in Rowan's words. She wasn't sure what answer she had been hoping for, but Rowan's response left the door open, at least a crack. As much as Simone wanted to probe further, to ask if Rowan would ever consider having a child now, the recovery room of a hospital, with a patient barely out of surgery, hardly seemed the appropriate place for such a conversation.

Simone continued to sway with the baby as a torrent of thoughts swirled in her brain. Realistically, as long as Rowan's quest for a new job could have her spending most of her time in Boston or beyond, a baby was out of the question. Surviving a mostly long-distance relationship would be hard enough on its own.

Simone's thoughts were interrupted by a soft moan from Fabienne. She quickly turned her attention back to the patient, gently placing the baby in the bassinet beside the bed.

"Fabienne? Can you hear me?" Simone asked softly, leaning closer to the woman's face.

Fabienne's eyelids fluttered, and she managed a weak nod. "My baby?" she whispered, her voice hoarse.

"She's right here," Simone reassured her in Creole. "She's perfect and healthy. You did an amazing job. You gave us quite a scare, but you pulled through beautifully. Your husband is on his way here now."

"Good." Fabienne offered a weak smile before closing her eyes again.

Simone let out a shaky sigh.

"Are you okay?" Rowan rubbed Simone's arm.

"Emotionally exhausted, but otherwise getting by. I'm finally starting to let go of some of the tension that had my muscles tied up in knots the whole way here."

"In that case, maybe I should wait to fill you in on everything I learned from an old colleague earlier." An edge to Rowan's tone warned Simone that whatever news Rowan had to share wasn't good.

"What is it?" Simone asked, her voice low to avoid disturbing Fabienne or the baby. "If you tell me, am I going to lose my shit and end up in jail?"

"Hopefully not, but I wouldn't mind seeing a few people at

a certain capital management company carted off to prison for what they're trying to pull."

"Hydra?"

Rowan gave a small nod, her jaw clenching. "It's so much worse than I feared."

"How bad?"

Rowan glanced around, as if wanting to make sure no one was within earshot. "They're not just looking to make cuts and maximize profits. They're systematically dismantling hospitals."

Simone's brow furrowed as she tried to see the benefit in this action. "I don't get it. Don't they want to make money? If you buy a hospital only to pull it apart, where's the profit?"

"Depends. How much do you think a few hundred acres of beachfront property on Cape Cod would be worth these days?"

"They're not possibly considering..." Simone's stomach dropped as the implications of Rowan's words sank in. "But that's impossible. The hospital has been there for over a century. It's a cornerstone of the community."

Rowan's face was grim. "To us, yes. To Hydra, it's just another asset to be exploited. They've done this before from what my colleague was saying. They buy struggling hospitals, strip them of valuable assets so investors get a big payday, and then either sell off the property or repurpose it for more profitable ventures."

"But what about the patients? The staff?" Simone's anger burned as her mind raced with thoughts of all the people who would be hurt if Marbury Hospital ceased to exist. "How can they justify putting profit over people's lives like that?"

"They don't care about justification." Rowan's voice was low and bitter. "They hide behind financial jargon and talk about *market efficiency*, but at the end of the day, it's pure greed."

"We can't let this happen. There has to be something we can

do." Simone sucked in a breath as a terrible possibility occurred to her. "Is Lance aware of this?"

"Almost certainly. If nothing else, he's the reason Marbury was out of the supplies needed to save Fabienne's life earlier today. He canceled a number of contracts with suppliers as a strong-arming tactic to renegotiate the prices, and he apparently didn't consider what would happen if the ER cupboards went bare in the meantime."

"How could he be so reckless? He's putting lives at risk!" Simone's blood curdled at Lance's callousness. "Maybe I shouldn't consider going for Candace's position when she leaves. He'd be my boss, and I don't know how I can be around him without smashing my fist into his face."

"I have to believe Lance will get what he deserves. For this, as well as for what happened in Florida." Rowan explained the details of his suspected involvement with the closure of the hospital near Pensacola. "All that's left now is an empty lot ready to become luxury condos."

"If that happens to Marbury, I'll lose my mind. What about your dad? Do you think he's part of this scheme?"

Rowan sighed, looking like she might be sick. "I honestly don't know. I hope not. But Mom's been telling me how cozy he's gotten with Hydra over the past several months. He's been going to these corporate events they host, even started using their jargon. I know one thing. If he's on board with what they do, he's not the same man I grew up with."

Simone's grip tightened on the edge of Fabienne's bed, her knuckles turning white. The thought of a pillar of the community like Harold Colchester being involved in such a dirty scheme was almost too much to bear. "I'm so sorry. This must have been incredibly difficult for you to hear."

Rowan blinked rapidly, her chin trembling as she fought to hold herself together. "I'm trying not to let my emotions run away with me. Right now, we need to be smart about this. We can't go charging in without a plan. I need to gather all the evidence so I can present it to my father. Or the board. I'm not sure which."

"I guess which approach you choose depends on who you can trust."

Before they could continue this conversation, a nurse rounded the curtain. "I need to check the patient's vitals before we move her to her room."

After recording temperature, heart rate, and blood pressure in Fabienne's chart, the nurse called for an orderly to help transfer the patient to the new room.

"What about the baby?" Simone asked.

"The baby will be moved to the nursery for now," the nurse explained. "Once Fabienne is settled in her room and feeling a bit stronger, we'll bring the little one to her. That is, unless you'd like to remain with the baby until the patient's husband arrives. It's not standard procedure, but given your connection to the patient and Dr. Colchester's history with the hospital, we could make an exception."

"Yes, I think Fabienne would prefer that," Simone said.

As the orderlies wheeled Fabienne's bed out of the recovery area, Simone and Rowan followed close behind, the baby securely tucked into her bassinet. They wound their way through the labyrinthine corridors of Boston General, stopping in front of a bank of elevators. When they stepped inside and the nurse pushed the button for the fifth floor, Rowan frowned.

"I think you meant to hit the fourth floor," she said to the nurse. "Unless they've completely redone the floor plan since I worked here."

The nurse checked the chart. "No, I have her going to the President's suite, room 522."

"What?" Simone's eyes widened. "There's been a mistake. She can't afford that."

The nurse consulted the paperwork once more. "Those are

the orders, and I'm showing here that her account is paid in full."

"How is that possible?" Simone demanded. The worried expression on Rowan's face mirrored her own concerns. Once the mix-up was discovered, Fabienne and her family would be on the hook for tens of thousands of dollars.

"It just is." The nurse shrugged. "It's way above my pay grade to know those kinds of details, but be happy. If I were in the hospital, this is where I'd want to be. She'll have the peace and quiet she needs."

Indeed, the hospital suite was the most luxurious thing Simone had ever seen, more like a high-end hotel room than a typical sterile hospital environment. A plush armchair and sofa sat near the bed, and a large window overlooked the Charles River.

As the orderlies carefully transferred Fabienne to the bed, Simone wheeled the bassinet to a corner of the room, her mind racing. Who could have arranged this? And why?

As soon as Fabienne was settled, the nurse left, and Rowan and Simone were alone. Simone sat down in the chair and held the baby, offering her a bottle the nurse had left.

"This doesn't make sense," Simone whispered, careful not to disturb the infant. "Who would pay for this kind of luxury for Fabienne?"

Rowan paced near the window, her reflection ghostly in the glass. "I have a hunch, but I'm not sure you're going to like it."

"At this point, I'm not sure I like anything about this situation," Simone sighed. "What are you thinking?"

"There are three possible explanations I can think of." Rowan paused, the lines on her forehead deepening as she chose her next words. "One, it's a clerical error that will be discovered and corrected soon. Two, Lance has been made aware of the situation and has pulled some strings in the hopes of avoiding the very obvious lawsuit headed his way when the family finds out all of this could have been avoided if he hadn't canceled the supply order. Or three..."

"Or three?" Simone prompted, teasing the baby's lips with the nipple of the bottle to get her to drink.

"Or three, someone is trying to buy her silence," Rowan finished, her voice tight with tension.

Simone's breath caught in her throat as she processed Rowan's words. The baby in her arms squirmed, and she adjusted her hold, focusing on the tiny face to ground herself.

"You think Hydra might be behind this?" Simone whispered, her eyes darting to the door as if expecting someone to burst in at any moment. "But why? Fabienne doesn't have the resources to sue."

"True, but Hydra may not know that. And even avoiding bad publicity might be enough of an incentive for them to shell out what amounts to peanuts for them." Rowan pressed her lips together, swallowing hard. "My colleague told me that secrecy is the key to these acquisitions flying under the radar. If they want to avoid public scrutiny, it's probably worth it to them to make potential headaches go away."

Simone nodded slowly, her mind racing. "So what do we do? We can't accept this, can we? It feels wrong to allow Fabienne to get caught up in what amounts to a bribe."

Rowan sighed, running a hand through her hair. "I know. But right now, she needs this level of care after everything she's been through." Her eyes fixed on the sleeping infant in Simone's arms.

"You're right," Simone conceded. "Anyway, just because Hydra pays her bills doesn't mean we have to sit back and let them destroy the hospital."

"Exactly," Rowan's eyes flashed with determination. "Once Candace arrives with Fabienne's husband, we'll head back home and get started building a case. We'll expose their plans before they can put them into action."

THE ANATOMY OF FOREVER

"But how? We're two people against a massive corporation." Even the thought of taking on a fight of this magnitude made Simone's head spin.

"We're not alone," Rowan said firmly. "We have allies, people in the community who care about the hospital as much as we do."

"Marigold would be more than willing to lead a picket line, I'm sure," Simone conceded, chuckling at the mental image of her landlady leading a march through the streets, her fiery spirit on full display. "And I bet your mom would be right there beside her, probably with a megaphone in hand."

"Which she would say was Marigold's idea because shouting isn't ladylike, but deep down, she would love every minute of it." A hint of a smile crossed Rowan's face. "We have a community behind us. People who've relied on Marbury Hospital for generations. Once they know what's at stake, they'll fight alongside us."

"That's something Hydra can't buy." Something like hope stirred in Simone's chest. If she hadn't been holding a newborn, she might have let out a battle cry. "Unlike the hospitals they've targeted before, we know their playbook."

Rowan seemed less convinced, raking her hand through her tangled curls with extra force. "What if that's not enough?"

Simone's eyes met Rowan's, and she saw the doubt and fear swirling in her partner's gaze. She took a deep breath, gathering her resolve. "It will be. I know you, Rowan. When you put your mind to something, God help the people who get in your way."

CHAPTER TWENTY-EIGHT

Printouts of financial reports, newspaper clippings, and hastily scribbled notes covered every inch of Marigold's dining room table. Rowan rubbed her temples, realizing for the first time how little she'd slept in the past few weeks. Ever since driving home from Boston General on New Year's Day, her research had become an obsession.

"This is everything I could find out about the inner workings of Hydra Capital Management," Rowan said. She leaned over, scanning the documents for what felt like the millionth time, as Simone, Marigold, and her mother took it all in. "I hope it's enough."

"If it isn't," Simone said, "nothing would be."

"Agreed. I feel like we need one of those murder boards to make sense of it." Marigold took a sip of a martini as she gestured to the cluttered table. "You know, with red string connecting all the pieces."

Rowan couldn't help but smile at the image. "Maybe we should invest in one for next time."

"Next time?" Grace raised an eyebrow. "Let's hope there isn't a next time to worry about."

"Yeah," Simone added. "Based on what I'm seeing, we need to put a stop to Hydra once and for all before they can do any more damage."

"You're right. They've gotten away with too much already." Rowan picked up a document, her eyes scanning the figures. "Hydra's been systematically targeting vulnerable hospitals across the country."

"How are they able to figure out which ones to go after?" Marigold asked. "Or are they incredibly lucky at guessing?"

"My theory?" Rowan allowed the paper to drop from her hands back to the table. "They're using their corporate retreats and executive wellness program—"

"You mean rehab," Simone interjected.

"Exactly. Rehab," Rowan corrected, rolling her eyes at the way Hydra attempted to cover up the serious addiction issues of the executives who took part in their program. "Under the guise of helping, they're gaining valuable insider information from vulnerable executives."

"Financial struggles, leadership conflicts, even potential scandals," Simone added. "All of it becomes ammunition for their takeovers."

Rowan nodded at Simone's summary, though she was hardly surprised by how well it had been explained. They'd spoken of little else for weeks.

"You mean, when Lance was sent to that place down in Florida, he wasn't getting treatment for his gambling addiction?" Grace asked, her voice tinged with disbelief.

Rowan shook her head, a knot forming in her stomach. "No, Mom. Maybe they were doing actual therapy, too. I don't know. But I think he was giving them everything they needed to target Marbury Hospital in the process. Maybe unknowingly but still."

"Poor Lance," Grace said, but Marigold made a tutting noise.

"Don't go feeling too sorry for him, Grace." Marigold's tone was sharp. "He's still responsible for his actions, addiction or not."

"I suppose, but—"

"No." Marigold held up her hand. "My second husband struggled with addiction, as people say nowadays. Back then, before I became the sophisticated lady you see today, I would've said he was a drunk. And a mean one, too. But even then, I understood he was making choices, that all his bad luck wasn't just being thrust on him by a vengeful god like he seemed to want people to believe."

"Even if Lance didn't know what was going on while he was at the facility," Rowan added, directing the conversation back to the topic at hand before Marigold could launch into an hours-long tale of one of her exes, "he definitely should've caught on when he started working at the hospital in Pensacola. He was sober then, and more than capable of understanding what was happening. But he chose to stay quiet, to keep benefiting from Hydra's scheme."

"Then he chose to come back here," Simone said. "And do it all over again, this time in a community he supposedly cares about."

Grace's expression hardened. "You're right. He doesn't deserve my sympathy. I hope when this all comes out, he gets what's coming to him."

"What's coming to him might be some jail time," Rowan said, the sudden vehemence in her mother's tone surprising her. "That's what has me worried."

"You don't want your ex to go to prison?" Marigold asked with a laugh. "Lord, I would've welcomed that outcome for at least two of mine."

"It's not Lance I'm concerned about," Rowan explained. "It's Erica. Simone and I are finally repairing all the damage the divorce and our subsequent dating caused in our relationships with her. I don't want her to resent me all over again if her father ends up behind bars because of what we're doing."

Marigold set her glass down on the table. "I haven't known Erica that long, but from what I've seen, she's not a child anymore. Since she started volunteering with the clinic, she's seen a side of Marbury she didn't know existed, and I think it's changed her. Made her more mature."

"I'm with Marigold," Grace said, picking up a photo of the empty lot in Pensacola. "No one—that is, no one with a heart," Grace corrected, "would want their community to lose a hospital. I'm sure Erica would feel the same if she were here."

No sooner had the words left Grace's mouth than a knock sounded at the front door. Rowan's heart skipped a beat as she exchanged glances with Simone. They weren't expecting anyone else.

"I'll get it," Marigold said, rising from her seat.

A moment later, Rowan heard Erica's voice echoing in the foyer.

"Sorry to barge in like this," Erica said, "but I was coming by to see if Simone wanted to go the Driftwood tonight. I saw all the cars here, but no one was answering the door, so I thought she might be over here."

Rowan's heart raced as Erica's footsteps approached the dining room. There would be no hiding the truth from her now. She locked eyes with Simone, who gave a subtle nod of reassurance.

"Hey, everyone," Erica said, stepping into the room. Her smile faltered as she took in the scene. "What's going on? Did you all decide to have a party and not invite me?"

"Of course not," Simone said, breaking the silence before it could stretch out for eternity. "It's actually good you're here."

"What's all this?" Erica edged further into the room with trepidation, as if deep down she sensed she didn't really want to know what was going on with the pile of papers on the table.

"Why don't you have a seat, dear?" Grace pulled out the chair next to her.

"You're all being weird." Erica remained standing, her eyes glued to the table. "Is this about the hospital? Some kind of fundraising plan? If so, I want to help."

"Not exactly," Grace said, her tone gentle with a hint of caution.

Rowan took a deep breath, steeling herself. "Erica, there's something you need to know. It's about your father."

Erica's eyes snapped to Rowan. "What do you mean? Is he okay? He's not sick or something, is he?"

Rowan felt a pang of guilt at the worry in Erica's voice. "No, he's not sick. But he is involved in something troubling."

She gestured for Erica to sit, and this time the young woman complied, sinking into the chair next to her grandmother.

"It's not good," Simone said softly.

Erica's gaze darted around the table, her brow furrowing as she locked eyes with Rowan. "I wish you would stop treating me like I might break and just give it to me straight, whatever it is. I'm not a child."

Marigold lifted her eyebrows in an *I told you so* gesture at this, and Rowan's shoulders slumped.

"I'm sorry. You're right." Rowan took a deep breath before plunging in. "Your father has been working with Hydra Capital Management to orchestrate the closure of Marbury Hospital."

Erica's eyes widened in disbelief. "No, that can't be right. Dad loves the hospital. Why would he want to close it?"

As Erica's eyes started to water, Rowan tensed for the inevitable meltdown that was sure to come. Instead, Erica sat quietly, blinking rapidly to keep her emotions in check but otherwise remaining composed. Rowan met Simone's eyes, and it was clear she had been waiting for the screaming or accusations to start, too. This new, mature Erica was most unexpected.

"Okay," Erica said, her voice steady despite the slight tremble in her hands. "Tell me everything. Walk me through it like I have no fucking idea what you're talking about. Because I don't. But I want to understand."

Rowan nodded, impressed by Erica's composure. She began walking through the evidence, explaining Hydra's pattern of targeting vulnerable hospitals and Lance's involvement. As she spoke, Erica's expression shifted from disbelief to anger to sadness.

When Rowan finished, Erica picked up the photo of the empty lot where the Pensacola hospital had once stood. "My dad worked here before this happened? He knew it was going on?"

"Yes." Rowan saw no need to sugarcoat it, nor to elaborate on what was an undeniable fact.

"You said that Hydra compensates all the people at the top, the executives and investors, as part of these schemes. That's how he was able to afford to buy the beach house and my car?"

"More than likely," Rowan said.

"Given the timing, he probably didn't get a payout until after you'd come home from Italy," Simone added.

"Or maybe the money is payment in advance for what he's been doing at Marbury," Marigold suggested with a shrug. "I'm not sure that part is clear."

"No," Rowan agreed. "I'll admit I don't have all the details on the financial side of things. But the pattern is obvious." Rowan explained what she had learned from Dr. Chen about the hospital in Rhode Island.

Erica let the photo slip out of her fingers. "This is happening to another hospital in New England? Right now?"

Again, Rowan nodded.

"Why isn't anyone stopping them?"

"Because only a few people know the full scope of it before it's too late." Rowan ran her fingers along her scalp, pressing hard to release some of the tension. "But it's clear from what I've learned that it's already underway at Marbury. Remember the young mother who had to be airlifted to Boston on New Year's Day?"

Erica nodded slowly, her eyes still fixed on the photos. "I heard she almost died."

"She almost did." Simone confirmed. "All because the hospital was lacking a simple device they should have had on hand. And because the patient couldn't get proper prenatal care after the L & D unit closed and all the doctors moved to Hyannis."

"She's going to be okay, though?" Erica asked. "And the baby?"

"Yes. They received excellent care in Boston." Rowan didn't feel the need to mention the presidential suite or how the bill had been paid by a mysterious third party since she still hadn't determined who was behind all that.

"What will happen to other patients if the hospital in Marbury closes?" Erica asked.

"People will die. Plain and simple." Marigold delivered the news in her characteristically blunt fashion, but it seemed to be exactly what Erica needed to hear.

Erica's jaw clenched, a fire igniting in her eyes. "We can't let that happen."

Rowan felt a surge of pride at Erica's determination. "You're right. We can't. And we won't."

"So what's the plan?" Erica leaned forward, her elbows on the table. "How do we stop this?"

"To begin with, I need to bring all the evidence to hospital leadership," Rowan said. "Meaning my father."

"Who might be caught up in all of this, too," Rowan's mother said, the pain loud and clear despite the low volume of her words.

Erica swiped some tears off her cheek. "If they're actually doing any of this, they both need to face the consequences."

"I agree." Rowan's heart clenched at the prospect of her own father's potential role. "I'm so sorry you're caught up in this, Erica. I know how much your father means to you."

Erica squared her shoulders. "He does. Just like your father means a lot to you. But you're being brave in facing this head-on, and I will be, too. When are you bringing this to him?"

Rowan had to clear her throat before answering. "Tomorrow."

Erica cradled her head with both hands. "Why do people suck?"

"Not everyone." Grace rubbed Erica's back.

"Was my dad always this bad?" Erica sought Rowan's eyes. "I'm really starting to hate him."

"I understand," Rowan said. "But that doesn't mean you have to stop loving him, too."

"How is that possible?" Erica scoffed.

"Trust me. You can feel a whole lot of ways about a person at the same time," Marigold replied. "That's the way life is."

Erica ran a hand over her face to wipe away the tears before straightening herself in the chair. "This will be a whole lot worse for other people than it is for me. I'm willing to do whatever it takes to make this right."

ROWAN AWOKE the next morning with a knot in her stomach. She'd barely slept, her mind racing with all the possible outcomes of her impending confrontation with her father. By the time she stood outside of her father's office, gripping a laptop close to her chest, she'd had four cups of coffee, and her entire body hummed like someone had plugged her into a generator. She wished she could put this off until she felt better, but there was no turning back.

It was now or never.

She was going to walk into her father's office and tell him

everything she knew about Hydra. It was either going to come as a total shock to him, or else she was going to discover that her father wasn't the man she'd believed him to be her whole life.

True, she and her father didn't always see eye to eye. He was old-fashioned in many ways, resistant to change, and often dismissive of her ideas. But she had always believed him to be fundamentally good, a man who cared deeply about the hospital and the community it served.

What if she was wrong?

Stealing herself with a deep, cleansing breath, she squared her shoulders and walked in to face the truth, whatever that turned out to be.

Her father glanced up, annoyance etched deeply in his brow, as she approached his desk. "Don't you know to knock? I'm very busy."

"I d-don't care." Rowan's voice cracked, and she sucked in her stomach to project her voice with more confidence, even if it wasn't real. "You need to hear what I have to say."

"Is this about your mother?" To his credit, Rowan's father sounded genuinely concerned. "We're both getting older, and I worry about her health. I really hope she—"

"No, Dad. This isn't about Mom," Rowan interrupted, her voice steadier now. "Well, not directly anyway. It's about the hospital."

Her father's eyes narrowed, and the openness that had crept into his expression faded. "Last time I checked, you don't work here."

"Will you just be quiet for a minute and let me speak?" Rowan had reached her breaking point. She refused to be cowed by her father's dismissive tone anymore. She set the laptop down and lifted the lid. "This is important."

"What is it?" Her father didn't bother to look at the screen.

"This is a laptop that belonged to Lance. I should have

brought it to you when I first discovered it several months ago, but to be fair, you would've defended him like you always do."

"Is this about his gambling and drinking? Because I've told you before that—"

"No. It's in addition to those problems." Her father glared at her, but she held his gaze and continued. "These are messages from a woman—although I'm using the term loosely because in catfishing scams such as this, the actual gender of the perpetrator is irrelevant. It could have been anyone behind this."

"Are you saying he had an affair? Because these dates on the messages seem to be well after you left the poor man. I don't see how you can expect Lance to have remained celibate when it was clear you had every intention of moving on. Finding your truth. Whatever the hell it was you were doing. There was a time when a marriage vow was—"

"Dad." The warning was unmistakable in Rowan's tone, so much so that even her usually unobservant father stopped talking and started to read.

He scrolled through the messages, his face getting closer and closer to the screen as the evidence built up. "Who is this person?"

"Like I said, I don't know. But it was clearly a scam. Often, the people responsible are part of organized crime rings," Rowan explained. "They prey on vulnerable people, especially those with addiction issues or financial troubles."

Her father's brow furrowed as he continued scrolling. "And you think Lance fell victim to this?"

"I know he did. You'll see."

Her father's eyes widened when he reached the final message: WHERE'S MY MONEY, BITCH?!?!?!?!

"I didn't know about any of this," he let out in a whisper. "Why didn't he tell me? How much did he lose?"

"From what I could tell, everything. Well beyond what he admitted to as gambling debt when I bailed him out by buying the beach house." Rowan took a quick breath and kept talking so her father couldn't interrupt. "As for why he kept quiet, would you tell anyone if you got yourself into an embarrassing scam like this?"

Her father shook his rapidly whitening face. "How did you find out about it?"

"When I was trying to make sense of the piles of paperwork Lance had left behind in his office, I learned of an apartment the hospital was being billed for in Boston. I paid it a visit, and that's when I found the laptop with all these messages."

"It's concerning," he admitted but didn't elaborate.

"That's only the beginning." Rowan pulled the news articles out of her bag. "There's this."

He picked up the paper. "What is it?"

"It's about a hospital in Pensacola that Hydra purchased and then destroyed. The community is devastated."

Her father's eyes skimmed the article, his face going paler.

"Did you know that's what they do?" Rowan held her breath.

"I've never even heard of this hospital," he said, though that wasn't technically what she'd asked. "I know nothing about Florida."

"No? Because in this article from the business section, there's quite a dashing photo of Lance along with an explanation of how he was excited to take a new role at the hospital. This was right after his rehab stint. The article doesn't mention that part of his story for some reason." She pulled out another paper. "Here's another outlining how Hydra had swooped in and saved that same hospital from bankruptcy. Fast forward to here." She set down another printout. "The hospital is being closed. Not too long after that, Lance swoops back into town, and you kick me to the curb."

Her father blinked but said nothing.

"I wondered how Lance was able to pay me back for the

beach house so quickly after his return," Rowan said. "In addition to the gambling, I knew he'd had his savings wiped out by the scammer. He sold his condo, but if he'd had any money left, I know he would've used it to pay Erica's tuition. And yet, he managed to send me three quarters of a million dollars almost instantly to buy back the beach house. Did you loan it to him?"

"Me? Of course not." Her father sounded genuinely shocked at the suggestion.

"In that case, it seems Hydra pays their accomplices well. He's probably expecting an even bigger paycheck for the Marbury sale. Beachfront property on the Cape is worth a fortune."

"Now wait a minute," her father said, his voice rising. "You can't possibly be suggesting Lance is involved in some scheme to close Marbury Hospital. That's preposterous!"

Rowan held her father's gaze, unflinching. "I wish it were. I bet these communities would've thought the same thing." She slapped the entire stack of articles Dr. Chen had sent her on the desk in front of her father as he flinched. "Luxury condos where community hospitals used to be. The rich need nice places to live, right? Never mind the little people. They're suckers for not being billionaires."

"Don't take that tone with me," her father growled.

She didn't care if he was annoyed by what she said. She needed to press on so she didn't lose her nerve. "I have to know, Dad. Are you in on it?"

"On what?"

"On the plan to sell Marbury Hospital to Hydra," Rowan said, her voice steady despite her racing heart. "Because that is what is going on. Their playbook is clear, and they're already acting according to plan. Are you knowingly participating in their scheme to strip this community of its healthcare?"

Her father's face flushed red. "How dare you accuse me of such a thing! I've dedicated my entire life to this hospital."

"Then prove it. If you care about this hospital, this community, or your legacy, you cannot sell to Hydra," Rowan said, her voice firm. "And you need to remove Lance from his position immediately."

Her father picked up the articles, rifling through them to find the one with Lance smiling in the photo. He shook his head slowly, visibly shaken. "How could a doctor do this?"

"Greed," Rowan answered. "Pure and simple. Along with a healthy mix of desperation."

Her father slumped back in his chair. "Lance assured me Hydra was interested in modernizing our facilities, expanding services. He said their investment would secure Marbury's future."

Rowan's anger was replaced by sadness for her father. He hadn't known; that much she believed. But his naivety had nearly cost the community everything. "They lied to you. Just like they've lied to countless other hospital boards across the country."

He nodded slowly, his eyes distant. "I suppose I wanted to believe it. Things have been difficult here for so long. I had no idea what they were really up to. I swear it."

"I believe you, Dad. But now that you know, what are you going to do about it?"

Her father ran a hand through his thinning hair, seeming to age ten years right before her eyes. "I'll recommend to the board that we walk away from the sale. Immediately."

"And Lance?" Rowan pressed.

Her father's jaw clenched. "He'll be removed from his position, effective yesterday if I have my way. I can't believe he'd do this to us, to the community. What are the chances of you coming back?"

"To replace Lance?" Rowan's heart skipped a beat. After the pain of being cast aside the instant Lance wanted to return, her father's renewed faith in her hit her system like a drug.

"Not Lance," her father corrected. "Me. Because if this incident proves anything, it's that I'm getting too old for this shit."

It was Rowan's turn to blink in stunned silence.

"You've been wanting this job since you were old enough to know what it meant," her father pointed out when she failed to respond.

"That's true." Rowan's mind raced as she considered her father's unexpected offer. The CEO position at Marbury Hospital had been her dream for years, but now that it was suddenly within reach, she felt conflicted. If she returned to a leadership position, what would that mean for her relationship with Simone?

There was no way Simone could be promoted to department head if Rowan became CEO. It would be a clear conflict of interest. Rowan had sworn she wouldn't ask Simone to prioritize their relationship over her career the way Lance had done to her. In addition to that, Rowan wasn't entirely sure she wanted to step back into the high-pressure world of hospital administration. Her time away had given her a new perspective on work-life balance and what truly mattered to her.

"Rowan, I really need you," her father pushed.

"I don't know what to say. This is a lot to process."

Her father leaned forward, his expression softening. "I know it's sudden, but you've proven yourself more than capable. You uncovered this whole mess when I was too blind to see it. The hospital needs someone like you at the helm. It always has."

She couldn't believe her ears. After all the years she'd watched him drool over Lance, suddenly she was good enough? It was enough to make her want to scream.

"I appreciate the offer, Dad. I really do," she began, choking back her bitterness. "But I can't step into this role without careful consideration. There's a lot that needs to be addressed first."

Her father's brow furrowed. "What do you mean? I thought this was what you always wanted."

"It was." Rowan admitted. "It is, I guess, but—"

"You've proved yourself worthy." Her father said this like he was bestowing a knighthood after she'd slayed a dragon or something. "You've been angling for this position for years. Why the hesitation now?"

"Because a lot has changed," Rowan explained. "I've changed. My priorities, my understanding of what I want from life—it's all evolved. And after everything that's happened, I need to be sure this is still the right path for me."

The only way to do that was to talk to Simone.

CHAPTER TWENTY-NINE

Simone peeked at the clock on the fireplace, noting the fading sunlight coming through the window. The meeting with Rowan's father had started hours ago. It was nearly four o'clock in the afternoon. How much longer would Rowan be? Her absence for this long was unsettling to Simone, who worried that the confrontation had taken an unexpected turn.

She tried to focus on the medical journal in her lap, but the words blurred together as her mind raced with worst-case scenarios. Then an orange kitten climbed across the pages, followed closely by her black and white sister.

"Hey," Simone scolded as Pepper curled into a ball, obscuring the graph she'd been trying to analyze, but her heart wasn't in it. The truth was the kittens were the best medicine out there for providing comfort.

Simone scooped up Pepper, cradling the purring kitten against her chest as she reached out to stroke Ginger's silky fur. The simple comfort of their warm, soft bodies helped soothe the anxious thoughts swirling in her mind. She knew Rowan was more than capable of handling the situation with her father, but that didn't stop Simone from worrying and wishing Rowan would come home. It wasn't just worry. Even with Ginger perched on Simone's shoulder and Pepper spread across her head, Simone was lonely.

There was a time in Simone's life when she would have mocked the way she was feeling right now. Giddily awaiting the arrival of her girlfriend despite literally seeing the woman every single day? Old Simone would have thought New Simone was a lovesick fool. But then again, Old Simone had never known a love like this. A love that filled her with a sense of belonging, of home, in a way she'd never experienced before.

As much as it frightened her to admit it, Simone never felt quite right unless Rowan was near. Sure, she functioned well enough, especially at work, where routine and expertise kicked in to carry her through the long shifts. But here at home, with nothing but her thoughts and the company of two rambunctious kittens, Simone felt Rowan's absence like a physical ache. There wasn't a second that went by when Simone didn't think, "This would be even better if Rowan were here beside me."

Simone found some comfort in missing Rowan, as it meant her absence was felt. If dread filled her at the thought of Rowan's return, that would be a bad sign.

At the sound of the key in the lock, Simone and the cats all turned their heads in unison. Rowan stepped through the door, her expression not giving any insight into what had transpired with her father. She dropped her keys on the side table and shrugged off her coat, hanging it on the rack before turning to face Simone.

"Now, there's a sight. All my girls cozy on the couch with a fire going." Rowan made her way over. Simone lifted her legs so that Rowan could take a seat, draping them across Rowan's lap once she was settled. Rowan's hand came to rest on Simone's knee, her thumb absently stroking back and forth as she leaned her head against the cushions and closed her eyes.

"How did it go?" Simone asked softly, studying Rowan's

face for any clues. The tension around her eyes and the tight set of her jaw suggested the meeting had been as difficult as Simone feared.

Rowan sighed heavily before opening her eyes to meet Simone's concerned gaze. "He's not going to allow the sale to go through."

"That's good news, right?" Simone asked, surprised by this turn of events. From Rowan's subdued demeanor, she'd expected the worst. "That means your dad isn't taking Hydra's side. He wasn't involved."

"No. He seemed truly shell-shocked by all the evidence I presented. Or rather, beaten might be a better word for it. He was so deflated." Rowan's voice softened, her gaze growing distant. "I've never seen him like that before. By the end, he looked so old."

Simone reached out to take Rowan's hand, interlacing their fingers. "That must have been hard to witness. Are you okay?"

Rowan squeezed Simone's hand, a small smile tugging at the corner of her lips. "I don't know. I'm relieved, I suppose. But also conflicted."

"What is it?" Simone studied Rowan's face, wishing she could smooth the worry lines away. "You're acting weird."

"He offered me a job."

"That was to be expected." In fact, Simone had spent most of the day preparing herself for this. It would be hard, but she knew what she had to do. "I'm sure the board will be relieved to have you taking over for Lance as soon as possible."

"No." Rowan let out a long breath, her gaze fixed on their intertwined fingers. "He wants me to take over as CEO of Marbury Hospital."

For a moment, Simone was speechless. This was monumental news, potentially life-changing for both of them. She searched Rowan's face, trying to gauge her reaction. "Wow. How do you feel about that?"

"It's good to know he respects me. After all this time, I finally earned his approval."

Simone tilted her head at the uncertainty in Rowan's tone. "Why do you seem sad?"

"Not exactly sad. I have all these emotions battling it out right now. I'm happy. Frustrated. Pissed. Relieved. Proud..." She circled a finger in the air, implying the options were endless. "Like, why did I have to work so goddamn hard to earn respect? He's my father. Shouldn't that have been a given? Also, why did I want it so badly? I've done a lot with my life. Why did I need my father to give me a thumbs-up in order for everything to matter?" Rowan rested her head against the back of the couch like trying to figure out the answers to these questions was exhausting.

Simone reached out to brush a stray curl from Rowan's forehead. "It's okay to feel all those things at once. Your relationship with your father is complicated, and this is a big moment. I don't want you to worry. I've already started getting my resume together so I can apply for positions elsewhere."

Rowan rolled her head to face Simone. "Why are you doing that? We haven't even talked about it yet."

Simone blinked, caught off guard by Rowan's question. "This is the job you've been chasing all of your life, and now it's finally yours. The hospital is your family legacy. I don't want to get in the way of that. There are plenty of options open to me. We must avoid any accusations of favoritism or—"

"Simone," Rowan interrupted, her voice soft but firm. "I don't know if I'm going to take him up on the offer."

"What?" Simone sat up straighter, dislodging Pepper from her perch. The kitten mewed in protest before curling up against Rowan's thigh. "But this is what you've been working toward, isn't it? The recognition from your father, the chance to lead Marbury Hospital. It's everything you've wanted."

"What if it isn't? What if I thought it was what I wanted

because it would prove—not just to him, but to everyone, myself included—that I was worthy? That I could live up to the Colchester name?" Rowan met Simone's gaze with a vulnerability that made Simone's heart ache. "I've spent so long chasing after this goal like it was a trophy I had to win that I never stopped to consider if it was truly what I wanted."

"You're not just saying this, are you?" Simone leaned closer. "Because of me? We both know we can't work at Marbury with you as the boss. I know you said you didn't want me to sacrifice my career for yours, but Rowan, I—"

"No." Rowan's tone was firm and unwavering. "Please trust me when I say it has nothing to do with you. It has everything to do with me not knowing what I want. Simone, as soon as my dad made the offer, I wanted to run as far away from it as possible. Would I have felt that way if it was what I wanted?"

"I guess not." Despite the lack of doubt or hesitation in Rowan's face, Simone struggled to process this unexpected turn of events. "Unless, it's the stress you've been under. Do you need a few weeks to think about it?"

"I don't think I do. You know what this feeling in here reminds me of?" Rowan pressed a hand to her chest. "It reminds me how I felt right before my wedding. That same sense of dread, of knowing I was about to make a huge mistake but feeling too trapped by expectations to change course."

"I get it," Simone breathed, reaching out to cup Rowan's cheek. "What do you want to do?"

Rowan leaned into Simone's touch, her eyes closing briefly. "Honestly? I don't know. Working at the mobile clinic is the one thing that has given me a real sense of purpose. That hands-on patient care, the direct impact we're making. It reminded me why I became a doctor in the first place. I don't know if administration is the right role for me." Rowan let out a sigh.

"Okay. I guess you can apply to other hospitals. Maybe look at your options in Boston?"

"I don't think I want to do that. I love it here in Marbury." Rowan tapped her fingers on Simone's knee. "After paying off the mortgage on the beach house, I'm left with enough in savings to live frugally until I figure out what I want to do. There's not a huge rush."

"Rowan, you know I can—"

"Please don't say you'll quit your job again. You love it. I mean, it frustrates you, but you still get a thrill knowing it's what you're meant to be doing. I want that for myself. I need the fulfillment of doing something I actually want to do. Not checking a bunch of boxes so my daddy will be proud of me." Rowan stared deeply into Simone's eyes. "The only thing I know for certain right now is I want us."

Simone's heart swelled. She leaned in, pressing her forehead against Rowan's. "You have me. Always."

Ginger let out a long, plaintive meow, making them both laugh.

Picking up the kitten for a cuddle, Rowan said, "Yes, I want you and your sibling, too. Don't worry. I wouldn't leave you out. This is what I need right now in my life. To be loved and to love. The rest is just gravy."

Simone smiled, warmth spreading through her chest at the sight of Rowan cuddling Ginger. She reached out to scratch behind the kitten's ears, her fingers brushing against Rowan's.

"What's next?" Simone asked. "When do you have to let your dad know?"

"We didn't really discuss that, but I'll do it soon. I even have a candidate to suggest if my dad's open to it, someone who knows exactly how much damage companies like Hydra can do and how to fight against them."

"You're honest to God serious, then? You really don't want the job?" Even now, Simone struggled to believe this could be true.

"I do not want the job." Rowan's posture softened, and she

let out a cleansing breath. "It would be hell on earth. What I needed, I already got. I stood up for what I knew was right, and by doing so, my father saw me not just as his daughter but his equal."

Simone nodded, taking in Rowan's words. She could almost see the weight lifting from her partner's shoulders, the tension easing from her face. It was as if Rowan had finally set down a heavy burden she'd been carrying for years.

"I'm proud of you," Simone said softly, squeezing Rowan's hand. "It takes a lot of courage to walk away from something you've been working toward for so long. Believe me, I know. I held on to my dream of working for Global Health Frontiers far longer than I should have, even when I knew it was the wrong environment for me. You were the one who helped me to see there were so many other paths I could follow. I want to be that support for you now," Simone finished, her voice filled with warmth. "Whatever you decide to do next, I'm here for you."

Rowan's eyes glistened with unshed tears as she looked at Simone. "I don't know what I did to deserve you."

Simone leaned in, pressing a gentle kiss to Rowan's lips. "You're you. That's more than enough."

Rowan smiled, a genuine, unguarded expression that made Simone's heart flutter. "For the first time in forever, I feel like I can breathe. It's strange, isn't it? I thought getting that job offer would be the pinnacle of my career, but turning it down feels so much better."

"We should celebrate."

Rowan's eyebrows lifted in surprise. "Celebrate? But I haven't actually done anything yet."

"You've made a choice to prioritize your happiness and well-being over external expectations," Simone countered. "That's worth celebrating. And if you play your cards right, I have a whole lot of ideas for more celebrating tonight when we get home from dinner."

Rowan's eyes lit up. "Oh really? What kind of celebrating did you have in mind?"

Simone leaned in close, whispering in Rowan's ear. "The kind that involves significantly less clothing and a lot more touching."

"In that case," Rowan said, her voice husky, "maybe we should skip dinner out and order in instead."

"You're the boss. Not actually, I guess, but..." Simone stopped as she realized what she'd said, but Rowan laughed.

"I may not be anybody's boss, but I think I can still make executive decisions when it comes to our evening plans," Rowan said, drinking in Simone's body with her eyes in a way that sent shivers down Simone's spine. "And right now, I'm deciding that takeout and an early night in bed sounds perfect."

Simone grinned, her heart racing with anticipation. "I like the way you think, Dr. Colchester. I like it very much. And I love you even more."

Rowan's eyes shimmered with unshed tears as she gazed at Simone. "I love you, too. More than I ever thought possible."

As Simone leaned in to kiss Rowan, a surge of contentment washed over her. This was what mattered—their love, their connection, their shared life together. Whatever challenges lay ahead, they could handle them.

The kiss deepened, and Simone found herself getting lost in the warmth of Rowan's embrace. Her hands tangled in those fiery red curls she loved so much as Rowan's fingers traced delicate patterns along her spine.

A loud crash from the kitchen made them both jump. They turned to see Pepper and Ginger skittering across the floor, a broken glass in their wake.

"I guess the kittens have other plans for our evening," Rowan said with a chuckle, rising from the couch.

Simone groaned but couldn't help smiling. "I'll get the dustpan. You corral the furry troublemakers and call in the takeout order."

"Fine. But I expect to see you in my office in thirty minutes, Dr. Doucette." Rowan nodded toward the bedroom. "No kittens. No clothes."

Simone laughed, her eyes sparkling with mischief. "Yes, Dr. Colchester. I'll be sure to follow your orders to the letter. I intend to pass my review with flying colors."

CHAPTER THIRTY

"It feels so good to have the sun on my bare skin." Rowan stretched her arms out, blinking behind her sunglasses against the bright midday sun. "I can't believe we're having lunch outside."

Simone laughed, stabbing a piece of lettuce from her salad with a fork. "I know. It's like the weather gods decided to give us a little preview of summer."

"Don't jinx it," Erica warned. "This time of year can be fickle. A week from now, we could be knee-deep in snow."

"Not today, though. Today is perfect." Rowan ran a finger over the brim of her wine glass. "This is one of the things I love most about the Cape. As soon as the weather shows even a hint of spring, everyone is outside."

"How could you resist when the ocean is right there?" Simone gestured toward the breathtaking view of the water that was visible from the restaurant's patio.

Erica's eyes darted to Rowan. "Can I ask you a personal question?"

"Uh, I guess so." Rowan took a sip of wine in case she needed it to prepare for a real doozy of an interrogation.

"How much did you used to get for renting out the beach house in the summer?"

Rowan let out a breath, relieved her stepdaughter's question had been so tame. "It may have changed a little since then, but if I rented it every week Memorial Day to Labor Day, it was enough to pay the mortgage and taxes for the year. Why?"

Erica took a sip of her iced tea before answering. "I'm thinking of doing it this summer to save enough money to pay for school."

"You're serious, then?" Rowan asked. "You're going to go for the master's degree?"

Erica nodded. "I love volunteering with the kids, and I think I could make a difference as an art therapist. I can take my last two psychology prerequisites at the community college, but after that, the tuition for the program I want is sobering, to say the least."

"You know, I can help you a little—"

Erica held up a hand, shaking her head. "I appreciate that, but I think I need to do this on my own. It's important to me."

"I understand. Renting out the beach house is a smart move." Rowan's body relaxed, the wine kicking in. She offered Erica a smile, hoping no sadness showed in it. Not that she wasn't happy for Erica and proud of the choices she was making. But as much as she understood Erica's desire for independence, it was hard to accept the teenager she'd once known was truly grown-up.

"Where will you stay this summer if the house is rented?" Simone asked. "I wish I could offer you the couch like before, but with the two of us living in the cottage—"

"And the kittens," Rowan interjected.

"Please," Erica said with a laugh. "I've seen those two furry beasts of yours, and they can hardly be called kittens anymore."

"They do seem to have some Maine coon in them," Simone

said. "We might have to start pitching a tent outside to sleep in because the two of them take up the entire bed."

"What is your plan?" Rowan asked.

Erica shrugged, looking slightly uncomfortable as she bit into her sandwich. "I haven't quite figured that part out yet. I was thinking maybe I could crash with a friend. Like, uh, maybe Pablo... or someone."

"Pablo?" Rowan raised an eyebrow but tried to keep her tone neutral. "My goodness. You two have been spending an awful lot of time together lately."

Erica's face flushed scarlet. "It's not like that. He's got a spare sofa bed in his living room. I mean, we've been hanging out a bit lately, but—"

Simone leaned forward, clearly not willing to let Erica off the hook. "Hanging out, huh? Is there something you haven't told me?"

"No." Erica shot a pointed look in Rowan's direction before lowering her voice and adding, "We'll talk later, okay?"

Rowan stifled a laugh at this obvious indication that her presence was making Erica uncomfortable discussing her love life. It was a blessing to be on speaking terms with her at all. Though Rowan was far too young to have been Erica's birth mother, she would forever be the parental figure in the woman's life. Simone, on the other hand, was Erica's best friend. Rowan would have to be content with that dynamic, even if it meant being left out of certain conversations.

"Regardless of where you end up staying," Rowan said, breaking the momentary silence, "I think it's a great idea to rent out the beach house. The place is huge, and tourists are willing to pay top dollar."

"It's way too much house for me," Erica agreed. "I would never sell it since my mom left it to me, but..." As her voice trailed off, Erica reached beneath her sunglasses to wipe her eyes.

"I think she'd like knowing she could help you this way,"

Rowan said gently, her own eyes misting. "It's like your mom's giving you a gift, even now."

"Both my moms," Erica corrected. "I haven't forgotten how you sacrificed to save my inheritance from my father's idiocy. Or how much you gave up to provide some stability to a bratty teenager who didn't always appreciate it."

Rowan reached across the table and squeezed Erica's hand. "You weren't bratty. You were hurting. I'd do it all over again in a heartbeat."

"Have you heard from your dad?" Simone asked, setting her fork on her plate and sitting back so the server could take it away.

"Not since he left for that new job working at Hydra's headquarters. How is what they're doing even legal?"

"Because laws are written for the wealthy," Simone muttered.

"At least you got out of having to work for him," Erica said. "Speaking of, how is the new promotion going?"

Simone's eyes lit up, a smile spreading across her face. "It's going really well, actually. I was a bit nervous about stepping into a leadership role, but I'm starting to find my footing. And, Dr. Chen is settling in nicely. He's even renegotiated our contract with HarborCare."

"It's amazing what can get done when a person is willing to check their ego at the door and negotiate in good faith," Rowan commented, not specifically mentioning Lance or her own father by name, but not needing to.

Rowan was about to ask Simone for more details about the HarborCare negotiations when she spotted two familiar figures approaching their table. Her mother, Grace, was walking arm-in-arm with Marigold, both women beaming as they made their way across the patio.

"Well, well," Rowan said, raising her eyebrows. "Look who's joining us for lunch."

Marigold waved enthusiastically as they drew near. "Hello,

darlings! We saw you from across the street and couldn't resist saying hello."

"What a lovely coincidence," Grace added with a trace of something in her tone that made Rowan think she might be hurt at not having been invited to join them from the start. Rowan was going to have to do better at remembering to include her, especially now that her father's constant presence in the house since his retirement was driving her mother bonkers.

"Considering this is the Cape in April and only two restaurants in all of Marbury are open for lunch, odds are good you'll run into half the town." Rowan stood. "Mom, Marigold, please join us. We were just finishing up, but I'm sure we could all go for another glass of wine."

"Absolutely. The more the merrier." Simone was on her feet in an instant, asking a table of three if they could spare the fourth chair.

"Are you two enjoying the nice weather?" Rowan asked as she resettled.

"We're celebrating!" Marigold flagged down the server. "We'll need a bottle of champagne."

"What's the occasion?" Simone asked.

"Grace has come on board as a full-time fundraiser for the Brewster Foundation," Marigold announced with glee.

"You're leaving Marbury Hospital?" Rowan asked, surprised by this turn of events.

"Not completely, but I'm taking a step back," her mother explained. "It's time for some fresh blood, and Dr. Chen's wife is eager to take on more responsibility with the hospital's fundraising efforts. This will allow me to focus on the mobile clinic project."

"Which is expanding rapidly," Marigold added. "With Grace's skills, we'll be able to add a fleet of RVs soon, not just the one I was planning. We'll be able to help more Fabiennes in the world, and if I have it my way, they'll never need to be flown to

Boston. Thank God her outcome was miraculous." Marigold grinned like a kid let loose in a candy store. "First the Cape, next the world."

"Why does that sound way more ominous than it should?" Rowan chuckled. "Just don't become the next Hydra. It's all I'm asking."

"Never," Marigold said. "We only use our powers for good."

The server came back with the champagne, popping the cork to a cheer from Marigold and a mortified look from Grace as several people stopped on the sidewalk to turn their heads and stare.

Following the pouring of champagne, Marigold raised her glass.

"To new beginnings and expanding horizons," Marigold toasted, her eyes twinkling. "Speaking of expanding horizons, Rowan, I have a proposition for you."

Rowan paused mid-sip, eyeing Marigold warily. "Oh?"

"We need a CEO who knows what they're doing." Marigold stared at her expectantly.

"Yes, I agree." Rowan wasn't sure where this was going, but now her mother was giving her an expectant look as well. "I'm sure you'll find someone excellent for the position."

Marigold laughed so loudly the sound carried across the patio. "I'm not looking for someone. I've already found her. I want to work with someone I trust."

It took a moment for Rowan to realize what Marigold was implying. "Me? You want me to be the CEO of your foundation?"

"We can talk the details later. Right now, I want to celebrate. To the mobile clinic!" Marigold hoisted her glass to the middle of the table for everyone to clink their glasses once again.

"Now that you'll be settling into Marbury for the long term," Marigold said, "you may want to consider finding a bigger place. Not that I'm going to kick you out of the cottage, of course, but the role of CEO does require a fair amount of entertaining. You may find—"

"I haven't said yes to the job yet," Rowan protested with a laugh.

"You will." Marigold spoke with total confidence. "The job is absolutely built for you, and I insist that you still volunteer when you want."

Rowan looked to Simone for help.

"It does sound perfect for you," Simone said, squeezing Rowan's hand. "And Marigold's right. We could use more space."

"And room for grandchildren," Grace chimed in, an almost crazed look accompanying this suggestion. Or maybe that was Rowan's interpretation.

Rowan nearly choked on her champagne. "Mom, please. One major life change at a time."

"I'm just saying," Grace continued, undeterred, "it's never too early to start thinking about the future. And speaking of the future, have you two set a date yet?"

Rowan's cheeks went hot as she exchanged a glance with Simone. They hadn't discussed marriage at all yet, and her mother's persistence on the topic was becoming increasingly uncomfortable.

"Mom," Rowan said, trying to keep her voice even, "Simone and I are happy with where we are right now. We'll cross that bridge when we come to it."

"If the cottage is going to be empty, do you think I could move in?" Erica asked, providing a welcome distraction.

"What's wrong with the beach house?" Rowan's mom asked.

"I'm going to rent it out this summer to help me pay for school," Erica answered. "But I'll need somewhere to stay from the end of May until September."

"From what I hear, you and Pablo are becoming quite an

item," Marigold said with a boldness that was shocking even for her.

"Pablo is such a charming young man," Grace added, her eyes on the horizon. "It's a good thing you're not doing something like selling that big house. You two may need it for all the great-grandbabies."

All the color left Erica's face, and she donned a deer in headlights look that made Rowan laugh despite herself. It was a lot funnier when uncomfortable conversations were directed at others.

"Mom, please," Rowan said, her voice strained. "Can we not discuss hypothetical grandchildren and great-grandchildren? Erica's barely started dating Pablo, and Simone and I are still figuring things out ourselves. Don't forget I've made that trip down the aisle before, and it didn't exactly go well."

"Pishposh." Marigold swatted away Rowan's argument like it was a pesky fly. "I walked down the aisle four times. When at first you don't succeed..." Marigold scrunched her face. "I don't remember how it goes, but don't let one failure stop you from having everything you want."

"I agree. I always wanted a baby sibling," Erica said, flashing Rowan an evil grin. "A sister or a brother. Either way."

Rowan felt her face flush even hotter. She snuck a glance at Simone, who was watching her with a soft smile. Rowan felt a flutter in her chest. The idea of building a family wasn't something they'd discussed, but suddenly the possibility seemed way more appealing than she ever would have expected.

Which was terrifying.

Rowan took a large sip of champagne, hoping it would calm her nerves. "I think we're getting a bit ahead of ourselves here," she said, trying to keep her voice light. "Let's focus on the present, shall we?"

Simone squeezed her hand under the table, a silent show of support. "Exactly," she chimed in. "We've got plenty on our plates already. I've only just been promoted, and Rowan will be starting a new job—"

"I still haven't said yes," Rowan interjected.

"You will," everyone at the table replied in unison.

Rowan laughed, shaking her head in mock exasperation. "I see I'm outnumbered here."

"Face it, darling," Marigold said, refilling Rowan's champagne glass. "You were born for this role. It's time you embraced your destiny."

"Destiny?" Rowan raised an eyebrow. "Isn't that a bit dramatic?"

"Not at all," Grace chimed in. "You've always had a talent for leadership and organization. Marbury Hospital's loss is definitely our gain."

Rowan was awash in emotions as she looked around the table at the faces of her loved ones. Their confidence in her abilities was touching but also a bit overwhelming. She was so used to fighting for every scrap of respect that to have it freely offered in abundance took her breath away.

"I appreciate your faith in me, all of you," Rowan said, her voice soft but steady. "I'm not for sure saying yes this second, but I'll give you an answer soon."

After the others had left, Rowan and Simone lingered at the table, savoring the last of the champagne and the warmth of the afternoon sun. Rowan leaned back in her chair, closing her eyes for a moment as she let the events that had unfolded over lunch sink in.

"That was certainly an eventful meal," Simone said, a hint of amusement in her voice. "How are you feeling?"

Rowan opened her eyes, meeting Simone's gaze. "Overwhelmed, honestly. It's a lot to process."

Simone nodded sympathetically. "I can imagine. It's a big decision."

Rowan sighed, swirling the last sip of champagne in her

glass. "It's not just the job offer. It's everything. The talk of moving, of..." A flush crept up her neck as she paused to swallow. "Marriage and children. I wasn't prepared for any of it."

"Hey, that wasn't my idea." Simone held up her hands in defense. "We've both been through a lot. There's no rush, okay? We can take things at our own pace."

Rowan let out a long sigh, her relief palpable. She sat for a moment, gazing out at the ocean, the gentle lapping of waves against the shore a soothing backdrop to her swirling thoughts.

"You know," Rowan said finally, turning back to Simone, "a bigger house might be nice. I mean, where we are now, we can barely fit all our books, let alone entertain."

Simone's eyes lit up. "I was really hoping you'd say that."

CHAPTER THIRTY-ONE

"All that's missing is the star at the top." Simone held the shiny brass tree topper out for Rowan. "Do you want to do the honors?"

"Are you sure you don't want to?" Rowan gestured to the stepladder next to the Christmas tree. "After all, your mom sent that as a housewarming gift. It's the star you used to have on your tree as a little girl."

"It was one of the few things we were able to salvage from the house after the hurricane." A lump formed in Simone's throat as her thumb traced the intricate patterns etched into the metal, remembering how her father would lift her up to place it on top of their tree each year. "But I think you should do it. This is our first Christmas in our new home together. I want you to be the one to make it complete."

"As long as you're sure." Rowan accepted the ornament and stepped onto the ladder.

"Of course, I'm sure. How would I be able to check out your butt if I was the one climbing up there?"

"I see. In that case, I'd hate to deprive you." Rowan climbed the rungs, glancing over her shoulder. "Getting a good look?"

Simone nodded. "Yes. Thank you."

Rowan placed the star atop the tree, adjusting it until it sat perfectly straight. As she descended the ladder, Simone wrapped her arms around Rowan's waist, pulling her close.

"It's beautiful," Simone murmured, resting her chin on Rowan's shoulder. "Just like you."

"It really is perfect. All of this." Rowan gestured to their spacious living room, made cozy with twinkling lights and festive decorations. "I never thought I'd have this kind of life. I can't believe we're already decorating the tree in our own house."

"Neither can I. But here we are." Simone leaned in for a kiss but was interrupted when the tree started to rustle.

"Ginger!" Reaching between the branches, Simone extracted a massive, struggling lump of orange fur. "Luckily none of the ornaments are breakable."

"Not with these two monsters." Rowan bent down to sweep Pepper into her arms before she could repeat her sister's mischief.

Simone studied the tree, which was still joggling, the ornaments swinging like the aftermath of an earthquake. "I think we might need to install a hook in the ceiling so we can wire the tree to it to keep it from falling over."

"Won't that encourage them? Maybe if they pull it down on themselves a few times, they'll learn."

"Have you met our cats?" Simone chuckled, shaking her head. "They have exactly one brain cell between the two of them. Speaking of cats, I heard from Poppy a little bit ago and—"

"No!" Rowan rushed to say. "Absolutely not."

Simone pouted. "But I didn't even tell you what she said."

"You didn't need to. This is Poppy we're talking about. That kid is a walking, one-girl animal rescue machine."

Simone held up her phone, pulling up the text Marigold had

sent on Poppy's behalf with a photo of the scruffiest tabby Simone had ever seen. "How can you say no to that face?"

"Another cat?" Rowan sighed, her resolve visibly weakening as she gazed at the photo.

"His name is Jiggles. His owner recently passed away, and no one has been willing to take him from the shelter because he's older and has a bit of a limp. He deserves a good home for Christmas, don't you think?" Simone's eyes pleaded with Rowan. "We have the space."

"What about Ginger and Pepper?"

"They'll adjust," Simone said, her voice soft but persuasive. "Besides, Jiggles is older and calmer. He might even be a good influence on our little troublemakers."

Rowan's eyebrows raised skeptically. "A good influence? On these two?"

Simone chuckled. "Okay, maybe that's a stretch. But it's almost Christmas. You won't even have to get me any other presents."

"You're saying all you want is an old homeless cat?"

"Absolutely." Simone insisted, and it was mostly true. Her job was going well, and with their new house, there wasn't much else she needed. The only thing that would make her Christmas complete wasn't exactly something she could ask for. Who knew when Rowan would be ready to take that next step? Simone pushed the thought aside, focusing on the matter at hand. "So, what do you say? Can we give Jiggles a home for Christmas?"

Rowan let out a long-suffering sigh, but her eyes sparkled with amusement. "Sure. But I'm putting my foot down if she wants to fob off Mr. Fuzzy."

"I'm with you on that." Simone shuddered as she recalled Poppy's prized tarantula. "Luckily for us, she would never part with Mr. Fuzzy."

Rowan's phone rang, and she pulled it from her pocket. "It's Pablo."

"Go ahead and answer," Simone encouraged. "It's probably something to do with the mobile clinic. I'm going to make some tea."

As Rowan stepped away to take the call, Simone made her way to the kitchen, humming along to the soft Christmas music playing in the background.

Simone filled the kettle and set it on the stove, her mind drifting as she waited for the water to boil. She couldn't help but smile as she thought about their growing furry family. Jiggles would fit right in, of that she was certain.

As she reached for the mugs in the cabinet, her eyes fell on the calendar hanging on the wall. Only a week to go until Christmas, and a new year was just around the corner.

A new year. New possibilities. New adventures.

So what if there was no ring on her finger? What she had with Rowan was more than enough. They had built a beautiful life together, and a piece of jewelry wouldn't change that. Even so, as she stared at the empty space on her left hand, an increasingly familiar ache tugged at her heart.

At thirty-three, she couldn't help but feel a sense of urgency. It wasn't about having a ring to show off or planning a big wedding. She couldn't care less about those things. It was about the future, about building a family together. Simone hoped Rowan was of the same mind, but they had barely discussed it since the topic first came up in the spring. What if she'd been reading the situation wrong the whole time? How would she feel if Rowan never came around?

The kettle's whistle jolted her from her thoughts. She poured the steaming water into two mugs, dropping a tea bag into each.

She wouldn't push. Rowan had been through so much with her divorce, and Simone knew better than anyone how important it was to heal at your own pace.

As she carried the mugs back to the living room, she found

Rowan had finished her call and was sprawled on the couch, looking pensive.

"Everything okay?" Simone asked, handing Rowan her mug and settling beside her.

Rowan nodded, wrapping her hands around the warm ceramic. "Pablo wasn't calling about the clinic. He wanted me to know he plans to propose to Erica when they come over for Christmas Eve."

Simone's heart skipped a beat. "Oh wow," she breathed, trying to keep her voice steady. "That's big news. I'm so happy for them."

Erica was her best friend, and she'd never seen her as joyful as she'd been with Pablo. So why was she on the verge of tears? Couldn't she be happy for Erica without feeling sorry for herself?

Rowan took a sip of her tea, her eyes fixed on the sparkling tree. "Pablo's a good man, and they're really good together."

Simone studied Rowan's face, noting the crease between her brows. "You look worried. Are you okay with this?"

Rowan sighed, running a hand through her hair. "Of course, I am. It just kind of puts a crimp…"

Simone's heart quickened as she spotted what looked like a small velvet box sitting beside Rowan on the couch. "Puts a crimp in what?" Simone prompted gently, trying to keep her voice steady.

Rowan set her mug down on the coffee table and turned to face Simone fully. "I had plans," she said softly. "I wanted it to be special. But I can't exactly steal the spotlight from my own daughter."

"What exactly did you have planned out?" Simone asked, breathless, her eyes fixed on the velvet box as Rowan picked it up and turned it over in her hands.

"Christmas morning. I was going to wait until everyone had opened their presents."

Simone's heart raced as she watched Rowan fidget with the small box. She hardly dared to breathe, afraid to shatter this fragile moment.

"I was going to slip this in your stocking and tell you that you'd forgotten to open one of your gifts. And right when you found the box, your mom was going to call."

"My mom? You talked to my mom about this?" Simone could barely keep her voice from cracking. The idea of Rowan reaching out to her mother, including her in this moment, touched her deeply.

Rowan nodded, a soft smile playing at her lips. "I wanted her blessing. And I wanted her to be part of it."

Simone's eyes welled with tears. "That's so thoughtful. Even if she couldn't be here in person, I know she'd—"

"That's just it. She will be here. What you weren't going to know when you answered the phone was that she was standing right outside."

Simone's eyes widened, her heart thundering in her chest. "My mom? Here? But she's in Oregon."

"She's flying in the twenty-third," Rowan confessed, her voice soft. "She and your stepdad. They're supposed to be staying with Marigold."

Tears spilled down Simone's cheeks as Rowan's words sank in. "You did all that for me?"

Rowan nodded, her own eyes glistening. "I wanted it to be perfect. But now..." Rowan looked down at the small box in her hands.

Simone held her breath, her heart racing with anticipation. "But now?" she prompted softly.

"You know what?" Rowan spoke with renewed strength, her determination clear on her face. "The perfect moment isn't about picking the right time and having a big surprise. I already waited longer than I should have. I've known for months what I wanted to do. I don't want to wait anymore. I don't care about perfect timing or elaborate plans. All I know is that I love you, Simone. I don't want to spend a day apart. Ever. Will you—"

"Yes!" Simone sealed the deal with a kiss. "Yes, yes, yes."

"I didn't even finish. I might have asked if you wanted to do the Polar Plunge with me this year."

Simone laughed through her tears, her heart overflowing with joy. "In that case, I might have to reconsider my answer. But if you're asking me to marry you, then it's still yes. A thousand times yes."

Rowan's eyes sparkled as she opened the velvet box, revealing a stunning ring. The center stone was a deep blue sapphire, flanked by two smaller diamonds. The band was intricate, with delicate swirls that reminded Simone of ocean waves.

"It's beautiful," Simone breathed as Rowan slid the ring onto Simone's finger.

"It's the color of your eyes. How does it feel?"

"Perfect." Simone kissed Rowan. "Everything is perfect. Well, almost perfect."

"Almost perfect?" Rowan raised an eyebrow.

"It's just, you know as soon as everyone finds out we're engaged—and Erica and Pablo, too—your mother and Marigold, and probably my mother, are going to have nothing but babies on the brain."

"It's become their favorite topic already," Rowan agreed.

"It has. But the idea has some merits," Simone pointed out. "We have a spare bedroom we're not doing anything with. And we'll need someone to take care of us when we get old. Plus, maybe if we have a baby, Poppy will stop trying to bring us cats."

"That will never happen. Poppy is a force that cannot be controlled." Rowan chuckled, but her eyes grew serious. "You really want to have a baby?"

Simone nodded, her heart racing. "I've been thinking about it a lot lately. But I wasn't sure how you felt about it."

Rowan was quiet for a moment, her fingers tracing patterns

on Simone's hand. "I'd be lying if I said I hadn't thought about it, too. And I think I'd like that. Starting a family with you."

Simone's heart soared. "Really? You would?"

Rowan nodded, a soft smile playing on her lips. "I would. I mean, it's a big step, and there's a lot to consider. But when I picture our future together, I see us with a little one. Maybe two."

"Two?"

"Yeah, two." Rowan's brow creased as her expression settled into a frown. "Aren't you supposed to have them in pairs?"

"Pretty sure that only applies to kittens."

Rowan laughed, pulling Simone closer. "We've certainly got the kitten part down. Maybe we should start with one baby and see how it goes."

Simone snuggled into Rowan's embrace, her heart overflowing with love and excitement for their future. "One baby it is. For now." She glanced down at her new ring, the sapphire sparkling in the glow of the Christmas lights. "Can you imagine how spoiled our child will be? Between your mom, my mom, and Marigold, that kid will never want for anything."

"Don't forget Erica and Pablo," Rowan added with a chuckle. "And Poppy. She'll probably try to sneak a kitten into the baby's crib."

"We'll have to keep a close eye on her." Simone grinned, already picturing their future. Family gatherings filled with laughter, tiny feet pattering through the house, Rowan singing lullabies as she rocked their little one to sleep. It was a beautiful dream, one she couldn't wait to make a reality.

As if sensing the joy and contentment radiating from the couple, Ginger and Pepper leaped onto the couch, curling up in their laps and purring loudly. Simone stroked Ginger's soft fur as she marveled at how much her life had changed in the past few years.

"I'm really glad I wasn't cut out for humanitarian work,"

Simone said. "Just think. Right now, I could be all alone in a tent in the mud, instead of here with you."

Rowan smiled, her eyes soft as she gazed at Simone. "I couldn't agree more. I thank my lucky stars every day that our paths crossed. You've brought so much light into my life, Simone. I can't imagine going through each day without you by my side."

Simone leaned in, resting her forehead against Rowan's. "You've given me a home, in every sense of the word. I never thought I could be this happy."

They sealed their declaration with a tender kiss, pouring all their hopes and dreams into the embrace. When they finally parted, Simone couldn't help but giggle as she glanced down at their now snoozing cats.

"Look at these two. Out like lights." She gently scratched Pepper behind the ears. "I think we wore them out with all the excitement."

Rowan chuckled softly. "Can't blame them. It's been a big day."

"It has. They have an entire tree in their living room." Simone stifled a yawn. "I think it's time for bed."

"I hope you're not too worn out," Rowan said, a twinkle of mischief in her eyes. "Because I was thinking, if we make a dash for it, we might get to the bedroom before the cats realize what's happening and get the bed all to ourselves."

"All to ourselves?" Simone teased. "Whatever will we do with it?"

Rowan quirked an eyebrow, a playful smirk tugging at her lips. "Oh, I'm sure we can think of something."

"Now to sneak away without waking them up." Simone carefully shifted Ginger off her lap and onto a plush throw pillow.

"Well done," Rowan said, raising herself from the couch

without making a sound. "This is good practice for parenthood."

Simone grinned. "In that case, I think we're going to be pros."

"Definitely. Now let's put those skills to good use." Rowan held out her hand, desire smoldering in her eyes. "Shall we?"

Simone took Rowan's outstretched hand, allowing herself to be pulled up from the couch and into her fiancée's warm embrace.

Fiancée! How amazing it felt to think of Rowan that way. Simone's heart fluttered as she gazed into Rowan's eyes, and she couldn't stop the giddy smile from spreading across her face as they tiptoed down the hall to their bedroom.

Soon, perhaps in the new year, they would announce their engagement to the world. But tonight was just for them. Tonight, and forever.

A HUGE THANK YOU!

Thanks so much for reading *The Anatomy of Forever*!

We couldn't have done this without the support of our generous Gold-level Patreon supporters, including: **Diva007, Jackie, Zaïna Adam, Patti B., Debster, Debbie, Georgia Becker Scheve, Kayla Bhadra, Marie Clifford, Julia, Rose H., Buzz, Erin Wade, and Tracey in WI.**

We've cowritten so many books now and we're often asked how we manage to work so well together. What many don't realize is that we go way back. How far back? We were actually born in the same hospital, just nine weeks apart, although TB keeps insisting it was only seven weeks because math is not her strong suit. While we may quibble about plot points, we're often laughing as we do.

In addition to cowriting, we also run I Heart SapphFic, a website we created that is dedicated to all things sapphic-fiction-related. You can search our massive database, the I Heart SapphFic Book-Finder, to find your next sapphic read.

A HUGE THANK YOU!

If you sign up for TB's newsletter, she'll send you a free copy of *A Woman Lost*, book 1 in the A Woman Lost series, plus the bonus chapters and Tropical Heat (a short story).

You'll also be one of the first to hear about her many misadventures, like the time she accidentally ordered thirty pounds of oranges, instead of five. To be honest, that stuff happens to TB a lot, which explains why she owns three of the exact same Nice Tits T-shirt. Yes, we're talking about birds here. TB loves birds.

And, if you want to follow Miranda, the voice of reason in this duo, to find out the full scoop of what really happens behind the scenes, sign up for her newsletter. Subscribers will receive her first book, *Telling Lies Online*, for free. The newsletters are heartfelt and funny, and often contain photos of her cats.

LET'S KEEP IN TOUCH

TB's newsletter: https://tbmarkinson.com/newsletter
Miranda's newsletter: https://mirandamacleod.com/list
I Heart SapphFic: https://iheartsapphfic.com
Patreon: https://www.patreon.com/IHeartSapphFic

Thanks again for reading our book. It's because of you that we are able to follow our dreams of being writers. It's a wonderful gift, and we appreciate each and every reader.

All the best,

TB and Miranda

ABOUT THE AUTHORS

TB Markinson lives in Massachusetts but dreams of moving to Vermont. When she isn't writing, she enjoys road trips in Pepper (her little red car) with Miranda, visiting historical sites, and reading with her furbaby, Sammy. Not necessarily in that order.

Miranda MacLeod is a California girl who loves living in New England. She spent way too many years in graduate school, has worked in professional theater and film, and held temp jobs in just about every office building in downtown Boston.

TB and Miranda were born in the same hospital (7 or 9 weeks apart, depending who you ask, because math is hard). They were childhood friends who lost touch and reconnected decades later to become a sapphic writing dynamic duo.

TB and Miranda also co-own *I Heart SapphFic*, a website for authors and readers of sapphic fiction to stay up-to-date on all the latest sapphic fiction news.

The duo won Golden Crown Literary Awards for *The AM Show* in 2022 and for *Midlife is the Cat's Meow* in 2024.

Get to know us better by following our Patreon account, where you can get weekly free content as well as opt-in for premium behind the scenes material you won't find anywhere else.

Printed in Great Britain
by Amazon